'So successfully has Molteno breathed life into her characters that we get a real sense of their vulnerability, their fury and their astonishing resilience.'

'Her writing has a poet's sensitivity and grace. Poignant and deeply empathetic.'

'She writes with intense sympathy of the bewildering experiences confronting Somali refugees.'

'This is one of those books I didn't want to end. It affirms the triumph of the human spirit in the face of adversity and honours the power of love. It is moving and beautiful, and if that sounds corny I don't care.'

e Simple

'Confi͟... ͟...osphere, the mix of sensuous beauty ͟... ͟...ism. The passages describing her characters ͟... are wonderful. At its darkest hour her plot has a Peter ͟... ͟...nes tragic potential.'

'This superbly well-written, intelligent book sounds not a jarring note as its deceptively calm prose leads the reader into a maelstrom of unresolved emotions.'

'Molteno's sensitive exploration of her characters' inner lives is the real treat of this novel, as she eloquently sketches a tale of desire, loss and forgiveness against a backdrop of indifferent sea and sky.'

FINANCIAL TIMES

'An intense, deeply personal novel. Molteno shows great compassion for and understanding of her characters, allowing the reader to care for them as much as she does. A muted, reflective meditation on the need for resolution.'

SUNDAY HERALD, NEW ZEALAND

A Language in Common

'She has an ability to fully create a world and draw the reader down into it so that one can almost feel and even smell it, it is so close. And what she says is of importance, of value, to our society and to our time.'

ANITA DESAI

'The most extraordinary book of short stories, straddling in fiction the social divide between white Britons and Asians. Her compassion never degenerates into sentimentality, and her sensitive perceptions come from a decade of getting to know her characters.'

AHMED RASHID, THE INDEPENDENT

'Powerful portraits. She has a remarkable understanding of her characters and their conditions.'

SUNDAY TIMES OF INDIA

'Written with honesty, determination and purpose. It is beautiful and wise.'

CITY LIMITS

About the Author

Marion Molteno's fiction reflects the breadth of her life experience. She grew up in South Africa at a time of political conflict, spent eight years in Zambia, pioneered educational projects in multi-ethnic communities in Britain, and has worked for Save the Children across Asia and Africa.

Her novel *If you can walk, you can dance* was awarded the Commonwealth Writers Prize for the best book in the Africa region and was selected for the top 20 books in the Women's Writers Festival in New Zealand. *A Shield of Coolest Air*, set among Somali asylum seekers, won the David St John Thomas Award for fiction. *Somewhere More Simple* explores tensions in an island community off the coast of Cornwall. She has won prizes for her short stories, and her collection, *A Language in Common*, has been translated into five languages. She has written and lectured on language, education and international development, and edits the work of Ralph Russell on Urdu literature.

www.marionmolteno.co.uk

UNCERTAIN LIGHT

Marion Molteno

Published by Advance Editions 2015
Advance Editions is an imprint of Core Q Ltd
Global House, 1 Ashley Avenue, Epsom, Surrey KT18 5AD
All correspondence: info@AdvanceEditions.com

First published as an advance ebook by Advance Editions 2015

ISBN 978-1-910408-04-9

Map by Kate Kirkwood
Designed and typeset by K.DESIGN, Winscombe, Somerset
Printed and bound in Great Britain by Clays Ltd, St Ives plc

www.AdvanceEditions.com

for Star

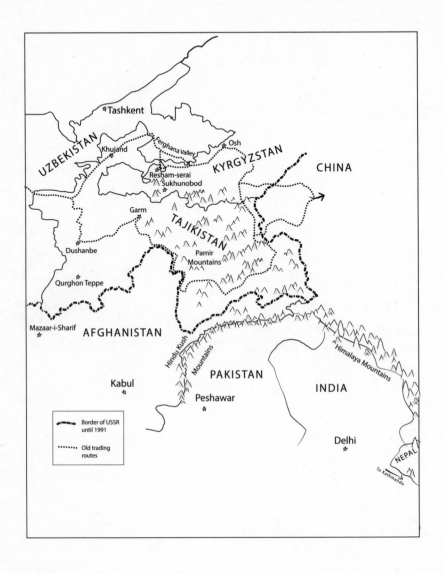

Contents

Part 1

This year it is the lightning, not the sun,
that marks time's course

GHALIB

The road into the mountains

You travel first through a flat valley, barren except for a trail of green that follows the bed of a river. The view is long, the spaces wide and empty; all you will see of human habitation is an occasional yurt, the squat round tent of a herder family, where sheep with long floppy ears and fat tails huddle together in the early morning mist. Ahead the mountains loom, rising abruptly from the valley floor. Nearer, and the road begins to rise into an amphitheatre of gaunt hills, with tracks disappearing into small stands of forest. Up further, and the earth closes in as the road winds up the side of a steep valley, with a dramatic drop to the river below.

It is from here that the road becomes treacherous – you would never venture up it without a driver who knew it well. The tarmac has fallen apart, it hasn't been repaired since before the end of the Soviet era, and the earth beneath crumbles. Each time you come round a steep bend you expect calamity. But when you can forget about the road you are caught by awe at the shape of the land. Look down, and it is all boulders and humpy earth, the remains of some long-ago landslide. Look up,

3

and the road winds constantly upwards. Hard to imagine that new valleys will open up high above, or that this mountain is a mere foothill to the massive barriers beyond: the Pamirs, that are called the Roof of the World.

You are touching ages past up here, for the road follows an ancient track that for centuries was a route over those mountains into China. But that fell into disuse, longer ago than anyone can remember, and the Silk Road traders found less hazardous routes across. In recent times it has had another function, for not far from here is a scarcely marked border with Tajikistan, a country so remote, so unconnected to the outside world that few elsewhere have registered its existence let alone know that its people have endured a traumatic civil war. For those fleeing from the fighting this was one possible route out; difficult enough in a vehicle, arduous beyond imagination for those who had to do it on foot.

If they succeeded they would arrive in a high valley, a place called Sukhunobod. Rahul Khan was one of the few outsiders to have been there, sent by the UN's refugee agency to check out the situation of those who had fled. When he and his team got up there they found over three thousand new arrivals, mostly women and children, crammed into the villages and former collective farms. It was September and if nothing were done they wouldn't survive the winter. Rahul had a month to get a camp set up, supplies in, and distribution systems in place before the road became impassable.

He had by then had years of experience of working with people displaced by civil war, first in Afghanistan and then in

Tajikistan itself, but something unexpected happened to him in that brief encounter with a remote mountain valley. The place itself moved him, he told his friend Lance, beyond what he could explain. There are huge boulders up there, Rahul said, with strange markings on them, that look as if the gods had rolled them down the mountainside, and here they landed, aeons ago. The markings could almost be a picture script but if they are, no one has ever deciphered them. The people who live in those valleys shrug and say, They are just scratches in the rock. How will anyone ever know how they got there? But he could not dismiss them so casually. Perhaps they had some religious significance, long before any religions we know of today? Or told a story? A long-ago herder giving expression to his artistic soul while he watched his sheep? To Rahul they represented something profound, a refusal of mortality. *I exist*, scratched the artist, the herder, the priest – perhaps the soldier who had been separated by blizzards from his army and wandered now alone in this valley, facing death by exposure and starvation. Today still I live, here, now, on this piece of earth. I ally with this rock that is older than all imagination, that will survive the obliterating force of time, to scratch some mark of my being here. I exist.

First light, 19 December 1996.

It's a freezing morning in the small mountain town of Gharm in Tajikistan, last stopping point before the road climbs deep into the Pamir Mountains. In a snow-covered yard five vehicles with UN insignia are parked, and their drivers wait as gradually small groups of men emerge from the low buildings that surround the yard on three sides. They are in leather coats and fur hats, and stamp their boots to keep circulation going as they wait for the last people to assemble.

Hugo Laval, a senior official from the UNHCR, the UN's refugee agency, stands a little to one side, watching. He is in his late fifties, Swiss, and not a man people immediately notice. Slightly built, with grey hair and a small beard already white, the lines on his face show the effects of decades of strain and of living in harsh climates. Among his colleagues he has a reputation for effectiveness under stress but few of them know anything about his personal life. Tajikistan, he reflects, is likely to be his last posting. He has no wish to retire but there are rules about this, as about most things. But before he is forced to stop he will see this peace process through to a conclusion. After years of painstaking negotiation a ceasefire has been agreed, and a group of UN military observers has arrived to monitor it. Today they will set off into the mountains to try to find the groups of armed men hidden up there, and make sure they know what their leaders have signed up to. With them are both Tajik government officials and representatives of the Islamic Renaissance Party – a historic moment, the first time that Tajiks from both sides of the conflict are taking part in a joint exercise. If they succeed, the end of the war may be in sight.

Yesterday they were all in Dushanbe, the capital of Tajikistan, where he was briefing them on the terms of the ceasefire. He has travelled with them this far to see that all the arrangements are in place, but when the five vehicles set off he will return to Dushanbe. His younger colleague, Rahul Khan, will be going with them.

Hugo observes the dynamics as everyone assembles. The two groups of Tajiks are keeping their distance from each other, old-style communist officials in one huddle, those representing the Islamic opposition groups in the other, the suspicions from the years of bitter conflict very near the surface. You could guess their political affiliation by their appearance, he thinks. The government delegation are Brezhnev throwbacks, their heavy-jowled faces clean shaven, their expressions unyielding, and underneath their thick coats they are in suits and ties. The Islamic opposition are full-bearded and wear long tunic-shirts with thick woollen waistcoats over loose trousers. The visiting UN internationals look strangely nondescript by comparison, and hover awkwardly at a little distance, not wanting to be seen to be associated more with one side than the other. Hugo is annoyed, for their separateness could so easily be interpreted as arrogance.

Rahul is – as so often – the exception. Hugo is his manager, but he watches him with something more engaged than the eye of a colleague. He has watched his progress since they first met in Delhi eleven years ago at a critical time in Rahul's life. Now at forty-one he has, Hugo thinks, an appealing combination of talents: the energy of one younger and the maturity of judgement of one older than his years. Physically he is not unlike the Tajiks: he has the same strong dark hair and marked features, but he is taller than most of them by a head and his trim beard is just a black line highlighting the shape of his jaw; enough to pass among the traditionalists as a beard, not enough to mark him as different when he is dealing with government officials. His clothes vary according to who he is working with. He adapts, without apparent effort; it is part of his function. Yet no one watching would mistake him for one of the Tajiks. They are all tired men, hardened by what they have gone through. Rahul's face has clean lines, unmarked by either defeat or aggression.

He has been talking briefly to the Russian journalist who is accompanying the mission, but now he begins moving between the groups of Tajiks. Hugo is not close enough to hear but from Rahul's body language he gathers that he is suggesting that there should be a mixed group travelling in each vehicle, someone from government, someone from the opposition. He's an instinctive mediator, Hugo thinks, whether officially required of him or not. Conversations get going; the groups begin tentatively to coalesce. Rahul pauses, then leaves them to it and goes over to join the five drivers who are standing at a little distance. That move seems to Hugo to capture something essential about the man. The drivers have kept themselves apart, not presuming to talk to the important people they will be driving. Rahul saw and moved over to join them, to disturb the division of status, to establish their commonality. A kind of courtesy, you could call it, something bred in him? But it is more natural, more specifically Rahul. He is as interested in the drivers as he is in everyone else. He lacks that instinctive filter that enables people to sort out who is 'one of us' and who isn't. Such openness is too exhausting for most people to contemplate but it is obvious that it doesn't tire him. It is what makes life interesting.

Now everyone is there, they are ready to go. They climb into the waiting vehicles. The drivers start up and one by one they set off, tailing each other, snaking up the mountain road. Hugo stands watching, curious now about what is happening inside those vehicles.

Hold the picture in your mind. Five white Land Cruisers with UN insignia, and in them twenty-three people: Tajiks, UN personnel, military observers, a journalist, drivers. Perhaps they are quiet as they watch the awesome mountains take shape around them. Perhaps they are talking, maybe even the occasional joke, a tentative camaraderie developing.

Then the squeal of brakes, as the front vehicle pulls to a sudden halt.

~ 2 ~

Dawn comes to the ancient Himalayan city of Kathmandu and the day starts for Lance Bergsen, Rahul's closest friend. For some minutes after waking he lies still, holding on to the warmth of his bed; and before he allows the day to intrude he takes stock of his life.

It is not, he decides, satisfactory. He is forty-six and single still, and not by choice. His last serious relationship ended three years ago, and nothing has arrived to replace it. It is probably his fault – he is awkward with women until he gets to know them; and he lets himself get too busy, filling the gap. 'Home' is an elusive concept. He carries a Canadian passport but he only started life there at fourteen and has never felt strongly about the place. His childhood memories are of England, cycling in the villages around Lincoln, but there is no one there now that he knows. Ever since he started work he has been moving from country to country, three years here, two there. How long can you keep that up? He does his job well but he's been doing it for too long. It's time he took a break. And it's far too long since he and Rahul saw each other. He decides he will phone today, see if he can pin him down to a date.

The last time he got him on the phone he was just about to leave for Moscow and the current round of the interminable peace negotiations.

'It's time we went walking,' Lance said. 'When you get back from Moscow, let's fix a time.'

'We can fix it,' Rahul said, 'but we may have to unfix it. That's how things go here.'

Lance lurches out of bed, pulls on a thick wool sweater in bright colours (knitted by women in a local community project) and socks as thick as slippers (likewise), and pads down the chilly corridor. He is an unusually tall man, big-boned, a craggy head with thick hair and a habit of bending forward to listen. You can imagine him walking in mountains but he seems too big to fit comfortably into a living room. Like his Viking ancestors he is an adventurer, but there any resemblance ends, for he is gentle, a bear who takes care not to use his strength. He has large hands that look as if they can fix things, competent hands, reliable. A man, people often think, it would be good to have near you in a crisis and crises seem to have drawn him. His first real job was as an emergency relief worker in Ethiopia during the terrible famine of 1974; mainly humping bags of grain, he would hastily add if anyone seemed to think this sounded impressive. When he was no longer needed there he became a volunteer with a Canadian agency working with landless peasants in Pakistan; and so it has gone on. Now he's getting near the end of his time in Nepal and once again he has foolishly allowed himself to be caught by love of the place, and he hates the thought of going.

In the kitchen he starts to prepare breakfast. He lives an expatriate life but without the usual support services; there is no house-servant here. He likes his comforts but he knows what they are better than anyone else, and he prefers to attend to his own needs. He switches on the kettle. No sign of life. He turns on a light switch. Nothing happens. Another power cut. He gets out the Primus stove that he keeps in the storeroom for such occasions, lights it and turns on the radio (battery run) as he waits for the water to boil. Wherever he is, breakfast begins with the World Service news.

Today he listens with more than usual attention for there is an item about Tajikistan. UN military observers are in the country to ensure that all sides are adhering to the ceasefire. The presidents of Russia and Iran have said it heralds a new era of stability for the region.

After that there is nothing of interest. He turns it off and gets ready to leave.

A fifteen-minute walk brings him to the office of Lifeline International, the development agency whose Nepali operation he heads. When he first joined to set up an office in India, Lifeline was still so small that no one there had heard of it. It has grown now, and he's not sure it's an improvement. The head office in Brighton is in the throes of restructuring, a recurring disease like malaria, and his in-tray is stacked with a depressing pile of memos. Organograms. Strategy papers. Policy guidelines. Monitoring frameworks. If he responds to all this stuff it will take the whole damn day and he has more urgent things to attend to. If he doesn't, the wrong decisions will go ahead without challenge and he will pay for it later.

'I thought you lot were committed to being un-bureaucratic?' He hears Rahul's voice, watching from the sidelines the mounds of paperwork that he processes. It was easy enough for Rahul to mock, he was the ultimate freelancer in those days, a journalist and a social activist, working to no master. To be unconstrained in using his own judgement, he said, was as necessary to him as the air he breathed. OK, Lance said, if you joined us you'd give up a degree of freedom, but you'd get something much bigger in exchange. You want to change things, and you know you can't work alone for ever.

Well, that was one argument I won, Lance thinks.

He takes a break from his in-tray to dial the number of Rahul's office in Dushanbe. Engaged. He tries again later. Still engaged.

As he moves through the day a vague anxiety lurks. The phones in Dushanbe often don't work, perhaps that's all it is. Tajikistan is a hell of a place to work. It's tricky enough here in Nepal with Maoists active in the villages near where Lifeline operates. He's having to take decisions about security all the time. His Nepali staff will come back from a project visit saying, 'It's all quiet,' and the next day they'll hear that two villagers were killed just after they had left. Was it a reprisal for being involved in a project supported by an international organization? But Rahul's job in Tajikistan is even tougher. If only they could get that damn peace treaty signed, and he could move on to something less stressful. But Lance doesn't have much hope. It's not just the political situation, it's Rahul himself. He's been like that since Lance first met him in India, never able to stay away from where things were going wrong and people getting hurt. There would be some new outbreak of rioting, Hindus and Muslims butchering each other, and Rahul of all people would choose to walk into those crowds. Son of a Muslim father and a Hindu mother, to the Hindus he would be a Muslim, to the Muslims a Hindu, he couldn't appear anywhere near the riots without becoming a target. But he wasn't listening to caution. 'I have a contact,' he would say. 'I need to get there quick.' And he would be gone. Communal riots, peasants being thrown off the land, women being raped by the police sent in to bring order – and always Rahul was there, interviewing people, writing it all, driven by an urge to tell what was actually happening. His report would come back, incisive, factual, the insistence on rigour doing nothing to dim the passion that underlay it. He had been doing it from the time he left university, he said, when Indira Gandhi declared a state emergency and took to herself the powers to rule by diktat. His parents' friends had started disappearing, there were police atrocities, and he was feeding stories to foreign journalists and sending off reports to Amnesty International. His parents had the same kind of history. His father had been jailed by the British, his mother had gone into dangerous places to help the victims of violence, but Rahul was their only son and they wanted him out of the country while things were so fraught. They offered to send him to London to do a further degree but he wouldn't go. He said he would go when the emergency was over, and that's what he had done. But from the day he got back he had been drawn right back into it. And from riots he had moved on to wars.

Lance presses the Send button on his response to Brighton and dials Rahul's number once again.

~ 3 ~

Early afternoon now, and several thousand miles to the south-east: in the tropical country of Laos where the Mekong River flows wide and slow, a young woman closes the door of the house where she has lived for almost four years. While her husband handles the suitcases that she has hurriedly packed, she lifts their two children into the waiting taxi. Everyone in, they set off for the airport. They are about to fly back to Ireland, where she has never felt she belonged.

Tessa Maguire is thirty-five, but she has the same slim youthfulness that Rahul first saw in her at nineteen – reed-like, he called it, flexible, bending in the wind – and the same light brown curls around her face. She has what she thinks of with some irritation as a typical Irish complexion, a hint of freckles on a pale skin that reacts too quickly to the sun. Her face seems to her to have nothing special to recommend it – a small nose, a possibly too-wide mouth, eyebrows so pale you can hardly see them – but it doesn't strike others as plain for it is alive with movement, a barometer of her every thought. If she is the least bit embarrassed, her skin flushes. If she warms to people, they know, for the responsive pleasure lights her face. If she is absorbed by some serious concern she seems to retreat into stillness. If she is amused, her eyes show it instantly.

It is those eyes that are the giveaway about the changes in her, for at any moment when she is not talking or listening they

15

revert to the alertness that sets a mother apart, a permanent consciousness of responsibility. She is aware of every nuance of their body-language, the tension in their small frames at this unexpected sudden departure. Sam, not yet four, sits bunched close up to her, unnaturally still. He's a child who feels things deeply, but doesn't always find a way to show it. There is something touchingly vulnerable about the way he accepts that it is his little sister who gets to sit on Tessa's lap. At two Alisa is already the more robust, secure as long as she is physically close. Her curls brush against Tessa's chin, her plump legs wriggle. Tessa has a momentary memory of her at the breast, looking up as she suckles, her small fist gripping one of Tessa's fingers.

Through the taxi window she watches the moving picture of lush tropical vegetation. This may be the last time she will see it. She loves this place yet she feels a strange detachment. Her mind is elsewhere, and not just on her children, or their sudden departure. She was woken early this morning by a line of poetry thrusting itself into her mind with the force of a troubling dream. It will not go away. It has been circling her brain ever since:

The wind blows hard, the night is dark, the stormy waves are rising –

It's part of a couplet but she can't remember the second line and it's nagging at her. It is a verse that Rahul once translated from an Urdu poem. Or maybe a Persian one? But what brought it back to her on this particular day, to wake her in the early hours?

She looks at her husband Ben, her partner of eleven years. His face gives little indication of what he is feeling. Until less than a month ago he was buoyant, absorbed in a job he loved. A geologist, he was monitoring prospecting applications on behalf of the Lao government, until in a remote mountain area he began stumbling on troubling stories about the activities of a mining company. People fleeing to escape oppressive working conditions, villages burnt if their men refused to take work on the mine. Back in his government office he began asking questions, to meet instant reserve on the faces of his Lao colleagues, buck-passing, silent withdrawal. Higher officials, it seemed, had been bought off to hear no evil. And before he could ask any more he was presented with a deportation order, forty-eight hours to leave the country. Since then he has been in a state of shock. Normally decisive, he has left all the arrangements to her, flights to book, suitcases to pack, arrangements with friends to take care of the rest of their stuff. Put it in store, waiting to be crated to wherever they might settle next.

They arrive at the airport, check in. The children are clingy. As they walk out onto the tarmac Tessa carries Alisa on her hip, Sam holds tight to her other hand. Ben follows, looking harried, loaded down with everyone's hand luggage and teddy bears. They find their seats, settle the children. The flight takes off. Now that they are actually in the air Ben seems to be recovering some of his usual personality and is showing the children the buttons for lights and the way the tables fold down. Grateful for a few minutes to herself she looks out of the plane window.

They are flying into the setting sun, and must be over India by now. In the toy town landscape, cities straggle along a snaking river. One of them will be Delhi where she and Rahul had their first chance encounter. Chance? Yes, of course it was chance, though looking back it acquired an air of inevitability. It was in a bookshop in a little lane in Old Delhi; Rahul was twenty-five, a journalist, and the bookshop was a place he often arranged to meet people, but that day the man he was supposed to be interviewing had not turned up. He'd decided to give him another fifteen minutes, he told her afterwards, and had perched on a stool near the counter to wait —

To Tessa, coming in from the searing light outside, everything seemed dark for the first few seconds. Gradually her eyes adjusted, to take in crowded shelves, books in several languages piled chaotically, people squeezed in between somehow, browsing, talking. She and her travelling companion Nalini felt like clumsy tortoises, their backpacks threatening to knock things over. She'd noticed a young man on a stool near the desk and assumed he was one of the staff, though he was taking his responsibilities remarkably casually. 'Can we put these in that corner while we look around?' she asked. 'Go ahead,' he said, and got up to help them. They started looking through the travel guides.

After a few minutes she glanced up and saw that he was watching them still. He seemed to be amused. At what?

At the unconscious irony of the picture they made, he told her later, an Indian girl in tight jeans and a T-shirt, and a pale-skinned tourist in Indian dress, a long *kameez* tunic over slim cotton trousers with a *dupatta* scarf at her neck, ends dangling down her back. He had been watching them with the idle curiosity of a young man sizing up female attractiveness without any intention of pursuing it. The Indian girl had the kind of conventional beauty that didn't appeal to him, possibly because his aunts kept introducing him hopefully to girls who looked much like her; but something about the other girl intrigued him. Perhaps her flyaway hair that gave her a windblown look even inside? And a sudden smile that lit her face as her friend said something that amused her.

He got off his stool and moved over to see what book they were so earnestly looking at.

'Ajanta,' he said. 'Have you been there?'

They hadn't yet, so he started describing it, how you come on it unexpectedly in a bare landscape, the curving face of an escarpment with its sequence of caves, and when you get inside, emerging from the dark are the most extraordinary paintings, centuries old. The girls abandoned the book. Who would not prefer a real-life guide, especially one whose relaxed confidence was undeniably attractive? She and Nalini were used to having to fend off unwelcome attention from the hordes of young men who seemed to populate India's streets but there was nothing pushy about this one; his manner was easy but courteous. His voice was English-medium-educated – a sign of privilege, making Tessa instinctively cautious. She didn't, on the whole, take to people to whom life came too easily. But there was something appealing about the way his hair fell onto his forehead, and his amused eyes made her want to smile back even though she didn't know what the joke was.

They got chatting. Where are you from? he asked, meaning Tessa, but it was Nalini who answered. From Sheffield, she said, surprising him – her parents were Gujarati emigrants and this was her first time in India.

'And you?' he turned to Tessa.

'I'm a nomad,' she said. 'I just keep moving.'

Nalini said, 'Actually she's Irish but she won't say so because she's lived in so many different countries. And she knows more Hindi than me. She's been learning it, before she came.'

'You have?' He switched to Hindi. 'And how come you didn't live in Ireland?'

Was he expecting she wouldn't understand? Piqued, she replied in carefully formed short Hindi sentences. 'My dad was an engineer. He liked Asia. We went where he was building roads.' But, damn, the verb endings were tripping her up. She said in exasperation, '*Dekhiye* – you see? I'm a complete beginner.'

He laughed and switched back to English. 'Let's go find a *chai* shop. I want to hear more.'

The girls looked at each other. Why not? They recovered their backpacks and followed him out and down the lane till he wheeled suddenly into a tea-house where he was clearly known. Over a succession of small cups of spicy tea, he drew Tessa out about the countries she had lived in as a child. It felt so natural describing for him the exotic birds of Indonesia, or wading through the flooded streets of Bangkok after the monsoon broke. How her mother had tried to keep Ireland alive for them, serving up in the steamy heat of Jakarta or Singapore vignettes of a land of cold rain and mists, of fresh milk from the farm down the lane. But she was her father's child, alert to the sounds and colours around her, excited to be taken off to experience half-forgotten history, a temple that emerged suddenly from the forest, a ceremony that took over a town for a day, a procession of monks in yellow robes.

The thing was done. Even then they knew, they both knew.

'It was your face,' he said later. 'It's incapable of pretence. I saw someone who was eager for life and wasn't going to let it pass her by. And your smile.'

(*It's still magic, the way it lights you up.*

Don't, Rahul.

I can't help it.)

He started telling them, both of them, but already Tessa knew it was mainly her, about a village project he was involved with. His Delhi friends were thoroughly bored hearing about it, he said, so it was good to have a new audience. The village, Hasilgah, was on land his grandfather had once owned. He was a follower of Gandhi and had responded to the call to give away a portion of his land to the people who lived on it, whose ancestors had for centuries been serfs there. As a child Rahul used to walk there with his grandfather, listening as he talked to the villagers, and he felt it a great thing to be the grandson of a man of such generous spirit. But even then he had puzzled over why owning the land seemed to have made so little difference: the villagers were still poor, still caught in the habits of feudal deference. Till gradually he understood that for them to improve their lives there would have to be others working alongside them, people who could imagine other ways of doing things, who could see what the villagers themselves might achieve by working together.

She was captivated. How could she not be? His enthusiasm was impossible to resist. He was articulate without being pretentious, full of ideals without being naive. He was twenty-five and had done things she knew she would not achieve in a lifetime, yet he was paying her the compliment of taking her seriously, when he could have dismissed them, backpackers, passing through.

'I'm going there tomorrow,' he said. 'You can come if you'd like to see it.'

Flying miles above the earth, the children need her attention. A meal is brought, stories read, games played. Now the cabin lights have been dimmed and they settle the children, who eventually slip into sleep, Alisa in the seat next to her, Sam across the aisle next to Ben. She watches their sleeping faces, and her protective instinct seeks to hold them safe. She is taking them away from everything they have known, from the place where she carried each of them in turn in a sling attached to her body, as Lao infants are carried. What is she taking them into?

Soon Ben too is deep asleep, exhausted by stress. For the first time in two days nothing is required of her and she is free to retreat into an inner life that has nothing to do with any of them. She pushes up the blind of the oval window of the plane to look down at the pattern of lights twinkling below, imagining she is tracing the journey to the village ...

She remembers every stage of it; she could still, all these years later, guide a stranger there. A train east from Delhi along the wide Ganges plain, watching through the train windows the fields that slipped by silently, the distant figures walking along the bunds, mud ridges between fields. They halted at each station, where barefoot young boys in threadbare shorts came running to the windows calling 'Chai, garm chai' – tea, hot tea, which they poured with practised speed into little clay cups that the passengers would toss from the window as the train pulled out again, earth to earth. Out at the station, through a dusty town, past market stalls and shops on spindly wooden legs, past a Buddhist temple where pilgrims prostrated themselves in front of a vast golden statue. We've arrived, she thought the first time, but the slow part of the journey was just beginning; a tonga ride, horse-drawn cart that carried them until the rough paths gave up and they walked the last stretch. His grandfather's house was still there, Rahul pointed, just over that rise; but inherited now by an uncle who regarded him as just such a naive fool as his grandfather. And now they saw the village, a collection of mud-brick buildings with pumpkin vines scrambling over corrugated iron roofs and a cleared space under an old peepul tree. Hasilgah.

Adults stopped what they were doing to watch their arrival. Children with skinny legs and matted hair gathered around calling, 'Rahul-ji, Rahul-ji', then stopped to stare at the two strange young women. Nalini, who had hardly ventured beyond the middle-class security of the homes of relatives, was almost rigid with shyness. Tessa, who in childhood was always among people who lived differently from her, sat down on the ground and waited for the children to cluster around her. She tried out her tourist Hindi on them. They giggled, and plied her with questions.

Rahul handed them over to one of the villagers and for two days she hardly spoke to him; he was deep in discussions with the project workers. A young girl called Maya shyly but proudly showed them around each of the activity centres. The communal dining area. The carpentry workshop. The clinic. The school that they were so proud to have built. They walked through a series of settlements that sprawled through cultivated fields down to the almost dry riverbed. They were shown the place where the villagers gathered reeds for baskets, which they sold to tourists who came to see the Buddhist temple; and with the money they bought tools they could not make. They traipsed across the 'jungle' area, tracts of land too poor to cultivate, being shown the plants that produced traditional remedies, then back to the experimental plots with plants that Rahul's friend, an agronomist, had introduced them to. The girls' minds opened wider as they listened to dilemmas they had never had to consider in lives where water came out of taps and food out of the fridge.

Two days of sitting cross-legged on the ground to eat meals prepared in huge pots, while Tessa tried to tune into the talk around her; two nights sleeping on string beds; and something had shifted in her. She had crossed some boundary of the spirit and would never be the same again. Rahul needed to get back to meetings in Delhi. Nalini had a flight to catch. Tessa had taken a year out before university and was making up her plans as she went along.

She looked up to see Rahul watching her with amused eyes. He had known her only a few days but he seemed already to have her measure. 'You're welcome to stay a while if you want to,' he said, 'I'm sure Chandra-ji will find something useful for you to do.'

For him, she thought, it was nothing special. He was doing it all the time, tempting his friends to get involved.

He was back in ten days, to see if she had had enough. She said, 'I don't have anything to get back for till September. There are things I could do here with the children. Can I stay?'

He said, 'I hoped you might say that.'

How do people find each other? What chance in a million was there that among the thousands of people she had passed in her travels across India, on the crowded pavements of Bombay, the cheap hotels of Rajasthan, the rattling seats of the train to Agra, she should have been noticed by the one person able to connect all the disparate, confused parts of her being and give them purpose?

Suddenly, cutting jagged across memory, the line of poetry is back:

> *The wind blows hard, the night is dark, the stormy waves*
> *are rising –*

She tries to remember when Rahul translated it. What was going on that made him choose that verse? Her mind moves over the volatile places he has chosen to work in. She holds quietly to herself the awareness of his ongoing existence and how despite everything that continues to separate them she is seldom unaware of where he is. Like migrating birds they have kept their own radar going, inaudible to others. His translations are part of this private language, fragments of Urdu poetry that he grew up hearing and delights to share. She has a stock of them in her mind, collected over years. They pop out at odd times, and often afterwards she will discover a link to something that is going on that she was hardly aware of at the time. She has come to think of it as akin to the perception of animals, beyond what science can explain. Like the stories her father used to tell when she was a child, picked up on his restless travels across Asia, about forest creatures that would sense the coming of rain, or lions in the zoo that had started roaring two hours before an earthquake struck.

But what *is* the second line?

Flight announcements break harshly into Tessa's semi-sleep. They are approaching Dublin; the present tense faces her. Wake the children, confused again and querulous. Fasten seat belts, ready to land.

Out of the plane they are greeted by a cold northern wind. Huddled in their inadequate coats they look, as they feel, like refugees. In the airport concourse she searches the crowd, to find her older sister Maeve waving windmill arms. And there

26

are Maeve's three boys, suddenly so large compared to when Tessa last saw them, and her mother behind them, looking frail. Hugs, hellos. Maeve and her mother lift Tessa's children up. Through her tiredness she feels humble. Four years ago they went off to Laos with hardly a thought about the people they were leaving behind, yet now that her life there has come to an abrupt end, her family are here for her.

Maeve says, 'We're going out to Uncle Flynn's summer house. It's for you to use, until you've sorted yourselves out.'

She drives them out beyond Dublin's south-eastern suburbs to a group of cottages a few hundred yards from the coast. The house is bleak, with the air of desolation that comes with not being lived in. Its only means of heating is one small wood fire; clearly no one thought to be here in winter. Maeve, the family organizer, has brought electric heaters and bustles about, shaking out blankets. Her mother worries after her. 'You're sure now there aren't fleas in here, so near to the sand?' Maeve's boys hoot and cavort around the echoing spaces. Alisa clings like a koala on her hip. Sam is close at her side, his eyes following every move of his big boy cousins. Ben stands just inside the door, as if none of this is anything to do with him.

She looks out of the window. The wind has flattened the few brave plants that have attempted to take over the waste land. There's a view down a short lane to a deserted winter beach where she can just see an upturned boat, and she remembers a beach in Thailand where once she watched the early morning light over the sea and sat on an upturned boat beneath banana fronds to write to Rahul.

Suddenly she remembers the second line of the couplet that has been circling her brain.

The wind blows hard, the night is dark, the stormy waves
are rising
The anchor's chain is broken, and the captain is asleep

The sense of unease deepens. Rahul, what are you telling me?

~ 4 ~

The morning of 21st December: Hugo Laval, in his office in Dushanbe, is finding it impossible to concentrate. His mind is stuck in Gharm, watching the five white Land Cruisers wind their way along the road, to disappear around a corner. They are equipped with radios, but there has been no news.

He decides to take a break. He wraps up well. Dushanbe's winters are mild compared to elsewhere in Central Asia but today there is snow on the ground and the air is cold on his face as he walks the streets of the city centre. He looks up at the tall winter trees and the statues of the square. He passes an elderly couple who stand huddled in long coats at a makeshift stall by the roadside, selling their bath taps and cutlery. What does it take to reduce you to that? Ragged children scavenge in dustbins. The windows of the technical college are like blind eyes – the government has no money to pay teachers. A factory stands closed, a monument to an experiment that failed. The centrally controlled economy was creaking for ten years before it finally imploded, and for this, one of the poorest of Russia's internal colonies, the fallout has been devastating. And on top of all that, the effects of civil conflict, the slow slide into loss of government control, violence escalating.

He remembers how it was in their first weeks here, his and Rahul's. No one went out at night; young men, gone feral, roamed the streets. Food supplies had run down, the hospital had run out of medicines. They have pulled back from that, but there is always the fear that it could come again.

His mind flips again to his last sight of Rahul, talking to the drivers, then everyone setting off. He is bothered for them all but he feels a personal responsibility for Rahul, for it was his decision to send him. Most of the military observers assigned to this difficult mission are new to Tajikistan and they are likely to be encountering some very antagonistic people. It was essential that there be someone with them who has the experience to handle that. Rahul does. He was out of the country when decisions had to be made but Hugo got him on the phone and explained the situation. 'Sorry about the short notice, but would you?' Rahul had other things booked but he cancelled them.

He has known Rahul since he was thirty, and even then he was juggling roles – journalist, social activist, running Lifeline International's operations in India. By the time Hugo got him his first job with a UN agency – in Afghanistan – he had way more hands-on experience than most of his colleagues, and a tendency to dismiss them as useless. He has learnt some tact since then, but the truth is, for anything involving negotiating with difficult people, he has skills Hugo cannot easily find elsewhere, and certainly not in one person. He is fluent in Tajik, from years of working just across the border in northern Afghanistan. He has been three years now in Tajikistan, and knows the terrain. He has travelled to the camps where the Islamic opposition leaders hold sway. He listens – that comes, he once said, from working in a village in India. There's a pace of change people can handle and it's not going to go faster because you get worked up about it. Yet for all that chameleon ability to fit in, he never lets go of the focus, what they are here for. There have been hundreds of thousands of people displaced by this war and until a peace treaty has been negotiated there is no way those currently in exile can come home. Rahul is the man he has selected to work alongside him in the small cross-agency team that services the peace negotiations. Together they draft proposals, carry them from one side to the other, try to edge people who are deeply threatened by each other towards a viable compromise. Rahul knows the terms of the cease-fire because he helped negotiate them. He has the strongest possible interest in making sure that the rebel leaders up in those mountains know what they are.

Hugo turns, to get back to his office – and finds a message is on his desk:

Please go immediately to the communications control room.

He sees as he enters the room that there is a senior official there from each of the UN agencies. All there, and waiting for him; by going for that walk he has held them up. He feels unduly upset by the incident. It is not his habit to be late.

He turns to the UN head of mission, Ruiz Pérez, a grey-haired Chilean, to apologize. Pérez nods and begins. 'You will know, I imagine, why I have called you here. Radio contact has been lost with the team that was sent to monitor the ceasefire. Their instructions were to communicate morning and evening. We are forced to conclude that they are not in a position to do so. Our assumption is that they have been attacked by rebel forces.'

No one moves. No one speaks. Hugo becomes aware that his pulse is slowing. A couple of times in recent years he has fainted. God, please don't let it happen now.

Ruiz Pérez has begun to speak again. 'I have met with the President. UN military and communications personnel are on their way to Gharm to assist local officials to discover what has happened. You will be called together again when there is anything to tell you. Until then, this news does not move beyond the people in this room.'

~ 5 ~

On the Irish coast – five hours behind – it is dark still, but Tessa is awake, lying with eyes open next to Ben's sleeping body. Jet lag, of course; if she were still in Laos it would be waking-up time. And disorientation. Their leaving was too sudden.

31

She gives up on the idea that sleep might return and slips out of bed, wraps herself in the dressing gown Maeve has lent her, and goes downstairs. Yesterday's fire has burnt down to a few glowing coals and the loveless damp of the house has crept back. She starts to get the fire going again. That's a legacy of her time in the village, she can always get a fire to revive. She piles on kindling, waits for it to catch, adds a log and holds a newspaper against the open front of the fireplace to funnel the air. A rush of wind in the chimney; the flames flare into life.

She rustles through their still-unsorted things till she finds some paper and an envelope and writes to Rahul to tell him what has happened to them, where they are. She ends by saying, 'Rahul, where are you? I keep hearing you quoting poetry. Something's going on.'

She is about to address the envelope when she turns, hearing something. Ben is standing at the door in pyjamas, hair tousled, eyes struggling out of sleep. 'What on earth are you doing?'

'I couldn't sleep.' She puts the envelope down on a side table.

'I woke and you weren't there,' he says. 'I couldn't work out where I was.'

'Me too. Come and warm up.'

He comes to stand close to the fire and looks around the unlived-in room. 'My head's full of all the stuff that was going on in Laos.'

She nods and says again, 'Me too.' Then, 'This place seems unreal. I'd imagined we would be staying with Maeve but they're crowded already.'

He starts poking the fire. 'So this is Uncle Flynn's place. Is he the one who thinks his own jokes are so funny? Who asked me if I was going to make the family fortune in oil?'

'Yes. But he's OK. He just gets like that when he meets someone new.'

Ben is not going to take easily to being surrounded by her extended family. He has done his best to avoid them ever since the first encounter, eleven years ago, when he was confronted by the aunts and their special combination of intrusive curiosity and disapproval. That she should have got married without telling them! And to someone she had only known three months! And not in a church. And he a Jew. Her mother was different; she and Maeve had taken Ben on trust, this man who had succeeded in persuading the restless Tessa to settle down.

Restless like her father, that's what they all said. Now that she is back in Dublin she is thinking of him again, the father who didn't live to see her as an adult, who all his life had to get away. Throughout her childhood she was brought back here almost every year, but marking time till they could get back to Jakarta, Singapore, Bangkok. She turns the pages of those constantly shifting homes and sees herself in them, caught in moments of her growing up by photos held in place by little corner-mounts. A child with skinny legs up a tree in the lush vegetation of an expatriate garden, or on her father's shoulders, standing in a crowd to watch a flotilla of ornately decorated boats move slowly down river. Strange that he could have been so interested in other people's processions and cymbals but he couldn't see a Catholic church without wanting to walk the other way. Maybe as an outsider he felt safe, free to be interested without any threat of being drawn in? For a moment she feels she has had an insight that might help her understand something, something about herself as much as about her father – she and Rahul. And then she isn't sure. Uncertain light, flickering, then gone.

Ben has given up with the fire. He puts the poker back in its stand. 'Let's get back to bed.'

'I don't feel sleepy yet. You go, I'll come soon.'

Wait to hear the bed creaking upstairs. Silence now.

She picks up her envelope and addresses it. In the morning she will walk to the shop to post it, but it will take a week at least to get to Dushanbe and then if he's out of town, who knows when he'll get it?

There's a soughing sound, wind in the chimney. Staring into the flickering flames she remembers winter evenings in Hasilgah, how they would sit talking at night after the village was asleep, huddled close to the charcoal brazier that was all they had of light and heat. Cocooned by night, he told her stories, his words weaving spells. Words, words ... Words are so powerful, he said, they affect how we see, and he told her how the villagers' first collective decision had been to rename the place where they had been born, where their fate was set in one form and now they were trying to change it. From before anyone could remember it had been known as Be-hasil-gah, the place where nothing can be achieved. No one knew what experiences had led its earliest inhabitants to give it so cruel a name, but in the new energy the project had released the

34

villagers decided to drop the *be* ('without') so it became just Hasil-gah, the place of achievement.

And what place am I in now? she thinks. The place of retreat. But it's not a chosen retreat, as in meditating; this withdrawal from the world has been forced on them and their psyches have yet to accept it. She has no spaces in the day to think about it, she is too busy – the house has to be made habitable, the children have no routine, their toys are still in Laos, her family are wanting her to connect. But Ben is still in a bewildered state, his known life snatched from him and no concept of what comes after this strange, suspended present. He thinks he is helping but all he does is move things about indecisively and then shift them again. Just take the kids for a walk, she feels like saying, and leave me to sort things. But she knows that she too is part of the problem. Her hands may be competent but her mind is not on it; and it is only now, alone at night, that she feels free to give space to what is preoccupying her. She cannot stop thinking about Rahul.

She seems to have hit one of those moments when her closeness to him, that is always hovering in the wings, comes right up centre stage. He was imprinted on her soul, she sometimes thinks, at a critical, deeply impressionable moment in her inner development. But she has learnt to live with it, to moderate it, to contain it where it does not disturb. He has taken himself off to a life of constant challenge in difficult places, she has settled for a quiet life with a man she started by liking and came to love. She is a wife, a mother. Where Ben goes, she follows, and she makes her own relationship to the life she finds there. It works. It has worked for eleven years. Yet now ...

Rahul needs something of her.

She dismisses the thought. It is irrational, it cannot be the case. He is self-sufficient beyond what most people could ever comprehend. Yet she feels it, and the pull cannot be resisted. She has always felt she understood him where others didn't, that they were intimately connected – it was why she stayed nine months in the village. He had never imagined, he told her afterwards, that she would have stuck it out so long. He couldn't have done it, he said; four days was about his limit. There were other volunteers, medical students who helped out at the clinic, people brought in to run training courses, but they came, they went. Tessa lived there. At first, perhaps, she had been sustained by amazement, by the possibility of living simply, by feeling a new language begin to work in her brain, gradually realizing she was saying simple things without conscious effort; and by the children, whom she found endlessly absorbing. But the concentration it all took was exhausting and claustrophobia began to threaten. To the women, the project workers, everything about her was an object of curiosity and comment, and except for Rahul's fleeting visits there was no one to talk to about her reactions. What held her there was that he did keep reappearing.

On his brief visits he was always busy but she knew he was aware of her, not asking for attention but available the moment he had time. She saw the amusement in his eyes as she picked up the village dialect, which he had never done; how she absorbed their code of behaviour, sitting with the women who laughed as she tried to learn the practical skills they took for granted. She was a nineteen-year-old, just beginning to engage with life, but he saw that she had capabilities and instincts of which she herself was still unaware and he assumed a mentor role, protective and encouraging. He used her as a foil for his own thinking – problems in the project, issues he was investigating, the tensions between the Hindu and Muslim parts of his family and the legacy it had left him. He belonged to both communities or neither, he said, lightly, depending on which he chose at any moment; but she knew it went deeper than his tone suggested, connecting in some difficult-to-define way with what he had taken on there. Isolated from her own kind except for his visits, had he been half the man he was she would have imagined herself in love with him. Being the man he was, she had no hope of ever becoming important to him.

Just once she met his friends. She was in Delhi going through the tedious bureaucratic hoops of trying to get her visa extended. Rahul said, 'There's a sitar concert tomorrow night, a fantastic player, there's a group of us going. You must come.' She was shy among his articulate friends but she was aware all the time of his proximity and took courage from his acceptance. There was a young woman in a green and gold sari, Devaki, a film-maker; poised, effortlessly elegant, a remote kind of beauty. 'Tessa's working in the project,' Rahul said, and Devaki's eyes as she assessed Tessa were cool. Then they moved on. Tessa had a momentary frisson of wondering whether her own thoughts were as transparent. She could not imagine Devaki in her silk sari doing anything practical in the village. Devaki knew only Rahul-in-Delhi. Tessa saw him whole, the man who looked at the child who brought him a plate of food in the village, and smiled as he took it in a way that met the child for who she was. A fleeting moment of uncle-blessing so gentle, so powerful in its potential. This man could light the world.

How had he been so slow to recognize what there was between them? You are lucky if you encounter it once in a lifetime, and it had been there before him for months, but he had simply accepted it, never tried to give it a name. Was he so caught up with his issues and plans, so unknowing about what was happening to him emotionally that he could delight in the like-mindedness they had found in each other yet continue to think of it as something that belonged there in the village, that didn't face him with having to resolve anything about his life with Devaki? Was it because he still thought of her, Tessa, as so young? Perhaps he had been afraid? Was there, even then, a sense of the illicit? Something too good for life to let him have?

The fire is burning low. She puts on another log. She watches as a flame licks its edges and slowly it catches. The vague premonition she has been carrying becomes an intense conviction. He is in danger.

~ 6 ~

In the UN communications centre in Dushanbe Hugo waits with his colleagues for Ruiz Pérez to arrive. No one speaks. When Pérez comes in it is clear from his face that the news is not good.

'Radio contact has been made by a group of rebels operating in the mountains beyond Gharm. They attacked the convoy of vehicles, probably towards the end of the day on which it left. All twenty-three people have been taken hostage.'

Hostage, hostage, the word goes round in Hugo's head, refusing to be absorbed.

'Their leader is a man called Sadirov. Their demands are safe passage back into Tajikistan for scores of their men who are currently in Afghanistan. They have planted thirty bombs around Dushanbe. If their demands aren't met in five days they will detonate them all, then kill the hostages.'

A pause, for them to absorb it.

'Immediate actions: The government will issue radio warnings to people in Dushanbe not to go out of doors unless it is essential. All non-essential UN staff will be relocated to Uzbekistan, for their own safety and to pre-empt further attacks. You will each see that this is done in your own agencies. The government is in contact with the families of the Tajiks among the hostages. For UN personnel from outside Tajikistan, UNHCR will phone through daily updates to offices in the relevant countries, who will liaise with the families.' He turns to Hugo. Hugo nods.

Pérez continues. 'Negotiations will be led by the Minister of Security; but no one has any doubt that the convoy was targeted because it carried UN personnel, so I will be involved at each stage. I will be setting up a core group from among you to support me in this. The press will be kept informed but no names will be released as yet. There is a fine line to be trod; a degree of publicity is necessary but too much may raise the stakes. As far as we have been able to discover this is a group of bandits, not allied to any of the major groups that have been involved in the civil conflict. In one way that might make things easier. In another it is more difficult; we have no leverage.' He pauses before he states the unavoidable, unpalatable truth. 'We will do whatever is possible to get them out safely but as everyone in this room knows, there will be little scope for manoeuvre. If we give in to their demands, everyone will be less secure in the long term.' He waits again. 'It's an impossible situation. Somehow we will have to navigate it.'

Hugo gathers himself for the task ahead. This is not the first crisis of this kind that he has been caught up in but it is different from any other because its implications are personal. From the day he and Rahul met it was clear that they shared an outlook on what was important. Hugo has been able to delegate to him tasks he would trust to few others. He needs him, they all need him, he is vital to the peace negotiations. But it is more than that, much more. Not just work.

He thinks of the calls he has to make: Moscow, Islamabad, Santiago, Oslo, Nairobi, the list goes on. Delhi. He leaves it till last. He cannot bear to have to say it.

~ 7 ~

The sun rises on Delhi, on the house where Rahul grew up. His father, Hamza Asadullah Khan, professor of sociology, sits drinking his morning tea and listening to the sounds of the day getting going. Voices of children in the servants' quarters of the next door garden, the first hum of distant traffic. A resonant voice intones, *Allah o Akbar*, God is great, the call to prayer from a loudspeaker at the local mosque. From an empty lot on the other side of the main road come the voices of Hindu *bhajan* singers. They have taken to chanting their hymns there every morning, deliberately positioning themselves opposite this largely Muslim suburb. The notes flow together and contend. He thinks, this could be the start of a peaceful Delhi day, or it could turn into an incentive to riot.

No radio disturbs his slow start. As he gets older he protects himself from the bombardment of unwelcome daily news. If there are developments of any significance, doubtless someone will tell him.

Today is December the 22nd. In two days he will be eighty-three, an astonishing thought. In himself he feels as he has always felt, no different. But his body tells him. He has to take more frequent rests and there is less progress on his writing each day.

His thoughts drift to Rahul. What is he doing this morning? It is a month and more since they saw him. He must have been busy, for he hasn't phoned. Perhaps it means things are going well with the peace negotiations, so he is in demand. Perhaps it means they are going badly, so, equally, he is in demand. A verse by the poet Ghalib comes into his mind:

> I grapple with that fragment of ill-fate that is my untamed
> heart
> The enemy of ease, the friend of reckless wandering

Rahul is not reckless but restless he certainly has been. Perhaps his mind is too quick? It seems that as soon as he has learnt what he needs to know to do something well, he begins to look for the next thing. 'There's a war on,' his sister said, when he told them he was going to Tajikistan. 'Why does he have to go there?' The answer was, because there is a war and he thinks there is something he can do.

At that time, Hamza reflects, few people in the West would even have heard of the place. The world map they had all grown up with had shown a vast undifferentiated area called the USSR; of its Asian reaches hardly anything was commonly known. He remembers those first distant earth tremors in the geopolitical map, words like glasnost and perestroika beginning to be used. Then it all seemed to happen so suddenly, the bloc that had been communist Eastern Europe was cracking, the Berlin

Wall came down, the world as they had all known it careering forward, a heavy lorry with failing brakes. Old governments were thrown out and new ones took their place. The world's atlases were redesigned and all those new -stans appeared. Uzbekistan, Kyrgyzstan, Tajikistan. Yet even then no one could have guessed that Rahul's future was written in those names, not till the Tajiks rebelled against the old-style communist rulers who had been left behind, and long-buried tensions flared into civil war. Then there were people fleeing to cross the river into Afghanistan, drowning in its icy waters, or arriving in a pitiful state in the refugee camps where Rahul was working. And when the UN agencies were called in, he was one of the first to go.

Hamza thinks of all that his wife Sushila has had to deal with in these years, fielding the incomprehension of her family at the path Rahul has taken. Pakistan, Afghanistan, Tajikistan, to them it is all one, lands dominated by mullahs and fanatics where no one in their right mind would want to go. She will have none of such thinking but her relatives change the subject when she challenges them.

His eyes move around the room. Every item in it bears the imprint of her eye, and care, and skill. Perhaps only he knows how the danger that her only son exposes himself to preys on her mind; yet she just says, 'It's his life. He must choose.' Take care, she says to Rahul at the end of each phone call; unnecessarily, for Rahul does take care. He trains the people in his team that it is their job to take all reasonable precautions. Risk-taking is not just foolish, he tells them, it is irresponsible. 'And your own security?' Hamza asked. Rahul said, 'We're surrounded by security guards, everywhere we go. I would get rid of the lot if I had my way. It simply aggravates the sense of violence about to happen. We're humanitarian workers, we are unarmed, and we *have* to be. If we have any influence, it's only through a kind of moral legitimacy.'

He hears Sushila moving about. She is coming through the door. She smiles a greeting and comes to stand next to where he sits. Her hand rests on his shoulder, a touch light and warm with familiarity. The day begins.

They are just finishing breakfast when there is a knock at the door. The cook-housekeeper comes to tell them that there is a woman to see them.

They invite her in, offer tea. She says she is from the UN's refugee agency. 'I'm afraid I am bringing difficult news.'

They sit very still, waiting. They have been waiting for years, knowing that one day this would happen.

Kathmandu: The receptionist in Lance's office tells him there is a call from Dushanbe.

'Rahul!' he says immediately he picks up the receiver. 'I've been trying to get you for days.'

'It's not Rahul,' a strange voice says. 'This is Hugo Laval.'

A shocked pause. Lance knows the name. He knows the man, slightly; they met in Peshawar some years earlier, Rahul introduced them, but they have had no independent contact.

A call from this man can only mean trouble.

Hugo waits for Lance to recover from surprise before he tells him, almost in the words of the press release that he himself has drafted and repeated now in so many calls. 'A convoy of UN vehicles was attacked by rebel forces on a mountain road. Twenty-three people were taken hostage.'

'Christ, I'm so sorry.' Small wonder the phones have been busy.

'I'm afraid that's not all,' Hugo says. 'Rahul is one of them.'

'Rahul?' His tone says, Impossible.

Hugo rescues him from misplaced hope. 'We are not releasing names to the press but I know you and he are close. I thought you should know.'

Lance puts the phone down. His hands are shaking. He looks at them as if they are not part of himself. He goes to stand at the window and stares out. Images of fear crowd in. He sees vehicles skidding to a halt. Doors are yanked open by men in balaclavas with scarves wound round their heads. Guns point in the faces of the people trapped inside. Stop it, he tells himself, but he cannot stop. He sees them driven off to a camp in the mountains, huddled together, Tajiks and foreigners, officials and drivers, role and nationality irrelevant, all with hands tied behind backs, the cold cement floor beneath them. Cattle, waiting for the auction.

Dublin: Maeve rushes around doing last-minute Christmas shopping; Tessa's unexpected arrival has thrown her plans. Presents for the children, an extra box of crackers, another pudding in case. She gets back, dumps her carrier bags and takes a few minutes with feet up to read the paper. *Hostages held in Tajikistan*, it says. Maeve knows only one thing about Tajikistan. She stops to read the article. Reads it again.

Half an hour later she arrives at the house on the windy coast, newspaper in hand. Ben and the children are out collecting driftwood; Tessa is alone, getting the house to rights. Maeve approaches this tentatively. It is dangerous ground, in more ways than one.

'Remind me, your friend Rahul, is he in Tajikistan?'

Tessa stares. Maeve shows her the article: Among the hostages is a UN official who has been negotiating the peace settlement. No names, but Tessa does not need names.

'That's him,' she says, and her voice carries no redeeming doubt.

> *The waves are rising high and wreckage floats on them.*
> *Why be afraid?*
> *With you I have no fear of fear. I'm not afraid I'll be afraid —*

But she is.

The wind blows hard

Three in the morning in Ireland, as Tessa huddles close to the fire. In Tajikistan it will be eight, his day will be starting. A day of – What? What is happening to him? Who is holding them? How are they treating them?

'You can't be sure it is him,' Maeve keeps saying. But Tessa knows it is.

'Did he say anything about going on that journey?' Maeve asked.

No he didn't, but he wouldn't have. He doesn't like her to worry.

She summons reason to defend her. This is not the first time she has been anxious about him, and whatever he has had to deal with, he has always come through it. Things happen all around me, he said when first he went to Tajikistan, but never until I've gone somewhere else. It's clear the planets conspired at my birth. But the planets are not to be relied on. What do they care if there is one more dead?

'Phone someone who will know,' Maeve says. 'Who does he work for?'

'UNHCR, the UN's refugee agency.'

'Phone the office,' Maeve orders.

She almost never does. It is understood between them. But she knows the number; in case. And now 'in case' has arrived. Her hand trembles as she keys in the international code. Who will she say she is? What standing does she have to enquire?

The number is engaged.

Maeve finds a number for the head office in Geneva, dials it for her, hands her the receiver. But Tessa cannot get past a receptionist who says they are closing for Christmas and there is no one to answer her enquiry.

This is me and you, he said once, *it involves no one else*. But it's gone beyond me and you.

Her mind moves back to the moment: they were in Delhi, at the station, had taken refuge in the anonymity of hustling crowds and rickshaw drivers calling for custom. They had just travelled together from Hasilgah – her last journey, for she was leaving for good. She had watched the fields slide past the window of the train, her small, safe world disappearing. She had zero interest in going to university. Everything she cared about was here, everything she longed for, and it was slipping away from her. Soon she would be on the other side of the world, in a place where it rained the whole time, constant miserable rain like weeping, never a real monsoon with some violence driving it.

Rahul started talking, not about them or about her leaving, but about problems in the project. He's in denial, she thought, he's just refusing to see. For two days he had been in the village but she had hardly seen him, he had been in closed meetings with each of the senior project workers in turn. Now he needed to offload. 'Chandra's been embezzling funds. He's going to have to go. It's going to be messy. I wouldn't want you to be exposed to all that. Maybe it's a good thing you're going.'

The moment the words were out she saw that he was caught by a rush of confused emotion. She said with sudden vehemence, 'I *hate* it. That I'm going.'

He said, quietly but with equal force, 'So do I.'

And that was it, the first statement to himself of what she had known for months.

They sat staring at each other. They were in a public carriage of a train, people on all sides; words were out of the question. But there were no words that would cover it.

Finally – out in the station, people milling about, no one noticing. They saw only each other. Rahul said, 'I think I must be crazy. I don't know what got in to me that I didn't see it sooner. You've been here all these months, and now – When's your flight?'

'Tuesday. But I can change it.'

'Make it a week later. No, ten days. I won't be able to get away longer, with this mess in the project. I've got to sort things out with the trustees before it gets even more out of hand.'

'What are we going to do?'

'Go away somewhere. What about Kathmandu?'

'Kathmandu!'

'It's a place not to miss. I'd love you to see it. But you'll need a visa. Go and start now.' He was talking fast, to beat time.

'What are you going to tell Devaki?'

'She doesn't own me, nor I her. This is me and you. It involves no one else.' He spoke fiercely. It wasn't about her, Tessa thought, it was his own need not to be controlled. But something had happened to him. He had seen her, seen her whole, as she had for so long been seeing him, and he had recognized himself in her responding eyes.

In the airport, waiting for their flight, there was someone he knew checking in. They behaved on the plane as if they were colleagues going to a conference. In the taxi from Kathmandu airport they held hands in the back seat like teenagers on a first date. For an instant it felt electric, then it became almost immediately ordinary; they had been holding hands in essence for all the months they had known each other. Durbar Square in Patan, Kathmandu's twin city. He knew a place overlooking the temples, he said, a hotel small and *desi*, catering for locals and only just beginning to be discovered by backpackers. But the manager remembered him and greeted him like a brother, so that removed his anonymity. He booked them into separate rooms. She was caught by momentary confusion. Did he not mean – ? He shook his head, eyes smiling. Don't worry.

The door closed behind them. Alone, finally.

And now shyness overcame her. He was gentle but definite. The recognition of what there was between them had come to him late, but powerfully. She guessed he was thinking of how young she was. Perhaps this was her first time? It's not, she said, but it's the first time it matters. The first real touch, touch with intent, a moment of breath-held awe – And the shyness was gone, their clothes were gone, on the floor, discarded like the barriers that had for so long kept them apart. They stood naked body to naked body, and she felt in that moment that they were the first man and woman ever to stand so since the world began, yet at the same time what was happening was something universal. Fingers trailing, hands moving, mouths seeking; lying together, face to belly, mouth to breasts, on top and beneath, limbs intertwining, back arching – impossible to get closer but their bodies pressed for it still. The smell of sweat, the sweet texture of skin. The rhythm took over, exploded in delight, longing become flight – the wetness of sex, enfolding and holding –

To lie spent and content, oneness achieved.

For days they lived and loved as if there were no future. He hired a car, paid off the driver who came with it, and they drove out to a village where they wandered between temples of deep red-brown, with multi-tiered roofs and intricate wood-carved shutters. Then out of the heavy air of the valley, up into the hills where every footpath was a steep slope and ahead towered mountains cut like white crystal against the sky, to a guest house with a room of their own, a double this time, to spend hours making love. They lay in the lazy afterglow and he recited words in Urdu, lines of poetry. Half the words are the same as in Hindi, he said, and he teased her to work it out.

Badan – body; *lutf* – delight; but she couldn't get the whole sense. He taught it to her, so it became theirs, the first of many:

> *Your body holds such joy, I know no longer*
> *Whether it is your body or my soul*

They woke to the realization that their week was nearly over. Tomorrow they would have to go back, he to Delhi, she to fly to Dublin. He stroked her hair, her face, her breasts, learning it all before it would be taken away from him.

'I don't have to go,' she said.

'You do. You know you do. You have your life to go to, and it's just starting. There's no way I could hold you here.'

'You wouldn't be holding me. I want to stay.'

'I can't let you, you're too young to know what you would be choosing. You've got to have experiences of your own, different ones from this, and work out what you're going to do with your own life.'

'And you?'

'My life is here, you know that. I can't distort the direction of that for you any more than I would want you to distort yours for me.'

'I don't want you to change anything, I want you to go on being yourself, doing the things that matter to you. And I could be part of it, like I have been this year.'

'And be stuck as an appendage on what I'm doing? You're far too big a person. This is my life; for you it's just a step on the road to finding yours.'

What we have found, he said, is different from anything else

52

either of us will ever know. But there's too much in the way. Without limiting who each of us is, we can't organize our lives around it. We just have to accept it as a wonderful gift, and hold on to that.

She fought against it. 'I don't have to go and experience another life, I want this.'

'This is a moment of escape,' he said, 'for both of us. It's real, but we couldn't have it for every day. And every day life here would put severe limits on you. I couldn't bear that. I want you to learn to fly, with your own wings.'

She said, 'I don't want to hear what you're saying.' —

A sound in the room above whips her back to the present. She is in Ireland, it is night in a cold house and the fire has almost burnt itself out. A bed creaks, a voice murmurs – one of the children is stirring. She waits, motionless. No more sound. Whichever child it was must have gone back to sleep.

She goes back upstairs, drops exhausted into bed next to Ben. But her body has taken charge. It holds itself apart; her terror cannot be shared.

~ 9 ~

Lance has not spoken to Rahul's parents but he can't put it off any longer. He dials the number. Someone whose voice he doesn't recognize answers, a woman. One of Rahul's aunts, maybe? The woman makes no attempt to introduce herself, she is simply a gatekeeper. 'They don't want to have to deal with calls.'

'Just tell them I called, that I know what they must be suffering.'

The voice relents. 'Lance, this is Rahul's sister, Yasmin.'

'Yasmin, I'm glad you're there. We just have to hold on. They're doing all they can to get them out safely.' He hears his voice, helplessly going on.

'We didn't even know he was going on that mission,' Yasmin says.

'None of us did.'

He remembers how it was when they were in Delhi, friends would phone, 'Do you know where Rahul is?' and he always did. But for years now it's been impossible to keep track.

He leaves the office early and goes for a long walk. He thinks of Rahul's mother, Sushila, who holds her anxieties to herself; but no mother can be calm through this. His father, Hamza, with his analytical mind; but when faced with feelings that words cannot encompass he is at a loss. When Rahul took himself off suddenly to Afghanistan and it was obvious he was in some kind of inner turmoil, Hamza gave him a volume of poetry to take with him. 'Our greatest poet, Ghalib,' he said to Lance afterwards. 'He has helped me through difficult times of my own.' Where else would that happen? A father is worried about his son's state of mind so he gives him a volume of poetry.

He is walking still, walking to keep something moving, through Durbar Square with its ornate temples, through familiar lanes that lead off it. It is evening, time to eat. His walking has brought him, unplanned, to a small local restaurant he knows, used mainly by Nepalis. He goes in, orders a meal, sits alone to eat it, his mind sifting through the years in Delhi when he and Rahul first became close. He had not expected it would happen – he had been frankly in awe of the cultured, intellectual atmosphere in Rahul's family, for his own could hardly have been more different. His mother's people had been agricultural labourers, and his father a mechanic with the Canadian air force, posted to an airfield near Lincoln during World War II. When Lance was fourteen they had moved to a small town in the Canadian prairies, flat, remote, where he lapsed into a moody adolescence, resenting having to help his father fix tractors, and disappearing whenever he could into the books his godmother sent him from London. Rahul, as far as he could see, had never had anything to rebel against.

But to Rahul difference was never an obstacle, but a stimulus. Lance needed a cultural and political interpreter; Rahul enjoyed the role. India was dense with issues and causes and confrontations; if he wasn't reporting on them he knew people who were. He gave Lance contacts with social development projects that Lifeline might want to support. He would drop by Lance's office on his way back from interviewing someone and say, 'You'll be interested in this,' and Lance would put aside whatever he was busy with, make them each a mug of coffee and settle in to listen. They were both often out of town for work and got into the habit of calling in on the other when they got back. Till a time came where he realized, this is a friendship like no other I have had. What was it? Common values – shared concerns – a similar sense of the ridiculous – but more than all that, a subtle chemistry of personality that just made things flow easily between them, till Rahul's companionship had become a fixed part of what made life worthwhile. However long it was since they had last seen each other, they always slotted back instantly. He had relied so completely on it always being there that he had let time go by, too much time, and now . . .

The Nepali proprietor of the restaurant comes up to him. Everything OK?

Everything OK? No, everything is not OK.

But the man is smiling hopefully. The food. He wants to know about the food.

'*Mitho*,' Lance says; delicious.

Hugo has switched to default calm, the competent persona that takes over in times of crisis. It is long-practised but this time he does not feel he can rely on it.

He and the others in the core group handling the crisis are working under minute-by-minute pressure. Get non-essential UN staff out of the country. Phone daily updates around the world. Discover whatever can be known about Sadirov and his group of bandits. Put technical experts onto locating explosive devices hidden in Dushanbe. But the one thing that really matters is to get the hostages released safely, and there is almost nothing they can do to make that happen.

Ruiz Pérez is now in Gharm, from where he is in radio contact with the hostage-takers. He sends through hourly updates. Hugo waits tensely for the radio to crackle into life. It is impossible to suppress hope that this time . . . Each time hope is shattered.

He takes breaks to get away from others, not to have to respond when they speak. Restlessly he walks the streets, which technically he should not do while the hostage-takers' bombs are still undetected. He observes the people around him with detachment, as if seeing them in a film. He has lived and worked here for over three years; it is, temporarily, his home. He knows its streets, its public buildings, the stark outlines of its trees in winter, the renewing hope of cherry blossom in spring. He has friends here, people he values. He has learnt the language, studied its history, been absorbed in getting to know how its people think and feel. Yet suddenly it has become alien. Or he has. He feels cold with distance.

Everything about the city seems artificial. All its architecture, its public institutions, are Soviet creations. The true heartland of the Tajiks lies far to the west in Samarkand and Bukhara, oasis cities that were cultural lights in the desert when Europe was still in the Dark Ages, yet when the Bolsheviks drew their boundaries the ancient cities went to Uzbekistan, and for Soviet Tajikistan a new capital was created here out of a small market town with no history. Russian engineers laid out avenues, Russian architects designed government offices, technical institutes, an airport, a statue of Lenin. Monuments to an alien way of life that sought to cancel all trace of old customs and beliefs. It is a bizarre transplant, grafted onto a people whose deeper culture is that of their cousins across the river in Afghanistan.

His mind flips. *'Sorry about the short notice, but could you?'*

He regrets intensely that he made that call.

A sudden change – the distorted radio voice brings news. As soon as he gets a moment alone he phones Lance. Within the space of two days Lance has moved from being someone he hardly knows to being the person he most needs to speak to.

'They're about to release most of the hostages,' he says.

There is a moment's silence as Lance takes in the word 'most'.

'They're keeping four back till their demands are met.'

Hugo can hear that his voice sounds detached, which he certainly does not feel. 'Two Tajiks, one from each side. The Russian journalist. Rahul.'

Silence.

Hugo says, 'We've given the names to the press. You should see it tomorrow.'

For nineteen families around the world the ordeal is almost over. For those close to the four that remain, the tension intensifies.

Lance listens hourly to the World Service news. He thinks about Rahul's name appearing in the world's press, being seen by people scattered across the world who know him. Greta most of all, his godmother in London – it is to Greta that he owes this friendship. He had stopped off in London to see her on his way to India, as he did at every major change in his life – briefing in the Brighton head-office of Lifeline, then overnight in London to see Greta. She had said, 'I have very special friends in Delhi, Hamza and I go back more than thirty years. They lived with me for a year when he had a visiting position at LSE, and Rahul came back when he was studying for a Masters. They're as close as family, you must *certainly* go and see them.'

Greta will be alone, seeing Rahul's name.

He dials her number, which he doesn't have to look up. Her voice is choky, or is it just the line? 'My dear boy, my dear boy.'

She sounds so much older than the last time they spoke. She is eighty at least. Suddenly he is afraid that one day she too will disappear.

'Poor Hamza, poor Sushila,' she says.

He feels bizarrely like a child again, needing her to make it all right. 'I feel like this has been coming to him all his life,' he says.

'That's how he is, Lance, you wouldn't want him any different.'

'I want him safe.'

'Of course. But hold on to what it means. He didn't say, I won't go there because it might be dangerous. Hamza's the same. When he was a young man, the time of the independence struggle, he didn't say I won't criticize the British authorities in case I land in jail. He just did what he had to do and coped with what happened.' Pause. 'Go to them, Lance. Help them to hold on to that.'

'I couldn't even get to speak to them on the phone.'

'Just go. You of all people can support them through this. Don't ask, just go.'

But he can't. He can't move from the phone.

He sits in the growing dark of his living room, not bothering to turn on the light, remembering how he had put off going to see them when first he arrived in Delhi. Should he really take up the time of an eminent professor of sociology? But when he finally got round to putting through the call, the deep voice that answered said, 'Greta wrote to us about you. We have been waiting to hear from you. Come today.'

He was still new to Delhi traffic and had a taxi driver who swerved between cars, tyres shrieking, hooting continually while he swivelled round to emphasize something he was saying. Lance said nothing in response, clinging to the faint chance of arriving unharmed. They turned sharply into a dusty side-road, the entrance barely visible, skidded to a halt and Lance climbed out, nerves shattered, to be met at the door by a large man in his sixties wearing the traditional loose *kurta* and *paijama* – Hamza Asadullah Khan. He received Lance with old-world courtesy and brought him into a house cool and quiet. He moved and spoke with quiet deliberation, until he laughed, a large generous laugh that shook his whole body. His wife appeared, Sushila, calm and graceful in a sari of homespun cotton. Lance observed them with interest, these people Greta had spoken of with such warmth, suddenly made real. Hamza, it was soon obvious, loved nothing more than to debate an issue. Sushila listened with an occasional smile to opinions that she had probably heard expressed many times. Grown-up daughters and young grandchildren were in and out, a house-servant wished to consult about the meal, her husband could not find where he had put the notes he was working on, and they were all sure that only Sushila could help. Through the bustle of it all she created a focused space for each of them in turn, making even a new and unexpected guest feel included.

The daughters and the grandchildren went out, the house-servant retreated to prepare the meal that Sushila had insisted Lance should stay for, and now it was just the three of them. She asked what he would be doing in India. He tried to explain but felt inarticulate in the face of her quiet intelligent questions.

Hamza tried to help him along. 'Greta wrote that in Pakistan you learnt Urdu?'

Lance said, in Urdu, 'Nothing special, just adequate,' but even that small offering was idiomatic for he had indeed taken learning Urdu very seriously. Hamza was delighted. He asked if Lance knew any Urdu poetry. Lance said no, but he'd like to learn. Hamza immediately offered to teach him. Then he moved on to telling him about the year they had spent in London living in Greta's house, they and their son Rahul when he was ten. And as if on cue, in walked son Rahul.

What Greta had said of him had left Lance feeling decidedly reserved. Rahul appeared to have everything. He had been nurtured on politics from infancy. He was astonishingly quick at absorbing information, Greta said, and sharp at analysing it. He was fluent in Urdu – his father's language, Hindi – his mother's, English – from his education, and to these he had added Persian out of an interest in the poetry. As the list went on and on, Lance's resistance to meeting this prodigy had increased. But there was something disarmingly natural about the young man who had just come in that made it impossible to hold on to envy. He was above average in height, though nothing like as tall as Lance, and undoubtedly good-looking, but he wore it like one who had never noticed. He draped himself easily on the low bench-seat opposite where Lance sat awkwardly, his knees getting in the way. His ease was itself relaxing, light banter with his mother, a lively exchange with his father, pleasant interest in Lance. He brought into the room a sense of engagement with the world outside; he had just been trying to arrange an interview with a police chief about their mishandling of a demonstration. His eyes seemed on the verge of a smile, as if challenging life to surprise him. And he surprised Lance by the fact that for one so obviously independent he was still living in his parents' home, the classic Indian extended family.

'It suits me,' he laughed. 'When you've got company as good as this, why move? And why burden myself with household possessions?'

'Rahul favours a simple life,' his mother said. 'He has the scorn of youth for people who care about material comfort.'

She was thinking, perhaps, of her friends who had him in their sights for their daughters – pointlessly, for Rahul showed no sign of getting what any sensible mother-in-law would consider a proper job. He was passionately interested in what he did but hardly focused on what he earned. Depending on how you viewed the matter, that was either admirable or foolish. Possibly both. It was certainly not a route to a comfortable married life.

Hamza was impatient to get to substance. '*Beta* – son – this man speaks Urdu.'

Rahul immediately switched languages. Lance was being tested, and luckily he passed. Rahul asked about his job. This time Lance found it a little easier to explain. They hoped to support local community groups that were tackling issues of inequality, but in a way that wouldn't create dependence.

Rahul said, 'Maybe I can introduce you to a few people you might find interesting.'

Lance said, 'That would be great,' and he passed Rahul his card.

Rahul looked at the words, Lifeline International, looked back up at Lance. 'Now that's an ambitious aim,' he said, eyes now definitely laughing. 'How do you plan to achieve that?'

~ 10 ~

Tessa watches her children. They have never seemed more precious. The terror of life and death hanging in the balance in the mountains of Tajikistan has infiltrated everything; she feels tearful just looking at the children, as if their hold on life too might be tenuous.

She is grateful for their life energy that carries on regardless, that requires a response from her, but she knows she is barely coping. Given any choice she would hand them over to Ben and go and hide somewhere. When bedtime stories are done and the children tucked up, she herself falls almost immediately into an exhausted sleep – only to wake in the early hours.

In the morning she leaves the children with Ben and walks to the shop, to buy the paper. She knows it is pointless, there won't be any international news, it's too near Christmas, the journalists are all on holiday. But there is.

> Rahul Khan, Indian national, humanitarian aid worker who
> has played a major role in the peace negotiations . . .

She stares, rigid. She knew, but now she realizes that still she had been hoping. For a frantic moment her brain rebels and she wills it to be someone else. The world is full of Khans. But there can be no other Rahul Khan. Rahul from his Hindu mother, Khan from his Muslim father.

She cannot go back to the house. She cannot face having to try to talk normally to Ben, to pretend to the children that nothing is wrong. She walks in the opposite direction, not knowing where. She has to hold on to Rahul, that's what she has to do, to think about him so hard that it casts a protective veil around him and no harm will come to him. This is primitive ritual taking over, and she goes with it willingly.

Everything that passes before her triggers a memory. She walks this street on the edges of Dublin and she thinks of the time she came back here, exiled after their week in Kathmandu. They were writing to each other every thought they had, but only they knew. When you live surrounded by extended family you devise strategies for privacy: he had an arrangement with the house-servant, Manzoor, who got to the post before his mother did and intercepted any letters with foreign stamps so no one else saw how many were coming from Ireland. And she? She was sublimating her thwarted intensity by playing Abigail in *The Crucible*, a young girl caught up in fantasy and sexual desire. Opposite, her friend Seamus played a married man, profoundly shaken that he could not stop himself from desiring her. On the last night the power of the fiction took over and they ended up in bed together. She was caught by surprise by her own physical abandon but it had nothing to do with Seamus. When they woke next morning he said, 'I had the feeling that I was substituting for someone else.'

Then suddenly the ground shifted. Rahul joined Lifeline, taking over Lance's job after he left India – and only she and Rahul knew that part of the appeal was that the head office was in Brighton. He would be flown in for an induction, and afterwards could take some leave in London. If she could get there . . . ? She absconded from university, took the ferry across the Irish Sea, then the train to London where he waited at the ticket barrier, laughing, their bodies affirming more clearly than letters ever could that it was all still there, the instant intimacy, the pull of desire, the spark of all that their minds responded to in the other.

She holds on to the memory of those times together – the elements of their lives made a pattern now, like iron filings reorienting around a magnetic field. She was dancing through time with someone who wasn't saying, as he had said in Kathmandu, 'This is an escape.' He was showing her London – another of his places, for he had lived there twice, he told her. Once as a child with his parents, and then for another year as a student, living each time in the home of a family friend, Greta, whom he called his 'English Aunt.' It was a joke between them, for she was no more English than he was, but Austrian, a wartime refugee. Greta's home was his base whenever he was in Britain, he said, but he wasn't considering taking Tessa to meet her and nor would she have wished it; her experience of the intrusive curiosity of aunts told her to keep well clear. 'I'll make a plan,' she had written before he came, and she had phoned her cousin Connor who had shared her need to get away and now had his own flat in London. 'A bed?' Connor said. 'Sure. For one or for two?' Connor was the perfect absent host. 'Here are the keys,' he said, 'here's the bedroom, here's the kitchen, help yourself to whatever you need.' He was out at work by day, popped in to get a change of clothes then spent the nights at a friend's flat; and he understood that no one in Dublin needed to know about the arrangement. It was only gradually that she realized that his friend was male and more than a friend; which explained a number of things, like his tact in not asking what he didn't need to know.

Strategy meetings, inter-agency workshops, conferences … Once people had heard him speak the invitations just kept coming. Tessa was working weekends to save money for fares to join him for the days off before or after. One summer it was a conference in Florence and she got a student rail ticket to follow him. While he was in conference sessions she explored art galleries; when he was free they disappeared together, wandering the city. The extraordinary light of Tuscany touched the warm colours of brick and stone, as the delight they carried with them lit their days.

But they were not part of each other's daily lives. His work was taking him off on an absorbing journey of his own, his days full of people she didn't know and challenges she could only half-imagine, while she was stuck in Dublin writing essays on child development. His visits were unpredictable and he did not want her waiting and pining. 'Focus on where you are,' he said, 'it's the only way to live.'

The remembered words jerk her back: Ben, the children, waiting for her, wondering why she has been away so long. She turns guiltily to walk back, to try to be for them the person she was three days ago, before all this happened.

~ 11 ~

The nineteen freed hostages have been driven under strict security back to Dushanbe, where Hugo is in the group of government and UN officials who are trying to make sense of the story they are telling. After their convoy was stopped they were taken to a building, blindfolded, so they had no idea where, and nor did they initially have any idea who their captors were. But they soon realized that this was a holding place only and the men pointing guns at them were not those in charge. Their leader was somewhere further up the mountains. They heard the name, Sadirov. Talking quietly among themselves, the Tajiks among the hostages pieced together what they knew about him. At the start of the war Sadirov had been a commander with the main opposition group in exile, the IRP – Islamic Renaissance Party – in their military camps in Afghanistan. But the IRP leaders got rid of him; the story was that he was unacceptably cruel. Then he tried to do a deal with the Tajikistan government, got weapons from them on the pretext that he would attack the IRP, then disappeared with them. Now he was anathema to both sides.

Rahul, listening, suddenly said, 'I think I've met him.' When he was working in Afghanistan he had visited the IRP camps. All attention now focused on Rahul. He said, 'Let's see if they'll let me go and talk to him.' A straw to cling to, but they were reluctant for him to go alone, so the Russian journalist offered to go with him. The men with guns went into a huddle and eventually summoned a driver and took Rahul and the journalist off. And that was the last the others saw of them. But they were convinced they owed their release to him, because some time later one of the armed men came back and announced that most of them were being released. They were keeping Rahul, the journalist, and the most senior Tajik from each side until the IRP released two of Sadirov's key men whom they were holding as prisoners in Afghanistan.

All the time Hugo has been listening his mind has been searching for what is not being said. There are things about this story that don't make sense. Maybe Rahul did persuade Sadirov that he didn't need twenty-three hostages, and perhaps he and the journalist offered to stay if they let the others go? But if Sadirov agreed, it was because he saw some advantage in it, and what is that? Even more puzzling, he is now asking for two of his own men to be released, but to start with he demanded safe transit back for scores of them. So what the hell has Rahul done to swing that? And there has been no more talk of bombs planted around Dushanbe. Maybe there aren't any?

A quick investigation takes place into the two men whose release they are demanding. One is Sadirov's brother, a criminal and big-time drug trader. If he is let back into the country, who can say what he might do? But if we refuse?

Don't give in to terrorist demands, all Hugo's training, his principles, tell him. But they are nothing compared to the urgency he feels to get out alive this man he values – no, face

up to it, use the word he shies away from – this man whom he
has come to recognize he loves. Whatever it takes.

He watches his colleagues' faces. Ruiz Pérez says, 'No
decision can be made immediately. We meet again tomorrow,
same time.'

Lance repeats, 'Rahul volunteered to go?'

'Yes,' Hugo says, 'he volunteered. 'If he had kept quiet no
one would have noticed him.'

He can feel Lance's thoughts across the crackling line as if
they were his own. Admiration, despair. Does the man have no
instinct for survival?

He *chose* to do it – Lance cannot get past the thought. He
can see, so clearly, of course that's what Rahul would have
done. And because of that, he is still in danger while the others
are free.

That night Lance dreams that he is back in India with Rahul,
and they are walking again in the foothills of the Himalayas. It
is beyond the reach of telephones, the only place in India he
has been where there aren't crowds of people. They walk for
hours and only pass a couple of villages. The hills – they are
mountains, really – are beautiful, covered in trees, alive with the
sound of birds they seldom see. Mists rise up from the ravines in
the early morning and swirl around them, gradually thinning as
the day warms up. They walk silently, both of them moved to

awe, a sense of things just beyond comprehension. At night they sleep in the guest house of an ashram to which one of Rahul's uncles has retreated, an uncle on his mother's side who has abandoned the world as per traditional Hindu custom. The men wander around in sandals and *dhotis* of homespun cotton. The only furniture is string beds and a few small box-like cupboards. There are no women to look after their needs, and they employ no one, an extraordinary thing to see in men who until they came here lived the usual waited-upon middle-class male lives. They cook for themselves, simple food that cleanses the palate so that by the end of a few days you notice the smallest trace of herb or spice; and each of them sweeps out his own personal space with a broom made of twigs. Lance asks Rahul about his uncle, how he came to make such a choice. Rahul laughs. He is not as impressed as Lance. Before this uncle took to the spiritual life, he says, he was a hard-nosed businessman.

As they walk Rahul talks about the group of civil rights lawyers he is involved with. There has been a series of distressing outbreaks of caste violence, with politicians stirring things and the police either standing by or taking sides. This group is trying to expose official complicity. Lance says, 'It sounds a bit like trying to act as a fire-brigade in a bush fire.'

Rahul says, 'Maybe, but that's no reason for not doing it.'

Hugo phones again. 'Did Rahul ever talk about the Russian journalist? Vitaly Ivanov?'

'I knew the name when I saw it in the press report. But I can't remember more.'

Hugo himself knows Ivanov slightly; they were together at the first round of the peace negotiations in Moscow. But now he has learnt that Ivanov and Rahul stayed in touch. 'Apparently they are friends, which would explain why Ivanov offered to go with him to see the commander.'

A man close enough to Rahul that he has risked his life by going with him into certain danger? Would I have done that? Lance does not know.

~ 12 ~

Christmas Day: they are at Maeve's. Tessa is trying to hold it together for the children but it is beyond her. She can peel potatoes and wash up and let the children climb onto her lap, but she can't do making-things-fun. Maeve is incredible, she just does it all. Then someone turns the radio on. What *is* it that carols in pure young voices do when you're vulnerable? The fear of impending loss overcomes her and she has to leave the room to go upstairs. Maeve comes up and sits next to her on the bed. She holds Tessa's hand. Maeve has guessed a lot over the years, though Tessa has told her so little. But in this crisis there are no words.

After a while Maeve says, 'Stay up here and rest. The kids will be fine,' and goes downstairs again.

Tessa looks blankly into the space Maeve has left. The carols drift up to her, further away than the places her mind keeps travelling to. She reruns time to keep him close, but memory is conspiring against her, for what besieges her are all the things that have separated them, the worms of unresolved questions that ate away at the life they should have had. Each time after he had gone it became harder to cope with the aftermath. Perhaps he never knew how hard, because she didn't write till she had climbed out of that trough, by which time she could talk about it as if it wasn't such a problem. Once, when they were lying together and she was feeling utterly safe, she told him properly and asked if it was like that for him too. 'No,' he said, 'there's nothing like a trough. I just feel light after we've been together, like everything's in the right place for once.' And he rode on that energy, back to the life he had momentarily put on one side. She tried to do the same. There seemed, for the moment, no other option.

So many things left unsaid … And in their short times together, bumping into misunderstandings. Time was always an issue; whoever had paid Rahul's fare required things of him. He pushed the limits to get the maximum time with her but still she seemed always to be waiting around for his meetings to finish. 'They only need me a couple of hours a day,' he would say, but things cropped up that they wanted him to stay for, and he said Yes each time. Once he was seriously late. At first she felt a mild irritation, but more time went by. She couldn't believe this, he had forgotten about her sitting there waiting. When he arrived he seemed not even to realize. 'We said four o'clock, surely?' but she knew they had said three, and even if it was four he was still half an hour late. He thought she was overreacting, and maybe she was, it was the week before her period; but knowing that it was partly hormones didn't make the feelings less painful. He tried to distract her, and when he got her to laugh and said, 'That's better,' she felt patronized. She flipped into anger, driven by the pent-up insecurity of all that was unresolved between them. Rahul didn't argue, he just said, 'Let's go back to the flat.' And only when they were making love did her turbulence subside.

Such small, small things, how did they seem so big?

'Focus on where you are,' he said. It was what he did naturally, caught up always in the immediacy of the issues around him. One year it was dowry deaths, people setting fire to their daughters-in-law because the families didn't pay all the dowry. She could hardly believe such a thing could happen. 'It happens,' he said grimly. And Tessa thought, other people see it and think, how dreadful; Rahul gets in there and trains volunteers to interview witnesses and collect evidence. How could she compete with an impulse so strong?

For her 'where you are' was a university campus where all her friends were pairing up. Sex was on everyone's minds. Their Catholic mothers clung to the belief that their girls would wait till they married but it had always been fear of pregnancy rather than principle that had held the line; and with England just across the water it was easy enough now to get contraception. She had plenty of options other than Rahul and occasionally she toyed with the idea of trying them out. She wondered, would he actually mind? He had unpredictable attitudes to so many things. Maybe he'd say it was up to her as long as she was there for him when he next came? The very thought made her insecure. Anyway, she couldn't seriously contemplate it. Sex, however compelling, seemed a minor aspect of the equation when divorced from all the other things that were part of being in love. It was the whole person she longed to be with, body and soul. Her willingness to wait grew out of their specific history, the long slow maturing of the year they had shared, the inner journey they had made together through the changing nuances of thought and feeling, the ease of their love-making. However brief and irregular their times together, they made anything less seem out of the question.

Her final exams came. And now? No more than in Kathmandu could he accept the idea of her simply attaching herself to his life. He talked about his mother, how she had let the momentum of his father's life substitute for her own. 'She proofreads his books, she keeps track of his meetings, always making his things happen. She was a doctor when she was young, way ahead for her time, but she gave all that up.' He'd tried to get her to talk about it but she was always vague. 'But the truth is, *meri jaan*, once she was married she bought in to limiting what she could be. And we're not going to risk that happening to you.'

Meri jaan. My love, it means; but literally, my life.

Her yearning was no match for his principles. She got a job in Sheffield, setting up playgroups in deprived areas of the city and involving mothers who knew scarcely any English in helping to run them. She pushed other desires to the background, as the stimulation of a new challenge released in her the energy she had first found in Hasilgah. Rahul listened to the stories of her work. 'You can do anything you set your mind to,' he said, the mentor in him there still, watching her progress.

'You know something?' said Nalini, who had been her travelling companion in India, 'that man's never going to stop. Just do me a favour and think seriously about it. Even if you went back to India to be with him he'd be gone ninety per cent of the time. A man needs to save *some* of his passion for his home.'

'We're not short of passion,' Tessa laughed.

'That kind of passion's not enough. You need someone who's *here*, and ready *now*.'

She went back to India – to his here and now. A holiday, they called it, but they were testing the ground, looking to see what might be possible. Were the stars against them? It was October 1984 and three days after she got there the Prime Minister, Indira Gandhi, was assassinated.

She was out of town when the news broke, visiting a community project in a small town half a day's drive from Delhi. In the project house everyone huddled round the radio in a state of shock. It was Indira's Sikh guards who had killed her and now Delhi had erupted in communal violence. Hindu mobs were rampaging through areas where Sikhs were known to live. Horrified, they listened to stories of Sikh homes burnt, Sikh men murdered in front of their families, bonfires made of the bodies, Sikh holy places desecrated. Rahul got them on the phone. Stay where you are, he said, till this is over.

For days she lived in a state of mental crisis yet bizarrely cut off from where it was happening. Eventually Rahul phoned to say that the violence had burnt itself out. The drive back into Delhi … signs of destruction everywhere, upturned cars, burnt-out houses. Fearful, alert, they made their way to the home of a civil rights lawyer where Rahul was surrounded by people who looked as if they had not slept for days and were running on adrenalin. There were half-eaten plates of food in odd places, half-smoked cigarettes stubbed out in saucers. Tessa did what she could to pick up some of the more mundane tasks, while around her there was constant, urgent movement. And from everywhere the horrific evidence came in, there had been nothing spontaneous about the uprising. Politicians were behind it, manipulating the crisis for their own advantage, promising money and alcohol to the mob, and instructing the police to do nothing.

His two weeks' leave turned into three days. He had no choice, that was obvious. Tessa was deeply affected by what she had been caught up in, and equally by his immediate and total response. She understood now, better than any words of his could convey, what it meant to him to live here and do the work he did. She did not doubt his love but she knew that what she had of him now was all he could give.

For them to have a life together she would have to have a role of her own, her own reason to be in India, but what she had just lived through had made her sharply aware of her ignorance, her irrelevance. More than that, she knew she could not cope with living in a situation where at any moment something could spark off tensions that could cause people to massacre their neighbours. For all the moving from country to country in her childhood she had been very protected; over-protected, she now understood. She was not equipped to cope even from the sidelines with the level of political tension that Rahul dealt with daily.

She needed a simpler life, which Rahul could not give her. She would have to find her own.

It is done. Eleven years done. She is a wife and a mother. Rahul is thousands of miles away, in the life that drew him, the extreme challenges that have taken him places where she could not follow. He is in certain danger, and she is utterly cut off.

~ 13 ~

The decision has been made. The men Sadirov wants have been brought from Afghanistan, to be handed over in exchange for the four remaining hostages. Tajik government officials will do the transfer. A vehicle arrives in Gharm, heavily armed, with the hostages; but in it are only the two Tajiks. The others are coming, they are told, in another vehicle, they will be here soon. The officials handling the exchange are confused, but they have their orders. They hand over Sadirov's men.

Hugo is appalled. The thing has been bungled, they have no

bargaining power now. His colleagues think he is overreacting; the other two will surely come soon. But they don't.

He leaves the communications centre, beside himself with tension, and phones Lance. 'Why didn't they do it at the same time? I keep thinking, if Rahul remembered Sadirov, it's possible that Sadirov knows enough to regard him as dangerous.'

'Dangerous? Rahul?'

'To them. Think about it. He has been talking to the Tajik opposition leaders. He isn't a Muslim but he knows how to use the idiom of Islam when he is talking to them. He is uniquely useful to the peace negotiations, and this bastard wants the peace process to fail. He's powerful while the place is lawless but once peace is signed he will be just a criminal. No amnesty is going to cover him.'

Twelve hours pass, and still the promised vehicle has not arrived. Hugo's emotions, usually within his ability to keep steady, have gone beyond what he can cope with. He recites to himself the catalogue of his responsibility. I set up Rahul's first job in Afghanistan. I brought him to Tajikistan. I assigned him to work on the peace negotiations. I arranged for him to be on this ill-fated mission. Please God let it stop there. Let that vehicle arrive, and Rahul and Vitaly Ivanov be safely returned.

Ben is in a depression. Tessa registers it dimly. It is nothing to do with her, he has been that way since they arrived. Forced to leave a place they regarded as home, losing a job he loved and felt was worthwhile – until a few days ago these were her issues too, but now she can't take them seriously, not with the enormity of what has happened to Rahul. She and Ben hardly address a word to each other. They do what has to be done to keep the day going, the children dressed, fed, occupied, got ready for bed.

She wonders in a strangely detached way if she is losing her mind. It keeps disappearing, looking for safety, something to hold on to. Out of the window she sees the luxuriant vegetation of Laos, the brilliant sunshine. She walks past gilded Buddhist stupas and monks in orange robes and shaved heads, and watches women in their straight skirts of hand-woven cloth carry baskets of produce to the market. Then, startled, she sees what is actually outside the window of this draughty house, a wasteland to which she feels utterly unconnected. A reality in which she does not know where Rahul is, or whether he is safe.

Maeve moves them all to her house. Tessa lets it happen, and registers what it means: Maeve and Ben between them have decided that she is not in a state to look after the children. Now Maeve is taking everyone except Tessa off to do things in town. 'Your mama is going to have some time on her own,' Maeve tells the children, and her tone makes it clear that there are to be no further questions. Tessa does not know what Maeve has said to the adults in the family, and nor could she care, but the barely hidden curiosity of the aunts who visit to say how worrying it must all be makes her want to shut the door on them. They need a category to put him in, they can't know how to react unless she gives them one, and she won't. An ex-lover? A friend? But to be *so* upset about him? How difficult for Ben.

Lest anyone else should decide to visit she pulls on a coat and sets off to walk down the lane. But the unease they have stirred pursues her. Defensively she tells the unseen aunts, Ben has known about Rahul right from the start. How could he not? It was the story of her whole adult life up till then, it was what had driven her to give up her job and go travelling, trying to get away from the love she could neither give up nor resolve. And but for that she and Ben wouldn't have met. Ben had taken it in much as she took in his lessons on rock structures; that is to say, he didn't understand but he accepted that Rahul was important to her and he didn't feel it necessary to get involved in the detail. It was obvious, he said, that no one was going to replace Rahul, but that didn't change anything for him. And he saw some things more clearly than she, that whatever Rahul's love had given her it had left her alone day by day, and that she needed companionship. He and Rahul occupied separate spheres, he said, that were hardly going to intersect.

Walking now to fend off panic, she is travelling that journey again, Thailand, Singapore, Malaysia, all her childhood places, searching for something that had made her develop into who she was, that could help her understand who she could be. She, Tessa, alone, not connected to Rahul. She trailed places once seen with vivid child-eyes, now revisited with adult questions. She moved through dense traffic where before there had been quiet streets, walked in the shadow of looming buildings where before there had been low white-painted bungalows. She looked for the house they had lived in, the route they had taken to school. When she found them, they seemed strangely peripheral. They were her places, yet they were not. She spent lonely evenings in low-budget hostels, briefly joined up with other backpackers to do tourist things, but mostly drifted around on her own, talking to almost no one. It was a state too isolated to be normal.

Fragments of the political dramas that had formed the backdrop to her growing-up years came back to her. American soldiers on leave from Vietnam, moving through the streets of Bangkok in their strange uniforms. Being with her mother and Maeve in town when police sirens started wailing, people massing, and her mother hurrying them away to safety. What was it about? They're angry with the government, her mother said, and that was all they got to explain the complex world around them, and then they were home again, home in the lush green of the garden and their carefully protected separateness. The point came when she understood. You're an outsider, all these places said. Move on.

Rahul too was travelling in those months, visiting the crisis points in the countries on India's borders to assess opportunities for Lifeline to become usefully involved. Pakistan, with millions of refugees fleeing from war in Afghanistan. Bangladesh, floods, tens of thousands of homes destroyed. Sri Lanka, civil war. She could picture him in each place; he would be staying up late each night talking, making notes. She knew he would think of her from time to time, but fleetingly.

At no time in the years since he had first seen her in a bookshop in Delhi had they been more cut off from each other. There was no way he could keep track of where she had got to; he could send a letter poste restante but that was about as reliable as putting a message in a bottle and sending it out to sea. She was trying to cure herself of the need to write quite so often. When she did, the letter went to his office in Delhi; perhaps an administrator forwarded it to a temporary address but he was gone by the time it arrived. For a dialogue on potentially life-changing decisions, everything was stacked against them.

Nothing had become clearer except her closeness to Rahul, and the impossibility of that ever being different. Weary of travelling without ever arriving, she had gone into a travel agent, looked in a desultory way at what was available, and booked a flight to New Zealand. The choice was arbitrary; and out of such choices are our futures decided. For on her second day there she met Ben.

She had been caught by a sudden downpour and taken refuge in a hotel foyer. Standing there, dripping onto the marble floor, she saw a young man running towards the hotel entrance to escape the rain, so preoccupied with some idea of his own that he tried to get into the revolving doors against the stream. He looked surprised, tried the other way and arrived in the foyer to see her laughing at him. They stood underneath a chandelier taking each other in, two dripping waifs mirrored in all that marble and glass. He was a little shorter than her, sturdily built, with dark hair and an intense expression in his dark eyes that was oddly innocent, like a boy whose mind is full of facts he finds absorbingly interesting so that he hardly notices what's going on around him. She felt a zing of attraction to something beyond that boyishness, and she saw from his eyes that his attention had zoomed in on her. He said, 'Let's look for something our own size,' and that made her laugh again. She realized with a jolt that it was a long time since she had felt like laughing.

They found a cafe and talked for three hours.

The weeks that followed were a blur. He was finishing an MSc in geology. Rock structures, he said, as if this were the most exciting thing life could offer anyone. He was passionate about rocks, always had been, he said, ever since he was a boy. He had overrun his deadline and was working frantically, staying in the library till they closed the doors, then dossing down in friends' rooms. But now that Tessa had been catapulted into his life he stopped, took time off. Hours of time. He got her out walking on unfrequented bits of coastline yellow with heath plants, braving the wind and ignoring the rain. He took her to South Island to give her a taste of real mountains. They became lovers – the amount of time they were spending together, there really wasn't any question of it not happening. At first she was hardly able to feel. Being body-to-body with Ben never carried the electricity of lying naked with Rahul, but she saw that there was another way, a less charged way. It felt good because he meant it, and because she had been a long time without it. Only afterwards did she realize that for Ben it had been momentous. Amazing though it was, she was the first. Whatever might have been going on beneath the surface, he had seemed, his friends told her, to regard women as peripheral creatures, interesting only if they happened to share his interests. Why it should have been she, who knew nothing about rocks, who broke through that protective shell was a mystery. He himself hadn't known until they met that he was ready for something like this, yet from the moment he saw her watching him and laughing at him, something in him woke up. She was the woman who had evoked desire and given it fulfilment, and he could conceive of no other filling that space.

Weeks turned to months. She knew they were too different to make a sensible couple. Ben had no interest in the things that for all her adult life had absorbed her. He had hardly ever read a novel, never seen a play, didn't think about relationships, had never considered how he could connect with lives different from his own. She could list in a long column on a piece of paper all the things that connected her to Rahul, and Ben shared none of them. Yet he was Ben – she felt comfortable and safe in his company, and his oddities made her laugh.

Time had stretched way beyond the point where she could say, I didn't mean it to go on this long. Ben was in love, and she had allowed it to happen. More than that, she had *needed* it to happen, to repair her damaged sense of self. He had everything Nalini had said she should go for, a man who was here, and ready now. He was offering her something she needed, that she knew Rahul never could.

But still she could not bring herself to take that decisive step that would shut off for ever the other possibility.

Then she fell ill. At first it was just an annoying cough, but she felt so wretched with it that she let Ben take her to a doctor. Whooping cough, he said. Whooping cough? She thought that had been eliminated, like small pox, but no. For three weeks she felt she was coughing her insides out and could barely move. Ben did everything. His attentiveness to her and her dependence on him were absolute. By the time she recovered she understood, the thing between them had been decided. They had gone too far, there was no unpicking it. She loved this man. Out of gratitude, yes, because he had so simply loved her and rescued her from being lost, but also for who he was, that combination of qualities that mysteriously makes each of us unique. The prospect of being always with him made her feel calm.

When Rahul finally stopped moving about and got back to Delhi, two of her letters were waiting for him. One said very little but had a description of a beach in Thailand at dawn that he said moved him deeply and made him feel suddenly lonely. Now that he was no longer being thrust from one intense situation into another it seemed a very long time to have been out of contact. The second was from New Zealand. It was shorter. She had been climbing mountains with a young geologist she had met, she said, and was learning about rocks. She hadn't heard from him for what felt like a long time. Maybe she had missed some of his letters? She hoped he had been getting hers. He wrote at length and passionately. No, he had received none of them. But more than that, he was unnerved by the almost detached tone of her last letter. As if to make up for it with his own passion, he poured out impressions of all the places he had been. They only reinforced what she knew.

There was no way now to say it except the bald fact. I have found another life, she wrote. I know now I would not fit into yours. I have found someone who can give me what I need.

For a few weeks there were more letters, following in quick succession, impassioned, disbelieving, hurt. They were extremely painful to receive but they did not alter what she knew. She knew that everywhere he went people would recognize his unique qualities and ask more of him, that Nalini was right, he would never stop, and there would be too little space for her. He denied it, but she knew —

She has walked so far that she is lost. She turns, staring about her. But it is not the way back to Maeve's that she is looking for. She wills her sense of direction to tell her exactly where Rahul is, what is happening to him.

There is nothing there, just space. Walking to fight off panic, she calls out into the silence, 'Rahul, stay safe, wherever you are, whatever is happening to you. I don't care what happens to us, I just want you to be safe. With you I have no fear of fear.'

But words have lost their power.

~ 14 ~

It is near midnight when the call comes. Lance has been sitting with his hand almost on the phone. Hugo's voice sounds tired beyond the telling of it. 'The vehicle that was bringing Rahul and the journalist –'

He stops. He cannot bear to go on.

He tries again. 'It hit a landmine.'

No, no, no –

'They're dead.'

Dead? No, no, no, please no. How can it be? How can he no longer *be*?

Maeve arrives before anyone has time to get out to buy a paper. Tessa is still upstairs in the bathroom. Maeve gets Ben alone and tells him what she is going to have to tell Tessa. 'Take the kids out for a run on the beach,' she says. Tessa comes down and sees them organizing the children. Boots, coats, hats, gloves, scarves. She starts to say, 'What's going on?' sees Maeve's face, and stops. She stands motionless in the doorway.

'Why aren't you coming, Mama?' the children ask.

Ben says, 'Mama and Auntie Maeve are going to have a civilized adult cup of tea. Come on, let's get going.'

Maeve waits till the last sounds of their voices are gone. Then she turns and says, 'Come and sit down,' patting the place next to her on the sofa. Tessa moves to sit, her face blank. Maeve hands her the newspaper, folded open at the page.

The UN head of mission in Tajikistan today conveyed the shock and sorrow of the international community ... Vitaly Ivanov, Russian journalist ... Rahul Khan, dedicated humanitarian worker.

Maeve hears a sound coming from somewhere as she rocks her sister's body in her arms, a weird sound, something between a child's cry of pain and the scratch of nails on glass. Only slowly does it penetrate. The sound is Tessa's voice.

~ 15 ~

Dead. Dead scared. Scared to death. A dead loss. Loss. Dead cold.

It is cold, cold in the night in Kathmandu and Dushanbe, where Lance and Hugo, each alone, walk the dark streets, unable to stay indoors. Cold in the house on the Irish coast that no fire will ever warm, as Tessa freezes in Maeve's arms and stares at the wall and does not know what she sees, and Maeve holds her sister whose lover has been taken from her and will never be there again for her to touch one last time and weep over. Cold in the house in Delhi, where Hamza moves from room to room, each one cold and empty, never again to be lit by his son's laughter, and Sushila lies alone between cold sheets and holds in her mind the child she bore, the boy she watched grow into a man clear of mind and straight of purpose, a son who transformed the world for her by his mere existence. Cold on that road in the mountains, a cold wind blowing over what is left of a man who lived so vividly, who loved so intensely. A man no longer. A body. Not even that, pieces of a body, burnt and charred, scattered in the snow.

Unfinished business

What does death mean? One moment life is there, the next it is not. Images move around Lance, bizarre fragments from way back in childhood. A winter morning in his boyhood home in Lincoln, and a mole he found dead behind a shed, its body frozen in an early frost, its small splayed feet pointing helplessly outwards. Meat on butchers' chopping boards, the moment of discovery that they had once been sheep, cows. Alive. A wild duck with an injured wing that he found by a lake in Canada, and made a safe place for in an old boat-shed. A creature he loved passionately as he cared for it. And then he came back one morning to find it dead.

He wakes at four in the morning with the first temple bells. He pulls on a coat and leaves the house, to walk the dark streets. He reaches Durbar Square and sits on the steps of an old building. He sits where he sat with Rahul the last time they were together. Bizarre in the half-light, the stone carvings of animals and gods are beginning to emerge. He hears Rahul's voice saying, in that light tone that disguised something serious, 'I love this place, it's got hallowed memories.' Now he will never know what the memories were.

The world is waking up. A woman appears with her children. He watches her prepare breakfast over a fire while her two little girls keep a casual eye on a toddler, who seems at some risk of falling into a ditch. A couple of boys arrive and start an impromptu football game with a Coke can. They are alive, these boys. In the face of death, all life seems miraculous. He watches them as if they hold the secret of how to stay living. There was a time when he lived with the same carefree élan these boys have. He and his friends would cycle out along the country lanes of Lincolnshire, dump their bikes at the edge of a field, scramble through hedges, shift stones to dam a stream. That was his place, as Kathmandu is theirs. But Kathmandu too has become his, and now his contract is almost up and he is going to have to go. I can't go on doing this, he thinks. I can't keep on moving, and rooting myself, and then having to leave. I need a different life, somewhere in one place, with people who I know will be there at the end of the month, the year, three years.

Men start work on one of the temples, repairing stonework. Bells ring, people walk purposefully across the square. The noise of traffic in the streets beyond begins to reach him, the city gearing up for the working day. They are all getting on with life, busy, normal. Rahul is dead, and everything here goes on as it did yesterday.

◆

In the UN guest house in Dushanbe Hugo moves around in the room where Rahul spent his last nights before going up to Gharm, and puts into a suitcase the small collection of possessions he left behind. Clearing up his effects. Why do we call them 'effects' when the man who used them lives no longer? It is a task that it would have been sensible to delegate to someone more junior, but he is doing it himself. Each object he touches evokes pictures of Rahul in action – signs of his existence, scratches in the rock. A wire-bound book, the reporter's notebook that he took with him everywhere. Hugo flips the pages, remembering how they pieced together fragments they were hearing about the appalling massacres that had caused people to flee. People avoided talking about it but the legacy lurked everywhere.

He lifts up some duplicated sheets of paper, briefing notes for the team that was heading into the mountains. History has made them redundant but perhaps it will comfort his parents to get a sense of the significance of what the man was involved with. They too go into the suitcase. And now he sees a small padded envelope, addressed in Rahul's handwriting. Something he intended to post when he came back? He lifts it to see. It is to his mother.

He flies out to Delhi, to hand the suitcase over to Rahul's parents. A suitcase, when they have lost a son. He gives Rahul's mother the envelope addressed to her. She holds it as if transfixed, opens it, lifts out a cassette.

She is overcome, and leaves the room. Rahul's father watches her go, then turns back to Hugo. Rahul occasionally recorded something for her instead of writing a letter, he explains. His voice breaks a little as he says, 'You have brought us his voice.'

In the taxi from the airport into Delhi Lance stares out at traffic belching pollution, death-wish three-wheelers weaving in and out, women in saris perched perilously behind young men on motor-scooters, whipping past advertising hoardings. New buildings going up, crammed in between crumbling old ones that no one has bothered to repair or pull down, and every corner of the pavement inhabited. The population must surely have doubled since he was last here, but it is more than pressure of numbers, it is the frenzy, the noise, so many people scrabbling to make a living.

Suddenly the tumult is turned off as the taxi leaves the highway, into a dusty lane of large cool houses, high walls, watered gardens. The lane is crammed with parked cars. Lance pays the taxi driver and approaches the house that Rahul grew up in. Manzoor, the house-servant, opens the door and when he sees it is Lance, becomes tearful. They stand for a moment, almost wordless, Lance's hand on the man's shoulder. Then he makes his way in through the bewildering mass of people, Rahul's sisters with their husbands and children, uncles, aunts, cousins, neighbours, old political comrades of his father, Rahul's friends. Some of them Lance knows, many he has never seen.

People arrive, hug, weep a little, bring food, sit to talk. There is no sign of Hamza or Sushila.

He moves from room to room, each so familiar and each suddenly crowded out of familiarity, the bulkier furniture pushed aside to make room for more and more chairs, brought in from who knows where. Tragic, terrible, such a shock, can't take it in, the same low-voiced phrases murmur across the room in several languages. Eventually he finds Sushila, who receives his hug and says, 'I'm glad you are here.'

He says, 'He was the best man I have ever known, or ever will.'

She nods, and looks lost. There doesn't seem any more to be said. He gets out of the way of the women and goes to find Hamza, sitting surrounded by older men. He takes Lance's hand and says, '*Beta, beta,*' – My son, my son – and Lance doesn't know whether he is talking about Rahul or addressing him. He finds a seat. Hamza hardly talks. He simply sits there, looking old.

Everything in this house evokes Rahul. It is the values he imbibed here that formed him. Lance used to watch him and his father talking, and think, I didn't know anything like this was possible between fathers and sons. And now the house has been robbed of its beloved son. There is not even a body for the Muslim part of the family to bury, or the Hindu part to cremate. Perhaps that will prevent a cultural crisis in their long, uneasy coming-together, but it leaves all of them empty, unable to do what they know should be done. He wonders about Hamza, the lifelong atheist with no gods to appease, no ritual to adhere to; what will he want done? Or Sushila. In her rejection of religious identity that divides, what does she want at such a time? He hears people discussing it. They ought at least to do this. For the family at least, something ought to be done. But each speaker only means their part of the family, their essential rituals. What does it matter, when Rahul himself is no more? Lance feels alien, not from this tolerant, embracing household that adopted him, but among the people who have come to occupy it.

Heading back to the airport, he watches through the car window as if he is seeing some other, lost world. In the plane he looks out to the line of Himalayas that rise white and razor sharp, as if marking the edge of the known world. But it isn't the edge, it is just part of a vast knot of mountains still being pushed up by clashing tectonic plates, and beyond lie the high valleys into whose troubled history Rahul poured his soul.

~ **17** ~

Tessa's sleep is shallow and troubled. She dreams that she is standing in an airport with Rahul waiting for a plane to take her somewhere. She is holding in her hands a strange, amorphous object, heavy as a cannon ball, wondering what she is supposed to do with it. Rahul is saying, 'You can do it, I know you can.' But she stares down at the weight, and knows she can heave it no further than the spot on which they are standing. She struggles into half-wakefulness and for a moment understands what is weighing her down. It is the future that she has no choice but to walk towards, but what kind of a future can it be that has no Rahul in it? Then she slips back thankfully into the dream and is with him again. She sees now that the airport is Kathmandu and he is seeing her off, back to Ben. He says, 'We'll find a way.' She shakes her head, 'You don't understand, it's not as simple as that.' He says, 'You'll be fine. I'll watch you. I still exist.'

She wakes suddenly, to his voice. 'Fire destroys, unless you take care to contain it.'

The sky is a permanent grey. Banks of clouds form out of nowhere, rain arrives and leaves. Tessa walks on the beach, pushing against the wind, willing the cold to block out the present and allow her to retreat, back, back, to before this emptiness. The light that she has followed for so long can guide her no more. The low, intimate light of the brazier that once held them close in the village in India, the translucent summer light of Florence where once they wandered, arms round each other in contentment and delight, the thin winter sunlight of a London February, walking in Regent's Park. The sudden flash of electricity each time he reappeared. It's real, he said, but we couldn't have it for every day. And now it is gone for good.

She cannot absorb it. He has never felt closer. He appears in her dreams, talking, laughing. He is there by day, just around the corner where she can't see him, but more real than Ben and the children. At moments it almost feels as if, by slipping the bonds of the physical body, he has shed also the barriers that she once thought stood between them – that he was so much more than she could ever be, more experienced, more articulate, sharper in his observation, more alert to what life asked of him. None of that matters any more. She touches now what she knows was always there, their equality of spirit. And yet he is gone, and will never be there again.

They spend a lot of time at Maeve's. Maeve is keeping each day moving on, meals, distraction for the children. All Tessa has to do is let it happen, which is in fact all she is capable of doing. Other relatives come and go. After the first day of hugs and 'I'm so sorry', no one has spoken of it. They are of course sad that she has lost a friend but since the exact nature of her relationship with Rahul is not, apparently, to be discussed, no one risks saying anything. Tessa's mother is particularly concerned that nothing be said that might upset Ben. Ben himself gives no sign of what he might be feeling. He has his own, unrelated, issues to contend with. He has lost his job and appears to have no idea how to move towards finding another. No one mentions this either.

It's Sunday. Tessa knows that, because Maeve and her boys went to church. She checks the wall calendar: Sunday 5 January. She is still checking time and date compulsively. Why? Nothing can stop the inexorable forward march of time. What has happened, has happened.

It's ten past four in the afternoon and dark outside. Her

mother has fallen asleep in an armchair and Maeve has taken the children off to the kitchen to feed the puppy. Ben and Maeve's husband, Tom, are slumped in front of the television. Tom is providing Ben with a running commentary to the match. It has apparently not yet got through to him that Ben has zero interest in football. Ben is letting Tom fill the spaces so he doesn't have to think. The two of them are almost like members of different species, she thinks, observing them as a zoologist might. Tom is loose-limbed and slightly uncoordinated and his mind is similar, meandering aimlessly. Ben, when he is not low, as he is now, is intensely focused.

Tessa feels utterly disconnected from them all, including Ben.

She tries to poke feeling back into life, to find again the warmth she has felt for Ben from the first time saw him, a dark-haired young man in jeans, hair mussed by the rain, muscles compact and efficient, like someone who scales rock cliffs she thought, before she had any way of knowing how accurate that was. And now? Where has all that packed energy gone? She looks at his body as if she hardly knows it. She remembers the sense of unreality the first time they made love; as now she feels, Is this me, still living with this man?

'The one thing I'm not going to do,' she had told Maeve when she gave up her job and went travelling, 'is become like Mam.'

'Meaning?'

'Packing and following. I'm going to find my own life.'

But instead she had found Ben, and packed and followed.

She despairs of ever getting past the state she has sunk into. Grief has taken up residence inside her, but for the sake of the children, for Ben's sake, has to be kept out of sight. She does not like what she has become.

She gets up and makes for the loft. Up through the trapdoor. She steps gingerly across an accumulation of old sports equipment towards a pile of cardboard boxes in the corner, to find the one that she left here before she went travelling. She sits cross-legged on the dusty floor to look through these old, old things, relics of life long gone. A book of Ajanta paintings, bought for her by Rahul on an impulse that first day in the bookshop. A little raffia basket, a goodbye present from the children in the village in India. She remembers the girls shyly presenting it to her. A card made by the playgroup mums and children in Sheffield, the paint cracking where it has been folded. A battered map of central London, with places marked on it. Their places. Right at the bottom, least likely to be seen by any unauthorized opener of the box, is the thing she has been looking for. She lifts out a bulky folder sealed with multiple layers of brown parcel tape, unlabelled except for the dates, October 1980 – February 1985. She looks around for something to cut the tape, finds a rusty old saw, begins hacking at it. Open it up, this fragment of their joint beings –

Onto the floor drops a scrap of paper with a verse written on it, Rahul's handwriting:

> *With us there is no talk of near or far*
> *Together or apart, we still must love*

100

She sees instantly the place, the moment he wrote it for her, a cafe near Regent's Park where they ate toasted teacakes, the last time before she went travelling.

It is done, she tells herself fiercely, as she sits in the dusty loft, surrounded by the paper remains of a love that went wrong. Time moves like the wind, never to be recaptured. It is finished. Accept it, move on. But she is weeping, now, weeping silently, the tears that would not come before, weeping for all that has happened and can never be changed. In the endless days when he was held hostage and she hoped her love alone could save him she was holding on so tightly, that even now that he is gone she cannot stop holding on. She *will* not stop. Something deep inside her urges her on still. It matters, holding on. He is gone but she is left, the sole guardian now of what there was between them, which only they knew, of what is possible between two people if they are exceptionally lucky. Now more than ever she needs to hold on to it, or it will be lost.

Back again in the house near the windy beach, just her, Ben and the children. She waits for Ben to say, 'We're going,' and numb as she is she will do what she has always done, pack and follow. But Ben isn't saying anything.

The children are getting fractious, she's late with supper. She goes into the kitchen, and sees that Ben has already done it. They eat. She responds to the children's chat. They do baths and bedtime stories. She thinks, to anyone watching this, I might seem normal. She gives herself silent lectures. She reminds herself how lucky she is to have Ben. She chose to be with him, for good reason. He is a good man, a good father. He is considerate. When he is not depressed as he is now, they are good companions. She can rely on him always to be there. They have moved around the world together, always each other's known person among strangers. He has given her space to do things that did not include him, and tolerated things in her no other husband would have. At a time when she was in pieces he saved her from herself.

But now she is in pieces again, and this time she cannot turn to him. They are separated by her misery, and they cannot reach each other.

She gets up in the small hours, still. Sits alone by the fire. She finds a half-used notebook, tears out the used pages, stares at the now-blank pages. She picks up a pen, hesitates. Begins:

I need to talk to you. It's been three weeks now, knowing that I can't reach you. I feel blocked up with all the things that need to get out. I hold on to Ben at night, needing that closeness as a defence against the things we can't talk about. Neither of us dares to put into words what's going on. We've hit a loneliness in the couple that's never been there before, and it's scary.

I can hear you saying, 'Don't worry, give it time,' and immediately I feel calmer. You can do it for me still, Rahul, even when you're not there.

I was afraid to start this, but it's so normal talking to you again. You were never here before when I was writing, so this is no different. I write as if I'm sure that you will listen and be there for me. Even though you are dead.

Dead. I make myself write the word, not some euphemism like 'gone'.

'I need to go away for a few days,' she says to Maeve.

'Away?' Maeve stares at her.

'To London. I've told Ben. But he may need your help while I'm gone. He and the children.'

Silence. Then, 'Where will you stay?'

'With Connor.'

'Connor? I didn't know you were in touch with him?'

'It was his place Rahul and I used. When Rahul came to London.'

Another silence. 'Tessa, are you sure you know what you're doing?'

'I have to do this, Maeve. I can't move forward till I have.'

'What did Ben say?'

'Nothing. We're not saying much to each other. Anyway, that's how Ben deals with difficult things. He just goes silent, and you have to guess. But right now I've got no energy for guessing. I'm no use to him, or to the children. I just need to get away from everyone.'

'And the children? What are you saying to them?'

'That I have some people I have to see in London. And I'll

be back in a few days.' More silence. 'I'm sorry, Maeve. You've been amazing, I can't tell you how grateful I am. I wish I could rise to it all better. But I don't know what else to do.'

~ 18 ~

Hugo will afterwards remember little about the weeks after Rahul's death. The organizational fallout from the crisis keeps him exceptionally busy, but his mind is on autopilot. He does what he has to do without it leaving an imprint. An investigation is set up into the UN's security procedures. The staff who have been flown out to Uzbekistan must once again be relocated. Several are unwilling to return; Hugo does not press them but that leaves endless personnel issues to resolve. Calls come in from cities across the world, many of them places Rahul has never been but where there are people who have once worked with him. He had no partner, his colleagues don't know his parents, so it is Hugo they call, to say, 'I can't believe it,' to share their sense of what they have lost. And perhaps, Hugo thinks, also to hold on to the living; for when unexpected death claims someone near us we all feel the tremor beneath our own feet.

He is more churned up than he knows how to handle. For years he has trained himself to keep his own counsel on emotional matters. Now the very strategies that have helped him cope seem to trap him. The extent of his tension is brought home to him when he faces the task of writing an obituary for the UN media. He will not trust anyone else to do it but he is stuck. How do you sum up a man's life in a page of A4?

They hold a memorial event. He sits on the platform with all the others who are going to speak, looking out over a sea of faces. Winter sunlight catches the particles of dust that swirl around, disturbed by the constant movement of people. The hall is packed to capacity. What would Rahul have thought of it all? He would surely have hated to be centre-stage. But we aren't doing this for him, Hugo thinks, we mark a death because *we* need to. We need the comfort of being with others who have loved the person who is no more.

Yet underneath all that, underneath the things that have to be done and the feelings that find no outlet, something else is disturbing him, stopping him from accepting what has happened and moving forward. He does not believe there was a landmine.

At the time the radio message about the deaths came through he was exhausted from ten almost sleepless days and nights. Caught in the intensity of emotion, he, like everyone else, accepted the story they were given. But within hours of making the phone calls to pass the news to the people waiting, questions came crowding in.

First, why were the four men not released together? Once the exchange was done there was no reason to keep Rahul and Vitaly Ivanov any longer. The vehicle in which the two Tajiks were returned could easily have carried them all. Something different was going on with the two they kept, for which there has been no explanation.

Second, they waited a further twenty-four hours before the message about the landmine came through. That had seemed long. Now, reflecting on it, it seemed if anything too short to be consistent with the landmine story. If there was only that vehicle travelling and all in it were killed on a road hardly traversed, how long might it have taken for news to have got back to Sadirov? So how did he know so soon, to be able to radio through that message?

Hugo was by now threadbare with lack of sleep and didn't trust his own judgement. He took a sleeping pill to break the cycle and descended into a blanked-out state that could hardly have been called restful, but from which he woke able to function more calmly. He retreated into the mountains nearest to Dushanbe and went for a long walk. And there, alone with nature, his brain suddenly presented him with a third, and to his mind conclusive, reason why the landmine story could not be true. They were in rebel-controlled territory. Government forces never got up there, so they couldn't have laid mines. And why would the rebels have done so, and risked killing their own people?

Something else had happened. Could it be that by the time Sadirov released the two Tajiks, Rahul and Vitaly Ivanov were already dead? And that the twenty-four-hour delay was because the rebels were arguing among themselves how to cover it up?

Back from his walk, he went to see Ruiz Pérez, the UN head

of mission. Pérez did not take much convincing. The phone calls started again, to New York, the UN security division, to UNHCR's head office in Geneva. Hugo was given the go-ahead to start an official investigation.

The obvious first step would have been to send someone up to travel that road again, to look for burnt-out remains. But by now there have been blizzards and the road is impassable. No vehicle will be able to get up there till April. It hardly matters, for he is by now sure that when they get up there, they will find no burnt-out vehicle.

He gets Lance on the phone. Lance says, 'I'm surrounded by packing cases.' He is on the point of leaving Kathmandu, for good. He will spend some days in Delhi, taking his leave of Rahul's family. For years he has been going back to Delhi to meet up with Rahul, timing their leave together so they could go walking. There will be nothing now to bring him back.

'And then?' Hugo asks.

'Debriefing in Brighton, then I'm heading for Vancouver. Taking a break.'

'Sensible,' Hugo says; but he feels unaccountably unsettled. Through all the trauma of the last weeks Lance has been just across those mountains, there at the end of the phone line. They have become closer than family, yet they have not even met since that one brief encounter years ago. Now he is going.

'Was there something special you wanted to talk about?' Lance says, hearing Hugo's hesitation.

'Yes, but I don't want to do it over the phone. How long will

you be in Delhi? I've been thinking of coming myself. I'll make
sure I get there before you leave.'

Lance walks out of the house that has just ceased to be his
home, casting off the line that has kept him moored. He tries
to feel nothing. Taxi. Airport. Wait. Board. Flight. Delhi
airport. Immigration. Taxi. The assault on the senses again,
traffic, noise, pollution.

When he arrives at the house, Hamza is at the door to
greet him. Lance is shocked at how old he looks. Until all this
happened it wasn't something you noticed. The life of the
mind and spirit was so strong in him, it was all you saw. Now
he is like someone wilting. Lance puts his arms around him.
Sushila appears. He does the same with her. He has no words
but his arms are not just sharing their sorrow, they are saying,
You are my family too.

She disengages. 'Manzoor has your room ready.' It is the
voice of someone who is going through the motions of life
rather than living. Time is the only healer, they say; but how
much time do you need? And what do you do with yourself
meanwhile?

Sushila leaves them. Hamza asks a few questions. Even at
a time like this the training in courtesy remains, always the
personal preamble. He hopes Lance has been bearing up. He
has had a wonderful letter from his dear friend Greta in London.

Then he raises himself out of his chair and says, 'Come, there is something I want to show you.'

He leads Lance back into the central area of the house, through an open door into Rahul's room, kept always for him to return to. Ever since Lance first came here it has had a spartan look; minimal possessions except for books and papers, and even those carefully edited. For a life as full as Rahul's, he accumulated extraordinarily little material clutter. Now its bleakness feels unbearable.

Hamza pulls open the top drawer of a filing cabinet. 'Look.'

Rows of files, as carefully labelled as an archive. The sign of an organized mind; but maybe more than that? Were the labels there not just for Rahul himself but to help other people find what they might be looking for? Did he have a sense of the importance of the papers he was filing, even once he himself would be gone? Hamza has clearly had the same thought.

'The cassettes, look at them.' Hamza gestures to the shelves above the cabinet, the rows of audio cassettes, just as meticulously labelled. 'Everywhere he carried his cassette recorder. This is a record of India's history in our times, in the voices of people who have been part of it.'

He opens the second drawer of the cabinet. Central Asia: Afghanistan, Tajikistan, Kyrgyzstan. 'Each time he came back he brought with him papers that he added to these drawers. He was building up a record of things that he thought mattered.' He turns back to Lance, looking lost. 'And now I don't know what he wanted done with them. Maybe there are things here that will be helpful to people in your kind of work? There may be stories here that we should keep hold of, for future generations.'

He has been standing all this time by the filing cabinet, looking shaky. Lance says, 'Come and sit.' Hamza moves to the chair at Rahul's desk. 'Open the next drawer.' Lance does so. 'See? Personal letters. Look how many people he was close to.' Merely opening the drawer feels intrusive. Lance shuts it. Hamza says, 'I worry about those letters. Rahul was discreet about his intimate life and I cannot bear the thought of anyone breaching that discretion. There are people in and out of this house, there is never such a thing as a locked door here. I do not want anyone learning things that he did not choose to tell them. Sushila feels as I do. Yet we cannot bring ourselves to throw those letters away. Perhaps they will be important to the people who wrote them.'

He begins talking about death; his own. 'I am eighty-three, it can happen at any time. Many of my friends have gone already. Before I go I want to make sure that Sushila is not left with any unnecessary burdens. You will do us both a kindness if you will take these papers so that there is nothing there left for her to decide. You have been his companion all these years, you will know better than anyone what should be done with them all.'

Hamza goes off to rest. Lance phones one of Rahul's friends, a historian, who comes over and joins him looking through the papers on India. There are files of his articles; the friend picks up a couple to glance at. 'He must have made a fair number of enemies writing this stuff,' he says. Reports on his fact-finding investigations, starting in 1975, the state of emergency – that was what kick-started his urge to tell what was happening. And on it goes, through the communal violence of the turbulent 1980s.

'Hamza's right,' the historian says, 'this is a historical treasure trove. I'll send someone to collect all this and arrange for anything significant to be archived.'

When he has gone Lance calls the Lifeline office, to arrange for someone to collect the rest and ship it off to Vancouver. He can sort through it all when he gets there.

Neither Hamza nor Sushila have reappeared. Lance feels a little trapped. There are friends he could be seeing in Delhi but he does not feel he can go out so soon after arriving. He returns to Rahul's files and starts dipping into the ones from the years in Lifeline, first looking with no particular aim but soon in a more pointed way, for clues to things he didn't understand at the time. When he was back in India and visiting friends in the Lifeline office he saw that all was not as it should be. Rahul was out of the office too much, leaving the rest of them to carry through the bewildering number of initiatives he generated. Lance saw to his surprise that for all Rahul's talents he was not a natural manager. He didn't need anyone's affirmation so it didn't seem to occur to him that those who worked for him might need his. Even with people outside the office he left a trail of disappointment. He would get them involved in things and then himself be off elsewhere.

He comes upon a file full of papers Rahul gave at international conferences. Far too many, Lance thought at the time, but when he tackled Rahul about that he just laughed and admitted he was running up air miles like the development consultants he had once scorned. Lance asked, 'So why do you do it?'

'It keeps my mind busy,' he said, 'relieves the tedium of strategy plans,' in that light, self-mocking tone Lance knew well.

Memories of that time are flooding back now. Rahul had begun erecting barriers of privacy that had not been there before. 'He doesn't even get his post here any more,' his mother told Lance, saying what she did not put in words in front of the family. 'It all goes to the office now, as if he's afraid someone will open it. When has that ever happened?' . . . He lifts out of the drawer a series of densely written notebooks: they are from the year Rahul was travelling to the countries on India's borders. Sri Lanka – civil war, Bangladesh – floods, Pakistan – Afghan refugees. How elusive he was in those months. Lance kept leaving messages in the Delhi office; Rahul didn't return the calls. He tried Rahul's home. His mother said, 'We hardly see him these days. When he gets home he sleeps or shuts himself in his room writing his reports.' Lance said, 'When he is back next, please tell him to phone. It's been far too long.' A week later he got a call. 'Sorry to have been out of touch, the new job has been unimaginably demanding.'

The new job, as Lance well knew, having helped to create it, left Rahul entirely free to set his own pace. If he was working himself into the ground it was of his own choosing.

He turns to the drawer with the letters. He feels, as Hamza did, that it is intrusive to be delving into these paper-remains of friendships that until so recently were live and active, but he needs to make a list of names and addresses so he can write to Rahul's friends and ask if they want their letters back. The names pass under his fingers, his list grows. About half-way through the drawer he comes to a file marked simply 'Tessa'. No second name, as all the other files have. Now he sees that the entire second half of the drawer is taken up with a series of such files, Tessa 1996, Tessa 1995, backwards through the years, each bulky, many, many letters, back to 1980. He stares, shocked. Sixteen years! That there should have been a woman with whom Rahul was on those kinds of terms, for so long, and he never once talked about her! And Hamza? Has he too not heard of her? Is that what he meant when he said, I do not want anyone learning things that he did not choose to tell them?

His eyes scan the file labels and he sees now that there is a gap, a long gap, nothing between 1985 and 1990. His mind is whirring: 1985 was the year Rahul went off to Afghanistan, so suddenly, right after that meeting in Brighton where Lance was worried about him—

High summer, it was. He remembers a haze over the sea, the shingle beaches crowded with families. In the Lifeline office people were assembling from across Africa and Asia, country directors flown in for a three-day meeting to discuss a proposed restructuring. It was like a family reunion, finding old friends, a buzz of conversation. But Rahul hadn't arrived. Each time the door opened Lance expected it to be him, but now the meeting was due to start and he still hadn't arrived. Eventually, the CEO said they should start anyway.

They were half an hour into the first session when Rahul came into the room. Lance was across the table from him and was shocked to see how tense and drawn he looked. He was scanning the agenda, and an expression came over his face that Lance recognized. He was about to challenge. At the first break Rahul went up to Glen Rogers, the Director of Programmes, and said, 'This is crazy, we have this rare opportunity when all of us are together in one place for three days, and we're going to spend it discussing departmental organograms? With the world changing around us faster than we can speak?' Glen, who himself had little interest in organograms, persuaded the CEO to give Rahul time after the break. Rahul launched into it. Outside this building, he said, the Soviet Union is in crisis, Islamic militancy is on the rise, civil conflict is becoming everywhere more an issue. We ought to be analysing what's going on. Where are the moments of critical change happening? And we should be preparing to support the people who are being buffeted by these events.

Lance was watching the faces around the room. Glen was tilting his chair back, pivoting his weight on its two back legs, watching Rahul with a look that no one could read. The other department heads were looking, variously, confused, intrigued and irritated. The CEO was decidedly put out. But the country directors were riveted and there would be no way now of pulling the meeting back to the original agenda. Several of them were looking to see how Lance was reacting. He had already said to Rahul earlier when they had talked about this, it was not possible for an organization with their limited resources to respond as rapidly or as widely as he was suggesting. But mostly he was concerned by Rahul's manner. He was over-assertive, not listening to points anyone else was making. Lance had seldom seen him like this and he began to feel sure that something must have happened to upset him. No one else seemed to have noticed, but none of them knew Rahul as he did.

Lance waited till he could get a moment alone with him and asked, 'Is everything OK?'

Rahul's defences were up instantly. 'What do you mean?'

'I just wondered if anything had happened?'

'I have no idea what you're talking about,' he said. And he took care not to be alone with Lance for the rest of those three days.

A week later, when Lance was back in Mali, Rahul called. 'UNICEF has offered me a job.'

Damn – but why be surprised? He should have seen it coming. It was a moment before he could ask, 'Where? To do what?'

'In Peshawar, north-west Pakistan, working with Afghan refugees. But I don't expect to stay there long. As soon as we can get in, they want me in Afghanistan itself.'

'To do what?'

'To find people we can work with to rebuild an education system.'

All Lance could say was, 'Well, I hope it works out that way.' He knew he was being churlish but he was still smarting from Rahul's behaviour in Brighton.

An hour later he had Glen on the phone. 'You've heard? About Rahul and UNICEF?'

'I have.'

'Who would have thought it, Rahul, leaving us for a UN salary!'

'Come on, Glen, you know perfectly well it's not the salary he's choosing and it's not UNICEF. It's Afghanistan. If *we* could have given him the chance, he'd have taken that.'

'And if I wasn't lumbered with a set of trustees who can't make a decision in under three months, we *could* have given him that chance. As it is, Lifeline has lost a man with the sharpest political mind we are ever likely to find.'

Phone down, Lance sat mulling over what had just happened. Rahul had taken weeks to be persuaded that he could make the transition to working for Lifeline and yet retain his mental independence. The leap from that to working for a UN agency was going to be far greater, yet he had made the decision in a matter of days and without wanting to talk it through. The suddenness was linked, Lance was convinced, to whatever had been causing Rahul's tension these last months. But what that was, he still had no idea –

And now here in Rahul's files for that same year is a sudden break in what had obviously been a long, intimate conversation. He has an almost overwhelming urge to read the last letter in 1985. But he stops himself; he cannot go there.

It is a struggle to push aside his confused feelings. He is compiling a list of addresses, that's what he is supposed to be doing. He looks at the most recent 'Tessa' letter for an address. *Meri jaan*, it begins, Urdu for 'my love'. But no address and nor on any of the earlier ones. If you write this often you don't need to give your address. Back, back. Phrases catch his eye, 'OK, you were right,' like they are in the middle of a conversation. Finally he comes to an address, and it's in Laos, of all places. It seems she has just arrived. The words are drawing him in and he can't stop.

> It's ten to six in the morning and I am looking out onto palm trees and tropical shrubs. It's raining, big drops, each one seems to land separately. I woke early, wanting to get out before anyone needed me so I could explore the track down to the rice fields, but I had forgotten about mosquitoes and dawn. I've been driven back inside behind a gauze door and am using these rare moments of aloneness to talk to you.

Lance shoves the letter back in the file, disturbed that he has intruded on this quietly shared moment. Except for the giveaway *meri jaan* the words say nothing of any significance, but the tone makes one thing absolutely clear. The woman who wrote that letter took it for granted that Rahul would want to hear even the smallest thing she was thinking and doing.

He shuts the drawer, a fierce sudden push. But he can't so easily shut out the sting of exclusion.

~ 19 ~

Tessa's cousin Connor is not yet back from work when she gets to his flat but he has left keys for her under a dustbin. Once in, she finds a note on the table: *Make yourself at home. You're to have the bed you and Rahul always used. I'll sleep on the sofa tonight.* She starts laughing, almost crying, and takes her things into the bedroom. There is a vase of daffodils on the window sill. Where had Connor found them? Daffodils in January? She lies on the bed, holding the memory of the shape their bodies made, right here.

Connor gets home. He says nothing on greeting, just puts his arms around her. Then she does cry, like it might never stop. He leads her to the sofa and sits next to her, arm still around her, till she is calmer. He says, 'It's unspeakable, being cut off in death. A friend of mine, his lover died. AIDS. The guy had never come out to his family, they had no idea until he was dying and it began to dawn on them. They wouldn't let my friend anywhere near him. Or to the funeral.'

'No one's doing that to me.' She wipes her wet face. 'Maeve's a lifeline. The others are all being so oppressively careful not to say anything. But it's obvious I wouldn't be so upset if he were just a friend or a long-ago lover. You can see it in Aunt Aggie's eyes: The wages of sin are death.'

'Keep away from them all. Stay here as long as you like.'

'I can't. The children.'

What will Sam and Alisa be doing now? Supper time, and Ben doing it all. Washing up, bath time, pyjamas, teeth. She feels redundant, confused.

She and Connor talk late into the night. He tells her things he remembers about Rahul. They only saw each other when Connor was back in the flat to get things but they were easy with each other, small, laughing moments. Once Rahul insisted on cooking an Indian meal for him, and he left him a bottle of wine each time. Excellent wine, Connor says. Tessa laughs, remembering. Rahul knew nothing about wine but the Indian in the off-licence down the road told him what Connor liked.

In the morning she goes walking where once they walked together. Primrose Hill, where his English Aunt used to take him to fly his kite. Tessa saw it that first time as the ten-year-old Rahul might have seen it, like something out of a children's picture book, a steep green hill looking down over banks of trees to where the tall buildings of the city clustered far below. Now the trees are bare as she walks all the way down and into Regent's Park, to watch the ducks on the lake and to remember walking here with him on their last time in London before everything changed.

They had woken to the thin winter sun slanting in through the window of Connor's flat, their bodies touching all the way down to their toes. Half asleep still, they slipped into love-making, luxuriating afterwards in their warm, naked closeness. She thought, I don't understand why we can't have this for ever. Every day. Suddenly he sat up and said, 'Come – it's sunny outside and the day's going to be short. Let's get out.' They got dressed and came to walk here, where she walks now, past people walking their dogs, a backdrop of leafless trees against a clear sky. Everything at work felt stuck, she told him. Her flatmate was leaving and she was going to have to decide something. Share with someone new? She was giving him every chance to see what she needed but he couldn't, or wouldn't. If he had said, 'Then come back with me,' she would have done it and made it work, overcome her own limitations. But she was too confused to ask for it. Love is something freely given. If what they had was enough for him, it would be pointless to press him to want more.

They came in from their walk, into a steamy little cafe where they ate toasted teacakes. The butter melted yellow and they poured tea from a pot that leaked from the spout. She said maybe she would give up her job and go travelling. He started asking her about where she might go. He caught the hesitation but didn't understand what it was. So clever a man, and so stupid about personal things. You'll be fine, he said, and he recited an Urdu verse for her and wrote it out as they sat there.

> With us there is no talk of near or far
> Together or apart, we still must love

That was what his hand was writing, that was what his words were saying. That was what his body told her whenever they made love. That, she knew, was what he really wanted. But something in him drove him on his own path, with no space for her.

The toasted teacake cafe is there no longer, the space taken now by a shop selling curios to tourists. She stares at them, bemused, buys a London bus for Sam and a guardsman with a bearskin hat for Alisa. Then she packs away the mother in her once more and sets out to look for the buses whose numbers she remembers. She takes one, then another. In each she climbs the stairs and sits as near the front as she can, looking down on the streets of London, the traffic, the people, so many lives, moving past. Will any of them one day revisit these streets that once were just on the way to somewhere, and try to hold on to something that is gone but that they cannot let go of?

She gets out on Waterloo Bridge and climbs down the stairs to the river level, the South Bank, looking out over the Thames. There are stalls with second-hand books under the bridge, and a cafe. She orders a coffee and sits down to wait for him to arrive.

She is being drawn back into silence, the silence that enveloped her after she had told him about Ben, and he had stopped writing.

No words travelling between them. How could that be?

Surely it was temporary? Surely they must be able to rescue something from the rubble?

She tried once to break through. Ben was taken on as part of an international geological survey team that was to be based at Liverpool University. She wrote to tell him that she was going to be in Britain for a few months. If he was still getting to London sometimes, perhaps they could meet?

More silence. Then a brief note. He was coming to Brighton for a three-day meeting, he said. They could meet the day before.

They agreed a time, a place. The South Bank, she suggested, a place they had often met. In the cafe by the bookstalls under the bridge. Where she sits now ...

She arrived early. No bookstalls set up yet, no cafes open. It was high summer and the morning was slowly getting going, people walking to work, women in light dresses, men in short sleeves, waiters setting out chairs, river boats moving slowly by. The cafe opened, she ordered a coffee, looked at her watch. He was late. Always her waiting, and Rahul late. She tried to hold on to fairness. Perhaps his flight had been delayed? But as with mounting apprehension she watched for him to come, she knew that it had been a terrible mistake to offer to meet. What more was there to say? The deed was done, she and Ben were together. How would they find a language to speak to each other beyond that?

She saw him before he saw her, saw him walking towards the place where she sat. But the walk was not Rahul's, not the long buoyant stride that she had watched each time he walked back into her days, lighting her world with joy. This was the walk of someone who was heading where he did not want to go. He saw her, waved, but no smile. He stopped a few feet from her, arms at his sides. No hug. The pain of having him stand there so separate, so distant, made her despair.

What had she hoped could be salvaged? Simple friendship? But how unrealistic was that?

His voice was full of hurt, anger. 'I can hardly believe that you, of all people, could do it like this' – and 'like this' meant landing it on him as a decision. But how else could it have been? Only she could know what she needed. But to say nothing earlier, while it was developing? She had no answer to that, except that she had been a coward, afraid to face up to the implications of her choosing. She had known when she wrote Ben's name in a letter and deliberately underplayed it, she had known every time she let the image of herself and Rahul lying together re-enter her mind, she had known there was no way to have what Ben was offering her without giving up the thing that was absolutely central in what she and Rahul had, their uniqueness to each other, the place they occupied together which no one else could ever reach.

Useless to say 'Nothing has changed, it means just as much to me as it ever did.' Then why had she given it up? Because there was something she needed more. What could there be, more than this? A quiet life, with nothing hovering in the air, unresolved. A settled life with someone who will be there when I wake, and not about to fly off. Having somewhere that I belong, because that's where he is, and he wants me to be there with him. But she struggled to say that to this man she had loved for so long, how through all those years when she was trying to live it his way, she had not been able to acknowledge to him how abysmally she was failing, so afraid had she been that if she claimed too much he would back away. Until eventually she came to understand that even if she could have told him clearly what she needed, he couldn't have given it to her.

Defensive indignation rose up to counter misery. 'Did you think I would wait for ever?' He could not reply. The intensity of that silence could mean only one thing: he had not considered the question. He had simply assumed, without doing anything to make it happen, that she would stay forever his.

Their cups were still half-full and the coffee cold. Their voices had been intense, probably loud, there were people staring at them. He got up and left. She followed, walking along the wide paved embankment; walking in silence. Gradually the movement released a degree of normality and he began to talk. He had been on the run these last two months, he said, staying away from his friends, trying to shut out feeling by working. He was hardly sleeping. She saw that it was as he said, he was worn out, no reserves. They went into a pizza place and he stared at the menu. She ordered them both some soup; neither of them could finish it. She tried to talk about other things; he brushed her questions away angrily as if she were patronizing him. Then the fight went out of him and he answered more normally; but a few minutes later he said, 'There's a meeting tomorrow morning in Brighton. I have to get the eight-twenty train,' and the hours between now and eight-twenty tomorrow morning loomed between them, full of questions. She reached out across the table to take hold of his hand. 'Rahul, we can't. Everything else can stay the same. Not that.' But she knew as well as he did that without that, nothing else would stay the same.

He pulled away his hand. In a voice hard and cold he said, 'Let's get out of here.'

They walked themselves footsore and ended up at St James's Park, walking past its lake with bright-feathered ducks and flower beds in full bloom and tourists consulting maps to find Buckingham Palace. They lay on the grass, bodies close but protected by the public nature of where they were from any dilemmas about how close. They lay arms touching, hands holding, looking up at the sky through patterns of leaves.

After a while she sat up and said, 'Put your head in my lap, I'm going to give you a head massage.' He shifted, and the feel of his head settling between her crossed legs was unutterably comforting. He closed his eyes and she began to move her hands through his hair. For the first time since he had come to stand a few feet from her, arms at his sides, she felt something approaching calm. He let her hands lull him into sleep.

When he opened his eyes she was looking down at him. She had been doing it for the whole time, memorizing his face. He said, 'I suppose I should say I'm grateful, for this small mercy.'

'Don't say anything,' she said.

Over an evening meal he started talking about the world-out-there, the political developments of which in her travelling months she had been oblivious. He was on familiar ground again and becoming less tense. As the meal came to an end he stretched out to take her hand and held it, wordlessly. She felt tears starting. 'Don't be sad,' he said. 'I can't bear you to be sad.' But the tears kept coming and her hand kept holding tight, holding on to the thing she had damaged, the thing of infinite value that she was afraid she might be losing for ever.

She was not afraid about her and Ben. They would keep loving each other in their own way, and make a good life together, an undramatic life of a kind that Rahul could never have offered. But the Tessa who sat here with Rahul was the person she had been for all the years before she ever met Ben, the one who followed the uncertain light within her, crossing borders, exposing herself to challenges. She was not sure that person would survive the blending into the couple.

She returns, slowly, to face where she is, the year it is, the woman she has become. She has been walking, retracing the route that they walked on that painful day. She walks to keep him there, till she reaches St James's Park and sits on the grass exactly where they lay that day. Everything else can stay the same, she had said, but not that. But what sense is there in saying, I will caress you, but only with my eyes? I will receive like an old friend the smell of male sweat that comes through your shirt but I will not touch the body that produces it? I will allow my ears to savour the sound of your voice, I will even let my arm touch yours, in passing, as it were, pretending that the moment of touch holds no instant electricity, I will take your head between my crossed legs and allow my hands to move through your hair – and still I will fool myself that I am keeping within limits. How desperate, thinking you can pin love to the ground with such fine threads of distinction.

'I'm still here, Rahul,' she had said, as they sat holding hands to ward off separation. 'I'm me, you're you, that doesn't change.'

He shook his head. 'I can't do this any more, Tessa. I won't be writing.'

~ 20 ~

It was to Hugo he turned when life had run out on him.

They had met just months earlier. Hugo had not been long

in Delhi and they had had no contact outside of work. Then he got a call from the airport: Rahul, asking if he could come to his house. 'I'm not in good shape and I can't go home. I can't handle people asking intrusive questions.'

Hugo left the office immediately so he could be there to receive him. He asked no questions, he had been warned, but it was obvious that whatever else had gone wrong, the man was exhausted. He phoned a pharmacist friend who came over with a sleeping pill. Rahul took it and passed out. Next morning he had still not woken. He phoned the Lifeline office to tell them that Rahul's return had been unexpectedly delayed, and asked them to let his family know. He went to work, leaving the cook with instructions to look after Rahul's needs and to tell no one that he was there.

For two days he barely surfaced. Hugo had seen burnout before and did not worry unduly but it bothered him that Rahul had still said nothing about the cause. He took a couple of days' leave and told him they were going off to a place in the hills. As Rahul recovered, the story came haltingly out. The years with Tessa, the shock of her letter about Ben, his own belated realization of the mess he had made.

Hugo let him talk till he had nothing more to say. But all the time he was thinking, Where does he go from here? He had hit one of those moments when only a dramatic change of setting could help him recover an ability to focus.

Afghanistan suggested itself. Rahul was already concerned with the issues, and Hugo knew that UNICEF was having difficulty recruiting good people for their work there. In Rahul's present state he was not someone he could honestly recommend but he pulled rank, a thing he rarely did. He phoned a friend and said, 'I've got someone who will be a unique asset. But he needs to start immediately, and he's going to need a tolerant manager for a few months.'

Within a week he was gone.

Hugo is thinking of it now as he waits in the International Centre in Delhi for Lance to come to meet him. He is looking out over the Lodi Gardens, remembering how he and Rahul walked there on Rahul's last morning before leaving, and that he tried to give him advice, a thing he rarely did.

Lance arrives. Hugo has no difficulty spotting him as he comes into the busy foyer – he is far taller than everyone else. His craggy head inclines slightly in greeting, strong arms around him in a hug.

Lance says, 'I wondered if we would recognize each other. It's been a long time.'

'Peshawar,' Hugo says. 'Holiday Inn. Nineteen eighty-nine. You had come to see Rahul. He was out from Afghanistan on R&R.'

'You have a precise memory!'

Hugo shrugs. 'I remember people. It's a necessary skill in my job.'

'His parents are expecting you. They're hungry for anything

that connects. You can tell them things about his life these last few years, that no one else can.'

'It's why I've come. But there's something you and I need to talk about first.'

At first Lance cannot take in what Hugo is telling him, something about an investigation into the causes of death. Hugo repeats it, leaving no doubt. 'We do not believe there was a landmine.'

But if it wasn't that … ? Lance's mind is groping for something to hold on to, when everything he has so painfully taken in as fact is now up for question.

Does this mean — ?

Hugo answers the question before he can form it. 'Don't go there, Lance. He is dead, that is not in question. These people do not lumber themselves with prisoners. The question is, *how* did he die?'

A different death? A different kind of horror?

Lance feels blank. 'Does it matter?' he asks.

'It matters a great deal. Countless Tajiks have lost their lives in this war but this was a calculated murder of an unarmed UN peacekeeper and an independent journalist. It cannot be allowed to go unchallenged. News travels, frighteningly. Each time a rebel force somewhere in the world gets away with something like this, it increases the chances of it happening to others.'

Lance is still struggling to adjust. 'His parents, are you going to tell them?'

'No. They have a kind of closure at the moment and I have no intention of disturbing it. If we find out anything, of course we will tell them, but until then there is no point in distressing them further. Which means I have to ask you not to talk about it.'

'Of course. But what – ?'

'The alternative theory? We're fishing in the dark. My suspicion is that there may have been someone up there who had a score to settle with Rahul. Maybe an angry encounter – things got out of hand – then they had to get rid of the journalist too. No witnesses.' He pauses to allow Lance time to take it all in, then comes to the point. 'I need your help. Rahul's father tells me you are taking charge of his papers.'

'They've just been shipped off to Vancouver.'

'That's a pity. A great pity.'

'I'll be going through them when I get there. What is it you're after?'

'Difficult to say. Leads, suggestions of hostility towards him. The commander is the obvious candidate – Sadirov. Check in the notes if there's any reference to him. But not just him. Look for any reference to some previous confrontation.'

Hugo is tracking a mirage, Lance thinks. A man is killed in the mountains by lawless bandits in chaotic times – what is there going to be in his papers that could lead them to what happened? But he says only, 'What could Rahul have been doing to arouse that kind of hostility?'

'Doing his job,' Hugo says bluntly. 'There were atrocities happening all the time and Rahul was a witness to some of them. He might have tried to intervene, or in some other way got up the nose of someone who later landed up with Sadirov's lot.'

Lance wants to go nowhere near all this. Hugo must surely feel the same, yet he is making it his business. Lance says, 'I admire your determination.'

Hugo shakes his head. 'You have to understand, this is my case. I sent him up there.'

'You had good reason to, I'm sure.'

'Yes, I had good reason.' In the weeks that have passed it has become no easier to face up to this. 'I asked him to do it because I thought that they might be meeting some very antagonistic people, and that his experience could be useful. And that is exactly what happened.'

'You're working with risk all the time, Hugo. It can't be avoided.'

'Of course. But it's the first time a decision of mine has sent a man I valued to his death.'

'His decision too. He knew what he was going into.'

Hugo cannot reply.

Lance says quietly, 'I'll do whatever I can. But we'll be lucky if there's anything in his notes that helps.'

'I'm not sure of that. Rahul was a note-maker – his reporter instincts, he never lost them. Anything significant happened, he recorded it, and he trained his team to do the same. They used to joke about it, said he was like the recording angel, like he thought it was all going to be used in evidence one day. And maybe it will be.'

They go back together to the house. An hour before Lance has to leave for the airport Hamza says he has something to show them both. He takes them into Rahul's room, even emptier now that the files and cassettes have gone, and hands Lance a couple of sheets of paper that he says he found folded into a collection of poetry. He and Hugo look at it together. On the first sheet is a working copy of a translation of an Urdu poem, with scratchings-out and alternative possibilities. On the second sheet is a written-out final version.

Hamza says, 'It was a poem I showed him on his last visit home. It is by Faiz, one of our great contemporary poets. But until I found this I had no idea he had translated it.'

> *I do not believe in miracles. But this I wish, that when the*
>> *time comes*
> *To lead me out from this bustling world, that I just once will*
>> *be allowed*
> *To leave the grave, so I can come and stand at your door*
>> *and call for you.*
> *And if you should need a partner in grief then I will be there,*
>> *to comfort you.*
> *If not, then I will turn once more to set out on the road to*
>> *oblivion.*

Their eyes lift to meet Hamza's. The questions move between them.

Lance says, as if to ward off the discomfort of the thought, 'They're not his words, they're the poet's.'

Hamza says quietly, 'But he chose to translate them.'

Stand at your door

Mountains half-circle the town, lifting out of the plain, their lower reaches shaped in strange humps as if by an earth's core that will not stop heaving. Beyond are more and more layers, the furthest ones white-topped. Blink your eyes, and you might see a caravan of merchants arriving at this oasis of civilized life after their desert journey from Samarkand, to rest their camels here before attempting the arduous crossing into China. And up there, on that barely visible track, surely that is a slow line of mules moving down, heavily laden? But it is a trick of the light. Look again and there is nothing.

Resham-serai. The name itself carries history, for *resham* is silk and *serai* is a resting place. But the only visible remains of those earlier times are a crumbling fort and a mosque with a blue-tiled dome. Whatever else survived the waves of invasion must have been destroyed in the earthquake thirty years ago, for mostly it is street after street of graceless concrete apartment blocks. The town centre is Soviet town-planned: a few imposing state buildings, a hotel that looks distinctly unwelcoming, and a statue of the national poet set in a square edged with formal gardens, dormant now in the slanted winter light.

In another way, less obvious to a newly arrived outsider, the town carries its history. This was for centuries the easternmost outpost of Persian cultural influence and the language lives on – in the streets, the markets, in people's homes. Here they call it Tajik, in Iran they call it Farsi, but it is the same language with only minor variations. Invisibly it links people back to the great Persian poets: Hafiz, Rumi, Bedel. The Soviet State sought to cut people off from their cultural roots by banning the 'old writing', the flowing Persian script and its more angular version used in the Qur'an. To use it became a crime punishable by exile, even death; and in the new schools children were taught to write their language only in the Cyrillic script which the Russians had brought. But old people secretly treasured handed-down copies of the works of Hafiz, though by now almost no one could read them.

Some stories refuse to die. Scratches in the rock.

It's a cold February day, more than a month after Rahul's ill-fated journey into the mountains. Across the town square a woman in her early thirties walks home from the small office of Lifeline International that she and he set up over a year ago. She has the features of Tajik mountain women, with high cheekbones and a clear complexion, but none of their natural grace. Her posture is too rigidly upright and she dresses for work in formal Russian style, a straight black skirt, a plain blouse, with her hair tightly scraped back; if she let it flow more softly she would possibly be attractive. Her eyes, unexpectedly, are blue, something not unknown in the mountains; a throwback, people say, to the Greeks, the armies of Alexander. But Nargis Suleimanova is not given to romanticism about her origins, nor about anything else. Life is tough. To survive it you need to be practical.

This walk is her one winding-down moment of the day. She is at no one's service, neither in the office nor at home, and she savours it. Everything looks quiet today, she observes, though until a few days ago this square was the scene of demonstrations that have made headlines in the world's press. Resham-serai is in Kyrgyzstan, but in its south-western end that looks on the map like a pointed finger protruding into the mountains of Tajikistan. Cartographers in Stalin's day drew lines on maps around a theory of nationalities: Kyrgyz this side, Uzbeks that, an enclave of Tajiks here, and the result is a surreal jigsaw that makes no sense on the land itself. And it particularly doesn't work in the town, where all groups co-exist. But when there is trouble in the mountains, its echoes are felt down here. Once again people have been fleeing across the porous borders, to take refuge in Kyrgyzstan; they need land, and that puts a burden on people already there. Naturally they get anxious. But the foreign journalists' talk of the war possibly spreading is nonsense. Either they didn't understand what people were demonstrating about or they were deliberately hyping it to get headlines.

Her irritation is a throwback to years working as a translator, constantly having to explain to foreigners what was going on.

It was OK if they really wanted to know but half of them didn't. At home she had tried not to talk about her frustration so as not to burden her mother-in-law, but the truth was she had become ground down by it. Until Rahul arrived, and offered her a job of a quite different kind.

He had come to see what was happening to an earlier wave of refugees, and the UNICEF office where she worked sent her to accompany him. He spoke Tajik and had no need of an interpreter but asked for one in case people were using a dialect he couldn't follow; that was the first sign she had that he was different from other foreigners. On the journey up he asked about the economic problems since the Soviet Union had collapsed, and what UNICEF was doing. 'Just lots of talking,' she said. 'And strategy papers.' Rahul laughed and asked what she thought they could do. She said, 'You're the first person who's ever asked me that. No one expects an interpreter to have ideas.'

The people she worked for had their eyes always on policy directives from New York, she said, and they wasted time trying to work with the government. They have to, Rahul said, that's their role. Maybe, she said, but if they want to get anything done it's useless. Government officials all have the old Brezhnev mentality, afraid even to say things are bad. So how can they fix them? And they're just looking for money. Not for the country, for themselves.

He was back a few months later saying that he knew people in an organization called Lifeline International that wanted to support local initiatives. Would she join them? 'They do things we in the UN agencies can't do,' he said. 'With a little support from outside, people like you could get great things done.'

How could she give up a safe job? No one here had ever heard of Lifeline International. Rahul said, 'They're small, but honest. I used to work for them. They'll match what you're getting now but you will have real responsibility. You'll be able to do the things you know are important.'

'And you?' she asked. 'Will you be in charge?'

'I can't leave Tajikistan till peace is signed. We'll set things up together, then it'll be over to you and the Lifeline head office, but I'll keep visiting. If there are problems, we can sort them together.'

She has no time for religious superstition but if she had believed in unseen powers she would have thought they must have noticed her distress, and she is every day grateful for the chance he gave her. In this job she uses her own judgement, and she has been entrusted with a task that could scarcely have been closer to her own fears and hopes, to find a way to answer the eyes of the child in her recurring dream. The child that is Layla and yet not Layla.

'I'll keep coming,' Rahul said.

But now he is gone, and she is stranded. Not even sure if that distant head office in Brighton will decide to keep them on. She left all that kind of thing to Rahul.

Insecurity threatens, all over again.

The house that she returns to each evening is in the old quarter of Resham-serai, one of the lanes near the market that has somehow escaped being bulldozed in the name of modernization. From the lane all you can see is a high wall with a huge door, and a smaller door cut into that. She goes through it into a yard that looks as if it might once have been home to chickens, but now houses the car which they never use any more because they can't afford petrol. As soon as the heavy door closes behind her, the noise of the world outside dies away.

Inside, the house is dark. She has never got used to it, in all her years living here. She grew up in a small apartment in a block built after the earthquake. The place she slept in couldn't be called a room, it was the size of a cupboard, but they were on the fourth floor and there was always light. In this, her in-laws' house, the main room is as big as that whole apartment, and would have held an entire extended family in the days when people had ten children, and scores of relatives would gather at the smallest opportunity. Now it has the air of a room where nothing like that has happened for years, or is expected to happen again. It folds her in gloom each time she comes in, and she has to work at keeping cheerful. At one end is a platform, and both it and the wall behind are draped with carpets of swirling red-and-purple designs. That is where her mother-in-law sits on a floor cushion to supervise Layla's homework. Nargis wishes they would do it out on the verandah where there is more light, but that is her father-in-law's place.

Each day when she gets in she spends a little time hearing about Layla's day and receiving her mother-in-law's litany of complaints about food shortage and the terrible cost of things in the market. On bad days her tone implies that it is Nargis's fault for being out at work all day. She tries not to let it get to her; her mother-in-law has a lot to deal with.

After a while she goes to make tea and takes it out to her father-in-law. He is a gaunt looking man, with something about the cast of his head that has always struck her as noble, some inner quality made evident through high cheekbones and old dry skin, and a look in his tired eyes of someone who has seen too much. They all sit to drink tea looking out on the courtyard with its vegetable beds and cherry trees, and a tap in one corner that drips slowly, the water collecting in a tin bath. Along one side is a storeroom filled with things no one uses. Over the courtyard walls they can see the tops of fruit trees in the neighbouring gardens, and beyond that the mountains, with snow still on the high peaks. To Nargis this courtyard is a refuge that nothing can spoil, not even the calamities that have befallen this family since she came to live here. The best time of year is when the cherry blossom comes out, a flurry of beauty so simple, so perfect, renewing itself each year, oblivious of the mess that humankind has made of things; the promise, constantly renewed, of small moments of sweetness ahead.

Layla, unaware of adult tensions, chats away.

In a pause Nargis says, 'We heard today they're planning on sending a new director to take charge of the office.'

Her mother-in-law asks, a little sharply, 'A foreigner? Will he speak Tajik? Or Russian?'

Nargis shrugs. 'Probably not. Rahul Khan was unusual.'

At the mention of his name her father-in-law looks up. Nargis waits, but he says nothing.

Her mother-in-law shakes her head. 'So you will go back to being an interpreter?'

'Maybe. Maybe not. We have to see.'

A disturbing presence has joined them here in the quiet of the courtyard, the memory of her husband Khaled's scorn when she started working as an interpreter. 'How can you work for foreigners?' he demanded. She told him, 'I can do it because we have to eat.'

And now? Will she once again be working to a stranger's agenda, set for her day by day? But she is tired, deeply tired. Perhaps it will be a relief not to be the one to make the final decisions when the situation around them is so volatile. Things are changing too fast, too fast for her feelings to keep up, let alone for her mind to run on after the feelings to try to make sense of it all.

Like what has happened to Khaled.

It is always Khaled that her thoughts return to; and they do so now, sitting quietly on the verandah with his parents, in this home that he has abandoned. She wishes she could simply stop thinking about him, but resentment, anger, fear keep surfacing. It's been like that ever since he came back from the war in Afghanistan. The Afghans invited us in, they were told, we are helping bring good things to their country, giving the land to the people, getting women into education; but by the time Khaled was called up everyone knew the Afghans hated the Soviet army. And anyway they are our cousins, Tajiks and

Uzbeks like us, why should we fight them? No one knew what things Khaled had seen, what he had had to do. They know only that when he came back he was hard, full of anger. She tried, but she couldn't reach him. With his father there was constant conflict. If they disagreed about something, Khaled would soon be shouting. His father would answer sometimes angrily, as you do to a son who is disrespectful, sometimes softly, like with someone who is not right in his mind. They kept telling themselves, it's the war that has done this to him, they tried not to blame him. But he didn't even try. Things were so bad in the country, there were people with university degrees working as drivers, but not Khaled. Even without a job there were things he could have done to help his parents, but no. She said, At least for our child you can try. But no. He paid Layla no attention. He would go away for long spells and not tell anyone where he was going.

That tap. That constantly dripping tap. They have to use it every morning to wash, each taking their turn, and Khaled could have fixed it, all it needs is a washer. She has never learnt that kind of thing and nor have Khaled's parents, but would Khaled stir himself to do even that? No. Now everyday as they sit here drinking tea that dripping tap speaks of Khaled's absence.

She looks at her father-in-law, wondering what goes on in his mind as he sits there, so silent. Each day she hopes that when she gets home she will find him a little less depressed, a little more able to talk as once he used to. He never is, but they keep up the ritual of tea together, so that something happens in his day. Momentarily today it seemed that Rahul Khan's name might have evoked something, but he has gone back into himself. The only person he responds to normally these days is Layla. She sees nothing different in him; he is her grandfather and she chats away to him as she always has, so for her he can be the same.

Nargis gets up and goes to the kitchen to begin preparing the meal.

~ 22 ~

The receptionist in the Lifeline office in Brighton is new and Lance's name means nothing to her, an unwelcome reminder of his dispensability. He starts up the stairs. New notices on the doors. Was that necessary, at a time of tight budgets? He is giving way once again to a familiar mixture of irritation vying with affection. From where he has been sitting in Kathmandu, or in any of the other cities in Asia and Africa that have been his workplaces before, irritation is always easily in the ascendant. The head office is on the other side of the world, seemingly unconnected to the pressing concerns of here-and-now, yet it keeps landing demands on people who are trying to get a job done. Then on each return to this building other feelings pop out to surprise him. Being back here, he sees the world map differently, with the place he has just come from no longer at its centre. From these offices emanate the intangible but essential things that link him and hundreds of others across the world, the point of it all.

He walks through the open plan area to the office of Glen Rogers, Director of Programmes. Glen is one of his oldest friends but certainly not the easiest. A large man, with large capacities. He's American and they have known each other since Glen was a Vietnam War draft-dodger and Lance helped him get across the border into Canada. Sharp, demanding, intolerant of fools. Loyal if you're his friend, intimidating if you're not. As Glen stands up to greet him Lance sees that there are signs of a paunch developing; not surprising, the man works relentlessly and takes no exercise. They have hardly got started when the phone rings and to Lance's irritation Glen takes it. I have come half-way across the world to see him but he can't let the phone wait. The adrenalin buzz is too strong. The phone call is an unknown, always a potential challenge.

While Lance waits his eyes move over the piles of reports and memos falling over each other on the desk. How can someone apparently so disorganized be so damned effective at getting things done? Maybe it's because he ignores half the papers that come at him, while people like me, Lance thinks, plod conscientiously through them even though I know half of them won't be worth reading. Yet you never catch him not knowing the critical things he needs to know to make decisions.

Phone down, Glen starts talking about Lance's next posting. Lance looks at him, despairing. They went through this on the phone before he left Kathmandu. 'I *told* you, I'm not going anywhere. I'm taking four months off.'

143

'I can't believe you're serious.'

'I am serious.'

'To do what?'

'Read. Spend time with friends. Let life pass me by for a while.'

'I can't believe what I'm hearing. What's come over you?'

Lance shrugs. 'Nepal in the last few months put the lid on it for me. The government's ineffective, development money pours in and it all dissipates into nowhere. Poverty gets worse instead of better, and our projects haven't the smallest hope of becoming sustainable.'

Glen waits for more.

'And there are far too many international agencies in the place anyway.'

'None of that's new. It's your attitude that's changed.'

'Maybe. It's not been a good few months. Rahul going so suddenly, it's forced me to think. One moment he's here and there are things we're going to do together, the next moment he's gone and we'll never do them. He was forty-one and his life is over.'

'Yours isn't, and it isn't going to be.'

'I have to stop moving around. I'm forty-six.'

'What's so mystical about forty-six? I'm fifty and I'm not quitting.'

'You've got a home and a family. I need a life of my own. In one place.'

'Which place? Some hick town in the prairies?' That is harsh, and Glen knows it. His tone modifies. 'OK, Rahul's death has been dislocating for everyone. But you know he would be the last person to think that raised queries about the work.'

'It's not about the work. It's about moving, constantly losing people. I've got to find a new kind of life.'

'You've forgotten something. You're good at your job. This job. *This* is your life. You're not just good, you do it like you were born to it, and have done since the day I sent you off with your first truck loaded with food in Ethiopia. How will you find anything else half as stimulating?'

No answer.

'Take leave later if you have to,' Glen says, 'but now is the wrong time.' He pushes his chair back. 'Come over here, I want to show you something.'

They stand in front of a wall map of Asia with pins in it, the places where Lifeline works. Next to it is a similar one of Africa. There's my life, Lance thinks, visually summarized. Glen's finger circles the vast unknown of Central Asia, till his finger hovers over Tashkent, capital of Uzbekistan. 'We have a small office here. It's the central hub of the region, and we manage a few projects from there. But here –' His finger moves south to where three -stans meet, their map colours crinkling round each other in surreal shapes. 'Here,' he says, pointing to a long stretch of Kyrgyzstan surrounded on three sides by Tajikistan, 'this is where most of the new work is that Rahul took on for us. Based out of this town, Resham-serai. You knew he was doing that?'

'Yes, we talked about it.'

'He took on a lot of projects, like he was in a hurry. I have wondered if he had some idea that he might not have much time.'

Lance's mind flips:

> *. . . when the time comes*
> *To lead me out from this bustling world . . .*

'I don't need to tell you,' Glen is saying, 'he wasn't the kind of person who needed to have you peering over his shoulder. But now he's gone it's different. I need someone to go there and assess whether we should keep all that on.'

'I'm sure you're right but it's not going to be me. What about the Tashkent office? Haven't we got someone there who can do it?'

'A new guy, he's holding things together until we can make some decisions, but he's under-experienced. We didn't have much choice, had to act quickly. He's got enough to do managing that office. I need someone with your kind of experience.'

'It's not on, Glen. I know nothing about the place.'

'You can learn it. You've done it before. What's the problem?'

Just that, *that* is the problem, the fact that he has done it before, too many times. 'I told you, I need a break, and I'm certainly not up for high-tension postings. For God's sake, look at what you're asking, it's across the border from where he died. Why would I want to go there?'

'For that very reason. This is Rahul's legacy. Every project we support there has been taken on because Rahul thought it important. All the people who work for us there were recruited by him. They are new to this kind of work and they are left now without a manager. I have held off asking anyone else to take it on because I thought you would want first option.'

Stumped. Silent.

He moves from office to office, doing a handover and catching up with old friends. 'Where are you off to next?' they ask, and he says, 'No idea. Taking a break, then I'll see.' No one else reacts as Glen did, but then no one else takes him seriously. They will see him again in a few weeks, they are sure. It is only he who knows this might be his last conversation with each of them. The thought is dreadful.

He is finding it difficult to shed the sense of responsibility for what happens here. There are signs of discontent among the staff. The new CEO has been introducing changes that Glen has been resisting, and making no secret of it. There are factions forming. I should talk to him, Lance thinks, it's divisive and he ought to know better. And I'm one of the few people he will take it from. Then he pulls himself to a halt. I'm leaving, and whatever kind of mess is brewing, it's not my job to sort it out.

The others aren't helping him detach. 'We're about to advertise for an Early Years Advisor,' they tell him in Human Resources. 'It's finally got through the system. You'll know some good people out there, get them to apply.'

He takes the details. Can't make himself say, 'Where I'm going, I'm not going to be bumping into people who want to do this kind of work.'

By the end of the day he is feeling torn between the desire to get out quick and fear of facing that final full-stop.

He goes back upstairs to tell Glen he is off. Glen says, 'I'll come down with you.' Down the stairs, out into the road. Standing there, delaying the moment of leaving, he puts his hand on Lance's shoulder, an untypically personal gesture. 'We go back a long way, Lance. You can't quit now.'

'I'm not quitting you, you old warhorse. Just all this.' His hand sweeps to take in the building behind them, and in his mind, the papers on Glen's desk, the incessant phone calls, the maps on his wall. All those pins.

Glen says, with mild irony, 'Not sure it's going to be easy to tell the difference.'

London now; the stopping point between all other journeys. Lance checks in at his usual small hotel, chosen for being a few streets away from where Greta, his godmother, lives. He has his own key to her flat and lets himself in. From the small entrance hall he can see through to the living room where she sits at her desk, absorbed in writing. She has not heard him and for a few moments he watches her, a woman in her eighties framed by the open doorway like a portrait in oils. She is small; when she stands next to him her head hardly reaches his chest. Her back is straight, set by a lifetime of determination. She wears a light blue blouse that he recognizes as an old favourite. Her hand grips the pen tightly, expressing the force of her feeling. Her white hair keeps up a constant accompanying movement.

'Greta.'

'Lance my dear, you startled me.'

He leans over to see what she has been writing. 'Your poor MP. What are you harrying him about this time?'

'Third World debt. There's a debate coming up and it's high time he asked a question.'

She is moving to stand. He puts his hand on her shoulder. 'Finish your letter. I'll put the kettle on.'

He carries the tea back into the living room. 'How's the arthritis?'

'It gets in the way. Not worth talking about' – and she changes the subject firmly. She wants first to hear about Rahul's parents, her friends of fifty years. When he has told her all he can he hands her a large envelope. 'Your letters. Rahul kept them all.'

She takes it but makes no move to look inside and after a moment she hands it back. 'I don't think I want them. Throw them away for me.'

'You keep them.'

'What for?'

'I don't know. Maybe one day someone will write your biography. Keep them.'

She laughs, but she takes them. He says, 'Hamza's asked me to sort through all Rahul's papers.'

'And do what with them?'

'I don't know. I'll think about it when I go through them.'

'Take my advice and throw them away without looking at them.'

'Greta, how can you say that? You, the arch hoarder.'

'That's while I'm alive. I'm giving you my instructions now, when I die just throw my papers away, the whole lot.'

'I absolutely refuse.'

'It's up to you. I won't be there to mind.' She turns her attention back to him. 'How are *you* doing?'

He lifts his shoulders.

'You have to keep talking about him, Lance. Keep him near.' And to help it happen she lifts up a framed photo from a small table next to her and passes it to him. It has been in just that position for years but Lance studies it now as if it were telling him something new. Hamza of perhaps thirty years ago, in loose cotton trousers and long Nehru-jacket, Sushila looking so youthful, hair still black, and a small boy looking up at them with a child's perky confidence.

Greta says, 'That was the year they lived with me. His sisters were doing exams, they stayed on in Delhi with grandparents.'

'He talked about it, often. He loved your place.'

'I used to lend him books and we would discuss them. Such a grown-up boy for his age, but sweetly childlike with it.'

Rahul at ten. He, Lance, would have been a teenager, and already in Canada. 'Good thing we didn't meet then.'

'Why on earth?'

'I would probably have been jealous of him, for being able to actually live in your house.'

'Don't be absurd.'

150

Absurd, maybe, but probably true. From earliest boyhood he considered Greta a charmed being, a woman with no children of her own but a way of being with other people's that put grown-ups in an entirely different light. He looks at her now, this frail-yet-tough woman who knows him better than anyone, with whom he can talk about absolutely anything, and is grateful for the accident of history that brought about her unlikely friendship with his mother. She had fled Austria the year the Nazis took over, and an organization that was receiving refugees found a place for her on a farm in Lincolnshire, lifting potatoes alongside a gang of local girls. Greta was from an intellectual family and had been politically active from her teens; his mother had little education and less political awareness, but she was a canny judge of character, and she took Greta home, giving her the thing she most needed, a family to replace the one she had lost. And it stayed that way after she moved away. One of his earliest memories was going with his father to meet the Friday evening train from London and Greta getting out, bringing with her such an aura of other places, of vigorously held points of view. He would stay up as long as he was allowed, and when eventually he was sent to bed he would slip into sleep to the sound of voices rising and falling in the room below. She found things to put in their tree house. She sat on the floor to play Monopoly and never said, 'That's long enough now.' In holidays she took him back to London, and her idea of entertaining a child was not just the zoo and the Tower of London, she took him on marches where they carried banners and sang songs about a world without nuclear weapons. It felt incredibly daring. There was his father working on planes that probably carried bombs. He would listen as she and her friends discussed things he never heard about at home, and he bugged her with questions, which she loved to answer. When he was a resentful adolescent in Canada it was the books she sent him that kept his spirit going and his mind curious.

'Godmother' is like 'English Aunt'– he and Rahul had each in boyhood found their own formula to explain her to other people. She herself refused the title; she told his mother she was delighted to do whatever she could for the boy but she saw no reason to bring God into it. But Lance has always suspected that she likes it that he claims her in this way. She has more adopted nephews and nieces than she can count, whose photos, like Rahul's, sit in frames around her living room. But he has always been more than that, an almost-son.

He puts back the photo, and tells her what he knows about Rahul's last days, how he volunteered to negotiate; and about Hugo's doubts about the landmine. As he does so he remembers Hugo asking him not to speak about it to anyone, but Greta is not anyone. She is tough and deals directly with life, however difficult; and Rahul had a special place in her life, she is entitled to know, as much as he is. He tells her that Hamza and Sushi have not been told, and that's enough. She had training in keeping secrets in her first years of adulthood – Austria in the thirties, the war, her generation's war, risking her own life to try to get others out to safety.

She turns to look out of the window, at the bare branches of the plane trees on the opposite side of the road, and says quietly,

'It's always the most valuable people who put themselves at the sharp end.'

He can guess where her thoughts are travelling. It isn't just Rahul.

'How did *you* cope, Greta? With what happened to people you lost?'

She shakes her head. 'It's beyond what our psyches can handle. But time helps.'

She takes his hand, holding it with her stiff, arthritic fingers, so small and pale against his. The touch releases him, and he begins to talk about himself, how Rahul's going has exposed things about himself that he was trying to ignore. 'I didn't have to think about who I was going to go walking with next time, it was just a question of us fixing a date. I was using a reliable friendship to cushion me from facing up to what I need, and don't have. A shared life, with someone I love.'

'So do something about it!'

The force in her voice catches him by surprise, making him laugh. 'You were always one for the obvious solution. There just doesn't happen to be an appropriate candidate.'

'The important thing,' she says firmly, 'is to recognize what you need, so that if a candidate presents herself you don't go into a dither, wondering if it's right for her. Like you did with that lovely girl Penny in Pakistan.'

'That wasn't just me wondering, that was Penny too.'

'Nonsense, she adored you. It was perfectly obvious the time you brought her to meet me. But you took so long I'm sure she wondered if you really wanted her.'

'You know something? There are limits to how much you can run other people's lives from this room. And you've just hit one.'

She smiles an acknowledgement. But he can see she is not dissatisfied with what she has succeeded in doing.

~ 23 ~

Tessa sits at the kitchen table trying to get Ben to talk about their future. A February wind whistles through the cracks between the walls and the roof beams. The children are asleep upstairs. Grief has given way to low-level dreariness, a state of non-feeling as featureless as the long northern night.

She looks at the jam jars on the shelf above the fireplace. Each holds a small collection of notes and coins, and each has a homemade label, Sam's child-writing, spelling assisted by Ben: Food, Things For House, Electricity, Phone. And a rather empty jar, Treats. Ben's idea, a means of making visible to the children the imperatives of the family economy. He can do that, but he can't make himself think about what he is going to do.

In all the years they have been together she has never known him indecisive. Now, it seems, the plug has been pulled and his energy for facing life has drained away. She cannot enter into it. OK, he has lost his job and a life he loved. She too loved it.

But to Tessa, dealing with one huge loss, all other losses seem hardly to signify. What is a job, after all? Or a place? Or friends? You lose them, you find others. They will manage, wherever they go. She will make a new home, she has done it many times before. They just need a plan, a 'what next' for Ben's work, and only he can come up with that.

He isn't listening to what she is saying. He is trying to balance a teaspoon on the tip of his finger. She watches, in growing irritation. The teaspoon drops. 'Damn,' he says, 'I thought I had that one.'

'*Ben.*'

He looks up. 'What did you say?'

'I said, Maybe we could go back to New Zealand.'

'No.'

She doesn't know why she bothered to suggest it. Ben always wanted to get away, and left as soon as he was able. Going back would feel like failure.

'The Middle East?' she tries.

'You know I'm not interested in oil.'

'America?' But she can answer that for him too. In Laos he saw enough of the power of the great mining corporations. Why would he want to put himself in their heartland?

'Europe?'

'And have to learn to operate in another language?'

'Ben, this is hopeless. We have to be *somewhere*. Geologists do get jobs, it's not impossible.'

'Geologists with the right kind of experience.'

'There are people who would help you find a starting point.'

'You don't understand,' he says brusquely.

She gets up, a sudden movement of irritation. She starts washing the dishes that have been piled up on the sink, her back to him. No, she doesn't understand. All she understands is that Ben isn't even trying.

'Do me a favour, just go to Liverpool and talk to Norman.'

It was Norman, his supervisor, who had fixed Ben up with his job in Laos. Maybe he can help him to find another. But Ben's unfinished PhD lurks, trapping him with failure. Theoretically he was writing it up in Laos, but his research notes could hardly compete with the lure of the mountains and the stimulus of a job that challenged him in unexpected ways.

Ben doesn't answer. She says, 'Well, I'm going to write to Norman, if you won't.' And he hasn't the energy to stop her.

A week later they come in from collecting shells. Ben is considering what to do with the towels that they had spread on wet sand. Tessa picks up the post, a card from Norman in Liverpool, brief, but enough: 'Looking forward to seeing you. Just let me know when you're coming.' She hands it to Ben. He looks at it perfunctorily and hands it back. 'Where do you want me to hang the towels?'

'Why ask me?' she flares. 'You're as capable of deciding as I am.'

He starts hanging them on the rail above the stove.

'Ben, they're full of sand. Shake them outside first.'

He turns on her. You see? his eyes say. I ask, you snap. I do it myself, you tell me I'm doing it wrong.

'Ben, tell me you'll go and see Norman.'

'I'll go.'

She can't even feel pleased. He sounds trapped. He is doing it for her, not to leave her alone, the only one trying.

She wakes to the sound of a storm lashing at the windows, creaking at the roof. The house feels as vulnerable as a ship out at sea. By mid-morning the storm has blown itself out and they see that it has damaged the roof of the coal shed. Ben gets going fixing it; the practical challenge seems to have released in him an unexpected spurt of positive energy. The rain starts again, quietly this time but constant, but Ben goes on doggedly. Tessa says, 'Come in, Ben, you can't keep working through all this,' but he isn't stopping. He is out there for hours, drenched.

By midnight he is shivering, unable to get warm despite a hot-water bottle and extra duvets. By the morning he has streaming sinuses and a temperature. He is so floppy he can hardly shuffle to the bathroom. Tomorrow he is supposed to be in Liverpool, but there is no way he is going to get there in this state.

Tessa's irritation borders on desperation. She phones Maeve. 'I feel like he did it deliberately, because he can't face Norman asking what happened to his PhD.'

Maeve says, 'You go. I'll come over and get the children.'

And so it is she, Tessa, who stands on the deck of the ferry as it heads out past the long pier wall and then out into the Irish Sea. What message will her coming give to Norman? Whatever she says to explain Ben's absence, Norman will know.

She watches the water lurch behind them as the ferry cuts through the waves, accepting the spray and mist on her face. She thinks back over their last weeks in Laos, and the story she is going to have to tell Norman. What it all meant to Ben. Laos was so remote, its people so poor, and they had suffered so much, with vast tracts of land carpet-bombed during the Vietnam war. Just across the Mekong River in Thailand the economy was booming; they wanted a slice of that but they were afraid of the social consequences. They had mountains whose mineral reserves could only be imagined but they had no experience of dealing with big corporations, and they needed someone with Ben's technical knowledge to monitor their activities. By comparison, writing a PhD came to seem irrelevant to life's real challenges.

But he had moved out of his depth. His passion had always been for the earth's structures, its own intrinsic processes – now he was watching primeval rock being blasted away, forests destroyed – for economic development, they said, but more and more what he saw was the drive for profit by the corporations. On his journeys up-country his driver talked to people in the villages where they halted, heard stories of a mining company that was forcibly evicting people from land they wanted to clear, and burning villages if the men refused to work for them. Some who took work and later tried to run away were shot as they ran. Ben was appalled, and at a loss what to do.

Then – a night visit from a group of students, linked to a covert human rights group, working with an ethnic minority in the far north. They suspected government collusion in covering things up. Ben worked in a government office, could he help them get proof? It can't be, Ben said, he trusted the people he worked with. But he followed the paper trail, the evidence began to stack up, then the trail fizzled out. He asked a cautious question – but not cautious enough. Next day two officials arrived at the house to hand him a deportation order. Get out, it said, now. No chance even to tell the students.

If Ben had been indignant she could have understood, but how to explain what has made him so *passive*? Is it the sudden disillusionment? A loss of role? Does he feel that he has failed in some way?

Or is it something to do with her? Her and Rahul? Why would the whole situation suddenly bear down on him now, when Rahul is gone? But he isn't gone, that's the truth. He lives in her still, a presence that is nowhere visible but everywhere immanent. His sudden removal has only intensified her awareness of him, raking up memories, leaving her raw and exposed. For Ben's sake and her own she longs to be able to close it all down – what is the point in holding on to something that is gone?

Liverpool is all around her now, the familiar smells, the sounds, the buildings crowding together. She faces a road roaring with traffic, tries to orient herself. On the bus she looks out at rows of brick houses, warehouses, grey February skies. It is all coming back.

She arrives at the university. Norman is courteous, kind. She knew she could rely on him for that. But how can someone whose days move as safely as his comprehend what drew Ben to get involved and out of his depth? She tells the story as simply as she can though it is difficult not to get flooded with detail. She is willing Norman to understand but she is sure she sees reserve creeping into his eyes, can hear him thinking, I gave him his chance and he muffed it. What can I do?

Norman's real voice cuts in. He asks about Ben's state of mind.

'He's very low.' She doesn't want to use the word 'depressed'; it sounds clinical, a diagnosis.

Norman says, 'Tell him to come and see me as soon as he's feeling more himself.'

But Norman was her one hope for getting him back to being himself.

When she arrives back her mother is in the kitchen fixing a meal, Ben is sitting up in bed playing a board game with Sam, and Alisa is trying to tie a paper garland around his neck. Tessa pauses at the door watching for a moment before they hear her. It all looks so normal, a father playing with his children. Then Alisa is running over to be lifted and Sam calls out, 'Mama, I'm beating Dad!' She bundles them both into her arms, grateful for the noise, the questions, the distraction of their insistent small beings. Ben's eyes meet hers above the wriggling bodies. She gives a small shake of her head, and he turns away, saying nothing.

It is a moment of seismic shift, one she will recognize when later she looks back, the point at which she knew that she could no longer pack and follow. *She* will have to strike out and find the route.

She lies for hours that night waiting for sleep to come. 'We're stuck, Rahul,' she tells him. 'Ben's opting out, and I can't see a way forward.'

~ 24 ~

Lance is in Vancouver, taking stock, considering his possible future.

He is surrounded by trees and not far from the coast. That has to be good. His sister Cora's house is where he comes back to after each stint abroad, the nearest he has to a base. His books are here, filling a wall. He is fond of his nephews. He is the uncle who played silly games with them and told them stories about elephants in Kenya, but it isn't easy to stay close when you only see them every couple of years. They ask sometimes about his work. 'It's all about poor people, isn't it? But how can you make them not to be poor?' A good question, to which there isn't a simple answer even for adults, let alone children.

Strange to have arrived at the age of forty-six and still be asking himself questions about how he wants to live. Without Lifeline, who is he?

He moves about the places where he once lived, a student, a hippy dropout, vacation jobs. He stands at the waterfront and looks south to the islands of Puget Sound, where he used to go sailing, once as far as Seattle where he fell in with a group of Vietnam War draft-dodgers. They had to keep moving about, no fixed address so they wouldn't get their call-up papers, dodging the authorities like criminals. But they were just kids who didn't want to go and kill and get killed for something they didn't believe in. Glen was one of them, but more clued up politically than the others. He understood why that particular war was wrong.

He goes to see his mother, who has been disoriented since his father died. She says, 'You never write any more.' He says, 'Look, Mom, there's one of my letters on the table next to you.' She looks at it in surprise, says, 'So there is,' but it doesn't seem to cancel the other thought. She says she can't understand why her friends don't come and see her, but she's thinking of friends from Lincoln, whom she hasn't seen for thirty years. 'Even Greta. You'd think Greta would come.'

'London's a long way, Mom.'

'But she used to come to us all the time. She used to play games with you children. Surely you remember?'

'I remember,' he says, and he joins her in the past as they remember together, which seems altogether more useful than trying to straighten out the confusing present.

Rahul's papers arrive. He starts to go through them, but he has little faith that he will find anything to help Hugo's investigations. First the files from Rahul's years in Afghanistan – notebooks, monthly reports. He becomes absorbed. This is a level of detail that he never heard, hadn't known enough to ask about. There is an account of Rahul visiting a camp

STAND AT YOUR DOOR

run by the Islamic Renaissance Party, but no reference to an encounter with anyone called Sadirov.

On to the files from the Tajikistan years. He is vaguely aware that there is something different about these, and then suddenly realizes what it was. There is nothing handwritten. Unlike the Afghanistan papers, these are all impersonal documents, memos, draft agendas, reports of meetings, details of ceasefire negotiations. He starts flipping quickly through the files to check. No, still almost nothing in Rahul's own handwriting. No personal notes.

He calls Hugo to tell him. Hugo is puzzled, and his disappointment is obvious. Lance feels unaccountably low. We are exactly on opposite sides of the earth, he thinks, the time gap is twelve hours. He feels far away from everything that for the past two months has mattered most.

He turns to the letters. There is already a small stack of replies from Rahul's friends around the world, saying they would like their own letters back. The saddest is a brief note from a woman called Parveen Jalali, an Iranian journalist Lance met once when he was visiting Rahul in Peshawar. She was a friend from his London student days, he said, 'And she's the reason I became fluent in Farsi,' with the definite suggestion that they had been more than just friends. Parveen was in Peshawar to interview exiled Afghan leaders, but also, perhaps, to meet Rahul again. A strange evening. Lance guessed she would have preferred to be alone with Rahul but he was making it clear that he wanted Lance to stay. To keep things uneventful? When Lance left them he wondered whether they would be going off to Parveen's hotel room together. It was obvious what Parveen wanted. Who could tell what Rahul wanted?

'Please destroy my letters,' she wrote. 'It would be extremely painful to have to see them again.' He lifts her letters out of the file and is dumping them in a bin when a sentence catches his eye. 'Ignore my last letter. I don't know what came over me, and I hate myself for it.' The date, late November, just weeks before Rahul died. Something painfully unfinished. He drops them in the bin. All that emotion, turned to dust.

Nearly all parcelled up now, but an entire box of letters is still untouched, for there has been no response from the mysterious Tessa. He shoves the box under his bed and tries to forget it is there.

Tessa has been working her way through vacancy columns. It is like scanning scripts of plays, she decides, trying to imagine herself in each of the roles, but her experience is so eclectic it fits none of them. Then she finds one she can do without thinking, manager of a day-care centre, here in Dublin. No, no, she needs to get Ben somewhere different. But there is nothing else, and their money will soon run out. Without enthusiasm she applies. She is interviewed. They offer her the job, and she feels instantly trapped.

She has not realized until now the strength of feeling that is pulling her away. Ireland is a place like any other, surely she can learn to cope with it? But she has, it seemed, absorbed her father's restlessness. Is it being so close to Maeve and her mother – people she loves, but she can't handle them knowing everything she is doing? There was reason enough in the past to put up barriers of privacy, but with Rahul gone, why does she still need to?

She has no idea what Ben is feeling about her having taken over finding a way to earn. Both relieved and guilty, probably. But he doesn't want to stay in Ireland any more than she does.

'They've offered me the job,' she tells him, 'and I realize I don't want it.'

For a moment he looks stuck, not knowing how to react. Then he says, 'So tell them no. Wait for something better.'

It is the warmest moment they have had since everything started unravelling, and she is grateful.

A letter arrives at Maeve's house, addressed to 'Tessa', no second name, forwarded from Laos. Maeve waits while she opens it.

'It's a friend of Rahul's. Do I want my letters back?'

'And do you?'

Does she? Will she want to hear her own voice, to be faced again with the fluctuations of her own intense youthful feelings? The letters from New Zealand when she was not telling Rahul about Ben? But if that's who she was in those years, that's who she was.

'Yes I do,' she says. 'There's half my life in those letters.'

But she knows what Maeve is thinking, It's the half that

165

doesn't include Ben. Are you sure you want them back, those outpourings to your other love? Another thing you can't discuss?

It's no one's business but mine, Tessa thinks, defiant.

The thought of her letters is deeply unsettling. Not just that they are in someone else's hands, but their very existence. Even if she doesn't want to look at them now, there might be a time, she has to keep them safe to have the option. They are fragments of her spirit, she can't let them be consigned to a recycling bin. Letters have marked each stage of their life together – even the five years of silence, defined by the absence of letters —

'I won't be writing,' he had said as he left, and then he had disappeared, into the void. She had no idea where he was, what he was doing. They had kept their life together so private that there was no one she could ask for news of him.

Starve the imagination of detail and it gradually turns to other things. 'Focus on where you are,' he used to say, 'it's the only way to live.' Now she had no option. Feelings that you can do nothing about do not necessarily go away but they get buried in the lower reaches of consciousness. If you have any sense of self-preservation, you take care not to go digging.

A year, two years, three years. Ben's work kept them moving, constantly somewhere new. Mostly it was South-East Asia, where his geological survey team was working in mountains in remote areas, and Tessa was being wooed by sensations familiar from childhood, the lush vegetation, the stimulus of different cultures, the warmth of the people. Ben was busy, and therefore happy, and therefore easy to live with. She had given up thinking she needed a plan for her own life, it suited her better not to have one. Wherever they went she found something to do; always with children, not often paid, but Ben was earning enough. It left her free to be creative. But in her inner life, Rahul had never gone away. He was there in how she thought, how she reacted, what she noticed, there as she watched women in the paddy fields standing bent from the waist as they worked, their broad pointed straw hats shielding them against the fierce sun; or fishermen flinging nets into the air, to land in graceful arcs; or young children looking after even younger children, their dark eyes set in perfectly oval faces. She saw it all as she would have seen it if they had been watching together.

1990: she and Ben were in northern Thailand, near the border with Burma. There was a settlement of refugees nearby, people from a persecuted minority, and Tessa was working with the children. A woman from the UNICEF office in Bangkok visited, watched Tessa training play leaders, saw the children's activity centres, and wrote a report. Tessa was sent a copy and then forgot about it. A month later she got a call from Bangkok. They were organizing an Asia-wide training workshop on work with children in conflict zones. Could Tessa come and talk about what she was doing? They would pay her fare and costs. As she listened she was thinking of the UNICEF conference in Florence where Rahul was asked to talk about getting girls into school in rural India.

He was using her work in the village as an example and he charmed the conference organizers into letting her be part of his session. Sitting there at a polished wood table in a beautiful Renaissance building, surrounded by development professionals from around the world, she had felt like a child allowed to stay up late with the adults. 'It's Tessa who should be doing this,' Rahul told them, and now this woman was asking her to. Silently she shared the joke with him.

'Sure,' she said, 'I'd love to do it. Where's the workshop?'

The woman said, 'Kathmandu.'

Her flight landed half a day before the workshop was to start. She checked in at the hotel and went wandering the streets, memories surging back powerfully at every turn. The hotel was only a few streets from where she and Rahul had first slept together. She went to the very place, and up onto the balcony, ordering a drink for the privilege of looking down at the same temples with their elaborate carvings, Durbar Square with people walking across it, stunning views of the mountains when the clouds lifted. When she got back to the hotel, her mind was having difficulty reassembling the present tense.

She registered for the workshop, was given a folder with papers, started looking through it. List of participants, their organizations, the countries they worked in. And there it was – Rahul Khan, UNICEF, Afghanistan.

~ 25 ~

He was at the far end of a reception room when she first saw him. There were people milling around, finding old friends. He was talking to someone, his back was to her. She couldn't see his face but every movement of his head and hands was familiar, the way he stood.

He turned, saw her standing there looking at him, went completely still, just staring.

Everything was silent, the people to left and right fell out of focus, there was only her, and him, and the line of sight between them. Then he recovered – he had the advantage over her of having had no warning, while she had for the last hour become paralysed with anticipation and awkwardness. He came across to her, stood in front of her, no more than two feet away. She felt the pressure of his closeness as if it were a physical change in the air. She had forgotten – how could she have forgotten? – the instant electricity each time he reappeared. Her eyes were taking in details, wanting to miss nothing. He was wearing an Indian shirt, no collar and embroidered around the neck, the kind he had often worn when she was in India. He had a trim beard now, just a glossy black line shaped around his jaw. It accentuated the shape of his head, made him look more considered, sober; and there were lines at his eyes that had not been there before.

Slowly a smile started up in his eyes. 'So,' he said, 'you still exist.'

She could say nothing, aware only of a surge of happiness. She didn't know she was smiling until he said, 'And it's still magic, the way you smile.'

The smile seemed to have taken over her whole being, but she said, 'Don't, Rahul.'

'I can't help it.' And then, as if discussing something completely ordinary, 'Funny, I thought it would be painful if this ever happened. But it's just you and me. The way it used to be.'

'Yes,' she said. 'It was too ghastly last time. I thought –'

'So did I,' he said.

A pause. Then, 'How's Ben?'

She was startled. 'You don't want to know how Ben is. Why do you ask?'

'I want to know how you are. That means I have to know about Ben. You're still together?'

'We're together. We're married.' Another pause. She added, 'We're happy.'

He nodded. 'And where are you?'

'Thailand. He's surveying mountains. I'm working with kids.'

'Of course.' His eyes were smiling, holding hers.

'And you?' she asked.

'Me?'

'Yes, you. I want to know how you are.'

He considered the question. 'Busy.'

'Of course.' They both laughed. She said, 'And in Afghanistan, I see. Where, exactly?'

'Mazaar-i-sharif, up in the north.'

'You live there?'

'I guess you could say that. It's not quite the way I think about it. But it's where I spend a lot of my time.'

Another silence, taking in once again the fact that they were standing in the same room, talking to each other. Eventually she asked, 'You live alone?'

'In a room in a shared UN house.'

'Shared with — ?'

He gave a short laugh, shook his head. 'With a bunch of time-servers whose main topic of conversation is what they're going to do on their next leave. Bangkok mainly, for the ease of finding paid sex with young girls. Conflict with their principles? No problem.'

She started laughing, at the vigour of his scorn and with joy at his continuing existence. 'And what about you?' she asked. 'You and women?'

He stood watching her, eyes appreciative, but challenging. 'You're being extremely direct.'

'No more than you.'

'Ah, but then your answer is simpler.' Then, in a neutral tone as if describing someone else's life, 'There have been a few. Short-lived.' Then, loosening up a bit, 'My mother still hopes I'll marry. She introduces me to someone new every time I go back.' Another pause. 'But the truth is' – he was speaking lightly now, that light voice she knew so well, masking something serious – 'I've never been tempted to settle for anything less.'

He reached out his hand, to rest on her shoulder. The shock of touch. His touch. She stood still, letting it become normal.

'Extraordinary,' he said. 'It feels like there's been no gap.'

She nodded.

He looked around him, as if suddenly aware of where they were, checking that no one was near enough to overhear. Quietly, his voice getting to practicalities now, 'Tessa, did you know I'm facilitating this workshop?'

'I saw in the programme. I'm glad.'

'Glad?'

'I've never seen you do it. I always wanted to.'

'It comes at a price. It means I can't opt out of any sessions, and there will be meetings at the end of each day with the organizers.' He laughed, a laugh of self-knowledge that demolished her last defences. 'Nothing much changes, does it?'

The resonances were simply too strong. They were taken back by the place, by the immediacy of look and word and feeling, the vividness of memory. Tessa had a fleeting thought that Ben was miles away doing his own thing and would never know, but after that she simply stopped thinking about him. This had nothing to do with him. She had been flipped back into a life that had happened before she ever knew him, and that had for this brief moment miraculously been given back to her. They had not asked for it, it had come as a gift. It changed nothing about the lives they had each made, but for the moment it was all that existed.

They slipped away before the evening meal, to eat on their own in a part of town where the other participants were unlikely to find them. They sat on low seats in a room where everyone around them spoke Nepali and paid them no attention, and they couldn't stop looking at each other, holding hands across the bowls of food as they talked and listened, laughing at small, ridiculous things, desire intensified by amazement at finding each other again.

They got back to the hotel late, when the foyer was all but deserted, collected their separate keys from reception and went up towards their rooms, to disappear into hers. They stood naked before each other, touching and exploring as if everything was new, but every point of touch was a rediscovery. When finally they lay on the bed and their bodies pressed against each other, it felt to Tessa that she was pushing off the weight of years of separation, emerging from a cocoon to find that she had wings, and was flying.

They lay for a long time after love-making, slipping softly in and out of sleep in each other's arms. Waking, touching, moving together, not wanting to miss a moment. Before first light an inner clock woke him. She woke to his fingers trailing over her breasts. She opened her eyes, they lay looking and touching until he said, 'And you're *still* here,' and they laughed and desire washed over them again. When they had made love again he disappeared, out of the room, down the silent corridor.

She next saw him at breakfast talking to the organizers about the day's programme. For the rest of the day he was a public person, and she simply one of the participants. At lunch he contrived to join the table she was at and to sit opposite her. They chatted with those around them; she was amazed at the ease with which they did it. Throughout the day she was aware each minute of where he was, who he was talking to, but she held it quietly in an inner space as she talked with the others, and she knew that he was doing the same. They could wait.

She saw, watching him interact, that he was a freelancer still. He was here on his terms – they felt lucky to have him – and without any awkwardness he made it clear that after the last session each day he would no longer be available – he had other things he had to do in Kathmandu in the evenings. The times they disappeared together were almost certainly noticed. He did not mind who saw them. For Tessa, he was protective, and took considerable care. But she hardly thought of it. These people had no connection with her daily life and at the end of the week they would all be disappearing to their separate countries.

In the small hours while others slept they held on to wakefulness, catching up on all the years that they had missed. He wanted it all. 'Leave nothing out,' he said. She felt the same about the time she had lost with him. She wanted stories about Afghanistan, pictures of the life he had moved to so suddenly to get away from the space she had left empty. Together in the dark, his words wove spells as once they had done over a brazier in the village in India. Gaunt mountains, rocky ravines, riverbeds dry for much of the year, a land so stark it was difficult at first to imagine how it could sustain human life. People herding goats and sheep up steep valleys, scorching in summer, and in winter cut off by snow. Unexpected places where the land flattens out and there are carefully tended fields, and pomegranate trees, apricots, nuts, or a mud-walled town where old men sit in a corner of shade, with faces that carry a lifetime of stories in their wrinkled lines. The shrine in Mazaar-i-sharif, a courtyard where white pigeons rise, their wings like moving light against the blue of the dome, the blue of the sky. Then you bring your eyes down, and all you see is the pressure, the poverty, the town crowded out with people fleeing the fighting.

'And what do you do?'

'What do we do? We try to mitigate the terrible effects of war. It's like building sand castles, only to watch the next wave wash them away.'

'Tell me. Properly.'

'OK,' he said, 'I work with local Afghans to try to get schools going. We find people we can train to become teachers. That's the easy part, the place is full of impressive people with no jobs. I spend a depressing amount of time in UN co-ordination meetings, arguing over budgets. More? I negotiate with warlords, because without their sanction nothing can happen. They are tough men, calculating all the time, suspicious. Their experience of foreigners has not been good.'

'And when you're not working? In the evenings, when the others are talking about getting cheap sex in Bangkok?'

He laughed but he had talked himself out. He began to caress her again, the closeness of bodies more compelling than words. For Tessa other needs were intruding. 'Tell me, Rahul. When I'm far from you again I'm going to need to be able to imagine what you'll be doing.'

He rolled to lie on his back, hands behind his head. 'OK, I'll tell you something I do in the evenings. I translate poetry.'

175

He turned his head to see how she was reacting. She was staring, repeating, 'You translate poetry. Which poetry?'

'Urdu poetry. And sometimes Persian.'

'Into which language?'

'English.'

'But you don't need a translation.'

He laughed. 'No. But I like doing it.'

Something in his tone reminded her of their first night when he had said, 'Nothing much changes, does it?' But something *had* changed, something that went deep.

'My father gave me a collection of poems when I first went there,' he said. 'Ghalib, the most popular Urdu poet. Every Urdu speaker of my father's generation knows chunks by heart. People quote his verses, they sing them, it was there in the air around me all the time I was growing up but I had never taken time to read it for myself. Then I was stuck in Mazaar with long empty evenings, and there was this book. I've spent a lot of time alone with Ghalib.'

'What kind of poetry is it?'

'They call them *ghazals*. It's like a series of couplets, each one can stand on its own. Ghalib packs meaning into each of those couplets, and images, and complex thought. They're amazing. Often you have to puzzle over the words, they're so condensed. Then you find one that cuts the air like a knife and I feel instantly, *Yes!* He's saying something I have felt but could never have said so well. And every time that has happened, I have wanted to share it with you.' He turned again to lie on his side facing her. 'You were gone and I had no choice but to learn to let go. But inside I have kept a private space, *meri jaan*, just for us. It's been there all the time. Putting the thought into English was a kind of fantasy sharing it with you. I knew I was never going to send it, but I wanted to translate it anyway. And it's become a habit.'

'Tell me one.'

'Name your topic.'

'What – any topic?'

'Just have a go, let's see what happens.'

'This. Finding each other again.'

'Ah, now that is so many things.' He was quiet for a moment, thinking, choosing. 'Try something else first.'

She considered. 'OK, how you reacted, after I'd gone?'

'Hmm. That goes in stages. Here's one:

> *Now let me go away and live somewhere where no one else*
> *   will be*
> *Where there is none that knows my tongue, where there is*
> *   none to speak with me.'*

He paused. She said nothing, but she was amazed.

'When I read that,' he said, 'I thought, yes, that's me, running away from hurt, going into retreat. But listen to this one:

> *To live in freedom does not mean to hold yourself aloof from*
> *   men*
> *Flee from yourself, and not from others, if you want to flee*

'It was like he was telling me, it's yourself you're trying to get away from. And I knew he was right. I was running from the mess I had made of things.'

'Not just you. We.'

'Maybe. It scarcely matters now. What matters is that I learnt that if it's yourself, you can't get away from it. It didn't help being angry. It didn't help feeling sorry for myself. You can grieve, but then you have to move beyond it. You have to live with whoever is around you.'

She felt stilled, beginning to be aware of how little she knew of the man he had become.

'How many have you translated?'

'I've never counted. But a lot. Several hundred couplets, probably.'

'And what have you done with them?'

'I collect them, in a notebook. But now you exist again, perhaps I'll send you some.'

Now we exist again. No way to walk away from that. They lay close against the coming separation, time ticking away. They had pushed aside any questions about the future, but the present was almost gone. Tomorrow after the workshop ended they would be heading for the airport, separate flights, he north-west, she south-east. And then? One extraordinary week did not change who they had become or the lives they had chosen or found. Ben was there still, expecting her back. Nothing in him had changed, and Tessa was the person still who had opted for a reliable, quiet life with him. Now Rahul travelled through the landscape of a disastrous civil war, and despite the frustrations of his role, she understood through everything he said his commitment to carry on. It was a life she could not contemplate trying to share, nor would he offer it. He knew himself better now. He would go back to it, and she would return to Ben, different from the woman who had left to come here; but return she would, and neither of them questioned it.

She was drifting into sleep when he said, 'Are you awake? There's something I want to tell you.'

'I'm here. Awake and listening.'

'That couplet you asked for, about us finding each other again. I've got it now.

> *No one can govern love. This is a kind of fire*
> *That no one can kindle, and no one can put out.*

'Actually, I couldn't do that one justice. In Urdu it has a repetitive sound pattern that you can't get in English. When you say "you can't make a fire start" it's *lagaaye na lage*, and "you can't put it out" is *bujaaye ne buje*. Still, the sentiment is what counts.'

He put his hand up to her face, gently moving his fingers across her cheek. 'Look back, *meri jaan*, all those years back to the village. What created the spark between us? It happened by itself, because you are who you are and I am who I am. As simple as that, as inexplicable. And what would it take to put it out? It can't be done. Look at what we did to ourselves. Five years of no contact, but even that couldn't dim our instant response to each other. We know now that nothing ever will.

'But that's only half the story. Fire has the power to destroy, unless you take care to contain it. I almost felt that happening to me once and I can't go back there. Nor can you. We are going to have to learn to contain our delight in having found each other again, so it doesn't disrupt what we have each been at great pains to create. When we leave this place, I will hold you in my mind, as close as I hold you now. But I will also have to leave you space to get on with your life. As I have to with mine.'

She said, 'I don't know if I'm going to know how to do it.'

'We'll find a way,' he said. 'We have to.'

~ 26 ~

'It's taking you so long to unwind,' Lance's sister Cora says. 'Even the boys have noticed.' She hands him a letter that came while he was out. Postmark, Dublin. She has never heard him mention an Irish friend and her intuition tells her the handwriting on the envelope is that of a woman. She has what she regards as a sister's normal wish that he will find a partner and settle down, and she hovers, hopefully, while he reads it.

He looks up, sees what she is thinking, and laughs. 'It's just another of Rahul's friends, asking me to send her letters on.'

Cora is sceptical. There is something about his expression that tells her this is not 'just' anyone. She is being fobbed off.

He retreats to his own room to read the letter again. Clues: She now has a second name, Maguire. She's not in Laos. She wrote, 'I would definitely like to have my letters, but if it's not too much trouble, don't send them yet. I'm applying for jobs and may be moving soon. I'll send an address when I know.'

He replies, choosing his words carefully to woo a little more information out of her: 'I couldn't help noticing from the files that you have known Rahul a long time. Almost as long as I have, which makes it surprising that we have never encountered each other. If you don't mind my asking, where did you get to know each other?'

'Another letter from Dublin,' Cora says.

He ignores the innuendo and waits till she has given up and left the room before he opens it. It says, 'We met in India.' But the first file of letters is from 1980, and he, Lance, was in India too at that time. How come Rahul never even mentioned her? 'I was a volunteer on his project' –

Ah, so Rahul *did* talk about her. 'We've got this volunteer,' he would say, and then things would slip out, like he wanted to say more but never clearly enough for Lance to cotton on. Stories trickle back … about girls in the village, the school. Since it opened Rahul had been working to get the parents to send their girls, but they were busy looking after smaller children. Then one day he was saying, 'I think we're cracking it. We've set up a pre-school for the little kids, so that frees up the girls.'

'And who runs the pre-school?'

'Right now this volunteer does, but she's training the bigger girls to do it on a rota so they'll all get turns at school. She's great with kids, and she's got this lateral-thinking mind.'

This volunteer. How could he have been so thick as not to realize Rahul was holding something back?

There are no more clues. It is so tantalizing, still knowing almost nothing about her. Somehow he has to keep this line open. Suddenly his mind does its own bit of lateral thinking. He replies: 'I remember Rahul saying you were talented with children. As you're looking for a job, I'm enclosing details of one that might interest you.'

There is a wind coming towards her, blowing through her so she can't think. The wind is her history and it is sweeping her up.

> Lifeline International is looking for an Early Years profes-
> sional to develop the organization's experience of work with
> children.

There's no point, she says out loud. I know nothing about how a development agency works. There'll be plenty of people who do. Why would they even consider me?

Rahul is standing just behind her, where she can't see him. He says, 'Because you're you. They'd be lucky to get you.'

That's what you think, Rahul, not everyone does. Anyway, I'm not up for working through riots and wars like you did. I never have been. And I *certainly* can't now, with the children.

Another day of vacillating.

'You're an initiator,' Rahul says. 'You're at your best in a new challenge.'

She phones her friend Seamus in Dublin. 'There's a job I'm thinking of applying for. Can I come and talk to you about it?'

Seamus was in Africa while she was in India and afterwards they shared their volunteer stories. Now he is working for Irish Aid, so surely he will know what an organization like Lifeline would be looking for.

She says, 'I feel a fraud even applying.'

'Why on earth? Come and see me, I'll sort you out.'

She gets the bus into the city centre, remembering the university drama group where she and Seamus acted in *The Crucible*, and ended up in bed together. A man sharp enough to know it wasn't him she was thinking of. She needs that sharpness now, she has lost faith in her own judgement.

She sits in Seamus's office high up above the road, and while he reads her application she looks out of the window to the offices opposite, the people working at their computers. In all the work she has ever done, she has only once before filled in an application form. Everywhere else she has just followed Ben and responded to what was in front of her once she was there.

Seamus looks up. 'It's no good.'

'I knew it.'

'I don't mean you. This application. We're going to have to rewrite it.'

He starts cross-questioning her, making her tell him what she actually did. Then he starts redrafting. Developing training in response to locally assessed needs – that was Laos, a mum with an infant in a sling, getting involved with local pre-schools. Meeting the needs of displaced populations – the camps in Thailand. Community-based provision in areas of urban deprivation – Sheffield and Liverpool.

'Seamus, stop, it sounds like someone completely different.'

'Is it true or isn't it?'

'That isn't the point. I'd never talk about it like that.'

He points to a pile of papers on his desk. 'See those? That's the shortlist for a job I'm interviewing for tomorrow. Five people. That's what they've whittled it down to from 170 applications, most of them probably perfectly well qualified for what the job demands. I never even see that first pile. There's an administrator who sifts through it and all she does is tick boxes when she sees the right words.'

Tessa shuts up. It is comforting having someone telling her what to do.

'Who are you giving as referees?'

'I'm stuck. There was a woman in UNICEF who saw what I was doing in Thailand, but she left soon after, I don't know where she is. And in Sheffield it was a community project, that folded years ago.'

'Laos?'

She lifts her shoulders helplessly, thinking of the letter that took two months to forward. 'It isn't how things work there. They wouldn't know what to do with a request for a reference, apart from the fact that someone would have to translate it before the people I worked with could respond.'

'You spoke Lao?'

'Sure I did. I had to. Hardly any of the women knew English. Anyway, it's quite close to Thai, and I knew that from when I was a child.'

'You speak Thai and Lao and Hindi, and you didn't even put that in your application? Stick it in. There are thousands of expats the world over who assume they can do it all through interpreters. How is anyone going to know you're different if you don't tell them?' Then, 'Referees. What about that guy in India?'

Bumping into it again – 'He's dead.'

'*Dead?*'

Dead. Will it ever become real?

'The car he was in hit a landmine,' her voice says, and she hears it as if it were someone other than her speaking.

'In Tajikistan. Oh my God, that was him?'

It is pouring out now, in relief at being with someone who can at least imagine the quality of the life that was so suddenly brought to a halt. She is weeping, and Seamus's arm is around her. The shock, the sorrow, the welling up of all that he has ever been.

'It was always so – so unresolved,' she says.

Unresolved. She is shivering now, half-laughing at herself through her tears. The sound of her own voice saying the word shocked her. But it is true. From that moment of rediscovery in Kathmandu there was a deep fissure in the certainty she persuaded herself she had achieved. Is it possible that still some part of her had clung to the hope of a different outcome? That somewhere deep inside she had been hoping still, even when she denied to herself that she was doing so, hoping that one day they would find a way to –

To what?

'It's ridiculous,' she says, shaking her head at her own contradictions. 'What kind of different future could there have been? There's Ben, the children. It's like saying I wanted two mutually contradictory things to be true at the same time.'

'We often do,' Seamus says quietly, his arm still holding tight. But she hardly hears him.

The shivering slows down, then stops. She wipes the moisture from her cheeks. Slowly Seamus removes his arm and goes back to his chair.

She reaches for the practical. 'About the referees. I've just remembered, Rahul did me a reference for my first job, the Sheffield one. He sent me a copy. I've got it somewhere. Do you think – ?'

'Yes Tessa, I definitely do think.'

'I don't know, it feels kind of – Everyone in that office will know about his death. I don't want it to seem like I'm trying to take advantage of that.'

'Tessa, do you want this job, or don't you?'

She laughs a little, still trying to free herself. 'Thanks,' she says, humbly.

His shoulders lift in a shrug, wordless now. They are silent a few moments. Then he says, 'I feel I was on the edges of this story right near the start.'

'You were.' Then, with an effort, 'Everything moves on. You can never go back.'

'You're following a path he helped you get started on. Hold on to that.'

When they have got the children into bed she says to Ben, 'I don't know what's got into me but I have to get out. I'm going for a walk.'

'In the dark?'

'Just down the lane. I'll take the torch.'

'Come here first.'

She goes over to where he sits on the sofa. He puts out his hand to pull her down to sit next to him, his arm around her, and holds her close. She nestles up against his shoulder, wanting to cry. She feels weighed down by all the complications she has landed him with these last six years.

He holds her. 'I'm sorry, Tessa. About everything.'

'It's all gone so horribly wrong. But none of it is your fault. It's me.'

'It's you doing everything. I don't know why I can't.'

'Forget it. We just have to get through this time, and it'll start getting easier.'

'If you're going for a walk, I'll come out with you. We can leave the kids for a short while.'

'No, I won't feel comfortable leaving them. I'll go on my own. I won't be long.'

It is unexpectedly calming being alone in the dark. Full moon, so she hardly needs the torch. She stands for a moment taking in the small night sounds, letting herself become just another part of nature. So much he has had to cope with, and then *he* says sorry.

She begins walking down towards the beach, moving carefully so that the crunch of her footsteps doesn't disturb the silence. She finds a sheltered corner next to a boat shed. 'Ben need never know,' she had thought fleetingly that night in Kathmandu. But as soon as she was on the plane heading back to him she had known that was not tenable. A divided life it was going to be; that would be enough to handle. It could not also be a secretive one—

An inner dialogue had begun chasing through her. Ben had accepted when they got together that Rahul wasn't going to disappear. 'I know he'll still be important to you,' he had said, 'but it won't get in our way. Our spheres will scarcely intersect.' But then Rahul did disappear, and for five years Ben hadn't had to think about him. Now he was going to have to.

'How was the workshop?' Ben asked. And before she could lose the moment she said, 'It was fine, but something unexpected happened. Rahul was there.'

A long silence. 'And?'

'It was like it used to be.'

She did not elaborate, and he did not ask her to.

He's working in Afghanistan, she said. My life is here with you. Rahul and I will be writing, like we always used to, but it's unlikely we will have the chance to meet again. If we do, it will be rarely.

Another silence. Her heartbeat seemed audible. She was afraid – but of what? Of this going wrong? Of it being too much for them to handle?

Of being asked to give up what she could not.

Ben said, 'This is going to take some getting used to.'

'Nothing has changed about you and me,' she said. 'Nothing needs to change. It's like something before we got together, a chunk of my past. I'd lost it, and I've lived without it, but now he's there I can't pretend he is not.'

Ben said, 'Let's leave it for a bit. Talk about other things.' –

That is how they have always dealt with it. Talk of other things.

She looks out over the sea, travelling in her mind south to the tip of Ireland, and beyond that to the open ocean, other continents. She remembers another sea, at another turning point in life, when she had gone travelling to get away from Rahul. She had retreated to a beach resort in Thailand that her father had once taken the family to. She slept in a thatched hut on stilts and was woken before dawn by the long slow repetitive crash of the waves, to take a solitary walk along the beach in the half-dark that, in looking back, acquired the quality of a rite of passage, a silent saying goodbye to any possibility of a life with Rahul. She feels still the air on her skin, damp, warm, salty, the sensation of bare feet on the stilted walkway and then as she jumped down off it, of the soft sand between her toes. The sea was just a dark space ahead with an occasional light bobbing but she sensed it getting nearer as the sand got firmer and wetter with each step. A dog emerged from the half-light and trotted past her, nose down, not stopping to look. She watched it go, trip, trip, heading straight for something unseen, a line of small footprints marking the wet sand and then disappearing as the water seeped back up. The huts of the resort were sleeping, dwarfed by palm trees. A rim of light touched the distant curve of the ocean horizon, pink now, getting lighter every second.

By the time it was fully light the magic had slipped away. What was she was doing here? Everyone else had a purpose. The fishermen were busy with their nets. On the thatched verandah the waiters moved around setting the tables for breakfast. Even the other tourists had a plan, a sense of why they were there. She went back for paper and pen and found a place to sit, perched on a derelict upturned boat, half lost under banana fronds, to write to Rahul. But what to write? She wanted to have something significant to tell him, a purposeful future to announce. She sat for a long time staring out at the sea, seeing pictures of him in all moods. Listening. Indignant. Amused. Thoughtful. Invigorating. He so driven, she so drifting, what was there to say to him? The pictures blurred through the waves. She began describing for him the early morning beach.

She returns to the present. It is night, it is the moon's light not the sun's that tips the shallow waves that wash towards her and out again, towards her then out, the shushing of the waves washing up fragments of her past, then washing them back out again. In the quiet rhythm of the night beach she begins to feel for the first time since Rahul's death a trace of inner calm. Touching and letting go. Being reminded and then letting it slip away.

Nothing that has happened is finished. The present moment is just the centre of spinning time, with all our yesterdays and tomorrows circling around us. He is here still, keeping her company as she adjusts to life without him; giving her courage to find her own way. 'I want you to learn to fly, with your own wings,' he said.

~ 27 ~

Lance is out in the yard chopping wood when the call comes. Wood chopping is a good way to deal with restlessness. It's physical, sweaty. You lift the axe, a big swing of the arms heavenwards, a fractional pause up in the air, weight above your head, then wham, down it comes, and the log splits. The concentration on the physical task becomes a kind of meditation.

The phone rings. He ignores it. It won't be for him, and the others are all out. Whoever it is can call back later. But the ringing goes on and on; the person at the other end is clearly going to hold on till it is answered. He puts down the axe and goes inside.

It is Glen. 'How's the reading going?'

Lance has to laugh. 'You're not just phoning to chat, I presume.'

'I am not. It's Kyrgyzstan. Have you seen the news?'

'I told you, I'm taking a break. From the news too.'

'Things are getting out hand, right in the part of Kyrgyzstan where Rahul linked us up with people. A new lot of refugees has walked over the mountains from Tajikistan, people are scared they'll take their land, they're demonstrating, the government's panicking. I've got the media people on my back for press releases and only now am I discovering the scale of what Rahul took on there. If things blow up, our workers and the people they're supporting could be in trouble. And I still haven't filled that post.'

'Glen –'

'Six months, Lance, that's all I need. No commitment after that. But we need you now. Send me a fax number and I'll get the briefing papers to you so you can think about it.'

Glen enjoys the adrenalin rush, Lance is telling himself. The places change, the characters, the scenario, but Glen's sense of imperative has been a leitmotif through the years.

Glen tries a new tack. 'What are you into these days?'

'Chopping wood. Looking at the ocean.'

'The town we work out of is called Resham-serai. It's on the old Silk Road to China, surrounded by incredible mountains, they tell me. You can't get more metaphysical than that.'

'And a load of people wanting to kill each other.'

'That too. But you know what these things are like. One per

cent of the time it'll be crisis stations, the rest you'll be waiting about for the next thing to happen. There'll be time enough to stare up at the mountains and think about the meaning of life.'

Silence.

'Just do one thing for me, Lance; go and buy a newspaper. You can't just disappear and pretend the world's not there.'

Lance drives to town and buys all the papers. Yes, there it is: Kyrgyzstan, ethnic tension turning into riots in the streets. Rumours that the government, still Russian dominated, is planning to invite Russian troops in to help patrol the sensitive border areas above Sukhunobod.

Sukhunobod. Where has he heard the name? Now it is coming back to him. It is the place he heard Rahul talk about, a valley high in the mountains, he said, with a lake of clear water, no one knew how deep. Lance feels the aura of it, feels Rahul suddenly near again, hears him describing the boulders with strange markings on them. *I exist*, says the herder, the priest, the soldier.

He finds a copy-shop in town that receives faxes and he phones Glen. Send me the stuff, but no promises. Then he drives till he reaches the coast and walks along a stretch of sand, still shining from the outgoing tide. At his feet is a line of sand-dollars, scores of disc-shaped shell-creatures washed up by the waves. He picks one up, marvelling again at the simple beauty of the star-shaped pattern pricked out in the perfect circle of the shell. It lies in the palm of his hand, light as air but its grainy texture marking its specific existence. He holds it as if it were an oracle. So exquisite a creation.

He looks out over the Pacific, feeling his life shrink to insignificance. We're all simply passing creatures, living as if we have all eternity ahead of us, till the ocean washes us up.

Cora is outraged. She has never liked Glen, whom she regards as responsible for having drawn Lance into his restless life. 'That man expects you to just drop things and go to the other end of the earth? And a war threatening! You promised yourself time off. You didn't have to say yes.'

'I know. But I realize now, it was too hasty. I've felt responsible for things that happen in Lifeline for twenty years. If I'm going to stop altogether, I can't just cut and run. I have to take leaving a bit more steadily.'

'This doesn't sound steady. This sounds like back in the maelstrom.'

'I have to do this, Cora. It's stuff Rahul left unfinished.'

But here he is leaving behind his own unfinished things. His promise to Hamza that he will make decisions about what to do with Rahul's papers – that is going to have to wait. His mother – he has made large statements to himself about being near her so he can take his share of the load. Now he is off again, leaving it all to Cora. 'It's only for six months,' he tells his mother, 'I'll be back for your birthday.' But in six days it will seem to her like for ever.

Euan, his eighteen-year-old nephew, wanders in to watch him pack. He picks up the Central Asia guidebook Lance

194

has bought and flicks through the photographs. 'Awesome mountains,' he says. Then, 'I might go travelling in the summer. A couple of my friends have been to India but I want to do something different. Could I visit you?'

Oh God, why is it a war zone he is going to? 'Euan, I'd love you to come one day, wherever I am, but not Kyrgyzstan, not just now.' The boy looks crestfallen. Lance says, 'You stick to India.'

Euan wanders off and Lance is left feeling confused. What am I doing, discouraging him? He's only a few years younger than I was when I went off to Ethiopia, and a life that the adults around me found incomprehensible.

It is after midnight; he is packed. He decides to take a quick look through Rahul's papers again and see if there is anything about the work in Kyrgyzstan. But when he opens up the boxes, unanswered questions start milling about his mind. Why did Rahul keep taking papers to Delhi? Why not leave them in his office in Dushanbe, or the Lifeline office in Tashkent, until there was a reason to clear his desk? Who did he not want to read them? What was he getting himself into?

A box labelled 'Miscellaneous'. He is about to skip it when something strikes him as odd. Miscellaneous is not a category Rahul would have used, his mind was too organized. Lance opens it, to find not the usual neatly marked files but a series of large envelopes, each stuffed with papers but unlabelled. The alert button switches on. The label is a distractor to keep off any curious eyes, and it almost worked on him. He opens the first envelope. No typed reports these, all of it is in Rahul's handwriting. Notes made after meetings, short references to remind him of things discussed, none of it making sense unless you'd been there. Every now and then a comment in Urdu, mostly scurrilous. *Badmash* – a scoundrel, not to be trusted; even the occasional *maderchod* – mother-fucker. Lance grins, remembering the first time he heard Rahul say it, about someone with power who used it aggressively.

And then – no more in English. All the other notes are in Urdu. Damn, it is going to take him for ever to read his way through this. It is years since he has had any reason to speak Urdu, and his reading was never that fluent, especially in handwriting; and Rahul's handwriting, neat in English, was in Urdu an often indecipherable scrawl. Then something more significant begins to register. Why did Rahul change languages? His language for work was always English. Urdu he used for letters to his father and short bursts of creative writing, but this was work stuff. The only reason for switching must have been that he wanted to make sure that people around him couldn't read it.

Lance gets out the green bag Cora has left in his room in case he needs it and starts shoving the envelopes into it. They are coming with him.

Part 2

We who are free grieve only for a moment
And use the lightning's flash to light our homes

GHALIB

Only for a moment

The child is in front of Nargis Suleimanova, a girl child, bedraggled from living on the streets. A child of about nine, ten – no, older, she must be older, look at her eyes. It could be Layla looking at her, but putting such distance between them. Right here, yet unreachable, her eyes giving no sign of feeling other than a now-habitual calculation, What can I get out of this person?

When the question comes it is like an echo, something she has heard before the child says it. 'Have you got any money?'

Her 'No' is instinctive self-protection, knowing she needs to save what she has for food for the household. But her brain is tearing at her, saying, 'Allah forgive me, this is my own child.' Then the child's eyes shift and she begins to wonder whether it really is Layla, and feels overcome that she cannot be sure. The face is so changed, but how would it not be changed, the life she is leading? Not just the eyes but the face hollowed out with permanent hunger, the skin calloused and dirty. She can't even be sure now whether the child is a girl, but deep hormonal knowledge tells her this child is *hers*. The love aches in her gut and leaves her mind fuzzy, barely coping with the pain of knowing she is doing it all wrong. Desperate to put it right, she reaches into her purse and starts saying, 'Here, take this.'

It is too late. The child has gone, soundless alley-cat disappearance. The sense of loss is overpowering. Why hadn't she said, 'Come home, there's food in the house and a warm place to sleep, and so much love, always there for you.' Why?

She turns to run down the street, desperate to find the child and hold on to her. Suddenly there at the end of the road is Khaled. He is climbing into a waiting car, the car is coming right past her. She has to stop him, get him to help her find Layla. If she jumps into the road in front of the car the driver is bound to see her and pull up. It gets nearer. The driver swerves to avoid her and drives on. She sees the back of Khaled's head as the car passes, and he never once looks at her.

She turns, to see Rahul standing there, quietly observing it all.

He says, 'I can see it's difficult for you. Perhaps I should stay away.' And then he too is gone —

She wakes, sweating, whimpering uncontrollably. And with waking reality comes the anger she cannot free herself from. Khaled should be here, helping to keep their child safe in a world in which nothing that they grew up taking for granted can any longer be relied on.

As the anger retreats an undercurrent of misery tugs back fiercely. About Khaled, the old Khaled, who is lost to them all. About Rahul. Wishing they had never met.

She waits until that too has all washed over her. Then, slowly, as if her joints ache, she moves to get out of bed and face the day, to pack her feelings away so they will not show in her face, will not alarm Layla, who is sleeping in the small bed in the same room, will not distress her mother-in-law as together they get food ready in the kitchen. Will not get in the way of her work once she gets to the office.

Another day, but this one different. She has heard from Brighton that the new director is about to arrive. She has to be sure that all the records are in order, all the accounts, that there will be nothing that he can find fault with.

~ 29 ~

The landscape tilts beneath the plane as it circles Dublin and then heads out over the sea. Tessa is still trying to detach. She has no illusions about why she has been shortlisted for this job. It is Rahul's reference that has made them pick out her application from scores of others, probably far better equipped than she. But from here on it is up to her alone, and it seems a mountain to climb. Seamus has been giving her things to read, heavy-going, demanding a kind of abstract concentration she hasn't exercised for years. She has been taking in jargon as if it were a new language, but fighting against it. An obstinate instinct has made her test everything. Would it make sense among the women in Laos? In the refugee camp in Thailand? In the backstreets of Sheffield?

It is only now that she is alone that she realizes just how tired she is, a tiredness that comes from deep inside. Those outside might see only the Tessa who is getting things in perspective again, the practical woman who is looking ahead, making plans. But privately she nurses the bereft lover, refusing to tell her it is time enough.

From the airport she takes a train to Brighton, travelling through countryside that Rahul saw each time he was here, crossing a viaduct that looks down over valleys, green fields, clumps of woodland. She watches it slip by in the winter sun. She wants the job now, too much. Her restlessness has found a focus but in its place is anxiety that she might not make it.

She checks in at the bed-and-breakfast that Lifeline has booked. Heavy furnishing and notices everywhere. Guests are kindly requested NOT to smoke / NOT to put anything down the toilet / NOT to open the windows more than two inches. She deposits her case, is tempted to leave a note saying 'I will NOT require breakfast', smiles as she shares the moment with Rahul, and is out.

She pauses outside the door like a cat on a threshold. Take this slowly, it might be your new life. The road slopes down towards the sea then becomes suddenly steeper till it is right there below her, inviting her with the smell of salt and of fish and the cry of wheeling seagulls. The wind is gustier with each step, till down at the front it is billowing everything in sight. The pier looms, its tall legs marching out in a sea washed pale green, flecked with white. She walks to the end of it, then turns to watch the light catching the sheen on the banks of shingle as the waves roll off them.

The children's voices come back to her, watching as she packed to come away. 'Is there a beach there?' Sam asked.

'Yes,' she said, 'but made of little round stones, all piled up.'

Sam considered. 'Dad will like that,' he decided. 'How long are you going to be away?'

'Four nights.'

Alisa said, 'Why?'

It's a long way, Tessa said, it'll take me a day to get there and to get back and I need a couple of days to do some reading in their office before the interview . . . But that wasn't the kind of answer the child needed. It was just *Why?* the great big generalized *Why* of being two years old and needing to make sense of all the arbitrary things that happen around you. Why are you going away? Why can't we all come? Why won't you be here at breakfast and bedtime?

The Lifeline building is a surprise. Odd that in all the years of hearing about Rahul coming here she formed no mental picture of it. It is a pair of three-storey houses, quietly elegant, with high sash windows and green shutters, that looks as if it might once have been a seaside hotel for respectable ladies. A set of stone steps with black railings leads up to the entrance, several feet above pavement level. She asks for the Resources Centre. It is at basement level so she looks out at the feet of people walking by on the pavement. She is intrigued, so many different kinds of feet. The woman who is showing her round says, 'We've been waiting a long time for this post to be created. Good luck to you.' There are boxes and boxes of reports. It could have felt intimidating but instead she feels a buzz of energy, as if she is being allowed into something that might open up worlds she can still hardly imagine.

OK, she says to Rahul, you were right.

A couple of hours later she takes a break from reading reports and goes out to find a phone, to call home. 'How's it going?' she asks.

'Messy,' Ben says. 'They're making seaweed stew. And you?'

'OK, but there's an overwhelming amount of information to take in. Everyone looks so competent. Heads in their computers, phones going.' She dries up. Maybe it is hard for him to hear, she about to have an interview, not him.

Noises off. Ben says, 'Alisa's got something to tell you.'

'Mama I've got a plaster. I hurt my finger.'

She listens and comforts her, but distance makes her helpless. Sam comes on the line, wants to know about the pebble beach. Then Ben again. Tessa asks, 'What happened to Alisa's finger?'

'Got caught trying to close a tin that wouldn't, then did.'

It all feels so close, far more real and important than reports in an office.

They talk a few minutes more, then Ben says, 'Sorry Tessa, the kids are climbing over me, I've got to go.'

Phone down. They are gone and she is alone. Suddenly it hits her – something so obvious she feels a fool that it is only now that the reality of it is sinking in. If by some miracle she gets this job she will have to travel, constantly. It will keep being like this, she miles away from them, only it will be thousands of miles not hundreds, and probably no phone that works.

She walks back. The sun is out and it's turned into a crisp, beautiful winter's day. As she gets to the entrance steps an unusually tall man arrives from the other direction with an airline travel bag. With old-fashioned courtesy he opens the door for her to go in. 'Beautiful day,' he says. She replies, noticing the hand on the door as he opens it. Large, competent; the person who first used the words 'in safe hands' must have been thinking of hands like these. In the foyer he is greeted by a woman coming down the stairs who says, laughing, 'I thought it wouldn't be long before we saw you again. Have you heard about ... ?' Office chat, people they both know. Tessa isn't listening to the words, she is watching the way his head bends forward as he listens, from being so much taller. It triggers the faintest of memories. Has she seen this man somewhere before?

But he is on his way upstairs now, and the wisp of memory, if it is that, has disappeared. She goes down to the resources centre.

On the third floor Glen briefs Lance on the issues he is going to have to deal with in Kyrgyzstan. Then he has to be off to another meeting. He leaves him with the numbers of people to phone for other briefings. 'Use my desk,' he says.

'Thanks,' Lance says drily. There isn't an inch of clear space on it.

Glen grins. 'Well use my chair and my phone anyway.' Then, 'Thanks, pal. I know you didn't want this but it's great you're doing it.'

An hour later Lance is done, says his goodbyes, and sets off.

Down in the resources room Tessa takes off the shelf a report on street children in Nepal. She looks to see who has written it. Two names, a Nepali one, and Lance Bergsen.

The tall man – of course! Switch to high gear, report back in the box, box back on the shelf, grab her bag, run upstairs to the receptionist, breathless already. 'Where can I find Lance Bergsen? He came in this morning.'

'He's just left. Literally, minutes ago. He'll be on his way to the station.'

A sound penetrates Lance's mind as he walks. Someone calling him? He looks round, sees a young woman tearing along the pavement towards him. She skids to a stop just short of knocking him over. He waits, puzzled.

'Sorry to chase after you,' she pants. 'But I – You wrote to me.'

'I wrote to you?'

'About the letters. I'm Tessa Maguire.'

He puts his travel bag down without being aware that he is doing so and takes her hands in his. Tessa of the bulky files has come hurtling into his life.

A coffee shop now, steamy from the breath of many conversations. They are staring at each other, still not quite able to take this in. A slow smile starts in her eyes. It carries a trace of shyness but also a definite hint of someone who responds warmly to life. Now that he has a real person in front of him he feels none of the hurt that stabbed him when he saw the letters, only the strength of what links them. But he still knows almost nothing about her. It's bizarre.

Across the table she is studying him, thinking, Rahul never told me he looked like someone who has just climbed Everest, facing into the wind. Funny about faces, sometimes they tell you nothing about the person inside, sometimes they speak to you, straight. His face says, thoughtful, unassuming, reliable.

'You know we've met?' she says.

'We have?'

She nods, the smile spreading. 'At a sitar concert in Delhi, 1980.'

'You're sure it was me?'

'No question.'

'This is terrible. I have no memory of it.'

'There was a whole group of you going. I was in Delhi unexpectedly so Rahul added me in at the last minute.'

'How mortifying that I don't remember.'

She laughs, a sound like her smile made manifest. 'I probably hardly said a word. Everyone else seemed to have a lot to say.'

'That's even more mortifying. We all talked to each other and ignored you?'

'I was happy being anywhere Rahul was.' She pauses, then

207

says cautiously, 'I should tell you, I wasn't just a friend. I loved him.'

The simplicity of the statement blows him away. Equally carefully he says, 'I thought it might be like that when I saw how many letters there were.' She looks startled, invaded. 'I assure you,' he says quickly, 'I didn't read them. But I had to find an address.'

'Of course.' Her invaded look is turning to caution.

'You were in Laos.'

'I left, just before Rahul –' She blocks the word. 'Died. I have to get used to saying it.' Then, a different smile this time, slightly wan, 'I've not had much practice. You're the first person I've been able to talk to who really knew him.'

He registers what that means. She doesn't know his friends. He says, half a question, 'Rahul kept you very private?'

Pause. Then, 'He didn't even tell you?'

He is grateful for the 'even'. He says, 'Not even me.'

She seems caught, not knowing how to proceed. After a moment she asks, 'Did you mind, when you saw?'

'I have to admit, it was a shock. So many years and not to say anything –' He reins himself in. 'I'm sorry, this is all so personal.'

'No, it's OK, it's just – Privacy is an odd thing, isn't it? We guarded it while he was alive. Now he's gone, I can't bear it being all stuck inside.' She pauses, then says impulsively, 'You shouldn't be hurt. It just happened that way. We had this extraordinary thing going between us but after I left India we weren't ever part of each other's daily lives again. Maybe he just found it easier to get on with his life without people knowing and asking.'

Tessa is waiting as Lance reacts, trying still to make sense of it. She sees it is going to be impossible not to say more. Very quietly she says, 'There's something else I think you'd better know. I'm married.'

'You're married.' He repeats it to buy time. His face speaks his incomprehension.

She has known since the moment he said 'Rahul kept you very private' that she will have to tell him or forgo the comfort of real connection that she so urgently needs. It comes out in short sentences like she's speaking a language she is still learning. Ben and I have been married eleven years. We have two children. We have our tensions but we have a committed life together. That's what the world sees, and it's true. But there's another bit the world doesn't see and wouldn't understand. Rahul and I lost touch for a long time but I didn't stop loving him or he me. Then we met again. So what to do?

He cannot find anything to say.

She says, 'So we didn't talk about it to other people.'

'Yes,' he says slowly, 'I can see that.' He is thinking, I can't see how you can have a situation like that without it being a disaster for everyone concerned.

She is waiting for him to say something more. The look in her eyes makes him walk around it, carefully. 'I'm not sure I under-stand exactly what there was between you. Before. And after.'

Before was easy. 'We had been lovers for five years before I met Ben.'

She stops, for she sees that for the moment this is enough for him to take in. He is, in fact, calculating. In 1980 she was in India. Add five years, 1985, the year the letters came to a sudden end. He sees Rahul's face at that meeting in Brighton, shutting him out. It is all so obvious now.

And the other question: After?

But she sidesteps. 'You were friends a long time.'

'We were.'

'And do you have a partner?'

He is disoriented by the change of topic. 'Not at the moment,' he says, and registers, regretfully, that he is being less honest than she is, for it has been a very long moment. Years.

She presses on. 'If you had met someone you wanted to share your life with, would that have altered the closeness between you and Rahul?'

It takes him a moment to work out that of course she isn't talking about him at all, but about herself. He says 'But –' then stops himself.

'But what?'

He was going to say, But it's different. We weren't lovers.

She does it for him. 'When Rahul and I –' she searches for the word – 'went our separate ways, nothing had been sorted between us, it had all just been packed away. When we met again years later, it was pure accident but it seemed like it had been bound to happen. And if you have loved someone a long time, if it's part of you, you can't just turn it off because it doesn't fit into your new life. It's there. So the only question is, what do you do about that?'

'And what did you do?'

'We said yes to it.' Her voice has become defensive. 'And I would have regretted it for the rest of my life if we had not.'

Silence. It is she who breaks it. 'I don't even know how to say this, but it wasn't like having an affair, he wasn't just a lover. I can't begin to separate who I am from who I became through being close to him. And his death hasn't changed that. I feel him there for me still. When I can be calm and sensible about things, it's because of his voice.'

He cannot speak. She has defined the thing he has never had, that he longs for.

She says, very quietly, as if afraid to be overheard, 'I talk to him still, all the time.' But now she looks alarmed that she has gone so far. 'Do you think I'm mad?'

He feels suddenly protective, thinking how young she seems, and troubled. 'No, not mad. Unusual. Brave.'

'Brave?'

'Telling me things that you're obviously scared to tell. I feel honoured. And I would say, in your situation, talking to him sounds an extremely sane thing to do.' He is hearing Greta's voice again: *You have to keep talking about him, Lance, keep him near.* He wishes he could hand this vulnerable young woman into Greta's care.

Quietly he says, 'It must have been complicated, living with all that.'

She looks at him curiously. 'Yes. For all of us, in different ways. But in a way it was also simple. I had chosen to live with Ben. I didn't feel anything less for him after Rahul reappeared.

Maybe more, because he was so generous. And I never had a choice about loving Rahul. So –'

'And Rahul?'

She thinks for a moment before saying, 'He was better than me at handling it. He was so – steady, and that helped. Like, this is who we are, this is what has happened to us, we just have to find the best way to handle it now. Things he said, they keep running in my mind. At the time I was too caught up to be able to hear properly. I'm only now beginning to realize, he understood things about how to live that few people do.' She searches her pockets for a tissue, blows her nose. 'I bet my nose is really red.'

'It's red, and it's fine.'

She laughs and impulsively stretches out a hand to take his. 'Thank you.'

'For what?'

'For being here.'

People come in, people leave, and still they are sitting there talking. The trust grows, and she becomes less cautious. They swoop over the years, matching things they have known, listening to things that fill in gaps, describing the road each is taking, opened up by having lost Rahul.

Lance says, 'And just think, if I had stayed in Canada and tried to live a normal life, we'd never have met.'

He tells her what he knows about Rahul's last days. Volunteering. The landmine that probably wasn't there. Hugo's search. Somewhat to his surprise she doesn't seem disturbed by it. She just lifts her shoulders and says, 'If it hadn't been this, it would soon have been something else. He was moving through dangerous places. That was the life he chose.'

Time is pushing. Neither of them wants this to end but he needs to get back to London and Greta. Tessa walks with him to the station and onto the platform. He stands just inside the carriage door looking down at her. 'Make sure you get the job. We need you.'

'I'll do my best.'

She is smiling again and he is thinking, They'll be fools if they don't appoint her.

The whistle is blowing. Too suddenly the train is pulling him away. Its departing wind blows her hair across her face as she stands there waving. Goodbye. Take care.

~ 30 ~

Greta seems unusually tired. Lance has planned to take her out for a meal but she says she would rather stay in. It is quite out of character but he makes no comment. She hates to be fussed over. He gets a takeaway instead, but as they talk he is watching her, assessing.

'Tell me about Kyrgyzstan,' she says.

'I know very little. Seems like, whatever else Rahul was doing, he didn't train the people he took on to keep Brighton informed. All I can tell is, it's going to be complicated.'

'I met a poet from Kyrgyzstan once, soon after the war. Look.'

She hands him a faded black-and-white photograph. A young Greta, fresh-faced in a cotton summer dress, an equally young Hamza in his Nehru jacket, and a dark-haired man some years older, in a suit. Greta's eyes look at him candidly. So young, yet so much character in her face already. He still has Tessa's face in his mind and he thinks, she's the age Greta was here. He has an odd feeling of an affinity between them. Maybe it's seeing Greta here with Hamza, thinking of Tessa with Rahul.

He turns the photo over. On the back she has written, Rahman Mirzajanov, Tajik poet from the Kirghiz Soviet Socialist Republic. Prague, 1947. He laughs, shaking his head. 'You're amazing, Greta. Wherever I go, there's some part of your life that connects with it. Tell me about this.'

'It was an international convention, just after the war and before the Cold War set in and made such things impossible. People talking into the night, singing songs in different languages. This poet, he recited in a deep voice that made you feel you were standing in the middle of the steppes. We talked a long time afterwards.'

Talked? But of course, Greta knows Russian.

'He wrote out a verse for us, from one of the old Persian poets.' She hands Lance a scrap of paper, bent edges, with two lines in Persian script and a translation:

Do not distress your fellow men and do what else you will
For in my Holy Law there is no other sin but this

Lance looks up. 'Unusual, surely, for a Soviet poet?'

'I think he was trying to tell us about things that no one could talk about.'

So much that no one could talk of: Stalin's purges, the resistance to forced collectivization, living with pervasive fear. And fifty years on, Soviet power has collapsed but they face another kind of crisis – the economy falling apart.

He says, 'I feel less prepared for this posting than any I can remember.'

'Don't be absurd. How can you expect to know what you have to do until you get there?'

One day he is going to come back and Greta won't be here any more to tell him he is absurd. The thought is intolerable.

'I'd like very much to know what happened to him,' Greta is saying. 'So would Hamza, I'm sure. You try and find out for me.'

'I'll do that.' He makes a note of the name. When he looks up she is watching him with an expression he can't work out. 'What are you brewing?' he asks.

'Just thinking that perhaps it's time I told you something. About Hamza and me, in Prague. That's where we first met.'

'I think he told me that.'

'The bit he won't have told you is, we were lovers.'

A stunned inner silence.

His first coherent thought is, This is a day for revelations. Then he forgets other things, just focusing on Greta. So utterly unexpected, yet it slots into place, a missing bit of a puzzle, the origin of their loyal connection over all these years.

Then comes a surge of anxiety – what about Sushila?

Greta is filling the space, her calm voice telling him what he might not be able to imagine. 'Just before that convention I was in Vienna looking for people I had lost in the war. I found none of them. At moments like that, you take love where you find it. And Hamza was lonely. He was teaching that year in Prague but Sushila had gone back to India. She found it too difficult, with a baby and no domestic help. He talked about her a great deal, his commitment to her was obvious. There was never a question of our doing anything to damage that.' She waits for him to react. He is still not ready to. She says, 'It was a present-tense-only thing. It gave us great joy, and no harm came to anyone.'

'Sushila never knew?'

'Why would she? It was worlds away.' Then, 'Are you shocked?'

'Shocked? No.'

The question doesn't arise. Greta has always been different from other people, he has never expected her to follow anyone else's path. Her goodness is an article of faith with him and nothing has ever happened to disturb it. But still this jolts, a different story from the one he has lived with for a long time.

'Why have you told me now?'

She shrugs. 'Privacy matters so much less as you get older. I'd have told you years ago but I couldn't while Rahul was alive. I didn't want to burden you with something you would have had to keep from him.'

The mention of Rahul makes him suddenly conscious again of Greta's own frailty. 'I wish I wasn't going so far away. You need to take care of yourself, Greta. Maybe it's time to drop a committee or two?'

'There's absolutely no need. Selma says my heart's good for another couple of decades.'

'Selma? Your doctor?'

She looks irritated with herself. 'You're too sharp, my boy, I should never have used her name.'

'Now you have, you have to tell me.'

She waves her hand dismissively. 'It's really nothing. Just that I had a funny turn a few weeks ago – felt a bit faint. Selma insisted on doing a whole raft of checks. It was a great nuisance, I had to cancel a lot of important things.'

'And the result?'

'I have the health of someone twenty years younger. Except for this damned arthritis.'

'I'm glad to hear it. But promise you'll let me know instantly if you have any more funny turns. I don't want any phone calls saying, Come quickly or you'll be too late.'

'Oh Lance, don't fuss. Anyway, there are lots of other people who nag me.' Her hand sweeps the room, the photographs on the bookshelves, on the bureau, on the mantelpiece.

'The more the better, but make sure they know how to reach me if they need to.'

'I promise,' she says, and he has to laugh at her unaccustomed meekness.

'And *you* take care,' she says. 'If Rahul was a target, anyone who comes sniffing around asking pointed questions could become one too.'

'I'll promise to be at least as careful as you've always been.'

Her turn to laugh.

Turbulence has overtaken Tessa. She is walking, hardly knowing where. There is no way she can go back into the office and read reports, and nor can she go and shut herself in that claustrophobic bed and breakfast room.

You're married –

She hears Lance's voice again, sees the incomprehension in his face. How did she let herself talk to him as she did? After so many years of saying nothing to anyone, why *now* has she let her defences down? But she was so beguiled by the glimmer of comfort he offered – to be able to be open for once, with someone who knew Rahul, who cared about him.

Without conscious decision she is heading towards the seafront. It'll be dark soon, the days are still so short. The windows of the hotels looking out to sea are lit and warm-looking. She chooses one at random, orders a coffee and positions herself in an armchair near a window. She will sit here and look out into the dark where lights from cars trickle by, soundlessly. She and her notebook.

But her pen will not move. She cannot write her confusions.

Her mind drifts back to the days after Kathmandu, the first letter from Rahul in five years –

I shall write to you even without cause
Simply to write your name fills me with love

Words flying again between them, chasing each other in the urge to catch up on lost time. They had done this before, it came so easily to do it again. They could be there for each other, they both thought, intimately connected once more, and it need affect nothing about her life with Ben.

She understood, better perhaps than Ben himself did, that the appeal of earth science for him was the security that comes from dealing with objective reality. Tectonic plates might clash, volcanoes might erupt and spew up molten lava, but these were phenomena you could analyse and understand. Facts, that was what worked for Ben. He needed to know where he was and then he could deal with it. To the extent that she knew, she had told him; but that extent was limited. She knew only that Rahul was back.

But nothing stays the same when you have let desire out of the cage where you had confined it.

Two months after Kathmandu, she and Ben had moved back to Liverpool for him to start work on his PhD. Rahul's life too was changing. In Afghanistan the conflict was escalating, and hundreds of thousands of people were displaced. He had left UNICEF and was about to start working for UNHCR, to help organize basic services in the makeshift camps. But they were sending him first to their head office in Geneva for induction, he wrote; then he would be taking some days leave and spending it in London.

That was all he said. He left it to her.

Liverpool, London, a simple train ride away. What chance was there that she could know he was there and not try to see him? But she knew what seeing him would involve. Kathmandu had been unplanned, not her decision. This time she would be deciding.

'You're going to have to choose.'

She heard the voices of her mother, of Maeve, the aunts; of common sense. But was it sense? She was important to both of them, as each of them was to her. To choose only one would cause unnecessary damage. Two things can exist at once, it was a practical reality. Ben had understood that from the start. She hoped he would understand it still.

She felt – to her own alarm, but she could not pretend she did not feel it – that what was about to happen was in some sense inevitable. Her history had caught up with them, and Ben had taken her on, knowing there was a chance it might. What went on between her and Rahul wasn't anything to do with him, Ben had said, when he had been pressing her to make a joint life. It was for her to work out.

She tried to harden herself against anxiety. Perhaps it is impossible to get through life without in some degree damaging those you love.

She told Ben. He did not try to dissuade her. He fixed up a

field trip for the week she would be away. She was impressed by his wisdom. He was smart enough to know that to have made an issue of it would not have resulted in Rahul becoming less important to her, and would almost certainly have resulted in damage to what they, she and Ben, had. If he had forced her to choose, she might have left him; if she had stayed, she might forever have resented him for what she had had to give up.

And so it went, each time. She switched lives on the train journeys as a woman who has been out at work all day switches to being a mother when she gets home. The first day back she and Ben were a little careful around each other, then they slotted back in together. She followed his lead, never talking about her times away. 'Tessa's in London,' he would say if anyone asked, leaving them to assume that it was something to do with her work.

But underneath all that – what was going on for him? He was gaining nothing, and whatever she said, he was threatened perhaps with losing something. By the world's standards jealousy was inevitable; but if he felt it, he did not express it. The most she could perceive was a kind of protective distance at certain moments. Perhaps in the times she was away he went back to how it had been before he knew her, a man so powerfully concentrated on his work that he gave little thought to relationships. Ben had an ability to block out difficult things, something he had learnt very young. She had spent little time in the household he had grown up in, but enough to see that if he hadn't protected himself from getting drawn into his parents' emotional tensions, he'd have gone crazy. His father had arrived in New Zealand as a stowaway on a boat from Eastern Europe at the end of the war, a Jewish boy who had survived traumas he could not talk about. He had dark intense eyes – Ben's eyes – and a piercing mind that fascinated Tessa as much as it intimidated her; and he could not get through a day without fuelling his tension with alcohol. Ben's mother was recessive and suffered. His father either ignored her or was unbearably cutting, and it was hard to decide which was worse. Small wonder that Ben had wanted to get away. Mountains were his escape but each one climbed opened out a further horizon, and Tessa knew that when she suddenly appeared in his life, she represented a world he was determined to reach, one in which people were simply kind to each other.

Ben wanted what he had wanted from the beginning, a shared life with her. He took what he could get of it. Who knows what else was going? He managed. They managed –

Until Rahul's death blew the whole thing open. For what must he have been feeling, watching her disintegrate, first in terror when Rahul was in danger, then in blind misery at his death, and now in this deep pain that she cannot shift? If ever in the past, in all those times she took herself off to London and he kept himself busy to block out thought, if ever he was able to persuade himself that what she had with Rahul was less than central to her being, he knows now that he was mistaken. For six years she managed – perhaps – to keep the depth of the love out of his direct view. She has not been able to do so with her grief.

222

~ 31 ~

Lance's flight is delayed. A minor technical fault, they say, the engineers are working on it, but hours pass and there they sit, grounded on the runway. It is like being stuck on a deserted road with a four-wheel drive that has broken down. Eventually they are herded for what is left of the night into an airport hotel; to start again next morning in a different plane.

'Check your baggage,' the airline staff call. It is all dumped in a pile on the tarmac. A scramble of people form round the pile. As each bag is identified it is pulled out by a waiting uniformed official. Scarcely a rigorous check, Lance thinks, and then goes cold. His own luggage is there but where is the bag with Rahul's papers? He starts creating a monumental fuss. 'I can't go without it,' he says. 'If necessary you are going to have to unload the whole lot again for me to check.' The uniformed officials are instantly suspicious. 'It's just papers,' he says. 'Zero commercial value but invaluable to me. Irreplaceable. My research papers,' snatching at professional respectability. And it is half-true. Rahul's biographer.

'What about this one?' A green-overalled man holds out Cora's old bag. Lance could have kissed him. He follows the other passengers up the metal stairway, into the plane. The adrenalin is draining slowly away, leaving him feeling foolish.

Tashkent airport. A dark anonymous world out there, lights around the airport building. Lance stumbles out, crumpled, groggy. He has missed his onward flight. It is the early hours of Saturday morning and there will be no one in the Lifeline office now till Monday. He has three words of Russian and none of Uzbek, and not the first clue how to get himself to where he is supposed to be.

He becomes aware of a man staring at him. Heavily built, dark-jowled, age possibly late fifties. The man comes towards him and says something incomprehensible. Lance shakes his head apologetically. The man speaks again, pointing to his own chest. He repeats a name several times: Ulughbek. Lance repeats, to test it. The man nods vigorously, lifts Lance's cases and moves towards the exit. Miraculous, the driver has been told to wait for him. Lance follows him out into the night. A plain car, no Lifeline International logo. A moment of hesitation: he has not told this Ulughbek his name, has not asked to see identification. But how can he check out the credentials of a man who has waited until two in the morning to meet him?

He climbs into the passenger seat. They drive off. Ulughbek starts speaking. The only word Lance catches is 'Russki?'

'Nyet,' Lance says; and then, pointlessly, 'English?'

'Nyet,' Ulughbek shakes his head. They both laugh.

They are driving through silent streets. The city feels eerie, deserted. Lance hopes he is being taken somewhere to sleep, but the streets continue to slip by till they are out the other side of town, a straight road heading through the night. So –

no flight till next week, so he is being driven there. How many kilometres? He has no idea.

Ulughbek makes another attempt at conversation. 'Rahul Khan?'

Lance nods vigorously. 'My friend.' He rustles in his hand-baggage to find the Russian phrasebook and looks up the word. 'Drook.'

Ulughbek nods back, pointing to himself, 'Drook, drook.'

They are both smiling broadly now. Lance studies him with renewed interest. It is Ulughbek who would have driven Rahul on long journeys like this. There are a thousand things he could have learnt from this man, and he has no words to ask any of them.

How did Rahul manage to speak to him on those journeys? Lance searches the phrase book again. 'Gavarit li Rahul pa Russki?' which he hopes means 'Did Rahul speak Russian?'

Ulughbek's smile widens. He lifts a hand off the steering wheel and gestures 'half'. Then he prods his own chest and does a me-to-him gesture. So Ulughbek was teaching him. Lance nods his appreciation, says 'Good', remembers that Ulughbek won't understand. The effort to say any more has become too much. He closes his eyes, and drifts off.

When he wakes a rim of colour lights the still-distant mountains. The land around seems empty of habitation, just grey-brown grassland and a few rocky outcrops. The mountains that edged the horizon have drawn closer, otherwise no change. The car slows down. Ahead is a long pole across the road, and to one side of it a concrete blockhouse. A soldier emerges, rifle pointed. Lance gives Ulughbek his passport. Ulughbek climbs out, his bulk towering over the slightly built youth. The soldier turns over the papers Ulughbek has handed him. Lance watches tensely. Now they are moving to the back of the car, Ulughbek is opening the boot for inspection. Lance's tension zips up another notch. He doesn't want anyone opening that bag of papers, they might think its contents politically suspect. And for all he knows, they may be.

The boot closes. Ulughbek gets back in. 'Tajikistan,' he announces.

Christ, Lance thinks, did we have to come through a war zone? Then he remembers the map, the long protruding bit of Kyrgyzstan that they are heading for is surrounded on three sides by Tajikistan. Maybe this is the only way.

The outskirts of a town loom ahead. 'Khujand,' Ulughbek says, but he turns the car off the main road before they get there, to pull up at a low airport building. So now he is going to have to trust himself to Tajikistan's planes.

The airport lounge is decidedly dispiriting. Rows of heavy armchairs stare emptily at each other down a corridor-shaped room. The large windows are overhung with heavy curtains even though it is now fully day outside. In the corner of the room a television flickers. Over at the bar is a group of heavily built men in suits, who look to Lance like members of some mafia group.

He walks over to the curtains and opens them a crack. He waits for a reaction. Nothing. He opens them a little further and peers through the crack to discover one very small plane on the tarmac and a few workers in overalls standing looking at it, without much conviction. Oh God, another case for the engineers. He goes back to his seat.

A loudspeaker shatters the gloom. Announcements in two languages, neither of them of any use to him. He looks over to Ulughbek for help, but he has fallen asleep.

About noon the airport lounge begins to fill up. A man in a perfectly pressed suit arrives with only a briefcase for luggage. He speaks to one of the men at the bar, in Russian, Lance thinks, and fluent. But his smile is a trifle too ingratiating; this is an outsider who wants to establish his credentials. When he turns, his eyes meet Lance's, hold them for a moment, then look down at the bag at his feet. Lance's hand has gone down to it instinctively, and the man with the unwrinkled suit noticed. Were they perhaps on the same flight into Tashkent? Maybe the man witnessed his panic on the tarmac and is curious about the bag? But he can't have been on the same flight, he has no missed-night look about him.

It's all nonsense, Lance tells himself firmly. But he can't shed the sense of something sinister lurking.

To distract himself he gets out the tourist guidebook and dips into the potted history. Every known group of people and many he has never heard of seemed to have conquered or populated Central Asia at one time or another. Buddhist monks walked the length of it carrying sacred scriptures. Marco Polo passed through on his way to China. The sweep of millennia makes the seventy years of Soviet rule seem hardly the flick of an eyelid.

A couple of young people stroll in, everything about their appearance announcing them as Westerners. They each have a large rucksack with assorted bedrolls and water-bottles attached. The girl is slim with coloured strands braided into her long blonde hair, frayed jeans sitting low on her hips, midriff exposed, and a series of top garments layered over each other, each a different colour. Her male companion is as dull-looking as she is colourful; the reverse of birds, Lance thinks, viewing them as he might a rare species. The male has an untidy stubble over his square jawline, and baggy khaki trousers with pockets all down the legs. Lance has a hard job not staring at the girl. She is beautiful, with even features, long hair swinging free, and eyes a colour he can hardly describe. Hazel-green is the nearest he can get, but it isn't the colour that is so striking, it's the life in them. Like she is at any moment about to comment on what she sees.

Baggy Trousers brings him back with a jolt. He points to the guidebook in Lance's hands. 'You speak English?'

Lance admits that he does. 'Not that that's going to help you. I have not the first idea what's going on in this place.'

The girl appears to find this mildly entertaining. She looks at him, unnerving him. I'm being assessed, he thinks. Only for a moment, then her eyes move on. He has been examined by a young woman who cannot have been long out of her teens, and found uninteresting.

Baggy Trousers sits down next to him and nobbles him in a slow mid-American voice. 'You going to Resham-serai? We are too. Annabel studied Persian. How about that, huh? She

228

says they've got a statue to one of their poets in the square in Resham-serai. Amazing, huh?'

Do they not know, these innocents, that the place might be on the verge of civil war? Lance's attention moves back involuntarily to the girl. She relaxes into a chair like a cat, her eyes travelling lightly over the decaying airport lounge, taking in the notices peeling off the walls, the stuffing coming out of the mock-leather upholstery of the chairs. She pauses to take in each of the men at the bar, just for a moment, the way she assessed him, then moves on. They are an unappetizing lot, he has to agree, but nevertheless he resents the easy wisdom of those eyes. They make him feel like one of the armchairs, part of an era whose time has passed.

Her survey completed, Annabel joins in the chat. Her voice is light, easy on the ears after her companion's, but the words are like her eyes, merciless with youth. He is torn between amusement at the accuracy of her observations and irritation that she should be so extraordinarily unaware of how she herself must appear to anyone else in this airport lounge, in her bizarre colours and fraying jeans, a young Westerner journeying through other people's lives, casually assuming her right to be wherever the mood of the moment takes her. Never an idea that what she does might have consequences for others.

My God, he thinks, I'm getting middle-aged. Correction: I am middle-aged.

The loudspeaker starts blaring. Suddenly it is all happening. Ulughbek wakes. The mafia men get off their stools and pick up bags. The man in the pressed suit is managing to look suave by simply standing in a queue. Ulughbek is at Lance's side, Lance's documents in one hand and in the other a scrap of paper with something written on it in Russian. He does a me-to-you gesture and gives it to Lance. He is touched; Ulughbek too has felt the frustration of not being able to talk. Lance smiles his thanks, puts the note in his pocket, pats it to show he values it, and puts out his hand to shake Ulughbek's. Ulughbek ignores the hand and puts his arms around Lance in a bear-hug, patting his back, saying, 'Drook, drook.' The girl and her companion hump on their rucksacks. 'See you on the other side,' she says. It sounds ominous, like a euphemism for dying. A woman in a severe black skirt waits to check tickets and papers. She stares at Lance's, hands them ungraciously back and motions him through. He turns to wave his thanks to Ulughbek, who looks solid and fatherly, and Lance feels confused by all the things he wants to say to him and has no words for.

The plane is perilously small. The noise as they take off is deafening. The whole plane shakes, loose fittings rattling violently. The folding table has come off its hinges; he tries not to think about what this says about maintenance standards for the engine. They seem to be going up almost vertically, battering through air-pockets, then suddenly the clouds clear, to breathtaking views down to gaunt rock faces and uninhabited snow-filled valleys. He turns to look for the backpackers behind him, now his only known people. Why did he react like a middle-aged bore? Maybe he is envious, for his own lost, freewheeling youth. Then the plane begins to lurch, wiping out all possibility of thought. He grips the arms of the seat and closes his eyes.

They land without his being aware that it has happened; the buffeting continued to the last minute. People are getting up, gathering their bags, but he cannot move, he is waiting for his stomach to stop lurching. He is the last to leave, climbing shakily down the steps, to find the two young people waiting for him. He is irrationally pleased. By the time they have wound slowly through the official queues Lance is tearing a page from a notebook, scribbling on it the address of the Lifeline office in Resham-serai and handing it to them. 'I don't know what kind of a place I'll be living in but if you're stuck for somewhere to stay, there might be some floor space.'

Annabel smiles, eyes warm and easy now. 'Thanks!'

Good, he thinks, I've passed. And then thinks, You old fool, and moves forward to face whatever it is he is coming to.

~ 32 ~

It is over, Tessa thinks, her brief flare of excitement. She has met Lance, and he is gone. She has had the interview, and that will be the last she hears from them. She has returned to marking time in a borrowed house in Ireland. But her mind will not move forward; it has got stuck in the Lifeline office in Brighton, in the room where her interview happened. A large table with a row of chairs, behind which three men in suits shuffled papers. How ridiculous, she thought, no one in these offices wears suits, so why are they wearing them just to meet me? Then she became aware that there was someone else with them, an elderly woman so small and birdlike that initially she had been hidden behind the large men. Everything about her contrasted with them. She wore a long soft skirt and a blue silk blouse and had a face full of wrinkles that seemed to smile, with eyes that said she was thoroughly looking forward to hearing what each of the candidates had to say. She was busy subverting the formal arrangement of chairs by getting one of the men to shift hers out from behind the table to one side of it. By this simple manoeuvre she transformed the stern row facing Tessa into an almost friendly semi-circle. 'Good, that's a little more comfortable,' she said, with a slight trace of an accent that Tessa couldn't place, and settled back into her chair. Tessa was so beguiled that she forgot to be nervous.

The man in charge introduced himself. 'Lionel Walden, CEO.' He liked the sound of it, Tessa could tell. He explained the procedure they would follow and Tessa, listening politely, could hear the management textbooks speaking through him. She thought, this is not the person I would choose to lead an organization like this. Now he was introducing the other panel members. One was a heavy-shouldered man who looked as if time pressed. 'Mr Rogers,' said the CEO, 'Director of Programmes.' Mr Rogers gave a brief nod, no smile. Gives away nothing for free, she thought. The CEO turned to the woman. 'Mrs Fielding, one of our founding Trustees. She has been a moving spirit in the decision to create this post and we are most grateful that she has agreed to help us with the selection.'

Mrs Fielding smiled. The room became more comfortable still, and Tessa felt an unexpected self-assurance settle inside her. For weeks she had been preparing for this moment, doubting whether she could do it. Now she felt the calm that comes over you as you walk onto a stage. Lights. Curtain.

The questions began. Back they went through Tessa's adult life. The CEO and the human resources officer listened politely but she had no idea what they were thinking. The Director of Programmes tipped back on his chair, assessing in a way that was decidedly unnerving. To steady herself she focused on Mrs Fielding's listening eyes, which made her feel that what she was saying was absorbingly interesting. It was perhaps not good strategy to half-ignore the men, but it was Mrs Fielding she wanted to talk to.

The interview seemed to be coming to an end when Mrs Fielding said, 'I have one more question.'

The CEO looked taken aback. They had been proceeding in an ordered manner through a list of prepared questions, and he had been nodding to each member of the panel in turn, indicating it was now their chance to say their piece. Mrs Fielding had spoken out of turn.

'Please go ahead,' he said, formally.

'Tessa,' she began; not Ms Maguire as the CEO had been so scrupulously calling her. 'You seem to be adept at finding ways to work within different cultural settings. Can you tell us how you learnt that?'

Now this was a real question. How do you learn things like that? She had learnt it in Laos by watching mothers with their children, but where did the instinct come from to want to learn from them? 'Perhaps from the kind of childhood I had?' she said, thinking aloud. A new culture every couple of years, taking it for granted that people were different from each other. But even as she described it she realized it was more complicated than that. 'Them' and 'us' wasn't primarily about cultural difference, the unbridgeable divide of life-chances was between the children of whatever race or religion who went to schools like hers, in uniforms, with school bags, and those for whom school was an unreachable dream. The children who sold things at roadsides, who carried heavy loads, girls who could be no more than five years old in charge of babies. Yet ever since she could remember she had felt some unspoken connection between herself and them waiting to be switched on, almost as if she *were* them, or could be, in another life.

'I suppose,' she said, 'growing up the way I did left me wanting to live in a way that didn't cut me off from others.'

'Thank you,' said Mrs Fielding –

And Tessa came back to where she was. She had been rambling on, far too personally, and the men were looking embarrassed. But Mrs Fielding's eyes had been intently on her as she listened, and she knew that this woman had recognized her for who she really was.

For the moment that seemed more important than whether she got the job.

When the phone rings Ben is outside and Tessa in the kitchen washing up. She has the tap running so she doesn't hear it. Sam answers, but it isn't one of Maeve's boys so he loses interest, lets the phone dangle on its cord and forgets to tell Tessa that someone wants to speak to her. So the woman from the Lifeline office is left bleating into unresponsive space while Sam goes back to roaring around with his aeroplane.

Alisa comes into the kitchen. 'Phone swinging,' she says.

'Swinging?' Tessa hardly focuses. Alisa likes experimenting with words and they are often unexpected. But this time she is definite. 'Swinging and talking.'

Oh my God ... 'Hello? Hello? Are you there?'

The woman from the Lifeline office has held on. Who knows how long it has been, but she has held on. Tessa's heart is thumping overtime – 'I'm so sorry, I didn't realize, I think my son must have answered' – so she can scarcely take in what the woman has phoned to say. She is saying, 'How soon can you start?'

Back to Brighton, to be given a pack of information for new staff, and to look for a place to rent. Furnished, cheap, immediately available. She sees basement flats with no daylight, cramped terraced houses where the gloom hangs like damp wallpaper, and a yard just big enough to hold the refuse bin. Not possible. Ben needs space, light, air, or his spirit will go further down the

235

plughole. She consults her map and estate agents' lists again, takes a suburban train that climbs up past more rows of houses zigzagging up the hill, till finally the world is green again. She gets out at a station of a small town that huddles under a cliff of chalk. A taxi to a village – 'Can you drop me somewhere where I can walk up those hills?'

'We call them downs,' the taxi driver says, 'and there's a path just there, by the church.'

In fifteen minutes she is up on the top, with the sky arching above her and views stretching miles.

The house to rent is part of a new development, already looking tatty, but she hardly notices. It is the place itself which speaks of a chance to heal. The village is set back about a mile from the main road and hidden from it by a rise in the land. A twenty-minute cycle ride from the station, she reckons. There is a school, a post-office shop, a pub, a Saxon church with moss on the gravestones, and a village green. In every direction there is a lift of the downs, their geological history showing through in the chalk on the bare hilltops, in the flint turned up in ploughed fields. Ben can survive here.

She phones him from Connor's that night, wanting him to be as excited as she is. But why would he be? For her this is a future she is positively choosing. What does her new job mean for Ben? Relief from financial anxiety, but along with that an irrational male guilt, that it is not him making that happen. His turn merely to pack and follow, and unlike her, he has had no early training for the role.

Connor is watching as she puts down the phone. 'You're tired,' he says, and he makes her sit down and hands her a glass of wine. It spreads through her. She *is* tired. It is almost three months since they flew in from Laos. The first month was a blur of misery, and since then it has been just coping. Now they are going into a future of changing roles, another thing for Ben to cope with – and for her to cope with the emotional tension of him coping.

She says to Connor, 'I don't know how it's going to be for Ben, stuck at home each day.'

'Tessa, my girl,' he says firmly, 'you've mourned your lover, you've found a job, you've found a house, you're going to earn the money, just you do what you have to do and let him get on with his part.'

Another flight, another life. Goodbye to the house on the windy coast. This place, that she so needed to get away from, it too has become security of a kind, and now they are leaving it, to start again. A last hug with Maeve, and Tessa feels suddenly tearful, bereft all over again. 'I can't tell you what you've been for me.'

From the airport they take a train to Brighton, another train on a branch line, and a taxi from the station to the village, that nestles in a fold of the chalk downs. They pull up at the house, hump their cases inside. The children start sniffing around like creatures in a new nest.

'Dreadful furniture,' Ben says. She has to agree. Cheap-modern and graceless, a sense of clutter like a second-hand shop. Ben knocks on one of the interior walls. A hollow sound. 'Cardboard,' he says. 'What these builders get away with.' Tessa doesn't want to know about the builders. Ben hasn't seen the grotty places she turned down.

Sam and Alisa are exclaiming excitedly. On every available surface in the living room is a collection of kitsch china ornaments, mostly dogs. Ben turns to Tessa. 'We've got to pack those away.'

'Oh Dad, please can't we keep them?'

'No we can't. You kids might break them.'

'We won't, we won't.'

Distract, to sidestep confrontation. 'Come and look at the bedrooms,' she says. 'Let's sort out who's going to be where.'

The children bag their beds and spread out their small collection of things. Then Ben supervises them packing away the knick-knacks and surplus crockery, to stack in the basement. He relents and lets them each choose one china dog to stay on the mantelpiece. 'OK,' he says, 'now let's find out what goes on outside.'

Instantly the sense of clutter and claustrophobia vanishes. A lane from the end of their garden leads up to the downs, with views of wave-like green and a tentative spring light to welcome them. Ben is explaining to the children how the chalk they are kicking up is magic stuff, formed from millions of shells of sea creatures, longer ago than anyone can imagine.

We can do this, Tessa thinks. The earth we stand on will do

it for us. We can learn the Englishness of this place the way we absorbed the Lao-ness of life in Vientiane.

~ 33 ~

Resham-serai's only hotel is gloomy and after a week there Lance is glad to escape. The apartment that the Lifeline administrator has found him is up three flights of dank stairs in a leaky concrete building. It is small, not to say cramped: a living room with a dining table and a sofa, a bedroom that just fits around a double bed, a kitchen the size of a cupboard, a bathroom you can scarcely turn around in, but compared to the hotel it feels like heaven. The previous resident was a Russian who fled in a panic after the demonstrations and left a lot of stuff behind, so Lance is surrounded by a ghost-life, pictures on the walls, a stack of old records of classical music. The disappeared resident was probably a high-up official – there is a phone. The first call he makes is to Greta. She doesn't encourage international calls; they spell Emergency. But she likes to get one call when he arrives in a new place, so she can picture him there, she says. For Lance it's so that she has the number, in case.

As he arranges his small collection of personal possessions, he is thinking about the perfectly groomed man on the flight from Khujand, who looked rather too pointedly at him when his hand went protectively to the bag of Rahul's papers. The same man was checking in at the hotel when he arrived, and next morning he was there again in the almost empty dining room. Lance took a seat at the opposite end of the room but the man had seen him and came over to his table. In an upper-class English voice he said, 'We were on the same flight, I think. May I?'

'Of course.' No escape possible.

'Duncan Eversley.' They shook hands. A firm handshake, too firm. 'What brings you here?'

Lance was having difficulty summoning civility. 'I work for an NGO. What about you?'

'Oh, I've been in and out for nine years, since things started loosening up. Russian studies was my field, but I've always been more interested in the Asian dimension, the parts other Russian specialists ignored.'

'So you're an academic?'

He smiled. 'I'm an observer, you could say. I follow events and write reports.'

'Reports for ... ?'

'Right now for the IMF.'

'This is a remote spot for the IMF to concern itself with, surely?'

'It's a question of the regional administrations. Difficult negotiations happening with central government. You know the kind of thing.'

Lance didn't; but if this man followed events he could be useful. 'What's your assessment of the security situation?'

'Difficult to tell. Very closed society, this. You don't hear anything until it blows up in your face. It was like that in Osh at the time the Soviet Union was breaking up. Kyrgyz and Uzbeks live alongside each other for generations, then suddenly they start burning each other's homes, chopping each other with butchers' knives. Incomprehensible.'

Lance's suspicion of the man was confirmed; too calm about observing other people's troubles.

'Did you mention the name of your NGO?'

No, he hadn't, and he felt an irrational resistance to telling him. But if the man didn't already know he could find out soon enough. He told him.

'Ah, yes. I heard about your colleague. Very tragic. I met him once.'

'You met him?'

'On one of his visits here. Information gathering, as I understand.' And that was all he would say about it.

A driver had arrived to fetch him from the hotel, a man about his own age with very little English. With him was a woman – in her early thirties, he guessed – her manner too formal for ease, her dress featureless and middle-aged. 'Nargis Suleimanova,' she introduced herself, 'Programme Manager, heading the Lifeline International office here in Resham-serai.'

Was it his imagination, or was that a touch defensive? Small wonder if she isn't overjoyed by his arrival. Where before she had Rahul flying in, getting things going and then leaving her to get on with it, she suddenly has a resident manager.

In the car she said, 'They told me you knew Rahul Khan?'

'He was my close friend.'

'We all mourn him. He was an inspiration, in all our work.'

They drove past the square with its statue of the poet, along a street of apartment blocks, then turned into a yard and came to a halt outside what looked like an old house. Nargis brought him into a large room with desks around the sides and a communal area in the middle where five other people waited to greet him. Three dark-haired young men, who at first meeting seemed indistinguishable – their functions, an administrator, a finance officer, a second driver – and two women who gave the impression of inhabiting completely different worlds. The oldest, in her fifties, was exactly Lance's image of a collective farm worker, sturdily built, in traditional-style long dress in florid colours and a headscarf to match. The younger looked to be in her early twenties, slim and in jeans. She would have looked at home in any office in a Western city.

These seven strangers were to be his daily companions for the next six months, his entrée into understanding what was going on in this place.

'What about the language?' he had asked Glen in his too-brief briefing. 'You won't need it,' Glen had said. 'All the staff speak English.' Maybe, but on first meeting they seemed struck dumb with not knowing who or what he would turn out to be. He tried to inject some relaxation into the situation, practising their names and encouraging them to laugh at his efforts. He asked Nargis about hers. Did it mean narcissus?

Exclamations: 'You know Tajik?'

'I wish I did,' he said. 'Only Urdu, but a lot of the words come from Persian.' But that seemed enough to have produced a general thaw.

It was time he made his intentions clear. 'You have heard, I think, that Rahul Khan was my friend. His loss is a tragedy for all of us, but we have to move past it. I am here to learn what you and he were hoping to achieve, and to see if there are ways I can support you to carry it on.'

It seemed to go down well.

Now in his apartment, Lance moves to the window, looks out over the town, and considers his work situation. What a bizarre thing it is to drop out of a plane into a country he knows almost nothing about, and from day one have to manage a group of people who have lived here all their lives. Each day he and Nargis spend hours together, but he is going carefully; they speak about nothing but work. She briefs him and he listens, taking in more new information than the brain can digest. He asks questions, about everything. Nargis patiently answers – he must seem *so* ignorant to her. He begins to notice that she has an attractive face; it was somehow hidden behind her initial tension. As she takes him around the town to see places where they support projects the sounds of Farsi/Tajik pass over him, tantalizingly evocative of Urdu poetry but making no sense. The first sentence he learns to recognize is 'Does he speak Tajik?' Then he hears the words 'Rahul Khan, *he* spoke Tajik,' and he gets a tolerant, slightly pitying smile. He is an inadequate substitute, in more ways than one.

They have driven out of town to see a project that Lifeline supports in a settlement on collectivized land, with buildings made of industrial materials, and on the way they passed Kyrgyz herders living much as their ancestors had done in portable

243

yurts, following the seasons as they move their flocks of sheep between the plains and the mountain pastures. The townspeople are predominantly Tajik but Russians still dominate official positions, and there are exiled groups, Crimean Tartars or Koreans, deported en masse to Central Asia in Stalin's time. The Lifeline staff itself reflects this ethnic mix, and jokingly for Lance's benefit they exchange historical stereotypes; but it is all good-humoured, and each day as he sees them working together the differences seem irrelevant. They are now all products of the same Soviet education system, working for the same international organization, lucky to have jobs when so much else around them is collapsing. The real political divide cuts across ethnic groups – it is between those, like all the Lifeline staff, who want democratic reforms, and those who cling to what they know, old-style communist officialdom.

What has happened to the crisis that so recently was headline news in the world's press? People are definitely nervous about the war spilling over and there are rather too many men in uniform around, but there have been no new incidents since he arrived. 'Seems like a false alarm,' he told Glen on the phone.

He moves back to the table, and opens up the bag with Rahul's papers – notes written in Central Asia, taken to Delhi, flown to Vancouver, and then making a huge circle in the air to be brought back to where they started, and still unread. He is daunted at the prospect of getting his brain back into reading Urdu; but within a few minutes he stops, puzzled. He can make out a place name at the top of each entry but almost no other words.

Damn, it isn't Urdu after all; it must be Farsi. Same script, different language. Which he can't read.

And nor, now he thinks about it, would anyone else around here be able to. Farsi is their language but for seventy years no one here has been allowed to use the 'old writing'.

He phones Hugo. 'Why would he keep his personal notes in Farsi? I know he spoke it well, but surely it must have been more of an effort than either English or Urdu?'

'No idea,' Hugo says, 'but send them to me. I've got a colleague here who'll be able to read them.'

'There are a lot of them,' Lance says, 'and I can make out that he started each new entry with a place heading. Maybe I'll just send you the ones from Tajikistan.'

So he begins to sort them. There's a growing pile headed Tashkent, another pile headed Resham-serai – and none from Tajikistan.

He phones again. Hugo is more than puzzled. 'You're sure?'

'Positive.'

This is getting more and more bizarre. It is simply not conceivable that with Rahul's intense involvement in what was going on in Tajikistan he made no personal notes. So where are they? He must have lodged them somewhere else for safe keeping. But Delhi is where he took these papers, presumably for safe keeping. Why would he have done something different with others?

The papers go back into the green bag, under his bed.

~ 34 ~

The notice on the door says 'Glen Rogers, Director of Programmes' – the man from Tessa's interview who tipped back his chair, assessing her. His door is open but he is standing at the window with his back to her, talking on the phone. His voice drums down the line: 'I need a report, in writing. Just telling me isn't enough.' All that punch in his voice, he probably hasn't the least idea of the effect he must have on others less robust. He turns, sees her, waves to her to come in. 'Thursday's too late,' he barks. 'The meeting is Friday, they're going to need a couple of days to read it first. OK, well make sure she does.'

Phone down. 'So, you've arrived.'

It is an odd greeting and she can't think of a reply, but he isn't waiting for one. 'You've caught us at a bad time, it looks like things are blowing up in southern Sudan again.' He talks for a few minutes about what is happening. Not to her, at her; she could be anyone. Then suddenly he interrupts himself to say, 'Come, let me introduce you to your fellow advisors.' The tone says, and let's be quick about it so I can get back to work.

She follows him back into the open-plan section. At each desk they have to wait for its occupant to get off the phone. No, John's in Addis. Did you see the report from Islamabad? Are you going to be in New York next week? Distance buzzes through the place names, giving their lightest words an air of importance, and she feels more of an innocent each minute. Then, phone down, introductions. This is Melvin, the Co-operatives and Livelihoods Advisor. Derek, the Refugees and Marginalized Groups Advisor, Jan, the Capacity Development Advisor. Hi Tessa, nice you're joining us, let's meet and talk properly sometime. Sorry I can't now, got a call coming from Delhi / a report to finish by this afternoon / a meeting in half an hour. They move on. Behind them the phone conversations get going again. The ICRC conference. The UNDP consultation. The NGO PRA Network. Each new acronym eats away at her fast-diminishing store of confidence.

They arrive at the far end of the open-plan area. Glen opens what looks like a cupboard door. 'Your office,' he says. It is shaped like a cell, thin, narrow, and as bare. A desk, a chair, a window too high to see out of unless you stand on tiptoe and peer. Is she to be stuck here, shut away from the others? At the far end is a strange metal-and-glass structure with a maze of wires visible through the glass. 'The computer network hub,' Glen says blandly. As if on cue, the robotic structure gives off a low buzz. Glen frowns. 'I hope that doesn't happen often, it could drive you nuts. I told them there was no space for another office on this floor but we have a Facilities Manager who is deaf to reason. At least you have the luxury of a door you can close.'

I don't want a door, she wants to say, I want people.

Glen is heading out again, into a small kitchen leading off the open-plan area. He puts the kettle on. 'I have to be frank with you,' he says as they wait for it to boil, 'I wasn't in favour

247

of this post being created. We don't have enough work with young children to justify it.'

She stares. She remembers the expression on his face at her interview. Now she understands, he was there under duress.

'The Trustees' logic,' he is saying, 'is that you don't stimulate a new area of work until you appoint a specialist. But it's not the right time, everyone's far too busy. You take milk?'

She accepts the mug.

'You'll find there's a lot of management nonsense talked in these offices but it isn't the way I work. I'm not going to have time to manage you. You've got the job description, anything you want to know, ask one of the other advisors. You're used to using email, of course?'

'Actually I'm not.'

That stops him. 'You're not?'

What to say? I've never worked in an office, I was running training sessions with pre-school teachers who've never seen a computer, I don't even know if they have email in Laos.

But he has recovered from the shock before she has to say anything. 'Someone will show you,' he says. 'Our IT department is way behind the curve. Here we are, 1997, and they only just managed to put our bigger country offices onto email last year. The smaller ones still aren't. Incredibly frustrating, an international organization and we're still sending each other faxes.'

He is walking her back to her room now. 'Sorry about this, but I have to get back to the guy in Sudan.'

And she is left to her mug of coffee and her box-cupboard of an office.

She stands looking at her new room-mate, the metal-glass-wire contraption in the corner. 'OK,' she says, 'so that's the way it is, I'm on my own. But I'm going to make this job work, whether he helps me or not.'

And so begins her new life.

Indignation has an energizing effect. She arrives for her second day at work with a small backpack of personal possessions. To reduce the cell-like feel of the long blank wall she hangs on it a length of woven cloth from Laos. Under the high window she pastes photos of the children, Sam running on the wintry beach near Dublin, Alisa on Ben's shoulders, laughing. On the wall above her desk she creates a collage of postcards, splashes of colour and cultural richness, the temples of Kathmandu, the cave paintings of Ajanta, a golden Buddha in Thailand, surrounding herself with the voices of people she loves, the places that affirm why she wanted to be here.

She stands back, surveys her work and feels several degrees better.

A man appears at her door. 'Hi, I'm Peter, Facilities Manager.'

Ah, the man Glen said was deaf to reason.

'Technically,' Peter says, 'you shouldn't be here. I told them it was never meant to be an office, the regulations say you can't share with our computer Charlie there in the corner. Your esteemed Director of Programmes had a month to shift things around, and he never got to it. Or maybe never wanted to.'

That figures, Tessa thinks. Peter might be an ally.

'Well, it's not my issue, I just follow instructions.' And he

249

gets busy with a screwdriver, fixing a sign on her door. Tessa Maguire, Early Years Advisor.

'There you are,' he says cheerfully. 'You now officially exist. Contrary to regulations.'

A few minutes later a young man appears; dreadlocks, torn jeans, trainers with giant laces. 'Post.' He hands her a pile of papers.

'Already? I've only just got here.'

'We've been keeping them for you. Internal memos, circulars to all staff. Most of your lot don't read them, your Director of Programmes doesn't think much of the CEO and his systems so they don't bother. I'm Chuck, by the way, post room. Your director's into IT, but my advice, don't try and send long documents by email, they'll just crash the computers in the country offices. Print out copies and use DHL. Goes three times a week. Anything urgent, fax it.'

'So would you be able to give me a list of staff? Here and in the countries?'

'We only do C.P.Ds.'

'C.P.Ds?'

'Country Programme Directors. But you could ask one of the D.Os.'

'D.Os?'

'You've got a bit to learn, haven't you? D.O. is a Desk Officer, contact person for three to four countries. Got it?'

'Got it, thanks. And is Chuck after Chuck Berry?'

'Well, so you do know something after all!'

She goes to find a Desk Officer. 'A list of staff?' He reacts as if she is asking for diamonds. 'It's like keeping track of a family of jellyfish. Funding ends, jobs end. New funding about to start, they take on someone temporarily – HR knows, Glen almost certainly knows, but I'm the one who's supposed to keep the regional systems functioning and I have to be a detective to find out what's going on.'

For days she moves about introducing herself, and when anyone has time, tries to find out what they do. She comes away with piles of paperwork and reads her way steadily through it, sinking under the weight of detail. But they have only tangential references to children and take her no nearer working out where she might slot in.

She tries Glen again. Whatever he said, he must have some concept of what she should be doing, and she needs to know it. He isn't in his office. The second time she tries he has someone with him. She mouths, 'I'll come back later.' The third time he is on the phone. This time a hunted look comes into his eyes at the sight of her once more hanging about his door. Finally she strikes lucky. 'Come in,' he says, 'sorry, it's been a crazy day,' and then launches into telling her all the things that have gone wrong, and the iniquities of the Finance Director. She listens, ready to pick up anything that might help make sense of this place. Just as she gets to her question the phone rings again and he waves her off.

Frustration wrestles with impending depression. She remembers Rahul talking about UNICEF, the organizational frustrations. You learn how to work the system, he said. OK, she can carry on gleaning bits of information from other people and try and piece it all together, but it makes no sense to have to go it alone. She needs to know what people in the country offices think a head office advisor is for. Glen knows, so why won't he tell?

She goes down to the post room to find Chuck. 'Can you show me how to send a fax?'

He gives her a lesson and watches in open curiosity what she is sending. It goes to the CPD, Kyrgyzstan:

> Hi Lance, I finally got here and I haven't an idea what I'm expected to be doing. Nor apparently does anyone else. Is this normal?

An hour later she gets one back:

> I'm in a similar state. Phone me if it gets too much.

Charlene, the administrator, appears at Tessa's door. 'You've got some interesting mail,' she says and gives her a pale mauve envelope, delicately scented. 'It's from Mrs Fielding, the trustee who was at your interview. She always uses that kind of paper, she must have boxes of it.' Curious, she waits while Tessa opens it. Inside is a card with a message in spindly, once-elegant handwriting:

Welcome, Tessa. I hope you are finding the new job very rewarding. Do let me know when you're next coming to London, I would be most pleased if you could join me for tea.

It is signed, *Greta Fielding*.

Her reason dismisses the possibility. But she stares at the signature on the card. She remembers the slight accent of the woman at her interview. She looks at the address. And reason is defeated. It is the home of Rahul's English Aunt.

She has been there, and she is the only person alive who knows it. It was the first time she and Rahul saw each other after their rediscovery in Kathmandu. I'll be coming to London, he said, and she was in Liverpool. It was years since they had needed to use Connor's flat and the only contact she had had with him in that time was Christmas cards. She phoned; an answer phone. She phoned again; the same. Perhaps he was on holiday?

She phoned Rahul. 'Don't worry,' he said, 'I'll fix up somewhere.' But somewhere turned out to be the home of his Aunt Greta.

'I couldn't possibly,' Tessa said.

'You're not going to have to meet her. She's going to be away, visiting friends. We will have the place to ourselves.'

She sees it still, how they walked from the underground station along a quiet street lined with plane trees, with last year's seed-baubles decorative against the bare branches and the winter sky. On either side were tall houses that must once have been the homes of wealthy families but were now divided, with entry phones to the flats inside. Rahul found a key under a flower pot. Inside, a lobby, three flights of stairs. Open the door to a small entrance hall, looking through to a living room. Everything in it spoke of a long life lived vividly, someone with decided tastes and wide affections. Comfortable armchairs in old-fashioned chintz, bookshelves spilling over with books constantly used, photos in standing frames on every surface. On a small writing desk lay open letters, in German as well as in English. Newspaper cuttings were piled on a side table.

For the first few moments Tessa felt she was intruding on this woman's life, or equally, that she was being observed by that absent presence. But Rahul's ease relaxed her; clearly, he was at home here. She stopped trying to imagine the woman whose home this was and simply accepted it as another gift from life.

This time there was no sense of amazement. They had been with each other again for months in spirit. But what luxury to have their own quiet space, away from observing eyes. What did they do, with five whole days to be together and no responsibilities to distract him? They took as long as they liked in bed. Breakfast didn't happen until it was almost lunchtime. A small expedition to the shops to stock up on bread and milk felt like a major outing. When the body-urgency calmed down they began to go out more, walking in their favourite places, Regent's Park, the South Bank, recovering them, cancelling the memories of false endings with present laughter. The days were short. When it got dark they drifted into whichever public building they happened to be near, to look up into stone arches or stand in front of paintings and discuss idly what they liked and didn't like and why, then out again to walk the lit streets and watch other people's lives go by. And then they would decide that was enough of the world for now and retreat back to Greta's place. Rahul taught her how to cook parathas. She entertained him by telling him about learning Thai and the mistakes you make if you can't distinguish tones. Rahul told her stories about Greta from the time he was a child and had lived in the big old house that was her home before her husband died, where bookshelves lined the walls, floor to ceiling; and how, when he had come back as a student to this so-much-smaller home, his first reaction was dismay at the loss of that wonderful library. Greta had said – and he echoed her trace of German accent – 'My dear boy, when you've lost someone close to you, you really can't be bothered about a few books.'

They listened, they laughed. They argued, they convinced the other or gave in. They visited the recent past and the near future – no need to go further, for they knew now there would be other times.

She woke to their last day feeling his warmth and solidity next to her. It seemed that they had lived all their times together in a succession of last days. He surfaced, saw it in her eyes, kissed away the sadness. They made love slowly, making it last. They showered, dressed, had coffee and toast. She began tidying up, erasing all trace of their joint presence, oppressed once again by the feeling that they had been living in someone else's borrowed space. Rahul saw her tension and said, 'Come and lie with me, one last time.'

They lay fully clothed; there was no time for more. 'I'm going to spend half my life waiting for the next time,' she said.

'No you won't,' he said. 'In a few days you'll get caught up in where you are again. And I will too. And so we must.' He took her face in both hands, holding her in his gaze. 'Rejoice, *meri jaan*, rejoice in what is possible, don't grieve for what we can't have.'

He sat up and pulled her up with him. His voice was firm and practical again. 'And if you definitely don't want to meet Greta, we need to go' …

And now she is about to meet her after all. Has already met her, without knowing it was her.

She looks up to see Charlene watching her, waiting to hear what is in the card.

'She's inviting me to tea,' she says. 'Does she do this for all new staff?'

'Never that I've heard of. What makes you so lucky?'

There can be only one thing that makes her so lucky. Mrs Fielding – Greta – will have seen Rahul's reference. But how much does she know apart from that?

~ **35** ~

Sukhunobod. Lance keeps hearing about it, the place Rahul talked about with the boulders with strange markings on them. It's beautiful up there, people in the office say, you must go as soon as the snow melts. There are projects up there that we support, very interesting projects. Rahul loved it up there, they say.

The snow melts early, plans are made, permits queued for. Finally all the preparations are made.

Dark still when the Lifeline car hoots outside the apartment block. Lance makes his way down to where the car waits. Nargis is in the front seat with Sultan, the younger of the two drivers. 'So you're the lucky one,' Lance says, and Sultan grins.

They drive out of the silent town. By first light they are out in a timeless world of space and light and clean air, heading into the mountains. Sultan is Kyrgyz and takes a personal pride in bringing Lance up here. In impressionistic English he explains that his grandfather used to move his flocks up to these valleys for summer grazing, travelling on horseback. The sheep are a kind Lance has never encountered, with a character all their own, thin pointed faces, ears that flop forward, unruly black or grey wool, fat tails. Karakul sheep, Sultan says, the oldest breed in the world. They can survive where other sheep can't and their wool is the best for carpets, for felt. For everything.

The road has begun to climb now, clinging to the side of the mountain as they look down into a deep gorge. An army checkpoint ahead; Lance tenses involuntarily. Nargis produces their permits and exchanges a few words with the young soldiers. They drive on, round a few hairpin bends, and when they can no longer see the soldiers in the mirror the car slows to a halt. They climb out, legs stiff, into the crisp mountain air. Breakfast is coffee from a thermos and some unleavened bread with curds and Lance feels that nothing could have been more delicious. They look out in the early light over long views of the land below that seems empty of people. Nargis says something in Tajik to Sultan, and her voice has the intonation of someone reciting poetry.

She turns to Lance to translate: '*If there is paradise on earth, it is here, it is here, it is here.* People have used that about so many places, but for me, this is it. Do you know what Sukhunobod means? *Sukhun* is speech, or poetry. Perhaps it is the place where once a great poet lived.'

Back in the car they follow the road a few more bends upwards till the land begins to flatten out. They're high enough now that the cold is getting to them. They pass a lake with water of unbelievable clarity, a scattering of yurts with horses tethered near them, sheep grazing. People in the fields are preparing the earth for sowing, and there's a wooden cart drawn by a donkey. It seems an ancient landscape. If these were once collective farms they were singularly unmechanized. Did Soviet control even penetrate this far?

Nargis has been telling him about the people they will be meeting. The refugees are there still in small settlements around Sukhunobod, still being kept alive by UN food handouts, but now growing some of their own food using seeds and tools that Lifeline has provided. Lifeline has also helped them set up a health clinic. But life is difficult also for the townspeople, she says, and it's important that they see it isn't only the refugees who get support otherwise tensions will build up. So Lifeline has encouraged them to form a citizens' committee and set up self-help initiatives. Like the one they are going to see, in the school.

She is getting used to Lance, Nargis decides. The situation is not as bad as it might have been. The week before he came they were all tense but now he is here, and appearing not to need to throw his weight around, she has to admit it is good to have someone to discuss her work with. Further than that she won't go at this stage. She has learnt not to trust people too far.

He asked her on his first day to tell him the story of how Lifeline had got started here, and she surprised herself by talking about it quite openly. The first thing she had asked for was to take on Fahmeda. She told Rahul, 'She is older, people respect her, they will listen to her more than to me.' To begin with it was just the two of them and Akbor, the administrator. But once they got going, the range of the work grew rapidly, and Rahul backed them, and somehow got them extra budget to grow.

'He had a way of supporting without controlling,' she told Lance. 'For us here, that was something very unusual. And every time he came I learnt something.'

'Like what?'

She thought for a moment. 'That it's people, not money, that can shift things. That's how the street-children's centre started. We got people together to discuss the problem, and there were enough of them willing to do things if we created the framework. People can be hungry for ideas, Rahul used to say, like they're hungry for food.'

She and Fahmeda took on anything they could find that showed initiative in responding to the economic crisis. She sees now, from having to explain it to Lance, it was a scattergun approach, because that was how the problems were coming at them. Lance is looking to see if she has a concept of where it might all lead, and she has to admit that she hasn't thought that far. She told him, 'Half of what we learnt under the Soviet system has turned out to be irrelevant. We face problems now we never had before, and we have to learn how others deal with them.'

He asked if she had ever been outside the former Soviet Union. No, she said, and only a few times out of Kyrgyzstan. He stared, and said, 'Then it's a mystery to me how your English got to be so good.' She just smiled. There was a reason it had happened, but that was a long story and she wasn't going to talk about it.

She still has to keep explaining systems to him. For every initiative they have taken on she has had to negotiate permission from several levels, political and bureaucratic, and now Lance has to be presented to each of them. He said, 'Is it necessary? What am I going to say to them? You'd have to be there anyway to interpret and to stop me showing my ignorance.' She had to explain to him, It's political reality. You just have to learn to work through it.

He has talked about Rahul's death. She knew it must come, was waiting. When he finally raised it, there were several of them in the office so she didn't have to say anything, which she was glad about. When he asked about the landmine Fahmeda

said, 'No one here believes that. That's bandit territory. It's
the government side that lays mines.' Lance asked, 'So do you
have any ideas about what could have happened?' Fahmeda
just said, 'He went into a dangerous place. Those people don't
care who they kill.'

And after that he stopped asking. He could see no one
wanted to talk about it.

The buildings get closer together. Sukhunobod town spreads
out around them, sheltering under a spectacular backdrop of
the mountains.

A large group has gathered at the school, the women all
in traditional brightly coloured Tajik dress. There is no coal
to heat the buildings, they explain, as they all shiver in their
coats in the echoing classroom while people make speeches.
They know Nargis well so the ceremony, Lance realizes in
embarrassment, is entirely in his honour. Nargis has to translate
so it all takes a long time. He lets the Tajik words roll over
him, oddly moved, and he remembers Greta talking about the
poet reciting, the sound of his deep voice moving her though
she didn't understand what he said. Then he tunes back in to
Nargis's English words. Because the roads have been closed by
snow, they are saying, this is the first opportunity they have had
to pay public tribute to Rahul Khan. He gave them courage to
tackle their problems. He showed by example that to be great
you do not need to be puffed up. Lance stands there receiving it
all, feeling frozen and unexpectedly choked. Such rough-hewn
men and women, faces weathered by constant exposure to the

harsh elements. He can hardly imagine what it must be like to have to struggle on in a place like this through the winter.

Speeches over, they hand round small glasses of vodka. Lance dislikes drinking in the daytime but there is no way to refuse. Now the teachers take over to tell him about their project. The government has run out of money, they explain; it is a long time since teachers here have been paid. The teachers of the older children have left but it is the young ones they are most worried about. If they miss the basic years and don't learn to read and write, nothing will be possible later. They will go back to the times of illiteracy and all the gains of Soviet times will be lost. They are doing everything they can to keep the classes for younger children going. All the parents contribute food for the teachers so they can stay teaching. And they are looking also for other ways to support the school. At this point an old man is brought forward to show Lance a tin bath with sheep's wool soaking in some dark liquid. He is teaching the older children how to make felt, he says proudly. Before Soviet times everyone knew how but the youth began to scorn such skills as old fashioned. Now they see it can be useful. From the felt they make slippers and jackets to sell in the market in Resham-serai. Nargis has helped them make the contacts.

It is all so brave, so desperate, and surreal for them to be standing there, a group of adults talking as if the school is still functioning but there are no children in sight. Eventually he asks, 'Where are the children?'

'It is too cold for them in here,' they say. 'We can only use the building in summer.'

He is led out to a yurt that the community has constructed in a cleared yard next to the school, insulated with thick mats of their own homemade felt. They lift the mat that hangs over the door, and he bends his head to avoid banging it on the wooden frame as he steps in.

His eyes adjust to the lack of daylight. He is in a large circular space, heated by a stove in the centre, its chimney disappearing through a hole in the felt-covered roof. Down at ground level small dark-haired children sit on low wooden benches, big eyes staring at this giant of a stranger, their high-cheeked faces red from wind and stinging cold. They are buttoned up in felt jackets that perhaps are never taken off all winter. Solemnly they accept the boiled sweets that Nargis has had the foresight to bring with her. With intense concentration they unwrap the twists of paper, put the sweets carefully into their mouths and start sucking. Nargis offers him one. It seems obscene for him to take one, the children need them; but she insists. He lodges it in his cheek as he has watched the children do and learns for himself the therapeutic effect of undiluted sugar on a hypothermic body. The children watch, big-eyed.

He is undone, emotionally completely taken over.

On the journey back they hardly talk. Lance is still overwhelmed, feeling intensely protective of those small people who have to grow up at a time when the adult society around them is so ill-prepared to look after them. Nargis has withdrawn into herself. From his seat at the back he watches her unmoving head. In the last hour up in Sukhunobod she was standing a little away from the others talking earnestly with one of the young men, and it was clear that she was distressed by what he was telling her. She didn't offer to tell Lance, and he did not ask. For all their growing ease with each other there are still puzzling things about her, moments when a flash of reserve appears in her face, as it did at their first meeting.

From Fahmeda he has learnt that before the economy collapsed Nargis was a research chemist at the university. 'She won prizes,' Fahmeda said proudly, 'she even had an article published in an international journal.' So why did she change jobs? It is the answer he is hearing to many questions – the university stopped being able to fund research. They didn't sack researchers but they couldn't pay them. After all her expertise in science, the prizes, the published research, in the end it was only the fact that she knew English that could keep her family.

Her family. That, he is beginning to realize, is off-limits. If he gets near, her face sends a warning signal, and he has stumbled sometimes on difficult silences. Perhaps Fahmeda has sensed his puzzlement, for when they were out together visiting a project she said, unconnected to anything, 'You won't hear this from Nargis but she has a difficult life. Her husband.'

What about her husband? But that was all she was saying. Perhaps she thought it useful at least that he should know there was a husband.

~ 36 ~

Tessa walks up the road from the underground station. Late March now, and it was February when last she walked here with Rahul, six years ago. There are daffodils in the small front gardens but the plane trees are still bare, with blotchy trunks and brown seed-balls dangling. She notes it all with an odd kind of detachment.

She has allowed so much time for the journey that she has arrived three-quarters of an hour before she is expected. Enough cause for nervousness that she should be coming to meet a trustee, whose first question will be, 'How are things going?' From a new member of staff, how far can honesty extend? Just this morning she sat through her first team meeting, hoping that this would perhaps throw some light on what she is supposed to be doing. Glen arrived late and they never got to the agenda Charlene had prepared because he took up all the airspace himself. Tessa asked a question. Glen appeared to regard this as a challenge and went on to the defensive. No one else attempted to get into the discussion. Meeting over, they all went back to their desks, their own deadlines. She watches them when she walks through the open-plan area, heads down, fingers furious on the keyboard, phones going. Obliquely she is beginning to get glimpses of what her job might one day entail, but how even to get started? Her diary is still empty. She has nothing to report on. No one needs her for conferences.

265

But this woman is not just a trustee. She is Rahul's Aunt Greta.

She arrives opposite the tall house and looks up to the window on the third floor that once she looked out of. The door opens. She panics. Perhaps it is her coming out? But it is an elderly man. He pauses as he sees Tessa, stares for a moment. She starts walking rapidly away, turns a corner, then another. She stops, recognizing a tree she and Rahul once stood under together, sheltering from rain. Keep steady, his voice says. Nothing to panic about. Inner freedom comes from learning to let go, that's what the greatest Persian poets all said.

I am trying, *meri jaan*, I am trying to let go. But it is all suddenly so *close*. Seeing the place where once we were alone together. Remembering ... Things you said. The quiet depth of our conversations in writing. The way you came back to me each time, knowing it would always be there, and how the months of separation dissolved into nothing. Love-making that was fuelled by being rationed – there was never a chance for the dulling of senses, for routine was a luxury we never had. Days speeding by, filled with pleasure in small things shared, autumn sun glinting on the dew on the grass, the crunch of frost under our boots as we set out for a winter walk, the scent of spring in the hyacinths flowering in a pot on Connor's kitchen table, the long, light summer evenings.

Rejoice that we had what we had, he says. Don't grieve that we can never have it again.

We who are free grieve only for a moment
And use the lightning's flash to light our homes

She knows that is what he is saying to her, but it is more than she can manage.

The minutes have passed, it is time to return, to walk up the steps to the front door, to press buzzer number six. To say, when it is answered, in a voice from which all panic has been stripped, 'It's me, Tessa Maguire.'

The door swings open to an echoing entrance lobby and stairway. Up to the third floor, where the Mrs Fielding from her interview is at the door to greet her, small and alert, like a robin – 'Welcome, welcome, come in, come in' – through to the living room with the photos on the bookshelves, on the desk, on the mantelpiece – it is all there, saved. She feels a surge of gratitude to this woman.

She uses 'Mrs Fielding' once and is promptly told to call her Greta. 'We have a lot to talk about,' she announces as they sit down facing a loaded tea tray. 'I want to know *all* about you.'

Tessa says, 'You had to sit through an hour's interview hearing it all!' as she feels the last remnant of awkwardness disappear in the face of Greta's complete relaxation.

'Interviews miss out half the things you're curious about when you meet someone. I want to hear about your children. You'll have been settling them into their new home, I expect.'

Tessa begins – Sam in the nursery class, still shy with the other children. The teacher says he's doing fine but Tessa

267

worries. Alisa has been waking at night since Tessa started work. Ben's adjustments —

She stops. 'I'm so sorry, I've been rattling on.'

'I'm delighted that you're sharing them with me.'

Tessa gestures to the photographs around the room. 'Tell me about *your* family.'

'Mine? I hardly know where to begin. Those beautiful girls on the mantelpiece, they're my late husband's great-nieces.' And round the room they tour while she conjures up children's names and personalities, children grown into young people, then into adults with children of their own. And none of them, Tessa now understands, hers. She is everyone's aunt.

'Now there,' she gestures for Tessa to fetch a photo from her writing desk, 'is someone I hope you will meet one day.' A tall man in mountain walking gear, shielding his eyes against the sun. Younger, but unmistakably Lance.

Greta misses nothing. 'You know him?'

'We met just before he left for Kyrgyzstan.'

'Excellent, so you'll know what an asset he is. And here –'

She lifts a photo off the small table next to her and passes it to Tessa. Rahul as a boy, with his parents in London. The photo was there, in just the same place, six years ago. She holds it in her hands and looks up at Greta, wanting to say, I was here once with him, we slept in your spare room, and you never knew.

Greta's eyes are watching as intently as she listened at the interview. Surely she knows?

Tessa says, 'He talked about you often, but I had no idea – at the interview —'

'Of course. Why would you?'

Tessa hands the photo back, struggling against renewed sadness. 'I know it's his reference that got me this job.'

Greta's eyebrows lift. 'I don't deny his opinion was a recommendation but I can assure you it didn't influence the decision. It was far too important to me to get the right person.' She pauses, leaning forward. 'You're not feeling anxious about it, are you?'

'I am, actually.'

'And why is that?'

It is coming closer. Greta's eyes are waiting for her answer. Lamely Tessa says, 'I feel so inexperienced.'

'Inexperienced? My dear, with all the work you've done with children, in I don't know how many countries?'

'Not that. I mean about how to work in an organization like Lifeline.'

'Oh, that.' Greta dismisses it with a wave of her hand. 'You'll learn quick enough. You've got the values, the ideas, the knowledge of your own area of work, the rest will follow. Did anyone tell you it was the second time we had advertised? The first time we didn't get anyone I could put faith in. Too many professionals with jargon. This post is something I've been hammering on about for a long time and I wanted someone who would do it with love. And that's you.'

It is exactly the kind of thing Rahul might have said. Carefully Tessa sidesteps the feeling. 'The trouble is, I have only the dimmest idea of what I'm expected to do, and no one seems able to tell me.'

'Ah.' A pause. 'I see. So you're having difficulty with Glen?'

And now what is she to say? 'I can see he's very experienced and I'd like to learn from him. But –' She hesitates. Oh, what is the point in holding back? 'He told me he didn't think the job was needed.'

Greta's indignation strides forcefully across Tessa's caution. 'I knew I'd better catch you early. I've known him twenty years and no one can imagine Lifeline without him but he has to be the one who knows, if he isn't he won't play. So male, so tedious. The thing is, my dear, you're a threat.'

'A *threat?*'

'Not because of anything you've done but because he hasn't the first idea about children.'

Whatever she expected, it isn't this. 'I thought he had children of his own?'

'He does. There they are, those two in the photo on the bookshelf, but they're his wife's job. You've seen the hours he puts in, he's hardly ever at home. It's been like that as long as I've known him. I told Lionel it wouldn't work, putting you in Glen's section, but he couldn't make that thing he calls an organogram look neat any other way.'

The picture of Lionel and his organogram, Glen and his disdain, is too much for Tessa. She starts laughing, and out it pours, all the frustrations. Nothing she says seems to surprise Greta. When the flow stops Greta says calmly, 'I quite agree, he is outrageous. But don't let it get in your way. As long as what you do makes sense to people in the country programmes, Glen will not stop you. If you need anything, just phone Lance instead.'

Tessa's vehemence has exhausted itself. She is amazed at this woman, her sharpness, her directness, her calm. 'Did you know it was like this when you wrote to me?'

'Not exactly. But I knew Glen wasn't the person to help and I didn't want you giving up before you'd given it a real go.'

'I've only just started, how can I think of giving up?'

'That's what I like to hear.' Greta pauses. 'Tessa, now listen. I have known for years that things are not the way they should be. But I'm not in the office, I can't follow the detail. Lionel ought to be doing something about it, that's what he was brought in for, but he's no match for Glen, and between you and me he focuses on the wrong things. Systems aren't going to cure the malaise, it's people who do it and he lacks the knack of getting the best out of them.'

She shifts in her chair. Tessa is suddenly aware of her again as an old person with a stiff, uncomfortable body.

'I should probably have retired as a trustee years ago but I'm obstinate. I have come to the conclusion that the kind of change we need is not going to come from the directors but from below. People who work for us, here and in the countries, who take the ideals seriously and who can still see clearly enough to challenge.' She paused and placed the next words into the space between them. 'Like Rahul constantly did.'

Again Tessa feels, She knows. But she can't risk responding.

Greta holds the pause, then says, 'And as I hope you will continue to do. Am I overwhelming you?'

'It's a lot to take in.' Tessa feels suddenly wet around the

271

eyes, and very tired. Wiping the moisture away with the back of her hand she says, 'This must be tiring for you.'

Greta sits back in her chair. 'Not a bit of it. I feel thoroughly invigorated.'

Tessa is laughing now, at this frail old woman having more stamina than her. Greta beams. 'And about what we appointed you for, if no one else is helping you work it out, I'm going to. You are already looking through the reports, I hope?'

'It's what I spend most of my time doing. But it doesn't help much, there's so little about children in them.'

'That is precisely the point. We work with some very inspiring groups of people but I hardly ever hear about them working with children. Whatever is going wrong in society, children are sure to be the most vulnerable. And if you want to change anything, you've got to start with them. So I keep asking, where are they in our work? And the directors keep thinking I'm an irritating old woman. Now at last we've got you, and you're going to change that.'

'I am?'

'You are. At the start of each new piece of work you're going to get people to ask, What's happening to children? In the war, the earthquake, the economic collapse. Or endemic poverty. Keep checking that they are noticing the children whom everyone neglects. And if Glen tells you these questions aren't relevant, ignore him. They're essential. But you want to reach a stage as soon as you can where it's not just you asking, everyone is.'

She sits back, waiting for a response. Tessa feels awed. 'I am so grateful to have found you.'

Greta nods. 'It's mutual, my dear.'

A moment of silence. The closer they have moved, the more the unspoken things loom. Rahul's presence is so real it feels as if he must be somewhere near, as if he has just gone into another room. Tessa remembers their last morning here when she was tidying up to go. His plane wasn't until that evening but he was keeping the rest of the day for Greta. He said, 'Stay too. I'd love you to know each other.' But she couldn't deal with anyone else knowing, and judging. 'Greta won't judge,' he said, 'she's seen a lot of life.'

An inner clock summons her. 'I wish I could stay longer, but I'd better be going. The children —'

'Of course. But come back soon and tell me how things are going.'

'I'd love to.'

Greta insists on standing up to see her to the door. Watching her stiff movements, Tessa remembers her first sight of her. 'I've been wanting to tell you, I loved the way you adjusted the chairs at my interview.'

There is a puckish pleasure in Greta's eyes as she replies, 'Those silly men. How do they think anyone can show who they are when they're facing a firing squad? Now you just do things the way that comes naturally to you, and you'll be fine.'

'That's what Rahul always used to say.'

'He was a wise young man,' Greta says firmly. 'And you're very like him.'

Tessa stands still, arrested in the moment of leaving by those words, spoken so calmly, signifying so much. Cautiously she asks, 'In what way?'

'My dear, I'm sure you know the answer. It's the way you live. Loving comes easily to you, as it did to him.'

She is unable to move. Greta seems to be waiting. The words come out. 'I didn't know how to tell you. I've been here before, with Rahul.'

Greta sways a little. Tessa begins to panic. I was wrong, she didn't know, she is upset. She says, 'I'm so sorry, I'm keeping you here standing.'

'Come back in.' Greta turns, gets herself back into her chair. Tessa follows and sits opposite her. Greta says, quietly, 'I was so much hoping that you might mention it.'

They sit facing each other, meeting properly for the first time.

'You knew?'

'Yes.'

'That we stayed here, the week you were away?'

'Yes. But he said you were shy about it so he didn't want to press on you the fact that I knew.' Pause. 'But before that, too. I've known about you a long time.'

Silence. Taking it in.

Greta asks quietly, 'Do you mind?'

'I'm grateful. Not to have to hold it alone any more.' She moves out of her chair and comes to sit on the floor next to Greta's. Greta's hand rests on her head. The gentleness of it makes her want to cry. She lets her head rest on Greta's lap, feeling the thin, bony legs through the fabric of her skirt. She closes her eyes. Greta's lap receives her, her hand strokes her hair. She feels acceptance in the silence. Greta won't judge.

And now her voice, coming through the darkness of closed eyes.

'I have thought about you a great deal these last months, hoping you were not too alone with it all. But I had no way of knowing how to reach you. Then you came to us. Even if you had not been the right person for the job, I was so glad.'

Tessa's own words start coming. 'Ever since he died, I do what I have to do, I'm living as if I'm holding it together, the job, the children, Ben. But inside I'm in pieces still.'

Greta's hand moves.

'He's gone – he's gone – he's gone. It just goes round and round inside, like I have to keep rediscovering what it means.'

She is rocking now, as she did when Maeve first brought her the news. Greta's hand moves rhythmically in time, her voice says, 'Be gentle on yourself. It will pass.'

How long later she does not know, but the movement of the hand on her head gradually slows down, comes to rest. Greta begins speaking again, this time almost as if to herself.

'He was an unusual boy, even when he was a child. So quick in his understanding in so many ways, and so childlike in others. Did he ever tell you about his kite?'

Tessa moves her head, a minimal nod. Keep talking.

'He explained it to me in great detail, how children do it in India, up on the flat roofs of their houses, with pieces of glass tied into the tail of the kite so they can cut each other's down if they are swift enough and skilful. He sounded quite aggressive when he talked about it.'

More. Keep telling.

It comes in short sentences, with silences in between, spaces, for her to take it in.

'He came back to me as an adult, the year he was studying. It was in the year after my husband had died and I had got too used to being alone. Then suddenly Rahul was here, giving my home life again. We used to have coffee together in the mornings and we would eat together in the evenings if we were both in. He often cooked. He liked to make things that reminded him of home. I would hear about what he was up to with his student friends. It was the seventies, you're too young to remember, but it was a vibrant time, Alternative this and Alternative that, and radical political movements of all kinds. Rahul was alive with it all. He never knew how much good he did me.

'Then there were your times. That was a few years later. Maybe three? I don't remember, it's all become a little blurred. All those meetings and conferences, but it was obvious there was something compelling going on. On his last day, he was here packing, and I said, Rahul, tell me about her. So he told me. Actually, he was dying to share it. About the village, and how you stayed for so long, accepting all the limitations, though it was so far from anything you had known. How you saw things there that he had never seen. How you understood things about him that no one else did. How you each knew what the other was thinking before you had to say anything.

Yet how slow he had been to realize. Afterwards he asked, Greta, how did you know? I said, My dear boy, your bed's not been slept in all week.'

Tessa's eyes are still closed but she is smiling, holding the picture of him and Greta here, in this room, and all those other pictures that Greta is giving back to her.

'Then he took himself off so suddenly to Peshawar, and I was one of the few people who knew why. I wrote to him, as soon as I heard. It was a while before he replied. I remember so clearly what he wrote. *I am having to learn a new way of being myself.* Then, years later it was, and he had been here only once all that time, he phoned to say that you had found each other again, and to ask if he could bring you here. I said, Rahul, my home is yours whenever you need it, you know that. But take care of her. She's the one who's going to have to deal with the tensions. He said, I know. We both know.'

Silence.

Greta says, 'When I listened to you at the interview, I knew.'

'Knew?'

'That you were what he had said you were. A very special person.'

She shakes her head, denying. 'It was he who was special, I was just lucky.'

Silence again.

Greta – 'You're troubled, my dear. By other things too.'

A nod.

'Talk about it a little.'

She doesn't think she can find the words, but then they

start coming. 'It's all so bottled up inside me. I can't mourn where anyone else can see. I've kept it so private, for so long, and you'd think that would end with death, but it doesn't, his death itself has to go on being private. Since he came back into my life, no one knew. Not my family, none of my friends. My sister guessed but we never talked about it. It was only Ben who really knew. Because he had to.'

'Tell me a little about that, you and Ben.'

What to say? 'When he and I met, I was at my lowest. I'd gone travelling. Did Rahul tell you that? To get away, because everything between us seemed stuck and I couldn't see that it could ever come unstuck. I was alone, and confused, and I thought I would never be able to love anyone again. And then Ben, he was just there, normal, thinking I was normal, loving me. Like it was all simple. He released me.'

'And you?'

'At the beginning I had no space for it, but it grew. He knew about Rahul and me, he knew it was part of me and it wasn't going to go away. But he just kept making it clear that nothing was going to change how he felt.'

'He sounds a man of unusual qualities.'

'He is. He never asked what went on between us. It was something he wasn't part of, and he just left it to me. I thought —'

'You thought?'

'That we'd managed to keep it that way, where it wouldn't damage us.'

'And now?'

She moves her head on Greta's lap, a helpless gesture. 'With Rahul gone, it's changed things, I can't explain why. Ben knows how huge it is for me but we don't talk about it. Neither of us can. Anything I could put into words would only make it harder for him. He was always so – getting on with things, keeping his own focus, but now – You'd think it would be simpler, but it feels the opposite.' The feelings are running wild, losing direction. 'Maybe I should try to talk to him.'

'Don't. Some things are easier to come to terms with if you don't name them.'

'Anyway, I can't.' After a few minutes she tries again. 'Maybe all the unspoken things between us are nothing to do with Rahul. Ben's got things of his own to deal with, maybe that's all he's thinking about. I've had lots of times without work and it's never mattered, I've just found other things. But Ben – Maybe he's always used his work to not have to notice his feelings. Now he's lost that.'

She stops, facing it again. 'I'm saying it all wrong. It's not Ben who has changed, it's me.'

'But of course.'

Tessa sits up. Opens her eyes. 'Of course?'

'How could you not be changed by his death? And of course it makes you withdraw from Ben, you're having to hold on to Rahul so much harder, because he's gone.' She waits for Tessa to take that in, then quietly she continues. 'Even if the whole world knew who you were to each other, grief is very private. It cuts you off, shuts you in a place of your own, there is no other way. But it doesn't stay that way for ever. You and Ben have survived bigger strains, you will get through this.'

Tessa lays her head back in Greta's lap, her eyes closed again, and lets herself be lulled into stillness.

The dark slowly closes around them. Dark in the world outside the windows, dark here inside, neither of them moving to turn on a light. Coming quietly through the darkness, Greta's voice again – 'You have been blessed, my dear, beyond what most people will ever experience. That's what you need to hold on to. Let everything else rest.'

A candle in the window

From the window of his office in Dushanbe Hugo looks out on a succession of white four-by-fours moving along the road, each with the logo of an international agency. The government hasn't the capacity to handle the mess the war has left without outside assistance, but having to rely on outsiders goes against their independent pride. International staff expect to live at a level few Tajiks can aspire to. They need housing, food, fuel, services that work, personal security; to provide all that distorts local supply lines and costs. It would have been extraordinary if there had not been an undertone of resentment.

This is not, at the best of times, an easy place to get things done. Political corruption is rife. Officials are afraid to take action. The legacy of conflict is everywhere evident, in a broken-down infrastructure, the loss of skilled technicians, communications that only half-work. The opium trade from Afghanistan passes illegally through, its knock-on effects disastrous. Tajiks in their personal lives are warm, hospitable people but anyone in a position of authority has acquired a certain deviousness; they would not have survived without it. To achieve a peace settlement requires compromise, power-sharing, and these are not things they have ever had to practise. As for his investigation into Rahul's and Vitaly's deaths, well, he can imagine several of his Tajik colleagues thinking, Thousands of Tajiks have died in this war. Why all this effort to investigate the deaths of two foreigners?

Everything about the investigation has been difficult. Hugo has interviewed each of the twenty-one surviving hostages, either in person or by phone in the case of those who had since left Tajikistan. They have gone over the story again and again but there are no clear leads. The people he needs to cross-question are Sadirov and his followers, and there is no way to get near them. The Department of Security nominated an official to liaise with him but within a week they had taken him off the case and allocated someone new, for no reason that Hugo could fathom. Mikhail Ivanov, brother of Vitaly who died with Rahul, has pressured the Russian delegation to allocate a security official to the case, but the man has been useless. Mikhail Ivanov is not surprised. Vitaly was a dissident all his life, he says, and was openly critical of the current Russian government. It solves a problem for them that he is out of the way.

Hugo has travelled to the south of the country, moving through the lowland valleys that suffered the worst violence. He has talked to people who worked with Rahul, listened for anything that might suggest a line of enquiry. There is no sign now of the transit camps that he and his team set up.

Houses have been rebuilt, the debris mostly cleared away, the memories buried as deep as it is humanly possible to do. But there are places still that people do not go. The Turkish baths in Qurgon Teppe are abandoned, the walls riddled with bullet holes, the memories of what happened inside unspeakable. The fields that once produced cotton have not recovered. Irrigation canals are clogged up. Women and children work small plots of land, guarding them as if there might be another attack. Too few men are left. Those who hold positions of authority are tense; apparent inter-clan calm can at any moment give way to suspicion born of fear. Peace has not been signed. Laws exist, but are not reliably enforced. Neither livelihood nor security can be relied on. UNHCR has handed over here, its work of resettlement officially done, but it is obvious at every turn that they left the district too soon. Rahul said it would be so, and he was right.

As to what might have happened in the mountains, there is a dark collective silence. No one wants even to think about it.

Except him. And he cannot free himself from thinking about it.

It is April now, three months and more since they were taken hostage. The snow around Gharm has melted early this year and now they are back in the same yard from which Rahul and the others set off that December morning, and a UN vehicle waits to carry him up the route of Rahul's last journey. With him is Mikhail Ivanov, also a UN munitions specialist, a Tajik government official, a local man from Gharm who knows the road well, and one of the men who was taken hostage. It is brave of him to be coming; it cannot be easy. Hugo watches the slowly changing shapes of the mountains through the windows of the Land Cruiser.

The ex-hostage identifies the point where the five vehicles were attacked, then they travel further, slowly, still looking for signs of a burnt-out vehicle. They travel for two hours and find nothing. Eventually the driver pulls to a halt at a possible turning point. They all climb out, and stand looking out. Spring comes late to the mountains of Tajikistan but when it does there is nothing more beautiful. Sunlight glints on the rocks in the stream. Alpine flowers hide shyly, a moment of colour in the grass. Rock faces are sharply etched in the slanting light. A more peaceful place could not be imagined.

The munitions man says that if a vehicle *had* hit a mine, the force of the explosion would likely have sent it tumbling down into the ravines so one wouldn't necessarily expect to see the remains on the road itself. There is constant earth movement up here, small earthquakes somewhere in the Pamirs almost every day. Searching the ravines is out of the question.

The Tajik government official turns to Hugo and lifts his shoulders. We're never going to know for sure.

It is almost dark by the time they get back to Gharm. They pass a house where someone has put a candle in the window. Perhaps it is to light the way for someone who has gone out and not yet returned.

~ 38 ~

Lance lets himself into the lobby of the apartment block. It's late, and he's just back from another out-of-town journey. Damn, the light isn't working again. He starts up the dank stairwell, barely able to see the steps. He stops, listens. He is convinced that he is not alone. He feels some ominous presence. He looks back quickly to check that he has not been followed. Nothing. He takes the last flight of steps two at a time and turns the corner to his door – to see someone sitting there, on the floor. A girl with blonde hair and a backpack next to her. It's the girl from the plane journey and she is holding the scrap of paper he put into her friend's hand at the airport.

'Hi, I'm Annabel. Remember? I bet you never thought this would happen.'

He stares at her, unable to think of a thing to say. She seems to realize a word or two of explanation might be needed. 'The guy I was with has gone back and I think I've sprained my ankle. I couldn't face any more walking, searching for a bed. I'd be really grateful if I could doss down on your floor for a few days.'

'Sure. Come in, come in.' He starts to unlock. The key is fiddly, slower than usual. He is still puzzling over detail. 'I gave you the office address. How did you find this place?'

'The security guard at your office told me. I hope you don't mind. You did say —'

285

'Of course.' The door opens. 'Afraid it's quite small.'

'No problem.' She dumps her rucksack. 'Thank God, that was doing me in.'

'I'll put the kettle on.' She follows him into the kitchen, where he fetches down a couple of cans from the shelf. 'I'm afraid the food's pretty minimal. I only get to the market at weekends.'

'No problem, I've been living off cans. Anything'll be great.'

'What happened to your ankle?'

'We've been in the mountains. I slipped in a stream.'

While he gets busy with the tin opener she sits down cross-legged on the floor, opens her rucksack and starts to spread her things. 'I haven't got a clean thing to wear. You got a washing machine?'

'There's one in the basement, for the whole building, it's like something from the early industrial revolution.'

'I'll give it a go. Is there washing powder down there?'

'I've got some here. How did you get up into the mountains?'

'Hitched. Had to wait a while, but worth it. Fabulous high valleys with little lakes in them. We got up to a place called Sukhunobod.'

Sukhunobod? He thinks of all Nargis's careful preparations, queueing for permits. And these youngsters just set off on their own. 'You didn't have any trouble?'

'Trouble?'

'The army?'

'Oh yeah, there were these soldiers half-way up. But they were bored out of their minds, hanging about with nothing to do. We chatted them up and they let us past.'

Chatted them up? 'They knew English?'

'No way,' she laughs, 'but I studied Farsi. They got pretty excited when I started talking. And we had some dried fruit we shared with them.'

The young walk through fire without even knowing they're doing it. You give up acting free when you know too much.

She describes how they came across a yurt in a lost valley, where the family gave them tea. 'With rancid butter in it. Ever had it?'

He has not. And even if he were free to spend his time wandering to lost valleys and finding yurts, he wouldn't be able to talk to that family as she did. There is no doubt, he is envious.

'What got you into studying Farsi?'

'Pretty arbitrary. I wanted to travel, so I reckoned that meant languages. And I had a book of stories about Persia when I was a kid with those gorgeous miniature paintings, all red and gold and highly decorated.'

He is entertained. 'You had good teaching?'

'The best. Our prof made us speak, not just grammar, and he was great on poetry. That was an unexpected bonus. I've always wanted to get to Tajikistan and into the Pamirs, but with the war it's not easy.'

'So you were driven to Resham-serai?'

She grins. 'I'm not saying I'm suffering.' She is massaging her ankle.

'Painful?'

'Yeah. I think I need to crash.' She looks around at the floor.

'Use the sofa. You'll be more comfortable.'

'Thanks, that'll be great.' She spreads her sleeping bag on it, disappears into the bathroom, and is back in a long T-shirt, legs bare, hair loose around her shoulders. Without waiting for him to remove himself she snuggles herself into position on the sofa. 'Stay up as long as you like,' she says. 'The light won't bother me.'

But there is no way he can stay in the room while she lies there, oblivious of the effect she is having. He takes himself off to his room and shuts the door.

When he wakes in the night to use the bathroom he tiptoes through the living room. She is curled up in the deep, trusting sleep of a child.

He has taken in backpackers in other places he has lived, so there is an expected pattern. You make a quick judgement before you commit – a stage that somehow got missed out this time – you show them how things work in the kitchen, give them a key, make it clear they are to look after themselves. There's an unstated trade-off. He works in places the young like to travel in, but he lives alone and it's a pleasant diversion to hear about their day's adventures on an evening when they happen to be in. Sometimes it has turned out to be more than that and he has made a new friend. Sharing the practicalities of daily life is an easier way in for him than small-talk at a social gathering.

This time it's going a little differently. He does not have at his disposal the usual expatriate more-than-comfortable house with a spare bedroom, so Annabel's arrival means he has lost all possibility of time alone. Short of retiring to his bedroom straight after they have eaten there is no way of avoiding spending every evening chatting to her. He tries not to show that he feels invaded, but it is symbolized by that moment when she opened up her backpack and spread the contents over the living room floor. He reminds himself how he was at her age, every bit as unaware of the needs of others. And the truth is, it is beguiling to have the company of someone who isn't living here and from whom he has to try and learn as much as he can in a short time.

It is also impossible to ignore the effect of having a young girl moving about in his home, her body lithe and naturally graceful. Those startling eyes, a complexion smooth with youth, a mouth that expresses her moods – lips slightly apart as she listens, puckering when she is thinking, opening wide when she laughs. But he knows his place. He is the convenient older-generation provider-of-accommodation.

He is bothered about her ankle, which is swollen each evening. He gets her sitting with it up on a stool, and makes her use icepacks.

'You're pretty clued up,' she says. 'Where did you learn this?'

'Walking in mountains, like you. And I know from experience, it's no use trying to short-cut it; it needs rest. You're gallivanting around too much.'

'It'll be fine. It feels a little better every day.'

There is no point nagging her. She is clearly not someone to stay in when the world waits out there to be explored.

Saturday, a beautiful spring day, blossom on the cherry trees. A day to shed work pressures and notice where he is. He gets out his camera and they set out to wander through the town. In the paved courtyard of the madrassa he watches the geometric shapes of stone arches reflected in a quiet pool, while Annabel talks to a young man who is rediscovering Islamic scholarship. In the market they weave their way between stalls where cheap plastic goods jostle with hand-crafted tools or piles of entrails and sheep's heads, and Annabel chats to two stout women who guard a stall hung with green-and-red felt mats. There are people with Mongolian-looking faces red from exposure to the elements, men dressed in quilted jackets and knee-length boots, some with embroidered caps and others with tall white-and-black felt hats, and soon Annabel is explaining to him which are Kyrgyz in style and which are Tajik. They buy food for lunch; Annabel by now knows something about most kinds on offer. They eat it sitting in the thin spring sun on a bench near the statue of the poet. She wants to know about Lifeline's work, so he tells her about the projects he has been visiting with Fahmeda, and the things he is learning from her stories. Fahmeda was a child through the war, when near-starvation levels were common. She remembers people disappearing, never being heard of again. But she is also an inheritor of what the Revolution has done for women; without that she would never have been educated, and she reminds the younger ones what they have to be grateful for.

Annabel listens, keen to learn. She is clearly something more than the casual traveller he took her for, and she seems to have an extraordinary facility with language. She can read the Cyrillic script and has picked up phrases in Russian, though she has been in Central Asia only a few weeks. 'It's really not difficult, Lance,' she says, surprised that he hasn't done the same. He discovers that she spent six months in Iran studying Farsi poetry. 'In Mashhad, home of Firdawsi,' she says, then she sees that means nothing to him. 'Great Persian poet,' she explains and switches into Farsi. The words are rhythmic, lilting. She laughs at his amazed expression. 'It says,

> Neither storm nor rain shall ever mar
> What I have built – the palace of my poetry.

And he wasn't far wrong. He lived a thousand years ago and people still quote him.'

'And how was it being there?'

'Mashhad? It was great. My professor had fixed me up to stay with a family he knew, and I made some amazing friends. When we did things together, it was fine. But I wanted to do some exploring alone. They all tried to tell me I shouldn't but I wasn't listening.' She pauses, seems to be reliving some experience, and not a good one. 'You remember Wayne, the guy I was with at the airport?'

'Baggy Trousers?'

'That's him. I picked him up in Bukhara, to fend off predatory men.'

'Baggy Trousers provided protection? I didn't think he looked the type.'

She grins. 'Any male companion is a deterrent. Simple evolutionary biology.'

A young man passes by on the other side of the street, and waves to Annabel. She waves back, turns to Lance and asks, 'Has Fahmeda taken you to the street-children's centre?'

'We're going on Monday,' he says; and then, surprise registering, 'How do you know about it?'

'That guy is one of the volunteers. I got talking to him and he took me to see it. Those kids, it really gets to you.'

His own work, and she has got there before him.

'They're struggling with their reporting,' she says. 'They asked if I could help.'

The street-children's centre is housed in the basement of the teacher-training college where Fahmeda once worked. She leads Lance past echoing labs with dusty equipment. Lifeline pays a minimal rent, probably just enough, he calculates, to keep the college director from having to abandon his job. In what was once a classroom volunteers serve a meal to children who hold their bowls to receive it with expressions of real hunger. In another Annabel is helping someone set out the accounts. There is a washroom, toothbrushes, lockers where the children each keep their few possessions. Helping them look after themselves, the project leader says, helps to build their self-esteem and gains their trust so that gradually the workers are hearing their stories, and considering if there are more long-term things they can do to help.

He is thinking, Do I recognize any of these kids? Has he seen them scavenging in rubbish bins, selling matches, offering shoe-shines, 'guarding' cars while their owners were in meetings?

292

Sometimes as he walks back home in the evenings he sees a couple of them huddled in moth-eaten coats over the gratings in the pavement where hot air emerges from the town's arcane heating system. The centre is open only for a few hours a day. There is nowhere safe to go at night.

Strange to think of them as 'kids', the word is too carefree. But 'children' also feels wrong for they are already so worldly wise in all the wrong ways. Forced into begging, presumably also stealing, learning to survive in gang culture, deprived of adults who can play the usual roles of control and socialization. So they evoke fear, not compassion, in the adults who pass them by on the streets. They have little reason to trust adults, yet here, receiving the most minimal of care, they respond like thirsty plants to water.

He heads back to the office, burdened by knowing that it is going to be hard to convince Glen that they should stay involved. Lifeline is going through a budget crisis. The projects here are among the newest Lifeline has taken on, and therefore the most vulnerable.

He faxes his reports.

He waits two days, then he gets on the phone. Glen starts with one of his usual gripes. 'Lionel's got some touchy-feely facilitator in to work with the Directors group and we have to spend the whole damn day on it.'

Lance makes sympathetic noises. 'My reports, did you see them?'

'I did. I have to say, it's hard to see where it's all going. Pre-schools, street children, we can't keep funding them for ever

293

and what happens when we have to stop? They had a street-children's centre in Kathmandu when you arrived and you closed it down.'

'In Kathmandu there were three other agencies working with those kids, all better placed than us. Here there's nothing, and the numbers are bound to increase as the economic crisis bites. Someone needs to be positioned with some experience.'

'I'm not convinced. Anyway, it's not our field.'

'Why not? They're all extremely vulnerable children and local groups are trying to do something about it.'

'You know what I mean. We've got no experience of that sort of thing.'

Lance thinks of Tessa's fax. 'So what have we appointed an Early Years Advisor for?'

No answer. He reads Glen's silence. 'How is she doing?'

'I couldn't say. I don't see much of her.'

'You know she worked with Rahul?'

'So?'

'So take her seriously. He had an eye for talent. If he thought she had something useful to contribute, you can be sure she has.' He waits, irritation rising. 'Glen, it's irresponsible to ignore her.'

Tone defensive now. 'Who says I'm ignoring her?'

'You did.'

The silence of someone who doesn't like being told. Enough for the moment, Lance decides. 'Listen, it's not just about the current projects. The whole society is under pressure. Rahul took on people who are showing some initiative but they're cut off from other sources of experience. For us to support their development is a strategic choice.'

'OK, OK. I'll leave it to you while you're there.'

~ 39 ~

In the days since Tessa sat with her head in Greta's bony lap, nothing has been the same. She can hardly find words for what Greta has given her, a sense of having been received and understood. Even at work things have changed. Colleagues who before were too busy to give her time now suggest that they get together. Phone calls have come from organizations based in London, 'Glad to hear Lifeline's getting into Early Years,' they say, and they invite her to come and meet their team. And Tessa knows: Greta has been talking to someone.

Glen remains unreachable. Everyone around her seems to regard him as a force of nature, beyond being held accountable, but her dogged streak is in the ascendant and she has begun to ask Emperor's-new-clothes questions. It's obvious that his range of knowledge is astounding and she doesn't see why she shouldn't tap into it. She sees him interacting with those he has let into his magic circle. There's an ease of good-fellowship that makes her exclusion doubly galling.

A meeting in London, and she ends up back with Greta. 'I'm

classifying this as my supervision,' she says. 'Since I don't have a manager.'

Greta's eyes are amused. 'Very well, report to me.'

Tessa off-loads her frustrations. Greta listens without comment, then says, 'Let me tell you a story about Glen. At the time of the terrible famine in Ethiopia, I was on a committee to raise funds. We were getting reports that made us desperate, about how slow the system of distributing relief was, all the cumbersome bureaucracies. We began talking about setting up a new organization that would go straight to local groups and support them to do these things themselves, but none of us had enough hands-on experience to get it going. Then Lance told me about Glen. They'd been together in Ethiopia. He said, "This guy just gets things done, he has a way of cutting through red tape and getting food to where it is needed." And now Glen had got himself sacked for challenging his managers about the same kinds of concerns we had. He's a man who is prepared to face personal cost for what he thinks is right. He had refused to fight in Vietnam, and couldn't go back to America. So we invited him to come and help us, and that was how Lifeline International got started. He was our first paid worker. We would probably have got going eventually, but without his energy and knowledge it would have taken us far longer.'

She pauses. Tessa is looking out of the window at the plane trees, now in first new leaf, tinged with russet. OK, it is useful to know, but it changes nothing.

'I'm telling you this, Tessa, to help you understand. He's an exasperating man but he's got qualities you will come to value.'

Tessa feels restless with all the things she needs to make Greta see. 'It's like he's guarding a huge iron gate, and he could so easily let me through, and he won't.'

'I know. It's utterly infuriating. Challenge him whenever you like and you'll have my full support. He's out of order and I shall tell him so. But people as self-driven as that take a long time changing, and for now, if I were you I would save my energy for other things. Just side-step him and get on with doing things your own way. Once he sees that people value what you can offer, he'll come round. And meanwhile there are others who can tell you things you need to know. Get me my address book, will you? There, on my bureau.'

It is no ordinary address book. It bulges with extra pages pasted in where letters of the alphabet have run out of space. Lifeline is the project dearest to Greta's heart but it is far from her only public activity. She has accumulated campaigning groups and advisory roles as she has accumulated adopted nieces and nephews. Perhaps, Tessa thinks, if you lose your most significant people early in life you never stop wanting to gather up new ones.

'Whatever anyone else is demanding of you,' Greta says, 'keep finding quiet moments for yourself.'

'I do,' Tessa says. She has taken to disappearing for short periods, creating moments that are neither work nor home. When others in the office do without a lunch break and eat sandwiches while they work, she walks down to the sea-front and stands looking out over the water, letting the wind whip her face. Sometimes at the end of the day she detours through streets with small shops and walks past Brighton Pavilion with its bizarre onion domes before she turns back towards the station to get the train. And once, lost in thought on the train, she missed her station and was carried on to the next one. She called Ben, full of apologies at her stupidity; but the truth was, she was simply happy. Another twenty minutes on her own.

More than anything, Greta creates space. 'You need to keep talking about him,' she says. 'It's good for me as much as you.' And Tessa sees that this is true, for Greta too has a journey to make. Calmed by Greta's listening spirit, Tessa talks. She talks of her confusions, that jostle for space with her certainties. She lets whatever is in her mind come out, and nothing now is too dangerous to say. During one visit she becomes tearful. Greta just waits till it is over and then says quietly, 'You wouldn't want to be without sadness.'

She wakes to rain battering the windows, looks at her watch, jumps out of bed. They have all overslept. Alisa refuses to eat her breakfast. Sam can't find his waterproofs. Ben is getting worked up. 'Tessa, can't you just stay until we've found Sam's things?' But if she does she will miss her train.

She pedals off into the driving rain. Why is it uphill going and uphill coming back, and the wind always in the wrong direction? At the station she locks up her bike, hands slipping on wet metal. A car pulls up in front of her, a woman driving, a man next to her, a teenage girl in school uniform in the back. The man gets out and without saying goodbye strides off into the station entrance. Tessa stands rigid. She can't see his face but the body language is unmistakable. The woman gets out of the car, dark-haired, in a red skirt, and calls after him, 'Glen, your papers!' He turns, hurries back, and without meeting her eyes takes the folder she is holding out to him, says a preoccupied 'Thanks' and turns immediately back. The woman stands for a moment watching him go; perhaps waiting in case he should turn. Then she gets back into the car, turns to face her daughter, their eyes sharing something they both understand without having to speak about it, are fed up with, and can do nothing about. She shrugs and drives off.

'He's hardly ever at home,' Greta said. And if after years of that his wife is coming to the end of her tolerance, how would he react? By blocking it off, ever longer hours at work, ever more resistance to changes that aren't in his control. Like anything Lionel proposes, which even Chuck in the post room knows that Glen is going to oppose. Like the trustees' decision to appoint an Early Years Advisor. He couldn't stop it, but he certainly isn't going to do anything to make it work.

When she gets into the office she goes to see Charlene, the administrator, and asks, 'When there's a new member of staff here in Brighton, who tells people in the countries?'

'Their head of department,' Charlene says. Their eyes lock as she realizes – no memo this time. So simple. Here is the answer to her empty diary, and why no one in the countries is contacting her. No one has told them she is here.

'Glen is impossible,' Charlene says. 'But I should have chased him.'

'You can't hold his hand for everything. Well, I guess I'll just have to tell them myself.'

Back in her cupboard-office Tessa shuts the door hard. She wants to throw a tantrum, the kind two-year-olds specialize in – *fury* at people who make decisions over your head and ignore what you are trying to tell them. Then she looks up at the picture of Alisa on Ben's shoulders, sunny, beaming. She sits down to type, her thoughts tapping furiously onto the keyboard. So much she wants to say to all those unknown people in the deserts of the Sahel and the foothills of the Himalayas, people who work in dust and monsoon rains, whose lives she can imagine so much more easily than she can fathom the ones right here in this building. She types, she edits, and now she is elated that she is able to do this herself, not have someone else speak inadequately for her. Eventually she has it down the way she wants it, and the way Greta has given her the confidence to imagine it – what she has seen, and not seen, about children in the project reports, her tentative ideas about what her job could be, and saying straight out, 'Please tell me how I can be useful to you.'

Within days the responses have started coming in. From Sri Lanka, where they are worried about the effects of the civil war on children; from Uganda, where the HIV epidemic has left so many children orphans, often destitute; from Nepal, Mali,

Pakistan. They are all, it seems, asking Greta's question, How does it affect the children? And they all want her to come and work with their staff. What was a drought has turned into an unmanageable flood. How can she respond to them all?

'You can't,' Greta says calmly. 'Just start where you can. And don't rush, first come to terms with the organization. There's no point arriving in the countries until you have a clearer idea of what we can realistically hope to achieve.'

But after that there can be no delaying it; this is what she is here for. She starts booking visits, starting three months ahead, a week away in every six. At one level it is difficult to take the idea of this globetrotting Tessa seriously; at another the prospect looms dangerously. How will it affect the children? And her and Ben? They have both known this would come but now that it is imminent, it threatens to create even more distance between them.

Ben. It comes back to him every time. Whatever the stresses of her job it fills her days with new people, opening up to her things she wouldn't have thought or done otherwise, but for Ben the horizon has closed in. The furthest he goes most days is a walk at Alisa's pace to the village shop and to fetch Sam from school.

'What do you do?' a mum in the village asks at the weekend. They are chatting while the children play on the swings, and it is Ben to whom the question is addressed. He says, 'Tessa's got a job in Brighton. I look after the kids.'

'Well done you!' But impressed or not, she can't quite take

it in, for a few minutes later she circles back to, 'What else do you do?'

Ben says, 'It feels like it's going to be pretty full-time. How about you? What else do *you* do?'

They laugh about it, but there is no escaping it, the change in their roles is changing something more fundamental between them. They are both tired, but he with the end-of-tether tiredness of a housebound parent. For her, being a mother at home came easily. She loved the playdough and coloured pens, the cuddles and laughter, the unexpected moments when she got a glimpse of what was going on in their minds. She didn't realize until she had to hand it over just how much there was to it, not the big things but the apparently minor ones, like getting the children to tidy up one activity before they started on another, that could make the difference between having a creative day and being surrounded by chaos. Now she has to set off each day leaving Ben looking harried with responsibility. When she is concentrating on work she can half-forget about it but each time she is cycling back from the station she is besieged by the feeling that she has abandoned the one role that really matters. She arrives, physically tired from pushing through the wind and rain, and tries to be super-mum to make up for having been away. When anything has gone wrong in their day, nothing can stop her feeling that she should have been there.

The times they have together are consumed in the constant tasks of keeping the family show on the road, dressing children and undressing them, breakfasts and suppers, bath-time and clearing up. There seem to be no moments for talking personally. She senses he isn't up for hearing the details of her days and she has no instinct to press it, but that only widens the gap. They are marooned on an island among people who know nothing of their past, more dependent on each other's company than they have ever been, yet their lives are becoming ever more separate. In bed too. That kind of loving is a language like any other and their bodies have become uncommunicative. Or is it just that they are both always so tired?

~ 40 ~

Annabel is showing no sign of moving on. Lance doesn't feel inclined to ask about her plans. She is really no trouble, they have worked out a comfortable way of sharing the space, and her company is cheering in the evenings.

Inspired by the street-children's centre, she asks if she can visit another of Lifeline's projects. Lance is cautious about letting personal things get mixed up with work ones but he can't think of any reason to say no. 'There's the weaving project,' he suggests. A group of young people have started learning from their grandfathers, reviving centuries-old patterns on looms that their families have kept from the days when handcrafts were ousted by the Soviet-era factories. An inspiring cultural venture, but Lance finds it hard to believe in the economics of it. Cloth piling up, such high-quality stuff, but local people have no money to buy. 'Tourists will,' Fahmeda says confidently. 'There are not many now because of those stupid reports in the papers but when they see there is no trouble they will start coming. They will come for the mountains, and when they are here they will buy something beautiful to take home.'

Tourists; well here is one, in his own apartment. 'The condition,' he tells Annabel, 'is you buy something.'

He gets back that evening to find her surrounded by metres of cloth of shining purple and green. 'They were just great,' she says. 'They let me have a go on the looms. Lance, what do you think about my writing an article about the project?'

'An article? For?'

'There's a travel magazine that targets gap-year students and backpackers. I've done pieces for them before. They said, If you get anywhere interesting, send us stuff, we'll see if we can use it.'

Well, why not? A bit of publicity wouldn't come amiss with the fundraisers back in Brighton.

'See what Nargis says. Come in tomorrow and I'll introduce you.'

Nargis and Fahmeda both think it a great idea. The young men can't take their eyes off Annabel. When Lance leaves the office for a meeting, she is joking with them in Tajik.

That evening she is excited from her interviewing and ready to start writing it up. 'Could I use a computer in the office?' she asks. He doesn't know why he hesitates, it is Lifeline's work she is writing about, but the picture of Annabel in there, doing an excellent job of distracting the staff ... ? He realizes with a jolt that the idea makes him jealous. That is so ridiculous that he immediately lurches the other way and agrees. After all, they do have to do something about fundraising, this project is so obviously unsustainable, it's on Glen's hit list if they don't.

Akbor, the administrator, fixes up a desk for Annabel. The younger members of the team cross-question her about aspects of Western lifestyle that Lance has proved useless to induct them in. Zohra discusses female fashion. The young men want to hear about footballers whom Lance has barely heard of but whose fame has somehow reached Kyrgyzstan. Fahmeda is pleased to have another curious foreigner to instruct.

At one point he comes out of his office into the central work area to find a vigorous discussion going on in Tajik, with Annabel at the centre of it. Fahmeda sees him and switches to English. 'Annabel is asking about the new mosques you see going up. I'm telling her, it's Saudi money and they are teaching people a kind of Islam we never had here before. Those people can't separate what is true Islam from negative custom. It is custom only that says keep girls at home, don't let them go to school. True Islam is not about rules and rituals, it is what is in your heart. It is about living with love and respect.'

Akbor quotes something in Farsi. Fahmeda nods approvingly and says, 'That's Sadi, one of our great poets.' Then, to Akbor, 'Tell Lance what it means.'

There's a discussion about how to translate one of the words. Akbor turns to Lance and says, 'You understand 'Sufi'? Most of our poets were Sufis. It means you try to get close to God.'

'I understand,' Lance says. 'So what did Sadi say?'

'*The Sufi way is nothing but the service of humanity.*'

Annabel's article is good. No question about it, she is bright and has an easy way of pitching it at the right level for the audience. Almost too easy. Some Puritan streak in Lance feels she ought to find some things difficult. Nargis makes a few factual changes and faxes the article off to Brighton. The answer comes back, the media team are happy for her to place it anywhere she can. And the fundraisers want to use it. Can she send them some photos? Lance is torn between amusement at seeing her so pleased with her success and a sense that he has allowed her far further in than he bargained for.

And not just into his work.

He is increasingly curious about her. She has arrived out of the blue but there must be a story behind what brought her here. OK, she's a traveller, but if that were the main motivation she would have moved on. One of the old tracks of the Silk Route leads out from this very town, she could be moving on to Bishkek, Naryn, crossing over into China. She wants to be somewhere where Farsi is spoken, to deepen her competence in the language? But if that was her aim she has friends in Mashhad, a family that hosted her, surely it would have been easiest to go back there. He remembers the suddenly closed look on her face when she talked about the difficulties of travelling alone in Iran. Had something happened that made her not want to return there?

He hesitates to ask directly. It's not a hesitation she shares.

'Have you never had a partner?' she asks as they clear up after their evening meal.

Lance plays for time. 'Define partner.'

'You know what I mean. Regularly sharing a bed.'

'Yes I have. Several.'

'But no one you wanted to stay with long term?'

'You wouldn't by any chance regard that as a rather personal question?'

'Of course it's personal. What's the point of not being personal?'

He is disarmed, as he so often is, by her directness. 'There have been a couple,' he offers cautiously, 'but neither of them was up for following me around the world. Or I them, I suppose, but somehow it never presented itself that way.'

'You don't have to be so cagey. I'm not going to the press with the story.'

That makes him laugh. 'OK, I'll tell you about one of them. Her name's Penny. She's still one of my close friends.'

'Go on, I love stories.' She settles into the sofa, lithe as a cat.

He gets carried away describing their times together in Pakistan. Annabel's eyes are fixed on him, waiting for more. 'Enough romantic ingredients?' he asks.

'Just fine. Why didn't it work out?'

He shrugs. 'I don't think she was ready to commit.' Then he remembers what Greta said – *Nonsense, she adored you.* 'Or maybe it was me, being too slow.'

'That's *so* sad,' Annabel says.

Her tone makes him smile. 'Probably more so for me than for Penny.'

Her expression gives him no idea what she is thinking.

Suddenly she jumps up. 'Dinner was a long time ago. I'm going to make pancakes.' He goes to join her in the kitchen that can barely accommodate two. It is like being a student again, spontaneous meals at midnight. One after another the pancakes fly up and settle, straight back into the pan. He says, 'It's amazing, the way you do that.'

'It's dead easy. Try.'

After a couple of attempts he hands it back to her. 'And I don't know how you can have a conversation while you're doing it.'

'Viv – my sister – she says I was born to be a juggler, keeping three lives going at once.'

'That sounds intriguing. What are they?'

'Guess,' she says. They sit down to the pancakes. Butter, honey, sticky, dripping and delicious.

'The traveller.'

'Mmmh.'

'The journalist.'

'Sounds good to me. The harsh reality is copy-editing, to fund the travelling.'

'And the third?'

'That's with Viv. She's an artist and I try and promote her painting. She's hopeless at it herself, just like she is about men.'

'Oh? What way hopeless?'

'She has an unerring instinct for men who don't know how to love anyone but themselves. Comes from living with my dad.'

He watches her face for a moment, then says, 'Maybe you'd better tell me what that means.'

She meets his eyes, unabashed, and says calmly, 'My dad is a charming shit.' The words are like a slap. She is watching to see how he is reacting. When he says nothing she goes on. 'He is an actor and his creative genius dominates his life. Everything else has to fall in line behind it. Including Viv and me, not to mention my mother. He left when I was only a year old but Viv had six years of him, and it shows.'

'Did you see anything of him when you were growing up?'

'Oh yes, that's the charming bit. He loved having daughters he could show off to other people. We were always backstage, meeting his arty friends, being made much of. And learning that being a little girl and pretty was a cute thing to be, if you wanted that kind of superficial attention. I'd have preferred to be stodgy-looking and boring, and have him *really* notice who I was. Maybe even listen to what was going on for me sometimes. But I grew out of that quite quickly, and learnt to just get on with my life. Viv never did. She still wants his approval.'

'Does she get it?'

'For her painting, yes. She's good, so that pleases his vanity. My daughter, my creative daughter. But her feelings? He couldn't care a toss.'

'You have sharp judgements, Annabel.'

He is rerunning their first encounter in the airport lounge, that clear assessing eye she turned on each of the men in turn. And the look she often has still, of being much older than her years. He feels a rush of protectiveness, wanting her to find something that will give her cause to be trustful.

When he eventually takes himself off to bed, sleep will not come. He lies in the dark, disturbed at his own state. At some point, probably quite soon, Annabel is going to get bored and move on, and his evenings are going to feel unbearably empty. He has known all along it was not wise to have allowed himself to be so beguiled.

He wakes after only a couple of hours, his thoughts instantly back to Annabel. He thinks of her facility with language, and his own uselessness. He has not made the slightest progress with Tajik. He is blind to even the notices around him because he has still not made the effort to learn the Cyrillic alphabet.

He checks the time: almost five. Pointless to lie here any longer. He gets up, moves quietly past the sleeping Annabel to the bathroom and then to the kitchen. While he drinks his coffee he opens his hardly used copy of *Teach Yourself Russian*, to read through the alphabet yet again. Then, book in hand, he sets out into the city to start practising.

The moment he is out of the apartment he is rewarded. There is mist rising from the ground and swirling gently. An elderly man on a bicycle wobbles past, shadowy in the half-light. A woman in a long coat, her head covered by a scarf, leads a goat on a rope down towards the market area. Outside the mosque a couple of watchmen huddle over a brazier. He greets them in Tajik, and they greet back. He arrives at the statue of the poet. This is as good a place to start as any. He looks at the words on the plaque:

РАХМАН МИРЗА ЯНОВ

He looks up each letter in turn. So confusing, letters that stand for one sound in English and something different in Cyrillic, and other letters that have no meaning for him at all. Slowly, like a child, he spells it out: R-A-H-M-A-N M-I-R-Z-A J-A-N-O-V

Greta's poet!

'I'd like very much to know what happened to him,' she said – and the poet has been here all this time, staring at him! He looks back at the plaque. No more words, just the dates, 1898 to 1947. Another cog whirs in his brain: 1947 was when Greta and Hamza met him in Prague. He died that same year – at forty-nine – and presumably not of natural causes.

He waits till the morning staff meeting is over before he asks, 'Would anyone like to tell me something about Rahman Mirza Janov?'

Every one of them turns. It is like an orchestrated movement, and they all laugh.

'OK,' he says, 'someone tell me why there's a statue of him.'

'He was a great man,' Fahmeda says.

'In what way?'

They all look at each other. How to tell it?

Fahmeda says, 'He inspired others, because he knew what was good and bad, in the old ways and the new.'

'The old ways?'

'He grew up in the time before the Soviet Union. He was

311

a scholar in the old learning but he was a *jadid*, a man with a modern mind. He understood the traditionalists, he could persuade them to accept new things, like sending their girls to school.'

They are all wanting to say their piece. Akbor, usually the quietest among them, says, 'His poetry, it's amazing. He found a way to write about things people couldn't openly say.'

'And he got away with it?'

'He was in a special position,' Fahmeda says, 'Nearly all the early Bolsheviks were Russians, he was one of the few Tajiks.'

Akbor says, 'And he was clever, he said everything through metaphors.'

'Do people know how he died?'

A collective hesitation; then Nargis says, 'In the end they got everyone who thought for themselves.'

Akbor says quietly, 'And he knew it would happen.'

Fahmeda turns to him sharply. 'How do you know?'

'His poems,' Akbor says. He quotes a few lines in Farsi. Nargis nods in agreement. Akbor turns to include Lance: 'It says, *Do not wait for me when darkness lowers –*'

He stops. They are all staring at him. This has the ring of a real translation.

Fahmeda says sharply, 'Say the rest of it.'

He recites:

> *Do not wait for me when darkness lowers*
> *Do not try to follow where I have gone*
> *Do not put a candle in the window —*

But he stops again, too embarrassed to continue. No one moves, stunned by the strangeness of hearing their poet speak in English.

Fahmeda breaks the silence. 'Where did you find that?' Then in her curiosity she forgets about Lance and switches back into Farsi. They are all talking, the conversation running away with them. He stands silent, absorbing it all, and has the strangest feeling of other lives intertwining around his – Greta – the poet – Rahul who brought him here, and who like the poet was taken away young – Annabel, whose facility with language sent him out to find the poet. And all these people, unknown until so few weeks ago, who are now becoming his.

~ 41 ~

Sunday night, the house asleep. Tessa stands at the window and opens it to take in the night noises. An owl hoots. The downs are out there beyond the lights of the last houses of the village, a brooding hump in the moon's strange half-light. It is a place of many moods, subtly changing with the winds and the clouds, or the mist rising off the grass in the morning. Its earth-history is there in the wave-like swell of green that once covered an ancient seabed. This bit of earth, this is their present tense now, hers, Ben's, the children's.

She will remember this time around pictures of the children,

313

moments captured on the retina. Wet days in wellies and anoraks, splashing in the mud pools of the lane leading up to the downs – the white of snowdrops that hide under the still-bare beech trees, the yellow of the first shy primroses nestling against a mulch of leaves and moss. A day of unexpected blue skies when they play out on the green, Sam in the fireman's outfit they found in a jumble sale, Alisa with her pudgy legs trying to keep up with him. Ben swinging them.

But there are things the camera will never show. The unavoidable imbalance; the unspoken thoughts.

A large parcel has arrived from Vancouver. She had almost forgotten – Lance's sister has sent on her letters.

Ben asked, 'Who do you know in Vancouver?'

She told him. He made no comment. She took the parcel, unopened, down to the basement. She had asked for the letters, she wanted them, but she so wishes it could have happened without having to involve Ben.

That night he was in bed before her. She lay next to him, searching for words to say she was sorry for all she had landed him with. He had his back to her and lay so still, but she thought he was awake. She moved closer, curling herself around his back, her arm across him, and said quietly, not to wake him if he was actually asleep, 'Thank you, Ben.'

He did not stir.

He went to bed early the next evening too. His absence was oppressive. She pushed it away, almost resentful now. I cannot undo what has happened.

She told Greta. Greta is her constant resource. She listens,

314

and does not judge. In her absence of comment Tessa senses the beginnings of the possibility of accepting what cannot be changed.

Her mind shifts to work. Last week Lionel, the CEO, asked to see her. He had made no move to speak to her since the day she started work. Why now?

He sat behind a desk twice as large as he could possibly need. 'Now, about the global meeting,' he said.

Global meeting?

'Glen will have briefed you about it at your induction?'

Induction? Was there one? Lionel saw what she was thinking. Perhaps had been expecting it. With only a trace of acidity he explained that all Lifeline's country directors were being flown in for four days in July, to get together with head-office staff and sort out major policy issues. A working group was being set up to prepare for it, and he was inviting Tessa to represent her department.

'Me? But I've only just started.'

'That's why I'm asking you. We want to ensure we get the perspective of people new to Lifeline.'

This means one of two things, Tessa decided as she listened to him expand on all that he hoped would come of the meeting. One, Greta put him up to it. Or two, he wants to side-step Glen. Possibly both. And someone needs to tell him that Lifeline will never get coherent policy direction unless he and Glen find a way to talk to each other. But it is not going to be her. She has no desire to get caught in the crossfire.

'I'll need to think about it,' was what she said.

He looked surprised. He hadn't thought he was offering her an option.

A few days later with Greta, she said, 'Tell me what you said to Lionel.'

Greta looked innocent. 'About what?'

Tessa told her about Lionel summoning her. 'Did you put him up to it, Greta?'

'I don't know why you should think that. I'm sure Lionel's capable of having good ideas on his own. And it *is* a good idea.'

'But did you?'

'Tessa, I put some cake out on a plate in the kitchen. Do bring it through.'

Tessa was laughing now. 'I'm only just getting to understand my own job and this will drag me into a whole other load of issues.'

Greta was unabashed. 'I've always found, it's the busy people you should ask if you want something done. And it will give you a chance to see the whole picture.'

But then she shed the woman who likes to stir in a good cause, saying in quite a different voice, 'Don't let yourself feel pushed, my dear, by Lionel or Glen or anyone. It's for you to decide what you can handle. Only you know what you're dealing with, apart from work.' And Tessa suddenly felt weepy.

She waits till she is sure everyone is asleep, then starts down the stairs to the basement, past the china dogs and spare crockery, to the far corner where the package from Vancouver lies. Alone in the dim, underground light, she begins to open it. Let in the past, calming the fear of the feelings it will expose. Beneath the brown paper wrapping is a sturdy cardboard box, and in it is file upon file, every letter she ever wrote him from 1980 through to 1996 and its sudden full stop. At the bottom of the box her hands touch something different. She lifts it out, a sealed manila folder. She is sure she has never seen it, that it cannot be anything she sent him, but there is something uncannily familiar about it. Suddenly she realizes what it is: this folder is sealed with layers of parcel tape, just as she sealed his letters that she packed away in Maeve's loft, and it is labelled in precisely the same way, just with the dates. Sept 1985 to March 1986.

It is a code that needs no key. Those were his first months after Hugo had sent him off to work with Afghan refugees. After he had stopped writing. She picks at the tape, opens it to find pages and pages in his handwriting:

> Peshawar. So it is done. The day before I left Delhi Hugo and I walked in the Lodi Gardens and he talked about the loneliness of working in tense situations. People learn to protect themselves by blocking off feeling, he said. Take care not to let yourself go that way. You won't want to talk about what's happened but you must process it. Write, every day, whatever you are feeling, and do it first thing in the morning, when

you are near to the self that surfaces in sleep. So here I am, having just woken. I write knowing that no one will ever read what comes onto the page. When I am through all this, I will burn it.

But he hadn't.

I kept a private space, he told her in Kathmandu, just for us, and he filled it with his translations. But he didn't tell her about this other thing that filled the space. Now these pages that he never meant to be read are in her hands. She cradles them, these scratches on paper, signs of a life once painfully alive. What will she do with them? Finish the task for him and burn them? She cannot. Read them? To stride uncaring across that tender privacy, this one thing that he kept from her? That too she cannot.

Write every day . . . It is months since she wrote in her own notebook, writing – as he did – so she could speak to him when he was no longer there. The notebook lies silent in a place where no one else will discover it. Why do we keep these words on paper, she asks him, these feelings that we strive through pain to capture? What good will they do us?

She looks around her. She is in a basement in a village in England that Rahul will never see, just her in a small pool of light, surrounded by dusty boxes. The dim light encloses her, till gradually the confusion of being bereft sifts away and she feels his returning presence. She holds in her hands something that was once his, but now it is hers. He has left it to her. Perhaps by accident, perhaps knowingly, by lodging it with her letters.

She will keep it. Safe. And one day, perhaps, she will read it, when she is as old as Greta, and has learnt as much about living.

She puts it back in the box and one by one replaces the *Tessa* files on top of it, taking care to put them in the right order.

~ 42 ~

On the verandah looking out at the cherry trees Nargis sits with her father-in-law. 'Our new director has been asking about Rahman Mirzajanov.'

Her father-in-law looks up. 'Asking what?'

'Why there's a statue of him. Why people admire him.' She waits, but he says nothing. 'Maybe you could write out a poem for me to show him?'

'Write? What's the point? You said he doesn't know Tajik.'

'But he can read the old writing. He knows Urdu.'

Her father-in-law says nothing. She thinks she has lost him again. But that night before she goes to bed he hands her a poem written out in the old script.

When she gives it to Lance he is surprised on so many counts that he doesn't know which to attend to first.

'Your father-in-law wrote this?'

She nods, smiling. 'Can you read it?'

319

The words at the top he knows —

بسم الله الرحمن الرحيم

'Bismillah ir-Rahman ir-Rahim,' he reads out. In the name of Allah, the Merciful, the Beneficent – Arabic words said traditionally by a Muslim at the start of any serious undertaking.

The next line – starting from right to left –

رحمن مرزا جانو

He looks up. 'Rahman Mirza Janov! This is one of his poems?'

She is smiling now, pleased at his excitement. 'Go on, read it.'

'I wish I could, but knowing the script doesn't mean I can read Farsi. But – your father-in-law, how does *he* know it? I thought the Soviet authorities suppressed it?'

'They did, but he's old, nearly eighty, and things didn't happen the way the history books say. Officially we became part of the Soviet Union from 1922 but it took a lot longer than that for things for change. By the time the first schools were set up he was twelve, he could already read the Qur'an and was studying Farsi poetry. Then he went to the new school also, so he has both kinds of education.'

'He must have extraordinary memories.'

'He does, and things we never heard when we were growing up. People didn't talk to their children in case they said things at school.' She points to the poem. 'Ask Annabel, she can read it for you.'

Annabel, as he might have expected, knows a fair amount about Rahman Mirzajanov. She is amazed that Lance has only just focused on his importance in this town. 'You never even looked at the statue?'

He says, a touch defensively, 'I've had one or two other things to keep me busy.' Then, 'And you know some of his poetry?'

'Sure! In Iran they think he's great. They know him there as Afaqi. You know Farsi poets always take a poetic name? That's his, and *afaq* is fate, so it's like saying, I am the fated one, or maybe the voice of fate. My teacher called him the lost poet of Resham-serai.'

'Lost?'

'Because a lot of his poetry is lost, maybe the best of it. He wrote his poems in Farsi script so the officials couldn't read them and somehow got them out to Iran, but there may have been lots that never made it out. Just think, there may be files of them in police records in one of those dreary buildings in town.'

That meeting in Prague in 1947, a rare chance to travel outside the Soviet Union. Had he used that time to make contacts and try to get his poetry out? And then been caught?

Annabel has been reading the poem. She starts explaining it but she has to keep stopping to think of the right English word. Soon she gives up, frustrated. 'It's far too subtle to show up in a literal translation.'

He is disappointed. From what he has heard it does not seem like great poetry. She sees, and is immediately defensive for the poet. 'I can't do it justice. And this kind of poetry *has* to have metre and rhyme, that's part of the power.'

321

Next morning she hands him a written-out translation. 'I sat up half the night with this.'

He laughs. 'I'm honoured.'

'Nothing to do with you. It was the poem. It just drew me on.'

> I shall write on the white paper bark of the birch tree
> And send it to sail like a boat on the stream
> My thoughts will be blown like almond tree blossom
> And no one may catch them or know what they mean
> But the water flows on. The wind will still blow.

He becomes aware of Annabel, waiting for his reaction. He shakes his head, then says, 'Annabel, you constantly amaze me.'

She is as delighted as a child. 'There are things I couldn't capture. The words have connotations you can't get in English.'

'Maybe. But it works. I'm going to show this to Nargis.'

Nargis is clearly impressed. 'I wish my father-in-law knew English so he could see this. But I'll show Akbor.'

'Why Akbor?'

'He studied with my father-in-law. Didn't I tell you? Khaled's father is a professor of Central Asian literature. He knows more about Rahman Mirzajanov than anyone. It was with him that he studied as a boy.'

Lance stares. 'That's extraordinary.'

'Why? Mirzajanov was a scholar. Teaching was how he earned bread.'

'No, I meant, extraordinary because ... A friend asked me to find out about him. She met him once, years ago. And someone in your family actually knew him!'

'More than knew him. They were close, right until the time he disappeared. It was that traditional relationship, revered teacher, devoted student.'

'So maybe he knows – Annabel says people in Iran think there were poems that were never published.'

She nods. 'There were.'

'Did any of them survive?'

She hesitates, then decides against caution. 'They did. But few people know.'

'But *he* knows?'

She nods again.

This is like pulling teeth but he cannot stop now. 'I hardly dare to ask, where are they?'

Very quietly she says, 'He has them.'

It is hardly more than a year since she herself found out. She was helping her mother-in-law sort out the outhouse that ran down one side of the courtyard, a lot of it things from Khaled's boyhood. Nothing was said, but they were both heavy with sadness about what had happened to Khaled. They each suffered in their own way, wife and mother, but for the first time Nargis felt a loosening of the tension between them, in the knowledge they were together in this. Her mother-in-law must have felt it too, for she said, 'There's something I want to show you,' and she opened a wooden chest that had a pile of mangy old sheepskins. Nargis thought, those should be thrown out; but her mother-in-law's arm was shifting the pile and delving right to the bottom, to lift out a tin box. She opened it. Nothing but old receipts. Why do they keep these things? Nargis thought. But her mother-in-law's hand was lifting them out, and there at the bottom was something different. A collection of sheets of paper, each with something written on it in the old writing.

'His teacher's poems,' her mother-in-law said quietly.

Nargis stared. 'Mirzajanov's?'

Her mother-in-law nodded. 'He gave him a copy of each one as he wrote it, to keep hidden. Until things changed, he said.'

Nargis stretched out her hand, but could hardly bring herself to touch them. All those years, imagine if they had been found with these! He'd have been sent away for life; maybe worse. She looked up. 'Who knows they are here?'

'Him. Me. Now you.'

Not Khaled? But she knew the answer already. Khaled had never shared his father's interests, and even before things went wrong, he was always careless about what he said. They couldn't have trusted him.

'I hate this box,' her mother-in-law said, voice low but vehement. 'I hate what it has done to him. All those years I was sure it was going to bring trouble and I wanted him to get rid of it, but it made him furious if I even talked about it. And now, look how he is. He has had too much to bear, his judgement has gone. I tell him, Give them to someone who can use them. But it has become a kind of obsession with him.

He says, He gave them to me, *I* have to take care of them. There are unscrupulous people still, everywhere you look.' —

Lance is staring at Nargis. 'And he's kept them all these years.'

She nods. 'He is afraid. But it's wrong to keep it a secret. He should transcribe them otherwise they're as good as lost. And Rahul said –'

She stops, caught out in something she did not mean to say.

A moment's silence. Lance says, 'Rahul knew your father-in-law?'

She nods.

So Rahul went to their home, was let in past the privacy she guards so closely.

She says, as if defending herself against some accusation, 'I thought it would help my father-in-law to have the company of a younger man who wanted to learn what he knew. And he could read the old script, so I thought maybe he could persuade my father-in-law to get them transcribed, maybe even help him. It was beginning to happen. Then –'

Another full stop.

'It upset my father-in-law very much. Now he won't even talk about the poems.' She hesitates, emanating again an air of defensiveness; but against what charge? 'I have been feeling so bad that I could not invite you home, but my father-in-law, he is very depressed. Since he retired he is too much alone. And my husband, he is away, and we don't –'

A knock. Akbor appears. 'The people from the disability project have come.'

'Just keep them busy, we'll come through in a minute.'

He turns back, but Nargis has closed up already, preparing herself for the task ahead.

~ **43** ~

Hugo has been summoned back to Geneva to report on progress, or rather, lack of it, in the investigation into the cause of Rahul's death. Thirty years he has been with UNHCR but its head office has always felt alien. He feels little connection to what this city has become, a confusing plethora of UN agencies and all the satellite organizations that have grown up to lobby them. These buildings, the cumbersome bureaucracies they house, the arcane intergovernmental processes they manage, have always seemed remote from the problems he has engaged with. Too many policy papers that don't get translated into action, too much networking of people who never get their feet dirty in the dust of refugee camps. He comes back for a short stint every few years and gets away again as speedily as he can.

He comes now particularly reluctantly. The New York office that deals with security issues has recommended that they put the case on hold, keep it as a watching brief but not waste staff time on it. Hugo has responded explaining why he thinks this a bad plan. Everyone in the Tajikistan government would be happy to forget it, and if he doesn't keep up the pressure there will be no motivation for their security people to listen out for leads. He has little enough leverage as it is, for they exert themselves only when there is a possibility of a significant pay-off.

His old head of department in Geneva has left and his replacement is not someone Hugo would have chosen to report to. She is strong on procedures, short on substance, and seldom sees the point of things he considers important. He himself could have had her job for the asking when it was advertised, but he refused to apply. So now he is stuck with having to report to this woman.

'I need to know where all this is going,' she says, and her tone says, Isn't it becoming a bit of a personal obsession? But she is fifteen years younger than him and considerably less experienced, which compromises her power. He says, calmly he hopes, 'We have several lines of enquiry. None of them, as yet, conclusive.'

'You have to slow down. You're constantly on a plane.' She waves at him the report of the medical examination she has insisted that he have. 'It's all here, you can't ignore it. Your blood pressure's too high. Your cholesterol level is shocking. Not to mention the stress you constantly expose yourself to. You're a walking invitation for a stroke.'

'There's nothing wrong with me that doesn't affect people my age who stay glued to a desk. And my stress level would be a lot higher if I had to stay here. I'll think about slowing down when this job's done.'

'We could put someone else onto it.'

'No we can't. This one's mine.'

But she has the last word after all. Tapping his medical report with a determined red-varnished nail, she says, 'I'm afraid it's no more flights into Tajikistan for a month.'

He is livid and phones Lance to offload. To his irritation, Lance says, 'She's right. You need a proper break.'

'Listen. I'm nearing retiring age and before I quit, this is something I'm going to do. I am deeply uninterested in staying in an office in Geneva and shifting papers. Anyway, who are you to talk? What happened to your break?'

Lance can only laugh.

A personal obsession. Did she actually say that, or did he just read it into her tone? He knows himself that there is something not quite rational about his need to pursue this search, but he is hyper-sensitive to anyone else suggesting it. From the day that Rahul came to him in a state of crisis he has felt a protective concern for him, but he recognized even then that it was his own need driving it. He was lonely. His nomadic lifestyle did nothing to help; no sooner did he begin to feel close to someone than they moved off elsewhere. But he knew that he was partly responsible. He emanated a reserve that he did not intend, and few of his colleagues had tried to get beyond it.

His alone-ness tracked back to the time that his ex-wife Oriel had left. Seven years they had been together, long enough to produce two sons, long enough also to discover that their ideas of what mattered could not be reconciled. She could not cope with the hardships of life in the places he chose to work, and her dissatisfaction was like shackles rubbing his ankles. She was constantly on at him to take a desk job in Geneva, which he refused to consider. So she had taken the boys back with her to France. He had worked hard at making holidays happen, skiing in winter, walking or boating in summer, but all too soon the time came when they wanted to do those things with friends their own age. Now they were young adults, able to make their own decisions, but it was too late to make up for those lost years. He thought ruefully sometimes that each of them had taken one quality from the model he had unconsciously held up to them, and turned it inside out. The older, Philippe, was a workaholic, but he applied it as an investment banker, making ridiculous amounts of money gambling with other people's life savings. Jules was a traveller, but he wandered aimlessly, dipping into other people's lives without any attempt to contribute. They were affectionate enough when he saw them but that was far too seldom; and they never communicated in-between. Why would they? He hadn't been there for them when they needed him.

He was in that state – an acute awareness of the loss of his own sons – when Rahul turned to him, expecting him to react as a human being not just as a colleague.

Since his death, Hugo's thoughts have returned often to that time, and to the months after he had sent Rahul off to make a new life in Peshawar. For only a few months later he himself arrived there, to oversee UNHCR's work. Was there a connection? He was careful not to let Rahul think so, for no grown man wants to be watched. But when the offer to relocate came, he hadn't thought long about accepting.

Peshawar: a hustling, overgrown place it was, struggling to cope with a massive exodus of population from Afghanistan. He and Rahul drove out together along the road between the city and the Khyber Pass, where new villages were still mushrooming. The city's streets were crowded with vehicles of humanitarian organizations. They fulfilled essential functions, providing shelter, setting up water systems, running emergency health services, tracing lost children; but the overall effect was to make him feel part of an invading army.

He saw that Rahul had changed in some quite basic way. What had once seemed a boundless store of energy had mutated into something harder. He still worked relentlessly, but the élan was missing. He had always been sharp in his judgements but now they were often underpinned by cynicism. Working for a UN agency, he said, was intensely frustrating. The procedures were despair-making. It was a culture where you got points for ticking policy boxes rather than getting anything practical done. The UNICEF office was full of people who wrote reports and preferred to stay at their desks. 'I'm a misfit,' he said. 'They barely tolerate me.'

From his international colleagues Hugo heard things that chimed with that. 'Definitely not a team player,' one of them said – in confidence, of course – over a whisky by the pool of the Holiday Inn, the focal point of their social lives. 'Has to do his own thing.' His own thing, as far as Hugo could see, was what they should all have been doing; he spent his days out in the refugee villages with the Afghan staff. But there was no denying that he was abrasive. Yes, Rahul said, he was perfectly aware that by refusing to spend time with useless colleagues he was developing a reputation for arrogance, but he really couldn't care. With a couple of honourable exceptions they were time-servers, lazy, there only for the high salary and hardship allowance that they got from working in a supposedly insecure place.

Then UNICEF began trying to move its staff into Afghanistan. Most of them resisted as long as they could; any excuse, any delay. Rahul was the opposite. At the first chance he moved to the far north of the country and reappeared in Peshawar only to take the compulsory R&R breaks. Rest and recuperation, for those working in high-tension situations. 'To stop us cracking up under the strain,' he said, voice heavy with irony as he surveyed the expatriates lounging around the hotel, sheltered from the noise and pressure and poverty just outside.

Hugo said, mildly, 'You're behaving like the classic independent traveller, complaining that there are too many tourists.'

Rahul said, 'It's not who they are that gets me, it's how they behave.'

Since their retreat to the hills he had only once referred to the crisis that had got him here, a passing reference, with the self-deprecating smile of a man who knew himself a great deal better now.

And then he had been invited to run a workshop in Kathmandu, and everything changed.

He told Hugo immediately what had happened. His joy was obvious but Hugo was unable to share it. He was, frankly, dismayed. It seemed madness to try to resurrect the relationship now that the woman was married.

'For Christ's sake,' he said, surprised at his own bluntness, 'you have, with considerable pain, pulled yourself out of a deep hole. Why risk falling back into it?'

Rahul said, 'There are just some things you can't say No to,' and he quoted a verse:

> As easy might I from myself depart
> As from my soul which in thy breast doth lie

'Shakespeare,' he said. 'A sonnet. That man knew something.'

'Shakespeare or not,' Hugo said with some asperity, 'it's simplistic.'

He knew there was no point pushing it. But what exactly was Rahul saying 'Yes' to? And how much destruction were they going to cause as they followed that urgent call?

What has become of the unknown Tessa? Where is she? What is she doing? If she has been as careful as Rahul was to keep their relationship private, there may have been no one that she could turn to. It's none of my business, he has told himself each time his thoughts have returned to this. But then he thinks of the poem that Rahul translated on his last visit home – *If you should need a partner in grief* – Perhaps he, Hugo, is the only person who knows who Rahul was thinking of when he translated that. He cannot shake off the feeling that he is neglecting something that he owes to Rahul.

He will have to try to find her. What he will do or say once he has done so, he has no idea.

He calls Lance. 'I'm trying to track down one of Rahul's friends, Tessa Maguire. Maybe you know where she is?'

There is a moment's silence before Lance says, 'She's with Lifeline, in Brighton.'

'I had no idea there was any connection.'

'It's only just happened.' Lance had thought he had got past feeling excluded, but if Hugo knew, that changed things again. 'How long have you known about her?'

'A while.' He can hear that Lance minds. 'Don't let it bother you, Lance. It was an accident that I knew. And the only reason was that I wasn't part of his circle of friends in Delhi.'

'I don't get it.'

'He had got into a mindset that he had to keep it private. I think he couldn't handle his mother knowing.'

'His mother? He was a grown man, for God's sake, not an adolescent.'

'He was the only son in an Indian family. You know what that means. The mothers never let go.'

'This doesn't make sense. Rahul lived his life the way he chose. And you've met his parents, surely you saw what they're like? There isn't a less controlling family.'

'It wasn't about control, it was about him not wanting to be burdened with her emotional pressure. His mother wanted to see him settling down with someone from her own world, who would fit in. Keep him there. He knew it was never going to happen her way so his defence was to keep all of that part of his life private.'

As Lance puts the phone down his mind is searching, and the memories come back. How Sushila reacted when Rahul ended his relationship with that young Indian woman he had been with. Devaki would have been the kind of daughter-in-law his mother was looking for, but that would have been a disaster. And years later, when he and Rahul were at his parents' house before setting off for the hills, Sushila said to Lance, 'You're the only person who can make him take breaks. Maybe I should get you to persuade him to look for a wife.' Rahul's eyes were issuing a warning and Lance had tried to joke past it. 'I know my limits.' But she was not to be deflected. 'And what about you?' she asked Lance. 'Don't you wait too long. A man needs to marry.'

Rahul said, tired, 'OK, *Ammi jaan*, you've made your point.'

Still Hugo puts off making contact. They have no business to discuss, nothing to shield against the uncomfortably personal undertones. She will know who he is, he is sure, but he has no idea what, if anything, she thinks about his role in Rahul's life. Perhaps she blames him for having led Rahul on the path that ended in his death? For his part, he knows too much about her but also too little. He has no image of what she might look like, how her voice might sound, let alone her as a person. She has lived in his mind only as the woman who complicated his friend's life.

But loss has brought humility. He has not handled his own personal life well. So, strangely, thinking about Tessa leads him to think about Oriel. No separation is absolute when you share children you both love. Even at the height of tensions they had to keep speaking, to make arrangements about the boys, and gradually the mutual resentment has faded and it has become possible to get back to something akin to cautious friendship. But there is still an unstated issue about how often they speak; too often, and she gets edgy. Is he trying to monitor what she is doing? Not often enough, and she thinks he no longer cares. He is no good at guessing his way through that so he has long ago taken refuge in routine. It is in his diary, once a month.

It is a week till their next call, but things can happen. Rahul's sudden death has taught him that. Without knowing quite why, he feels suddenly moved to speak to her.

She says, 'Have you lost your diary?'

They talk, as they always do, about their sons. When the call is over he goes for a long walk. When he comes back he finds he can do what his nagging conscience has been telling him to.

The voice on the phone in Tessa's office says, 'This is Hugo Laval, calling from Geneva. You'll have heard my name, I think?'

Silence. Then, cautiously, 'This is a surprise.'

'I thought it was time we got to know each other. I'm coming to London for a meeting next week. Could I come and see you?'

She has no chance to consider whether she wants this or

335

not. It is there, in front of her, but instinctively she tries to keep him at a distance. He is not coming here. If this has to happen, she will meet him on neutral ground.

'I can come up to London. Where will you be?'

'No need, I'll be coming to Brighton anyway, there are people there I'd like to see. I could come to you, meet your family. Sometime at the weekend?'

'Actually we're not in Brighton, we're in a village outside.'

'Sounds lovely. Perhaps we could go for a walk on the downs.'

When she puts the phone down she sits looking blankly at the postcards above her desk. He has made it clear he knows she has a family. She was trying to say, 'Don't come and complicate my life,' but he won. What does he want? Whatever it is, she is not ready.

~ 44 ~

'I've booked my flight home,' Annabel says.

They are in the middle of breakfast. Lance is shocked at the stab of pain it gives him. He has to stop himself from saying, 'Surely not yet?' She has to go sometime, and when is it ever going to feel the right time?

'When?'

'Monday.'

In three days! He tries to gather himself to respond. 'It's going to seem very quiet without you.'

'And it's going to feel pretty strange being back home. I've loved being here.'

'To think, when you arrived, I felt slightly invaded.'

'I know.' Her eyes are laughing at him, her beautiful, beautiful eyes. 'If I'd had any sensitivity at all I'd have moved on. But I've been enjoying myself too much.'

'Cancel your flight,' he says, made bold by those eyes.

'I can't. I promised Viv. She's got an exhibition coming up; she needs me there.'

Of course. She is going back to her own life. He feels more bereft than he can cope with, and painfully inhibited. All he can say is, 'You have unusual talents. I hope you find some way to use them that satisfies you.'

'I know what I'd like to do, more translating. Just think, all this poetry that people here know and no one in the West has even heard of it. I never thought I could do it, until –'

'You *can*. Stay, do it!' And then a blindingly obvious thought hits him.

'You OK?' she asks.

'I'm OK, just unbelievably thick.'

Rahul's notes, sitting in a bag under his bed, notes that he can't read because they are in Farsi. For weeks he has had someone right here in his apartment he could have asked to translate them for him, and now she is leaving in three days' time.

For the first time since arriving in Resham-serai he phones the office to say he is going to be late. He gets out the papers, but before Annabel can make sense of the task he has to tell her the whole story. She listens so appreciatively that it becomes a much deeper conversation than he was expecting. He finds the words to express, to himself as much as to her, the impact Rahul's death had on him; but saying it out loud he realizes he is using the past tense. He has moved on, the loss has become vaguer; and it is Annabel's presence that has done it, by giving him the illusion of a shared life.

'If a candidate presents herself,' Greta said, 'don't go into a dither.' I'm not going into a dither, Greta, you can see for yourself it's out of the question. She's young enough to be my daughter, how could she possibly consider it? But he sure is going to miss her, miss coming back to find her rustling up something in the kitchen, telling him about her day, pressing him for stories. Miss watching her beautiful, youthful ease as she moves, her eyes that are sharp beyond her years, her – Stop it, you old fool.

Annabel's mind is focused entirely on sifting through Rahul's notes. 'There are two sets, quite different. This Tashkent lot seems to be notes to himself, things people have told him, but in a kind of personal shorthand, tricky to decipher. The Resham-serai papers look like a continuous text, maybe a story written in instalments.' She looks up. 'Which do you want me to start with?'

'The Tashkent ones.' Tashkent was Rahul's base for his Lifeline work. These might be notes he made when he was back from his travels. If they are going to get any clues, it will be there.

338

He leaves her to it, and goes into work.

She is still at it when he gets back that evening. The notes are frustratingly cryptic, she says, but that speaks of their significance. There are place names, dates; no names but some initials keep cropping up ... Namangan, 21 July, B had unexpected visit at night, got message to R in time ... Andijan 27 July, B & others taken at Friday event ... U has tried to get official information, none forthcoming ... M has left for Tajikistan, families being harassed for details but they don't have any.

The recurring place names are the Ferghana valley towns, the economic heartland of Central Asia – in Uzbekistan but close to the porous borders of both Tajikistan and Kyrgyzstan. Since the Soviet collapse it has been hard-hit by economic decline and Rahul would very likely have tried to stimulate community initiatives there. But there is nothing in these cryptic notes that suggests they are about Lifeline's work. As he moved around he must have been doing something else, something he couldn't write about openly.

It can mean only one thing: he had gone back to where he started adult life, as a human rights reporter. But to do it in Uzbekistan is another matter altogether. Dissidents there are still as ruthlessly hounded as they ever were in Soviet times. Those who publicly criticize are subject to constant, violent pressure. Torture of suspects is commonplace. Several have disappeared. No one can say these things in Uzbekistan yet Lance knows, because it has been reported outside. Because, despite the risks, there are people secretly sending reports out. People like Rahul.

His thoughts move back to the driver who met him at Tashkent airport, Ulughbek. Is he perhaps U? 'But it could also be O or V,' Annabel says, 'they all use the same letter in the Persian script.' It's U, he would bet on it. Ulughbek would have driven Rahul on those journeys to the Ferghana valley towns, he would know who he was meeting. He remembers the note Ulughbek put into his hands on parting. He got Nargis to translate it for him and send a reply. 'Any friend of Rahul Khan is my friend,' it said. 'I hope we will meet again.' Now his desire to keep contact suddenly assumes a possible new significance.

Annabel says, 'I can't see how any of this would link with what actually happened to him.'

'Perhaps it doesn't. But maybe it explains something else.'

He tells her about the poem that Rahul translated on his last visit home; about Glen saying, 'I have wondered if he had some idea that he might not have much time.' Now these notes. At the very least he must have known he was living in a way that exposed him to risks, not from one direction, but from several.

'And does that help, knowing that?' Annabel's voice is – He doesn't know the right word; caring, he supposes, and it makes his heart lurch.

'Yes, I suppose it does.'

He looks helplessly at the pile of papers still untranslated.

'Lance, I want to finish this for you but there's no way I'm going to get through it before I leave. Let me take them back with me.'

He wrestles only for a moment with the instinct that made him hold on to that bag on all the stages of the flight. 'Take them,' he says. 'Sitting here they are useless.'

Sunday – the last day before her flight: afterwards he will remember it, every detail imprinted in sunlit pictures. He booked an office car and they drove out towards the foothills to a point where people had told him they could go clambering up the side of a stream. They had brought a picnic and sat to eat on some huge boulders, looking down the valley and out over the flat plain beyond. I will remember this, he thought, I will feel the clarity of the air, see the wild almond trees, the water sparkling over brown stones. He told her about the boulders in Sukhunobod and they looked for marks on these, but found none. Still, the solidity of the rocks spoke to him. We exist, they said, Annabel and I, together for this moment.

She asked, 'Did you ever go through a time when you didn't know what you were doing with your life?'

He laughed. She had no way of knowing how recently he had been trapped in that state. But he decided to answer only in the long-ago past. 'Years of it.'

'You're kidding.'

'I am not. I escaped from home in a grand gesture, telling them all I was going to do something better than stick around in a small town where nothing ever happened, and then I landed up with a lot of long-haired dropouts wearing beads, and we none of us had the faintest idea what to do next.'

She was entertained. 'Go on. What did you do?'

'What did we do? We sang songs about peace. We made love rather promiscuously. Got stoned occasionally, though in my case not as often as I allowed my parents to believe. And we took political stands. Demonstrations, sit-ins. I can hardly remember what we were demanding, but it felt pretty radical at the time.'

She was wiling it all out of him, the story of the Vietnam War draft-dodgers and how he helped get Glen out of the US to safety in Canada. Annabel was wide-eyed and he realized he was in danger of appearing in a heroic light. 'I was just the driver, it's Glen who has the crossing-borders mentality. He only has to see an obstacle to feel challenged. But it changed my life. He joined our collective house and woke us all up, got us reading political theory and arguing about how to change the world. Not, of course, that we found any answers.'

'And then?'

'Well, that was 1974, and then Ethiopia happened, the famine, and we went and volunteered.'

'The famine?'

He saw from her face that she had never heard of it, that seminal event in his life that had shaped his whole future. 'Of course, you wouldn't know, it was before you were born.'

She looked mildly indignant. 'In 1974? I was five.'

He calculated, in disbelief. 'You're twenty-eight?'

'I know, don't tell me, I look eighteen.'

'Good God.' And here he had been comparing her with his nephew Euan who was still in his teens.

She was watching his face, amused. 'So you can stop thinking I'm a kid that needs looking after.'

He was startled. 'Have I been?'

She passed the question back. 'Haven't you been?'

'I deny it. You're manifestly capable of looking after yourself.' But he was unnerved.

She held his eyes a moment longer, then said, 'You know what I was telling you about my dad? It's had its uses. I can tell easy charm a mile off, and the opposite works too. I can't tell you how, but I knew from the moment I saw you in that airport that you were someone whose goodness I could rely on.'

It was so sudden he felt as if he had been winded.

'And even with a sprained ankle,' she said, apparently unaware of the effect her words had made, 'there's no way I would have landed myself on you otherwise.'

'I'm glad you did.'

'Me too. But I can tell you, if you'd made one move to encroach, I'd have been out.'

He saw again that look in her eyes at the airport, turned on each of the men in turn. He said quietly, 'You've had some difficult experiences, I'd guess.'

She turned to look at him squarely. 'What makes you say that?'

'Just a look I've caught sometimes, as if you've stumbled too near something you don't like to remember.'

She looked away, out over the plain below.

343

He prompted. 'While travelling? Iran?'

'That had its moments. Once quite scary, when I got stuck in a town and hadn't fixed up a place to sleep by the time it got dark. But mostly it was just tedious pestering, men on the streets not knowing how to make sense of a woman travelling alone.' She paused. 'But no, the big one was on home ground. Culture no excuse.'

She was silent again. He said, 'If it's difficult to talk about, skip it.'

'No, I'd like to now we've started. It was a stupid teenage party where things got out of hand, and everyone was so intent on demonstrating how cool they were that no one tried to stop things before it was too late. It was in this girl's house, her parents had gone out for the night, left us to it. Liberal parents. Someone should have told them long ago they were doing no one any favours. The deal was, only beer and wine, no spirits, no drugs, but the word got round, and a bunch of tossers turned up with vodka and brandy. Stole it, probably, from their parents. There was all this swaggering and proving who could mix their drinks and stay upright, and girls being taken off to rooms upstairs, and too pissed themselves to know when to say no. And then –' She stopped. When she started again, her voice was unnaturally detached, as if she was describing something very distant. 'There was this ghastly guy, the kind who thinks he's God's gift to women and you just know he measures the length of his cock. He started draping himself over me, he had his hands on my boobs and breathing his foul breath over me, and I was telling him as straight as I knew to get lost, and the next moment he was flat on the floor.' She stopped again. 'He fell, like a tree. Because I pushed him. He was out. Like dead. And everyone just standing around, too pissed to know how to react. The next thing I remember, I was fighting to get to the phone to call an ambulance, and people were trying to stop me in case the police came, and I saw people were leaving – those arseholes who'd brought the vodka, they were gone by the time the ambulance came. Someone else called his parents.' She stopped again, then said quietly, 'He didn't die, but for days it looked he might.'

'And you?'

'Me? I thought I'd killed him. I hated him, couldn't bear to have him near me, but I didn't want him dead, I didn't want the burden of it. It was weeks before my brain eventually took over and I knew it wasn't me, it wasn't the push, it was what he'd done to himself with all that alcohol. And since then –' She shrugged. 'I won't go near a party where getting pissed is the way to have fun.'

She looked up, smiled in self-deprecation. 'It's ridiculous, he didn't actually *do* anything to me, but I felt dirty for months afterwards, and I hate instantly any man who's looking at my boobs and looks like he might want to touch them. You asked about travelling alone. I have a strategy. I check out what's going on, till I spot a man who I can trust not to look at me that way, and I stick around in his vicinity. Then I feel I can cope.'

'Like Baggy Trousers?'

'Actually, I meant like you.' Again she went on talking, as if she had said nothing special. 'And what set me off travelling

345

again was I'd just extricated myself from a messy relationship and I had to get away.'

'What way, messy?'

She lifted her shoulders, a gesture that said, *How to explain?* 'Most of the men I've known wanted to move to sex so quickly. I see it coming and I know it's got nothing to do with me as me. If I like the guy I can't help hoping there's something more but nearly always I'm left feeling lonely. I taught myself to handle it like they did, like sex is just something you do, nothing to do with emotional commitment. When I realized that was happening I began to see my father in myself, and I thought, I have to get out of this. And the only way seemed to cut loose and go.'

He was moved; by her honesty, her vulnerability. She turned to face him. 'It's been great being here. I haven't relaxed like this for ages. Just having you let me be part of your world and not expecting anything in return. It's restored my faith that people can be like this with each other.'

And what could he say in the face of that simple trust? That you've got me totally wrong, I have desired you from the moment I first set eyes on you. And only now that I know you are not the naive twenty-year-old I once thought you were, am I letting myself fully face up to it.

They cooked together that night. Annabel had the plan, he was sous-chef, chopping vegetables. She was quieter than usual. He said, 'You're tired?'

'I guess so.'

346

'Me too. I'm shocked that one day's walking has taken it out of me like this.' But he knew it was more than physical tiredness, he was fighting sadness, and having to resist the urge to express something at least of what he was feeling. In the end all he said was, 'It's going to be hard to get used to living alone again. I've never been good at change. It always seems safer when things stay the same.'

'You haven't exactly lived your life looking for safety.'

'Of a certain kind. But maybe you never find it.'

'You will, I'm sure.'

But she had her back to him as she said it, busy over the cooker, and he couldn't be sure what it meant.

Monday morning. Annabel stood ready to leave, loaded like a Sherpa with her backpack, Rahul's papers safe inside it. The night's sleep had revived her. She was looking bright and ready to engage with the world again. Lance had booked a driver to take her to the airport. They heard him hoot his arrival.

At the top of the stairs she said, 'Don't bother to come down.'

'Of course I'm coming down.'

But she wanted to do the goodbye where the driver wasn't watching. 'It's been fantastic. I can't tell you. You're a star.'

He laughed it off as he responded to her hug, holding her just a fraction longer than he thought permissible, but so much shorter than he wanted. He said lightly, 'Who else is ever going to call me a star?'

With a fling of her beautiful hair she started off down the

concrete stairwell, with him following. But before she got to the bottom she tripped and crumpled under the weight of her backpack, and he rushed to pick her up, this woman he desired but could not tell, and he carried her out to the waiting car, and they drove to the hospital, where, many hours later, they told her what was already obvious from her level of pain: that she had broken her ankle. They put it in a plaster cast that was, like the Soviet version of everything, massive, and he supported her as she hobbled out on crutches, and he and the driver together got her back up those stairs and into his apartment, and he settled her in his own bed because there was no question of her being on the sofa with that cast. Then he took his things out of the room to camp on the living-room floor, until she would be able to walk again, back onto the next plane.

Beating against the wind

He is with her again as she sleeps. It has not happened for a long time. He has been waiting, it seems, till she has journeyed far enough on her own that they can be properly alone again.

They are walking together along a path that runs along the side of an open field, green like the tops of the downs. The cow parsley is out, lining the verges with white blossom, the earth fresh-smelling from recent rain. A flock of starlings lands to graze, their black oil-slick-speckled bodies dotting about against the green. Then something startles them, and suddenly they rise from the earth just a few yards away. First one bird, then a few more, and more, more, till the air is filled with small wings beating against the wind, beating, rising, until they are simply black specks against the sky with little sharp calls to stay connected as they fly.

She turns, to see Rahul turning to her at the same moment, and she knows that they both understand. The flock moves, without it we cannot survive; but each of us has to make that decision to rise and beat against the wind to keep up, summoning our own energy.

Then, and now.

She explains to Ben who Hugo Laval is and that he will be coming to see them on Sunday. Sam's four-year-old antennae are alert.

'Who's coming? Do I know him?'

'No, poppet. Nor do I yet.'

'So why is he coming?'

What to say? 'We both had the same friend, so we thought it would be nice to get to know each other.'

'Is the friend coming too?'

Tessa looks over to Ben. Ben says, 'No, he's not alive any more.'

'Why not?'

'There was an accident and he died.'

'What kind of an accident?'

'He was in a car, it hit a landmine.'

'What's a landmine?' 'Why do people put them there?' 'Why was there a war?'

Tessa listens, grateful, as Ben handles it all. How do you balance not pretending there are no hard things in life, yet not creating fears they are too young to deal with?

Ben says, 'Let's think about where we should take him for the walk.' He gets out the map and is down on the floor with them, explaining contour lines.

Thank you, Ben, Tessa says silently, as she clears away the meal.

'What is it you're afraid of?' Greta asks.

'I don't know. I'm just so unused to anyone knowing about us.'

'And what does he know?'

'I don't know. But whatever it is, I don't want him saying anything in front of Ben.'

'My dear, the man is hardly likely to be so stupid. If you don't trust his sense, trust Rahul's. He will not have talked of you to Hugo in any way that could cause you problems.'

'It's not that. It's the whole situation.'

'Life can throw nothing more complicated at you than it already has, and you have managed, you and Ben and Rahul between you. It's no one else's business how you did that.'

Hugo watches the fields of Sussex slip past the window of the train. There has been rain but the sun is out again and everything glistens, the trees budding in lightest green, with wild flowers shy on the grassy banks. At the station he gets a taxi to the village. He has no idea what Tessa and Ben might be feeling about this, but he has learnt over the years to try not to speculate about things he cannot influence. Once a process has been set in motion, you go with it, steering as best you can.

In fact it is the children who steer in the first stages. Sam checks out if Hugo knows how to play snap. He does, and so they do. Alisa sits firmly on Ben's lap, staring at him. Eventually she announces solemnly, 'You've got hair on your chin.'

He says, 'It saves me from having to shave. It's a very boring thing, having to shave every day.'

'My daddy shaves.'

'He's probably much better than I am at doing things he has to do.'

They set off along the lane by the church and up onto the downs. Hugo stoops to pick up a chunk of flint and says to the children, 'There are some beautiful stones here. Do you collect them?'

'I don't need to,' Sam says, 'there are tons of those here. My dad knows all about them. He's a geologist.'

Hugo turns to Ben. 'That is something I've always wished I knew more about,' and he gets Ben explaining about the probable dates at which the fossils in the chalk were laid down.

Tessa, a few feet away, is keeping the children occupied. Their young voices blend with the sound of skylarks spiralling and seagulls mewing. Ben has moved on from fossils to the scarcely tapped mineral resources of South-East Asia, and from there to what he was doing in Laos, and what made them leave. She is scarcely able to credit what she is hearing. Ben has *never* talked about their troubles in Laos, in all their time here. No one in the village would even have known where it is. But Hugo has been there and he seems effortlessly to be drawing Ben out. Now Hugo is saying that he heard similar stories from Burmese refugees in Thailand, about an oil pipeline being laid in remote areas and the company's horrific treatment of villagers. Ben says, 'It could be the same company. Someone's got to track those bastards, expose what they're doing.' And now he is saying things that he has not even told Tessa, how he felt he had failed people there.

'I had it so easy, just being thrown out. I keep thinking of the students who came to see me, they're still there, trying to find a way to tell the world. Or maybe they've been shut away by now.'

'It's not too late,' Hugo says. 'You could still tell what you know.'

'Who to? Anyway, they threw us out before I could get proper evidence.'

'But others could, if you share what you know.'

Sam is plaguing Ben to stop talking and watch him do handstands. Tessa takes Alisa's hand and says to Sam, 'Race you to the bottom of the downs.'

They are back and tea is ready before Ben and Hugo arrive, Ben still talking.

Time to go. Ben has taken the children upstairs to get bathed and ready for bed. Tessa stands outside with Hugo, waiting for the taxi he has ordered to take him to the station. There has been no chance to talk about Rahul. Is she relieved or disappointed? She doesn't know. What happened instead has been so much more useful.

She says, 'You were very good for Ben.'

He says emphatically, 'He should tell his story.' He gives her his card. 'I'll phone tomorrow, Tessa, to make another time, just you and me.'

'I'll be glad to. When you phoned, I thought that's what you ... But then I was confused, because you wanted to come here.'

'I didn't mean to be mysterious. I just felt I should get to know you and your family a little before we got talking.' The taxi has arrived. He gets in and winds down the window.

'Thank you, Hugo, for making the effort to come all this way.'

He shrugs. 'The only thing we can do is be there for one another.'

~ 46 ~

Lance watches Annabel move awkwardly around his apartment on her crutches, a brightly coloured bird trapped in a small cage.

She has phoned home to tell her family about her ankle, her missed flight. There was a long discussion about the things her sister should be doing to publicize her coming exhibition. Then a silence while Annabel listened, which ended with, 'Just forget about him, you've just got to stop letting it bug you.'

She put the phone down, visibly distressed.

'Boyfriend trouble?' Lance asked.

'No, father trouble.' But she didn't want to talk about it. 'At least this stupid ankle means I'll be able to get on with the translations.'

But she was still on painkillers and clearly not in a position to tackle anything requiring concentration. He didn't have much difficulty distracting her into reading a novel instead.

The office, luckily, is only a short walk away and he comes back in the middle of the next day to check she is OK. As he brings the lunch through she says, 'I hate having to be waited on.'

'You're on a rest cure. Just relax.'

'I wish there was something I could do to help.'

'OK then, teach me some Farsi,' he says, and she says instantly, 'Done!'

That evening she starts him off as if he were a total beginner, unimpressed by the fact that he knows something of the grammar. 'What use is that if you can't ask the time of day?' She makes him repeat basic questions and answers until they begin to come easily. She quizzes him on what he has done in his day, then gives him the words to tell her in simple Farsi. By the next day he is scribbling down phrases he has heard and brings them back to her. None of the others are much good at explaining.

'You're a great learner,' Annabel says.

'Thank you,' he says, in mock humility, 'I didn't expect such praise.'

Her eyes laugh back. 'And I didn't expect someone your age to learn so quickly.'

Now, is that teasing? Possibly not.

The inflammation recedes, the ankle becomes less painful. She is hobbling around the apartment more, and gets started again translating Rahul's notes. Lance no longer tries to dissuade her; it is at least a way of keeping her mind occupied while she is so immobile. He curses the absence of a lift. Three flights of stairs is just too much to navigate with that heavy plaster, even with him helping her. 'We'll get you down at the weekend,' he says. 'I'll book the car again and take you for a drive.'

But when he is on his way back at lunchtime her crutches are lying at the base of the stairwell and Annabel is bumping down on her bottom after them. He leaps up the stairs two at a time to reach her. 'For Christ's sake, what are you up to?'

'I have to get moving. It's weeks till this plaster comes off, I can't stay up there all that time.'

'And how do you imagine you're going to get up again?'

'Hop, if necessary.' She has reached the ground floor, with him helplessly following. 'But I thought if I got down on my own, someone might be able to help me up again. Just be an angel and hand me my crutches.'

'Where are you going?'

'To say hello to Sultan and Taimur.'

The drivers. But they are her friends now.

'Don't worry, it's their lunch-break, I won't be distracting them from work.'

He and Nargis have a visit planned to the refugee settlements beyond Sukhunobod and will be away overnight. He lays in food and asks Zohra, the young woman in the office, to pop in at lunchtime and at the end of each day to check Annabel is OK. 'And do me a favour,' he says to Annabel, 'don't do anything crazy like trying to navigate those stairs alone.'

'Stop worrying, I'll be absolutely fine.'

They are back in Resham-serai mid-afternoon. He walks into the office to find her sitting with Akbor unpacking a box of equipment, chatting away in Farsi, their faces lit with laughter. The entire office seems to focus around her, all of them sharing in the joke. Lance gives a short answer to their greetings, goes straight into his office saying he needs to phone Glen, and leaves Nargis to tell the others about their trip. He does phone Glen, but it could easily have waited. He just needed that closed door to hide what he was feeling.

And what is he feeling? Trying to adjust his fond picture of Annabel stuck in his apartment, waiting for him to return to cheer life up; and facing up to a number of stark facts. One: that she got on, as she assured him she would, perfectly well without him. Two: that a young woman as attractive as she is will never be short of people to cheer her up. Three: that she will naturally gravitate to someone her own age like Akbor. That, in short, he has stupidly allowed himself to be beguiled into fantasies of the impossible.

That evening she accepts without comment his explanation that he is tired from the journey and not in the mood to talk. 'The situation in the refugee camps is quite stressful,' he says, and then despite himself starts telling her about it.

Around mid-morning next day her arrival is announced by the sound of crutches on the gravel outside the door. The drivers, he discovers, have added her to their list of duties. Whoever isn't out driving helps her down the stairs. Akbor seems to have a string of practical tasks he can delegate and has assumed the role of crutch-carrier when she has to make her way back up the stairs to the apartment. In the short time Lance has been away her presence in the office has acquired an air of comfortable routine.

He feels an unaccustomed inability to grapple with what should have been a simple situation. He does not want her moving in to become part of the office, yet without revealing his feelings he can hardly start telling her now that she should take herself off elsewhere. He has for weeks shoved to the back of his mind any concern about what the others might be thinking about the whole set-up, and they have had the sense to leave his private life to him. But it is not going to help to have Annabel stepping so casually across that personal/work border.

Annabel's attention is on other things, other people, but for him every moment they are in the same place has become charged. In the evenings he is constantly aware of her closeness, her body movements, her expressions. In the office he is on his guard against showing in front of others what he feels must surely be obvious. Ever since they sat on the boulders on the side of the mountain and she said, 'Men want to move to sex so quickly' he has been almost painfully aware of his own desire.

But he has had a warning call.

~ 47 ~

Hugo's base when in London is the home of an old friend, Karin. She is out at work so he and Tessa will have the place to themselves. Lunch, he suggested, 'and it'll be simple', but he has got in a good French cheese, has walked to a baker which Karin says does the best bread, and is going to some trouble over the salad. He surveys the results with quiet satisfaction.

When she arrives he takes her through to the doors that open out onto a patio and a surprisingly large garden, a secret oasis in the city. She stands framed in the doorway, caught by surprise. 'This is beautiful.'

He nods. 'Karin is an artist with her garden.'

They sit to eat. He asks about her work, how she got into it, what she thinks she might achieve in it; simple questions, obvious ones even, but after a few minutes she says, 'In all the time I've been in that office there's never been one conversation like this.'

He feels, ridiculously and to his own surprise, momentarily happy.

They have come to a pause. A moment of awkwardness. He smiles and says, 'We have so much to talk about but it's hard to begin. There's a park nearby. Shall we walk?'

It is a soft day, a light wind with scudding clouds that hide the sun for a few minutes then move on, letting it shine through again. The horse chestnut trees are already in full leaf, their white candle-blossoms celebrating. They find a bench looking out over a pond and sit watching children throw bread to the ducks. It is unexpectedly touching, speaking the continuity of life.

'Lance told me about what you have undertaken,' she says, 'trying to find out what happened to Rahul.'

'Yes.'

'Have you got anywhere?'

'Not with any certainty. But I've not been able to be in Tajikistan for the past few weeks. Maybe my colleagues there will have discovered more.' He pauses before saying, 'It was my decision to send him up there. I don't know if you knew that.'

She shakes her head.

'It is difficult not to feel responsible.'

She turns, surprised. 'No, Hugo. You did what you had to do. As he did.' Then, 'So that's why you feel obliged to – ?'

'It's more than that. I felt the breath of his life, the thing that gave it value. I cannot just say, he is gone, and get on with other things.' He turns to ask, 'You have an Irish name; did you grow up a Catholic?'

'My mother would say so, but no. My father was a much stronger influence, and to him the Church was something oppressive, dragging people down with sin and guilt.'

'I came to that point myself but I still understand the appeal of ritual. In a world with no God we have to find our own way to mark the passing of a life. This seems to be mine.'

'And if you do find who was responsible? What then?'

'That will be in the hands of others. In a way I don't care.

What matters is that the crime be known for what it is.'

He feels released to talk more easily. He talks about the difficult times he and Rahul lived through together, how being in such situations creates an unusually strong bond. There were so many damaged people, people who had done terrible things, people who had seen those things happen and did not try to stop them because they were afraid. 'We didn't see the worst of it,' he says, 'but the aftermath was terrible enough. Few internationals lasted long. Rahul stayed and he kept his detachment, so he remained useful. When we were faced with bitterness he could hold on to compassion. When people talked of revenge, he tried to steer them to compromise. He sensed the humanity in each person he met, and because of that he had an influence few of us ever have. In a few weeks I will be in Tehran for the next round of peace negotiations. How will I sit there in those negotiations if I know that he died in the attempt and that I did nothing?'

She nods, to say, I understand.

'Tessa, I know I am intruding on very private territory. But I want you to know, Rahul was very discreet. I think none of his Delhi friends knew about you, and certainly no one else in Tajikistan. And I knew only because it was me he came to when he was in trouble, when he realized that he had lost you.'

Lost you. A dog trots past. She watches it, mesmerized. She is seeing again a dog trip-tripping its way along the early morning beach in Thailand, where she lost her bearings, where she sat on an upturned boat under banana fronds and tried to face up to her failure.

'I wrote him a letter from Thailand, the last one I wrote before I met Ben. I remember sitting there thinking, what do I write? I had never before had to think that, at all other times writing was just the way we were going to be together until we could next meet. But I thought he wanted me to have something major to say, about what I was going to do in life, and I didn't have anything. All I wanted to say was, I tried to find my own way, Rahul, and I can't do it. Please can I come back now? Maybe if I had written that, he would have heard, and understood.'

But she didn't. And he didn't. It is all so long ago now. Inevitable, almost. That was the way they were then, so that was the way it had happened.

She shakes herself out of the memory. 'It'll help me to know what Rahul told you about me.'

He chooses his words carefully. 'That you and he had a long history together before you met Ben, but that things had happened to stop you getting together.' He waits for her to react.

'And later – he told you that we met again after I was married?'

'Yes. But that you were managing to make space for him.'

How must it feel, he wonders, to hear years of her complex life summarized in so few words?

'That was why I felt I should meet you and Ben together first. And I'm glad I did. It gave me a chance to see how things are.'

'To see – what?'

362

'That you are anxious about Ben. I can imagine that dealing with your loss has had an impact also on him.'

She nods, the smallest movement of her head, but he has the impression that she is glad to have it out. But she is still waiting. The unspoken question: What did you think?

'You will not want me to be anything less than completely honest, so I will tell you that I was worried for Rahul. It seemed madness to try to continue the relationship once you were married.'

She nods. Of course. That's what everyone would think.

'Life is full of complexities, Tessa. Don't feel that I judged you.'

But he had.

She is looking out over the pond. He doesn't know if she has heard him.

'It was always complicated. So many ways. There was me and Ben, that was my issue and I had to deal with that on my own. But I also worried that it was wrong for Rahul. I could offer him no future. He knew that, but he wouldn't think of letting go. This is us, he said, you and me. Everything else has a place, but it can't cancel us.'

Hugo sits unmoving on the bench next to her. His very presence seems an intrusion, yet he knows it is only because he is there, and that he has admitted his negative feelings, that her own vulnerabilities are coming out. He does not want to move a muscle in case he disturbs her process.

I never doubted that I was safe in his love, not after we found each other again, but there was always this fear that I would lose him again. It seemed impossible that it would be enough for him, waiting months for the small doses of intimacy that was all we could snatch from life. He must constantly be meeting other women who could offer what I could not, a lover for every day. I was in no position to expect otherwise; I had Ben, after all. But if that happened, where would it leave me?

He was always the one to steady me, but the strain was there for him too. I saw it in the poetry he translated:

> I have not ceased to struggle; I am like the captive bird
> Who in the cage still gathers straws with which to build
> his nest

'What's the cage?' I wrote back. And he replied, 'The disaster that is the world. The complexities of life, which no one can escape. Fill in the details yourself. I'm sure you can.'

There *were* other women; he never pretended otherwise. He tried to laugh off my anxiety. It's ridiculous, he said, you've not the slightest need to feel threatened. How can you doubt that? But doubt is easy when you're not free to be there all the time. There was his lover from his student year in London, Parveen Jalali. Iranian. There were things they had in common, that I didn't. Work – she was a journalist. Speaking Farsi, he owed that to her. In the years we lost contact they drifted into becoming occasional lovers. Occasional was the operative word, he said, they were not often in the same place, and he had always made it clear that even if they had been he wasn't up for more. But even after I was back she kept reappearing, like she was trailing the places he moved through. Is it her work taking her there, I asked, or does she find reasons to go? He said, A bit of both.

When we were together everything was simple but each time our days together were coming to an end the insecurity would surface again. He couldn't understand it. Nothing touches what we have, he said, and I will never give you tactful half-truths. I won't say it'll never happen, but what will it matter? It can only happen if it is clearly understood on both sides that it's brief, and carries no implications for the future. It would be an entirely limited thing. And what you and I have knows no limits, except practical ones …

She turns to face Hugo, noticing him again, letting him back in. 'You cared about him. I don't wonder that you wished I wasn't there.'

On the train back to Brighton she stares unseeing at the moving landscape. Her mind sifts through the fragments she has gleaned of the life that Rahul and Hugo shared, which she could never be part of. She has taken them in, thirsty for anything that connects; but at the time she never felt excluded. They had their own direct lines of communication, thoughts and words spun fine as spiders' webs – light as air, catching drops of water to reflect all the colours of the spectrum – visible only to themselves.

She remembers the first time Rahul went to Tajikistan to assess the effects of the war on the civilian population – he routed himself back via London so he would have time with her while he wrote his report. He was bursting with facts and impressions, urgent to tell the world what was going on, but she was his only audience. She too had something to tell him but she knew it would have to wait until he had offloaded. They walked while he told her of the people who had fled into the mountains, places their own parents had come from until in Stalin's time they were forcibly transported down to the plains to work in the cotton fields. But the numbers up there now were overwhelming, there was no way the place could sustain them. Desperate people, hardly able to talk about what had happened, others who couldn't stop talking. Children with no shoes, and winter coming. How could you walk away from that? He ordered several thousand pairs of children's shoes, paid for them up front and got someone in government to promise to distribute them. Had to be done on trust, hurriedly, but it all could go wrong, there's always someone ready to profit from other people's misery.

They had reached the embankment of the Thames, outside the Royal Festival Hall. Tessa interrupted the flow. 'Let's get some coffee.' They sat near the plate-glass windows that looked out over the river. There were people milling about, a party of schoolchildren, their voices chirpy, their teachers harried. A jazz group was playing. Rahul looked around him as if he couldn't work out where he was. 'This could be on another planet from where I've just come from.' Suddenly he focused on her properly and stretched his hand out to take hers. He talked more calmly now. 'All that human misery,' he said, 'is happening in one of the most beautiful parts of this earth you could imagine.'

She knew as she listened that he would be going there, to the middle of that war. She took it all in, preparing herself, learning through his eyes this new place that was soon to become his, the awesome grandeur of the road that wound its way into the mountains.

Gradually his over-intensity diminished. He said, 'It's so good to be back. Tell me about you.'

She talked first about inconsequential things, till she felt he was quiet again and was simply there with her and listening. Then she said, 'Meri jaan, I've got something to tell you.'

She and Ben were going to have a child. She was careful to tell him in a way that left no possible scope for misunderstanding. A month after Rahul had last been here they had decided to stop using contraceptives. He nodded slowly. Of course, the obvious next step for you and Ben. But what was he feeling as he sat there, eyes holding hers? Was it the jolt of recognizing that she was moving towards an experience beyond what he could envisage for himself? Had he imagined, once, a future in which she would be the mother of his child?

She held his hands across the table and willed his vulnerability to vanish. He pushed himself past the point, saying – and meaning it, she was sure – 'You'll be a fantastic mother.' But in those moments of hesitation she had felt something so unaccustomed that she could not immediately name it – compassion. Compassion for this man whom she loved, who could not stop going out to do battle, and had not known when to say, 'There is something else in life I need.'

~ 48 ~

The very air seems heavy, Lance thinks as he walks to a meeting in town. Sign of a summer storm approaching, echoing his sense of unease about a looming political crisis. For weeks now there have been rumours about a new group of armed rebels up beyond Sukhunobod, young Uzbek men who have been persecuted for practising Islam and have fled into the mountains. There's a certain sympathy for them, but they are men with guns. No one wants them there. You watch for the lightning, and hope it will strike somewhere else.

He arrives at the hotel where he spent his first week in Resham-serai. He is about to meet an unknown man on an undisclosed mission, and feels like an extra in a cold-war movie. Two days ago he got a call from a man in the British embassy in Tashkent. We have a friend in common, he said, but he offered nothing further. I'm going to be in Resham-serai for a couple of days, he said, can we meet?

The hotel foyer is crowded. There's a conference going on, people arriving, harried organizers trying to direct them. A man moves out of the crowd towards him; slim, about his own age, in a neat suit. A pleasant but unremarkable face. A natural diplomat, he thinks.

'Lance? I'm Francis MacKay. Let's get out of here. I thought we might take a stroll?'

Does a stroll mean out of range of hidden microphones? Who is going to bother to monitor the conversation of two foreigners? Outside, Francis says, 'Sorry if this seems a bit paranoid. In Uzbekistan you learn to exercise caution as a matter of habit.'

'So I understand. I've not been there, just passed through once at night.'

'Yes, Ulughbek told me.'

Lance stares in surprise.

'The driver in the Lifeline office,' Francis smiles. 'He's our mutual friend.'

'So. I had guessed it was someone else.'

'Rahul Khan? No, I never met him. But I heard about him from Ulughbek, and what happened to him. I'm very sorry.'

'Thank you.' He is still taking it in. 'You and Ulughbek are friends. You know Russian, then, or Uzbek?'

'Both, actually.'

'I hardly know him. Did he explain that? We've only met once and couldn't exchange more than two words.'

'He told me. But he has a way of sizing people up very quickly and he's almost always right. He has heard you were close to Rahul Khan, and he's keen to have time with you. He is hoping you will be coming to Tashkent at some point, and can keep an evening free for him. Have a meal at his house.'

'I'll be delighted. Someone from their office will interpret?'

'If I'm there I can do it, but if I'm travelling, bring your own interpreter. There are people in your office in Tashkent he doesn't trust. So don't mention there that you'll be going home with him.'

Lance looks at him curiously. 'How do you find it, working in a place like that?'

Francis shrugs. 'Politically tense, no getting away from it. Too many uncomfortable compromises. I salvage my conscience by doing what I can for people like Ulughbek.'

Lance takes back his thought about the natural diplomat.

Francis says, 'He's a poet – did you know?'

'A *poet?*'

'Why not?'

'I don't know. Just – You meet someone as a driver, you don't think past that.'

'He's a serious poet, a dissident writer from the time it was very dangerous to be so. As it still is in Uzbekistan. He writes in Uzbek but he translates his own work into Russian and it circulates privately. He's highly thought of among a small group of writers in Moscow. When I was posted to Tashkent one of his Moscow friends gave me an introduction.'

'So what is he doing working as a driver?'

'You can't earn a living as a poet, can you?'

'OK, stupid question. But you'd think –'

'Not such a stupid question, actually. He did have a more responsible job but he lost it. Politically suspect. It's difficult to find anyone else who'll employ you after that.'

'Rahul knew all that when he took him on?'

'That's why he took him on. They met through a friend, who knew they would have a similar outlook.'

It is enough. He tells Francis about the notes written in Tashkent.

Francis says, 'It was probably Ulughbek's daughter giving him the leads. She was involved with an opposition group, technically legal but hounded by the police. People came to her for help when relatives disappeared and she asked questions. Too many.'

'And now?'

'She got out of the country.'

'How?'

Francis shakes his head, smiling. 'You don't ask such things, my friend, even of people you know well.'

A pause. Lance ventures, 'It's not impossible Rahul had a hand in it.'

'Nothing is impossible.'

Or you? Lance wonders.

Francis moves them on. 'The Russian journalist who died with Rahul, did you know him?'

'No.'

'He was the friend through whom Rahul and Ulughbek met.'

Lance stares. It all comes suddenly closer.

'He and Ulughbek had been students together in Moscow. In the early days of *samizdat* they produced a journal with poetry and political satires.'

'So he lost two friends up in those mountains.'

Francis nods. 'It hit him very hard. It would mean a lot to him to meet you.'

The apartment is empty when he gets back. He is shocked at the sharpness of his disappointment. He wanted to tell her all he has just learnt. Is he losing the ability to live alone?

He takes a can of beer from the fridge and sits down with it. On the table is a pile of papers Annabel has been busy with. He picks up the top sheet:

> *Who sees into the soul? Not you, not I. We pass as strangers*
> *Yet still the taunting memory of what we could not grasp*
> *Pursues us –*

He reads no further; replaces the paper with a vehement movement, drains the rest of his beer and goes to take a shower.

In the office next morning he asks Nargis if they can have a word. Closed door. She registers it; something important.

'Tell me what you know about Ulughbek,' he asks.

Why is he asking? 'What do you want to know?'

'Have you met him?'

'Of course. He was the first person Rahul took on in Tashkent. He wanted the three of us to plan together what Lifeline should be doing, so I went there a few times.' She pauses. 'He is smart. If he knew English he could run that office, better than that useless Sanjar. But Sanjar doesn't even ask his opinion.'

'Because?'

'Sanjar, consult the driver? And there was the accounting thing.'

'Accounting?'

'Money was disappearing, not being properly accounted for. There were rumours, everyone in that office must have heard but they were all too scared to say. It was Ulughbek who asked the question. Sanjar acted like he had known nothing, made a big thing about setting up new procedures. They never found where it had gone. I don't believe he didn't know, nor does Ulughbek. Sanjar keeps control of everything. Rahul sorted it out best he could but with Sanjar still there, it'll happen again. And since then, Sanjar hates Ulughbek.'

'Rahul must have seen that?'

'He did. He realized it had been a wrong appointment. But Sanjar knows people in government, if Rahul had tried to get rid of him there could have been repercussions, for Ulughbek. Bad ones.'

'Christ, what a mess.'

She nods. 'Rahul knew he had to sort it out some way. But then –' She stops. 'Has something happened?'

He tells her about the notes. She says cautiously, 'Rahul knew a lot more than most foreigners about what was going on politically. That can be dangerous.'

'Nargis, if there's anything you know that might help us find out what happened to him, please tell me. There are people who are not going to be able to put it to rest until we find out what really happened.'

He sees immediately that he has gone too far. Voice

uncharacteristically harsh, she says, 'Wars destroy people and we never hear the full story.' Then, with no warning, she puts her head in her hands. She is silently weeping.

He feels completely at a loss. She is usually so in command of herself. Eventually she lifts her head, brushes her hand across her eyes and says, in a voice that is now simply tired, 'If you will excuse me, I must go. I have someone coming for a meeting.'

~ 49 ~

Tessa gets back to a living room strewn with a chaos of shredded paper packaging. The children are wrapping themselves in it, Ben is horsing around with them, and scattered everywhere are objects she hasn't seen for months. Two huge crates have arrived from Laos, their things, packed up the day before they had to fly out. Light summer clothes, but will they ever wear them in this climate? Children's toys, all but forgotten. All that clutter they have lived without, coming back in to crowd them.

Eventually the excitement calms down, the shredded paper is cleared up, the children settled in bed, and she and Ben start unearthing what the crates have really landed them with, boxes and boxes of his research papers. The unfinished PhD. Data collected in the years tramping around Snowdon and never analysed in Laos because the lure of unexplored mountains and a new kind of responsibility was too strong. He has gone quiet at the sight of those boxes. He has learnt to exist at a low level without his intellectual life; opening them is going to confront him painfully with what he has been, and is no longer.

'Get it behind you,' Norman, his supervisor, said when Ben finally got it together to go and see him. 'You'll have the evenings. Just do it, then you'll be ready to move on.' And Ben had briefly believed it might be possible; but that was before he faced up to how exhausting full-time childcare was going to be.

For hours he pages slowly through the papers, musty with the smell of things left in the middle. Tessa moves around quietly, not wanting to interrupt him. Eventually he packs them up and starts taking them down to the basement, box after box. She doesn't know whether to offer to help. Maybe he is waiting for her to say something? Maybe he is relieved that she doesn't? Maybe he isn't even conscious of her?

When he comes back upstairs after carrying the last box down she says, 'Ben, we need to do something so you can get a bit of time to yourself. We could put up a notice in the village shop for a childminder, maybe one day a week?'

He says, 'Just leave it, Tessa,' and he takes himself off to bed.

The very smell of Laos was in those crates.

She lies awake, seeing the bungalow that was their home, the wide verandah, gauze-covered to keep out the mosquitos, looking out onto a garden of luxuriant tropical growth. She hears again the whirr of the ceiling fans as slowly they stirred the sluggish air, and the Russian air-conditioner that rattled so clankily that she usually chose peace and turned it off. She remembers how sometimes at night, when Ben's work had taken him up-country and she lay alone and wakeful under a mosquito net, she would play mind games, imagining herself a bird travelling the distance between her and Rahul. She would spread wings and feel herself lifted on air currents, to look down on Buddhist temples and the roofs of village houses clustered along the bank of the meandering Mekong River. With slow flapping movements she followed it north through the borderlands of Thailand, Burma, China. She soared above gorges carved by rivers through forested mountains, where people lived remote from governments and spoke in a hundred different tongues. She tacked against the wind to rise by difficult stages up over the highest mountains in the world, sailing over the prayer-flags that flapped around the temples of Lhasa, then west over Tibet's cold deserts to the vast, inhospitable spaces of the Pamir Mountains, where Kyrgyz nomads tended long-haired yaks. Till finally she began her descent into the valley where Dushanbe lay, its parks and Soviet monuments and wide streets unable to counter the pervading sense of things falling apart – to where Rahul slept in a room in the UN guest house, having chosen not to be bothered with a house of his own.

And now she sees him, there, in his place, the life he made. How he rose early, to step outside and breathe the early summer air, and then go back inside to settle at his desk with a mug of tea and a pen. For a few moments he would sit and wait, feeling her presence, and then the conversation between them would begin to flow onto the page. Each day the same, till at the end of the week all he had written would be sealed in a large envelope, and travel with UNHCR's mail delivery to their office in Vientiane, from where Tessa would collect it, and find a moment when the children were asleep or playing, to read it; and the circle would be complete.

She holds in her mind what all this writing meant to him. For the rest of the day he was having to be over-alert, to take small openings and hope to edge them slightly wider. There was no natural end to the working day. He lived with the tensions because he lived surrounded by the people. Even in sleep his mind was sifting, sorting out significance. Then he would wake, and whatever had surfaced in the night would be channelled through his pen. It was for himself that he wrote, she knew, but that did not make it any the less for her, rather more so. Through all that had happened between them, and through their acceptance of all that could never happen, the boundaries between their minds had become so porous that 'I' or 'you' scarcely made any difference. 'We've become co-extensive,' he wrote. 'The things that move me, move you. The things you care about, I care about. In whatever I do, I feel you with me.'

Sunday. They wake to a sky of perfect blue and Ben decides to take Sam out for an ambitious cycle ride. Tessa and Alisa wave them off and then go down to the basement, and while Alisa rediscovers the china dogs Tessa delves into the crates. At the bottom her hands touch the contours of a wooden box, hand-carved, forest-scented, that she found in a market in Vientiane and bought to store Rahul's growing pile of writing. She holds it for a moment, her hands recovering its familiar weight and texture.

Upstairs with their booty, she with her box, Alisa with her china dogs, and out into the garden where she spreads a rug on the grass. Alisa becomes absorbed in her imaginary world. Tessa starts paging through the letters. Words and phrases conjure places she herself has never seen but knows from his descriptions as intimately as an imagined land of childhood. The gaunt mountains, the fertile valley floors. The dust of a desert summer, heat building to intolerable levels, and winters to freeze your bones. Fields that once grew cotton, now neglected, mulberry trees that once nourished silk worms, now stripped of their leaves. And against that backdrop, the intense experiences he was living through. Stories, stories ... Here is one of a woman in his team, a war-widow, being challenged by someone from her own clan: 'Why are you helping these children? It's *these* people who killed your husband.' She said, 'We will probably never know who killed him. But I know it wasn't these children.'

Translations from Ghalib lie scattered through the pages, a voice commenting from another life on the human condition that does not change:

> *The flames of hell cannot give out such a heat*
> *For hidden griefs burn with another fire*

I felt the breath of his life, Hugo said, the thing that gave

378

it value. In these pages that breath has been transmuted into words. What is she going to do with all this? Who is there that she can trust to make sure that this living record will not be lost? Only Hugo is close enough to it all to be able to judge significance, but he is too preoccupied with his search.

Alisa has lost interest in her china dogs and has been picking the miniature daisies in the grass. Now that too comes to an end. She climbs onto Tessa's lap.

Tessa starts packing the letters back. Alisa watches. 'What are those papers?'

'Just some old letters.'

'Have they got any pictures?'

'No pictures.' Tessa smiles, for it is only half true.

'Why are you putting them in that box?'

'I'm keeping them carefully.'

'Why?'

'It's a story, a very special story that I don't want to lose. You help me pack them away, then we can take them down to the basement together.'

'Carefully,' Alisa says, starting to help.

The pictures follow her, are with her still when Lance phones. He is pressing her to come to Kyrgyzstan.

'There are so many children at risk,' he says, 'and society is changing so fast. We need help thinking through where best to put our support.'

'I'd love to come,' she says, 'but I'm already booked up with country visits for the next three months.'

'That's far too late. I'll be gone by then and I have to be part of it. Postpone one of the others. Say we got in first.'

'But you didn't!'

'Sure I did. In that café in Brighton. I remember distinctly saying, We'll have to get you to Kyrgyzstan.'

By now she is laughing. 'Lance, are you always this pushy?'

'I just know this is what my staff here need so of course I'm arguing for it. But you'll thank me for it. This is a special place, you'll learn an amazing amount.' A pause, then, in a different voice, 'Tessa, people here talk about Rahul often. When you come we'll be driving you up into the mountains he loved. You owe it to yourself.'

'I'll have to think about it,' she says.

But what is there to consider? She has come this far; how can she back away?

She checks her diary – what can she juggle? Early June she can do it, before she goes anywhere else. She calls him. 'I'll come.'

~ 50 ~

Nargis and Fahmeda start planning Tessa's visit straight away. Lance hears how they talk about her in capitals, the Head Office Early Years Advisor, and he tries to defuse it. She's a simple person, he says, and tells them about her living in a village in

India with no facilities. That interests them. When she comes, they say, we can arrange for her to stay in a yurt when we are in Sukhunobod. That's more like it, he thinks.

Then he brings them the news that Tessa has found a donor to fund new developments in the street-children's centre, and she becomes again a person of power, defending them from the threat of budget cuts. 'These things are partly luck,' Lance tells them. A company that designs children's clothes (Toddlers Plus, they are called) approached Lifeline looking for a project with children in Central Asia, to adopt as their charity of the year. Why Central Asia? 'They have been sourcing cotton from here since the markets opened up,' he explains. 'It's good publicity to show they're giving something back.' And Tessa's role? 'She presented them with examples from our reports, and they chose the street-children's centre. It's a perfect grant, no strings attached. We provide them with stories and photos for their promotional material, and you are free to work out how to use the money.'

Nargis and Fahmeda start discussing options. Annabel is nearby, listening. Lance is avoiding looking in her direction but willing her not to get involved. He knows very well that she will have ideas of her own from the time she spent helping with the accounts, and very likely her ideas will be good ones. But this is Nargis and Fahmeda's project, it was they who got it started out of nothing and he wants them alone to have the satisfaction of planning for something more ambitious.

Fahmeda says, 'These stories they want, the project workers have so much information, it's just a question of writing it up.' She turns to Annabel. 'Could you do that?'

'I'd love to,' she says.

Lance is piqued, but what possible objection can he make? Writing anything in English is a challenge for the staff, and these stories will need writing of a very particular kind. Without any idea about the audience they will make heavy weather of it and he will end up having to edit it. They all know Annabel can do it. The weavers' article showed that.

Sultan, the younger of the two drivers, is summoned and drives her off to talk to the project organizers.

Evening now in his apartment. Annabel talks animatedly about her day. Lance is less than responsive. The fact is, she is tackling the work sensibly but he is perversely determined not to encourage her.

After a few minutes she asks, 'Are you bothered about something?'

He is too full of contradictory feelings to be able to answer honestly. 'I'm just preoccupied,' he says, and retreats into reading.

Annabel shrugs, hobbles across the room to fetch some papers, then settles back with them. His eyes lift involuntarily to where she sits, sideways on the sofa, with her plaster-cast leg stretched out full length. He marvels at how she always manages to look at ease despite the encumbrance she has to carry around. She is reading something on a sheet of paper, and making marginal notes. Curiosity gets the better of him. 'What's that you're working on?'

She lifts her head, as if to say, So we're talking again, are we? For an instant they hold it there, neither saying anything. The temptation to make some move towards her is almost overwhelming; but so is the fear of rejection.

The moment passes, and is lost. She says, 'It's just something someone asked me to look at.'

He gets up and goes to the kitchen to make coffee. When he comes back she starts talking about something else, and the ease between them returns. She says, 'There's something I've been wanting to show you. And now you've stopped being huffy —'

She passes him the sheet of paper she has been looking at. It has writing in Cyrillic script, presumably Tajik, and in short lines. A poem, and below it an English translation.

'Another of Rahman Mirzajanov's?' She nods. 'And you translated it?'

'No. Akbor did.'

'*Akbor's* translating Mirzajanov's poetry?'

She nods, smiling. 'He says he quoted a couple of lines from one in the office, the day you asked about the statue, but he was too shy to tell them it was his own translation.'

Lance remembers it well – *Do not wait for me when darkness lowers* – and Fahmeda saying, Where did you find that? Akbor wouldn't tell Fahmeda, but he has told Annabel. 'You have an extraordinary way of getting people to open up.'

'I didn't have to do anything. He came to me with it because he'd seen my translation. Turns out he's been doing them secretly for about a year. The only other person he's shown them to was Rahul.'

'And what was his reaction?'

383

'That it's difficult to translate poetry except into a language you've spoken from early childhood. So they sat together and revised a couple of them. This is one.'

Lance reads:

> *I hear the echoing silence, the sifting wind*
> *I watch the kestrel hover, then plunge to the kill*
> *I feel the shadow behind me, breath of a stranger*
> *Be still, my heart, be still.*

He looks up. She says. 'Rahul promised that they could work on a few each time he came, maybe put together a collection. Now Akbor's stuck. He has asked if I'll work with him.'

'And will you?'

'Sure I will. It's an amazing opportunity. Together we can do what neither us could possibly do alone.'

So now they will be spending hours together after work, becoming ever more intimate. Lance tries to shake himself out of vulnerability. If it is going to happen, it is going to happen. Just get used to it, he tells himself fiercely, and be glad for her. He doesn't have a monopoly on her company.

'There's a bottle of wine in the cupboard,' she says. 'Why don't we open it?'

He goes to fetch it, grateful for the excuse. Did she see what he was feeling and want to ease it? But every thought of that kind is fragile as a butterfly's wing. Try and hold on to it and it breaks.

He pours the wine, hands her hers. 'Cheers. Is there an equivalent in Farsi?'

'Not that I ever heard, but plenty of poetry that celebrates wine.' They clink glasses, 'Here's to Afaqi. And to Fate, for tripping me up on the stairs.'

'I thought it was your backpack.'

'It's more appealing thinking it was in my stars.'

She is laughing at him. Thinking what? Did fate intervene so she could stay longer with him? Too much to hope. To see more of Akbor? Please God, no. She is daring him to guess and he is certainly not going to do so out loud. 'I give up,' he says.

'So that I could get into translating,' she says. And leaving the merest wisp of a suspicion of teasing, she changes the subject.

~ 51 ~

Hugo ponders the line of enquiry Lance has opened up for him. Cryptic notes, Uzbek dissidents, a poet-driver.

'I can't see that any of it's relevant to what I'm looking for,' he said.

'Nor can I,' Lance said. 'But I thought I ought to tell you, in case it fits with things you come across.'

Could there be a connection? The only person who might have some idea is Tessa. So he calls her.

Tessa knows nothing about the notes but yes, Rahul did talk about the Uzbekistan government persecuting people. And she assumed he would have made it his job to pass on what he knew.

'To — ?'

'I'd guess Human Rights Watch. He knew people in their London office.'

'Anyone in particular?'

A slight pause. 'He had a friend there, Parveen Jalali. I don't know if she's still there.'

They have hit sensitive ground, but he can't stop now. 'You know her?'

'No. She was around a long time but we never met.'

He calls Human Rights Watch. Parveen Jalali is still there; but when he explains why he is calling, her voice becomes distinctly cold. Is that because she finds the subject painful, or does she know something?

She says brusquely, 'I can't possibly talk about this on the phone.'

Now he definitely wants to meet her, but it can't be until after the peace negotiations in Tehran. 'Perhaps when I'm next in London we can meet?'

She doesn't say, 'I'd rather not', but virtually.

Is there more to her tense reaction than political caution? A lover who hung on, Tessa said. As he moves to other tasks his mind shifts to Tessa and her complexities. And Ben's. Ben is going nowhere, and that is dangerous for them both. It is the mirror image of the inequality that brought the painful end to his own marriage. Can anything be done to lift Ben from his intellectual isolation?

He finds the article about the oil pipeline in Burma that he told Ben about, and posts him a copy with a note encouraging him to write about his own experiences. 'Send it to me,' he writes, without any idea of what he will do with it. He just wants Ben to feel someone thinks it important. And having posted it, he has one more idea.

Tessa is on her bike ready to set off for the station when Ben appears at the door. 'I forgot to tell you, I have to get up to London sometime soon. Could you take a day's leave to be with the kids?'

To London? What about? So out-of-the-blue. Ben doesn't know anyone in London; but clearly he does. Before she can ask there is a piercing cry from inside the house. Ben disappears back inside and a few moments later he is at the door again, carrying Alisa. 'She slipped.'

'Oh poppet.' Tessa feels helpless, stuck there standing over her bike.

'She's OK.' He brings her out for a quick kiss and cuddle. But she can't stay any longer, or she will miss her train.

For the first hour in the office she is hardly able to concentrate. She can make plans to meet people in London whenever she needs but Ben has to ask her before he can move. She is in revolt against days so time-structured that when Ben has something important to say to her she can't stop to hear it. Why? A mindless sense of obedience. Who would have noticed if she'd come in twenty minutes late?

She calls him. He sounds surprised that she has worried. The London thing? It's just that there is someone Hugo wants him to meet, to talk about Laos.

Ben sets off on his bicycle, heading for the station and his day in London. Tessa stands with the children, waving goodbye. They were all chirpy at the novelty of reversed roles. She has a chance to talk to Sam's teacher and meet his new friends. Alisa is at her most delightful, excited to have Tessa to herself.

The children are asleep by the time Ben gets in. Tessa knows from the energy in his footsteps that it has gone well. He can hardly speak fast enough. 'It's a group called Ethical Economics, a research outfit that tracks the doings of big companies, for people who want to be sure they aren't investing in a company that sells arms or has horrendous employment practices.' Extrincor, the company he came up against in Laos, is already on their radar. 'They said my knowledge of mineral prospecting would be really useful to them. They're going to try and raise funding so they can take me on.'

Real work? That's wonderful. But in London? Before she gives voice to any of her swirling thoughts, Ben says, 'I told them about the children, your job. They said I could work from home, as long as I can get up to the office one day a week. I have to do it, Tessa, even if they don't raise the money.'

That night they make love again the way it used to be. It is heady and loving and simple all at the same time, and such a relief to feel it so. Afterwards Ben goes straight off to sleep. Tessa herself is completely awake. They have come so far from the house on the Irish coast, the jam jars labelled Food, Electricity, Phone, Treats, but the sums aren't going to be any easier. They will need a childminder not just for his day a week in London but for any day that he is going to try to work. Fine, if Ethical Economics can come up with a salary. But if not?

It is two in the morning, her brain is going very slowly, but eventually she does the calculation. Their savings will cover childminding three days a week for three months. By that time, either Ethical Economics will be paying him or they will all have to think again.

'Start right away,' she says in the morning. 'Until we find a childminder we'll just make it work somehow.'

The passivity that for months has been dragging him down has vanished. His voice is punchy with energy again as he tells Tessa about his first task, tracking the corporate links of Extrincor and its parent company. They are picking out countries that have been cut off from the global economy until recently, he says. Zero experience of trading internationally. Economies nose-diving. Governments desperate. Any Western company can more or less dictate terms.

She phones Hugo. 'You can't imagine what you've done for him.'

'It was just luck that I knew the right people. I hate to see a man not using his abundant talents.'

But you shift one problem, another raises its head. Her

notices advertising for a childminder have brought no response and they are having to fit three jobs into the human capacity for two. Tessa is gone before the children wake, getting into work by six when only the cleaners are there so that she can walk out early afternoon when everyone else is still hard at it. Even though she has explained the situation to her colleagues it still feels embarrassing. Home, to Ben waiting to hand the children over the moment she walks in the door. He disappears upstairs or sets off for the university library, working until late; and one day a week she brings work home so he can get to London. By the time he gets back she is asleep.

She does it gladly, it is so much better than what went before. But communication is no easier, for they hardly see each other. They are just shift workers on a parenting conveyor belt.

~ **52** ~

Lance calls Tessa to confirm arrangements for her visit. When they are done she says, 'And you can tell Annabel I'll be bringing her dictionary.'

He is too stunned to speak.

She laughs. 'I've just had a visit from her sister. If Annabel looks anything like her, you must be enjoying having her there.'

'Listen, Tessa.' His voice sounds like that of a man struggling to fend off a charge. 'How did she — ?'

'Annabel's doing some translation work for you, right? Well, apparently she needs her Farsi/English dictionary. She heard I was coming and got her sister to come and ask if I could bring it.'

'She really shouldn't have bothered you. I hope it's not too heavy.'

'It's twice the size of the complete works of Shakespeare. But I'll bring it in my hand luggage.'

'Well, thank you.' Curiosity gets the better of him. 'Did her sister say anything else, about Annabel?'

'She did actually. She said you never know what mad thing she's going to get into next. And she hasn't a clue about limits, if there's something she wants, she just goes for it.' Pause. 'Does that figure?'

'It certainly does.'

'Sounds intriguing,' she says hopefully. But he is saying no more.

Phone down, Lance realizes his hands are sweaty. Annabel behaves each day more as if she were part of the staff. He *has* to set limits. But he can already see her surprised eyes, hear her saying, 'But I do really need it, Lance. And Akbor said it would be fine to ask her.'

He cops out; simply passes on Tessa's message.

'That's great,' Annabel says, with no trace of awareness of having stepped over the line.

And there's another issue, the drivers. He himself chooses to walk rather than be driven and he would have liked to lay down the law about her being driven about, but with that damn plaster cast of hers, what can he say? Her journeys are always one way or another on Lifeline business. And, he has to admit, she has an ear for gossip that is useful to him. Zohra listens to daily radio and television news, reads all the documentation that comes into the office, and presents him each day with summary briefings, but Annabel does something more: she has been getting Sultan to take her to the market where she hobbles about on her crutches while they listen to what people are saying. People have heard of new armed groups in the mountains near the border with Tajikistan, she reports. Summer is a dangerous time, the time when men with guns can easily move about. And once peace is signed in Tajikistan perhaps they will be tracked down with the help of UN troops and forced to hand in their arms. They may try to act before that.

It is always Sultan, he notices, who drives her. He is a perky young man, full of jokes and zip. Once he saw the two of them entertaining a couple of drivers from other organizations as they stood at their cars waiting for their employers to appear. Her complete lack of concern for status is one of the things that most appeals to him about her. But she already has Akbor in her pocket over the translations, now here is another of the young men he employs constantly with her. And what about the third one, Oman, the finance officer? Stuck in the office with no special excuse to hang out with her? If jealousies start developing, it will seriously disrupt everyone's work.

Nargis sleeps only fitfully, and in the mornings she is short on patience. Today Layla refuses to go to school. Nargis expects of the child what she expects of herself, that she will do what has to be done and not make a fuss. Usually she does, but not today. 'What's the problem?' Nargis demands. Gradually her sharpness gives way and she takes the sobbing child onto her lap and cuddles her till she calms down. Then she comes out with it. One of the children has been asking where her father is, saying nasty things about him. Nargis's protective anger sweeps her to the school, and to talk to the teacher.

Then she is late for work.

They have started the staff meeting without her. She has never been late before, ever.

'Very sorry,' she says. 'Some problem at home.' Her face says, *Please don't ask.*

Meeting over, she follows Lance into his office. 'I'm very sorry about that. My daughter was crying. She didn't want to go to school.'

Lance sees that she was more than anxious. He closes the door and says quietly, 'You're worried. About other things too?'

She cannot deny it. 'I have not been sleeping well.'

'Nargis, I know that things at home are not easy to talk about. If you tell me that's the way it has to stay, of course I'll accept it. But I would be honoured if you would let me understand what it is that you are dealing with.'

She looks past him, out of the window. He sees that her eyes are wet. Eventually she says, 'I – It's very complicated.'

'Just take your time.'

'I don't know where to start.'

'Your husband, he is away?' She nods. 'Do you know where?'

'Not exactly. But we know he has gone to Tajikistan.'

'Ah.' This is beginning to make sense. 'To fight?'

'I don't think so. He –' She is stuck again. 'There's been trouble a long time, from before he went away. Since he came back from Afghanistan he has been angry all the time. Paying no attention to his family. And when Rahul offered me the Lifeline job —'

She stops, looking at him in some alarm, so unused is she to talking about it. 'The thing with Rahul –' She stops again. A small, difficult smile. 'This is not easy to talk about.'

'It's OK. Just take it slowly.'

'It wasn't anything that I – Khaled was jealous before he even met Rahul. Who is this guy? Where does he know you from? Why is he offering it to *you*? What's been going on between you? I said, Nothing's been going on, he just offered me a job.' Now it is bursting out of her, a stream of hurt and anger. 'It was such traditional husband behaviour, it made me furious. There's supposed to be equality for women, I was the one earning the money and doing all the women's work at home, he did nothing to help anyone, and the moment another man talked to me out this came. But because I was angry, to him that was an admission that he had cause to be suspicious. I knew, whatever I did he would find something to object to.'

'But Rahul came to the house?'

'Khaled was away most of the time, with his new friends. Friends?' Her voice becomes cold as she rejects her own word.

'You couldn't call them friends. The men he used to spend time with. When he heard Rahul had been he accused me of doing things behind his back. In one way it was true, I wouldn't have invited him if Khaled had been there, I would have been ashamed for him to see the unpleasantness. Once when he got back Rahul was there and he behaved so –' She can find no words for it, just shakes her head. 'He said everyone could see I was infatuated with Rahul. I wouldn't answer him, I just felt cold and angry. So he got – Next day Rahul said to me, it'll be better if I don't come; but my father-in-law wouldn't agree.'

But now her face has closed up, retreating into protective privacy. Pushing to keep the line open, Lance says, 'Your husband, what has happened to him?'

Blankly she says, 'We hear things, but we don't actually know. And if I think about it too much it makes me go crazy, so no more, please, no more.'

She can block off Lance's questions, but not the memories they stir ... Rahul asking her, 'Do you know where Khaled gets his money from?' He and Ulughbek had seen him in the market of a town across the border in Uzbekistan, in an argument that seemed likely to turn into a fight. Rahul had a meeting to go to but he asked Ulughbek to stay and watch. It was a dispute about territory. Two gangs of drug traders ... The time Khaled got back drunk, or high on drugs, she didn't have the experience to know the difference, but she could see that just the sight of Rahul talking with his father flipped something in his distorted brain. He started attacking him about the peace negotiations. It was a sham, he said, the UN was just supporting the government side. Rahul said, 'We talk to both sides, we just want them to talk to each other.' But Khaled was looking for offence in every word. He let loose a landslide of abuse. Her mother-in-law was overcome by shame. Her father-in-law said, in a voice she had never heard him use before, 'If you can't behave decently to our guest, leave this house.' Khaled stormed out. Rahul left soon after. Late that night Khaled came back and attacked her physically.

Stop, stop remembering. But it is out now, she can't close it down –

Next morning she was unable to move for pain. No sign of Khaled. She heard her mother-in-law's voice, getting Layla off to school: 'Your mother is tired, leave her to rest.' She knew. How could she not? Their rooms were next door to each other. But no one had come in the night to stop him.

When eventually she got up Nargis said, expecting no sympathy, 'I can't share a room with him any more.'

Her mother-in-law said, 'I will move his things into the storeroom. I cannot tell him he cannot come back. But if he does, he will sleep there.'

But he didn't come back.

~ 53 ~

Tessa watches the rain through the train window as it carries her to work. It is three months she has been making this journey. Without consciously noticing, she knows the moment when the green folds of downs give way to the suburbs, the terraced houses climbing over the hills. She sees them and sees nothing, for she is thinking about the changes in Ben. She watches him these days as if he were someone she still needs to get to know. In their too-brief moments together he is talking more, and about things other than practicalities. She is beginning to understand better the connection between their intense last weeks in Laos and the low state he fell into once they had to leave. The stories he was hearing in the mountains unearthed another that for years he had sought to deny – what had happened to his father. All his boyhood he had lived with the effects of his father's distorted spirit, and not wanted to think about what had made him that way, and anyway, what was there to consider, for his father would never speak of it. All Ben knew for certain was the fragments that his mother had heard early on, and passed on to him – how somewhere in Eastern Europe the boy not yet thirteen had heard that the SS were coming to his village and that all Jewish men were to report to them. His mother had sent him to hide in the forest, while the men were loaded into trains. Trains sealed; airless; the men left to die. He had seen that, and he alone of all those men and boys-not-yet men, had survived. Had found his way to another life; but never been able to shed the damage it had done.

And then, in the mountains of a country far from any his father had known, Ben had come face to face with a similar evil. Men were burning other men's villages, putting them to slave-like labour, shooting if they tried to run away. It was inconceivable that people could do such things, yet it was happening. The aggressors were different, their motives were different, the victims were different, but the story felt like a continuous loop that repeated itself in endless new configurations. And this time he was *there* – on the outside, watching, but with just the sliver of a chance that he could do something to stop it happening. That insidious thought was planted in the quiet night-time meeting with the student group in Vientiane. Help us find evidence, they said, and we will know how to use it. The sense of failed obligation has never left him.

This job Hugo has opened up to him has given him the chance to do what then he couldn't. Yet now, just when he is so motivated, she has to go away and he will have no time for his own work. For they still have not found a childminder.

'Nargis has been sending me briefing papers,' she tells Greta, 'like an avalanche. And the more I read, the more ignorant I feel.'

'My dear girl,' Greta says, at her most acerbic, 'they don't need you to know all that, *they* know it. What you bring is an outside eye, so keep it clear. Don't clutter your brain with detail.'

Fine for Greta to say. She doesn't have to climb off that plane and justify her existence as a head-office advisor. But Greta sees beyond that to the real cause of her anxiety about this journey. 'It's Ben that's worrying you, isn't it?'

Greta takes matters into her own hands – that amazing address book again. A young girl called Fern cycles into their lives, the daughter of an old friend of Greta's who once worked for Lifeline and still lives nearby. 'She has dropped out of art college,' Greta tells Tessa, 'and is mooning around at home driving her mother crazy. You'll be doing them all a favour.'

Fern is long and leggy, shy with adults but easy with the children. For two days she works alongside Ben, learning the routine. By day three she is on her own. There are no tears as they do goodbye hugs and Tessa and Ben set off together to cycle to the station.

'Every family should have a Fern,' Ben calls, as they pedal against the wind.

Tessa pushes to catch up with him and cycle alongside. 'Now I won't have to worry about you sliding into a depression while I'm away.'

'Depression?' he calls. A car is heading towards them. Tessa slows down to single file. As soon as it has passed Ben screws his head around, wobbling precariously. His voice sails into the summer air. 'When have you ever known me depressed?'

Greta is amused, and considerably pleased with herself. Tessa says, 'You're a born fixer, Greta.'

'Well, it is gratifying when things work out. There is so much more I would like to do, but I just don't get about as much as I would like.'

'You seem to do fine just sitting here, letting people come to you.'

Greta moves her onto other things. They slip into talking about what being in Kyrgyzstan will signify in Tessa's own inner journey. She is following him into the heart of Central Asia; his place. The light beckons.

Greta says, 'You never got there while he was there, did you?'

'It wasn't possible. The children.'

'Of course.' A pause. 'The arrival of a child changes everything.'

Greta has never had a child of her own, Tessa thinks. Yet she knows.

The miracle of birth, no one can prepare you for it. The onrush of love, the delight in watching this child's every movement, the instinctive realigning of all your priorities – all these were hers and Ben's alone, deeply shared, forever binding, excluding all others.

And for Rahul? What did all that mean? 'What we have knows no limits,' he had said, 'except practical ones.' But now the practical limits had become formidable. She had been grounded, by her own maternal instinct.

He had no choice but to get out of the way. 'Don't try and

write,' he said. 'You'll be tired. I'll phone when I get the chance.'

But when he phoned it was, of course, Ben who answered, so they finally had to encounter each other, at least in voice. 'Tessa's just feeding Sam. Can she call you back in about half an hour?'

A gatekeeper. No possibility of direct access. He withdrew further, immersed himself in his work.

He was handing over his job in Afghanistan and preparing to move to Tajikistan. Tessa and Ben were getting ready to move to Laos; they would be leaving when the baby was six weeks old. To Tessa, in love with her child, all loving feelings seemed to blur into one. When Rahul phoned next she said, 'Come and see me before we leave. I want you to meet Sam.'

But that would also mean meeting Ben.

Rahul said, '*Meri jaan*, are you sure you want that?'

'It's time, Rahul. Something is going to have to shift.'

Tessa was busy with the baby when he arrived so it was Ben who received him. She heard their voices in the next room. Sorry the place is so chaotic, Ben said, we're packing up to go. Rahul said, I know what it's like. Normal conversation, as if there were nothing bigger going on. When she came in to join them Sam was a shield; they all talked about him, watched him. Rahul took a turn holding him and was clearly at home with babies. She had been getting hardly any sleep. She said, 'I should warn you I'm incapable of intelligent conversation,' but perhaps that was no bad thing because it left Ben and Rahul to find their own level. She watched from the sidelines as they searched for common ground and tried not to show that they were trying. There was a moment when she was in the kitchen putting the next load of nappies on to wash, looking at Sam in the rocking seat and thinking, 'You're the only person here who is completely relaxed.'

The phone rang. A call from New Zealand, a thing that never happened. Ben's face said, calamity. When he put the phone down he spoke to Tessa as if Rahul were not there.

'My dad has died.'

Awkwardness became an irrelevance. Ben was devastated. For years he had blocked his parents out to survive; now suddenly it broke through to him, all the things about his father that he valued, all the things he knew were part of himself, all the things he could now never hear or try to say.

Rahul took Sam out for a walk in the buggy, to give them time alone.

Ben had never considered going back but a death leaves you few options. He would get the first flight he could, stay on with his mother after the funeral to sort things out, then go from there straight to Laos. Tessa would, somehow, get the packing done alone and then fly out with Sam.

Rahul said, 'If you need help I could stay on a few days?'

There was no time for anyone to consider feeling complicated about it; it solved a practical problem. They started work straight away as a trio. Ben sorted out his papers while Rahul took over booking flights, first for Ben, then changing his own. Overhearing, both Ben and Tessa got a sense of the size of what he was putting on hold for them. He was heading into a war where hundreds of thousands of people had been displaced and he should have been there, getting emergency systems going.

Ben said, 'Leave this, you go.'

Rahul said, 'A couple of days isn't going to make any difference.'

After that he spent most of his time holding Sam, to free Tessa up to help Ben. The self-consciousness of that first evening had been wiped out.

Ben flew off. There was a moment after he had gone when Tessa and Rahul stood looking at each other, each waiting for the other to decide how to go forward. They were alone, this could have been one of their moments, but Ben and his father were filling the air between them, Sam was right there, the packing still to get done. The question mark didn't last more than a minute and then they both knew how it was going to be.

Rahul said, 'OK, so what needs to go from the kitchen?'

They worked together in a companionship that needed no words to define it, till tiredness made them stop. While Tessa settled Sam to sleep Rahul got a takeaway. When she emerged he said, 'Stop working now, we're going to eat in civilized leisure.' He poured them each a glass, wine for himself, grape-juice for her, and they clinked to the unknown future. What she would be doing was simple, it would focus around Sam, and now that Rahul had spent so many hours with him, that would be easy to share. But he? The chances of their seeing each other for the next few years were slim and she didn't want to struggle to imagine his days. 'Tell me,' she said, as once in Kathmandu she had said, Tell me about Afghanistan. 'What will you do?' she asked now, 'about all those people in the mountains?'

'A lot of it's just practical arrangements,' he said. Setting up systems so that people get shelter, food; tracing people who have been separated in the confusion. There are human tragedies all around you but you've got a job to do, and that keeps you from getting overwhelmed.

> *In all this suffering stay calm,*
> Ghalib says,
> *Breathing with even breath*

He talked about the things that renewed him through the pressures, little interactions that made him laugh, or feel moved at seeing how resilient people could be in hard times. 'And inventive. The children especially. I wish I could waft you there to see.'

Sam woke. Another feed, and it was past midnight by the time he had finished. Normally she would have drifted off to sleep with him but the sand in the hourglass was running down and she came back, to find Rahul up still, waiting for her on the sofa. She came to sit next to him. He said, 'It's your turn. I want you to tell me about Ben and his father.'

She began, things she had not been able to write at the time and had never had occasion to since; now it came out naturally. She described his father, his brilliant, unhappy mind, wanting closeness but unable to connect. The tension that crept up in Ben as he watched his father fill his wine glass yet again. How little Ben knew of his early life, not even the name of the country he had grown up in or those of the people he had lost. It was a dark space between them that there was no way to cross.

'Then on our last evening in New Zealand something astonishing happened. Ben's father came into town and took us out for a meal.' A meal for his father meant wine, and for Ben, deep embarrassment. But something was different that night. Ben's mother wasn't there to be anxious about so instead of being prickly at the things his father said he began picking up the challenges, the two of them winding each other up in unaccustomed repartee till they were laughing with the release of years of pent-up reserve. Beneath the laughter Tessa was fighting off sadness. If things had been just a little different Ben and his father could have had this kind of companionship over all the years past. Ben's father turned his attention to her, leant across the table, took her hand while his own trembled, and said she was a Fine Young Woman. She knew it was only the sentimentality of bleary-eyed alcohol but she had never seen it take him that way. Just as she was thinking she must find a way to get her hand back, he said, 'I had a sister once, a spirited girl like you. Her name was Alisa.' Then he fumbled with his napkin, knocked over his glass, and they all got to their feet in a confusion of wiping things up ...

Suddenly Tessa realized what was happening. She was sitting here in the home she and Ben had made, and Rahul was asking her to help him begin to understand the man whose life he had circled but never until now got near. After her years of loving them both and having to keep everything separate the dam of tension was crumbling. She was crying now, in the relief of having the two parts of her divided life brought together, crying in sadness for Ben, that the simple life he had wanted with her had turned out to be so far from simple. Rahul held her while she wept, and stroked her hair.

When she was calmer she took the handkerchief he was holding out to her and wiped her face, laughing at herself a little now. She said, 'I don't know what came over me.'

'Life came over you. It just does sometimes.' He kissed her wet eyes and held her face, smiling, waiting for her to relax and smile back.

'Don't be afraid,' he said. 'You and Ben are going to be OK. I'm going to be OK. Sam's going to be OK. He's got you as a mother, how could he not be?'

She laughed and said, 'You're ridiculous.'

The last morning. Just two hours to go before the packers would arrive to collect the crates that dominated the stripped room. She put Sam in a sling and they went walking along the canal, noticing the early buds on the willows, watching the birds skim the water. She was moving to Laos, out of range of his flying visits. He was going into a war, and who knew what might happen. But for these quietly moving moments, they had this.

They got back to the flat. Sam was asleep. Careful not to wake him, she took him out of the sling and laid him down on the bed. Then they made tea and sat close together on the sofa to drink it. Rahul had his arm around her. She said, 'You can't drink your tea like this, it'll get cold.' He said, 'Let it.'

The doorbell rang. The removal men, to take the cases away. Sam woke and was suddenly crying fiercely. Rahul went to pick him up while she signed documents. He was holding Sam up against his shoulder, rocking him, and managed to get him to calm down. The removal men left. Still holding Sam in one arm, Rahul put out the other to draw her into a hug. He held her there, neither of them saying anything. Then he disentangled, said quietly, '*Meri jaan*,' handed Sam back to her, picked up his case, and was gone.

Part 3

In that house where a lamp burns bright you need
    feel no uneasiness.
In this dark corner of the earth I have my heart.
    Why be afraid?

GHALIB

Waiting for lightning

On the train to Brighton a man opposite Tessa is reading a newspaper. Idly she looks at the page facing her, international news. A headline catches her eye: 'War threat over Kyrgyzstan.'

The man turns the page, the item is gone. She has to wait till the train pulls in at Brighton station. The man gets out, leaving his newspaper on the seat. She picks it up, turns pages to find it: *Guns have been found in a mosque in Kyrgyzstan, near the border with Tajikistan, raising renewed fears that the four-year civil war may be spilling over.*

As soon as she gets in she goes to see the desk officer. What if things escalate and they cancel flights and she can't get back? The children –

For the desk officer this is just part of the day's work. He has already phoned Lance and discovered that the story has been somewhat hyped. The guns were not found in a functioning mosque but in a small abandoned one, in a village just beyond Sukhunobod. Nevertheless it is a sizeable stockpile of lethal weapons and its discovery has thrown the whole valley into a panic of apprehension. Who put them there? The valley is

411

desperately poor, it cannot be anyone local. Clearly this is a temporary storage place, waiting for someone to collect them. It can't be Tajik rebels, they would have gone the other way. It must be the Uzbeks. If they are planning to make a raid back into Uzbekistan they will have to cross Kyrgyz territory.

'He says if things stay tense they might have to call off the part of your visit up into the mountains, but everything else should be OK.'

Right. This is what I let myself in for. Just get on with it, Tessa.

Ben stands in the kitchen while she gets supper ready. 'I don't want you going into a war zone.'

'I'm not. There's nothing actually happening. And the people I work with go into far more high-wire situations all the time.'

'Something could happen any time. Men with guns aren't predictable.'

'Ben –' Tessa gestures with her head to the living room, where the children are playing within hearing distance. 'We can't talk about this now.'

But she is too late. When they are sitting to eat Sam asks, 'Is there fighting where you're going, Mama?'

'No, poppet. I'm just going to work with people there. They help kids who don't have lots of good things, like you do.'

Ben steps in. 'I'll tell you what there is where Mama's going, the highest mountains in the world, made by two mega bits of the earth called tectonic plates. They push up against each other like this.' He starts demonstrating with two plastic plates.

Tessa is not sure this is an improvement. 'It goes so slowly you can't even see a tiny movement.'

'Not always,' Ben says, refusing to compromise science. 'Sometimes it's very sudden.'

'Why do you have to go, Mama?'

'It's my job, Sam. But it's only ten days.'

Ben says, 'And grown-ups have jobs so they can earn money. You're expensive to feed, you kids. Alisa, eat those carrots. They're not Lego.'

'Are carrots expensive?' Sam asks.

In the Resham-serai office there is a buzz of discussion. It's all because of the drug trade from Afghanistan, Akbor says. The Taliban have stopped opium getting out through Pakistan so now instead it simply comes north. Trucks loaded with it get across the river that is the Afghan border, bribing and maybe worse to get past military posts and officials. They drive through to Uzbekistan where it is sold on to others who take it on to Russia and the West. And that fuels the war. It is money from opium that buys the guns that have been taken back into Tajikistan. And now here.

Fahmeda for some reason doesn't like this discussion and tells them all to get back to work. Nargis, Lance notices, has already withdrawn to her office.

They wake next morning to the news that in Uzbekistan, just across the border, a prison has been attacked. The officer in charge and several guards have been killed, and scores of prisoners escaped; most were in for offences relating to practising Islam.

It is all anyone can think of. The Uzbekistan government is going ballistic, demanding that its neighbours arrest Islamic militants. How? Kyrgyzstan has thousands of kilometres of mountainous borders and no chance of patrolling them. In Tajikistan the government long ago lost control of those mountains.

The rebels must have passed through Sukhunobod; or if not through, very near. 'OK,' Lance says, 'we have to start thinking of the implications for people we work with. Fahmeda, you get up to Sukhunobod to find out what happened there. Nargis, see what you can find out from local government officials. I will talk to people in the UN agencies. Akbor, call the Tashkent office, see what they can tell you. Once we have a better picture of what actually happened and the likely fallout, we will work through possible scenarios and options in response.'

He moves back to his office. Annabel follows him. He is not pleased. This is one line she hasn't yet overstepped.

She asks, 'Do you think anyone in Sukhunobod might have been hurt?'

'Unlikely, but not impossible, if the rebels demanded food or shelter and someone didn't co-operate. Why?'

'Just, I was thinking – If Fahmeda's going up there to check it might be useful to have someone with her who has first-aid training.'

414

He is about to say, 'Annabel, this is not your business,' but she has a point. He will check with Fahmeda. If she isn't first-aid trained, she should be, and Nargis and the drivers.

Annabel says, 'I am.'

'You are what?'

'First-aid trained. I could go.'

'Annabel, there is *absolutely no question* of your going to Sukhunobod. Is that understood?'

The fierceness in his voice shocks them both. For a moment there is silence. Then with some difficulty he moderates his tone to say, 'I know you want to help, but it's not your place. Now get on with something else. I have calls to make.'

All day he is busy, but the miserable taste of tension is there, constantly. Of course he had to say what he said, but to anyone else it wouldn't have come out with such sudden heat.

He doesn't see her again all day. He asks Akbor if he knows where she is. 'Maybe at the street-children's centre?' he says, but his voice is reticent, and Lance knows she has told Akbor. He feels exposed and angry.

When he gets home there is no sign of Annabel. He cooks a risotto, trying to release his tension.

He waits. She doesn't come. He decides to start without her.

Sounds of her crutches coming up the stairs, her voice and Akbor's. Then Akbor's footsteps going down.

She comes in, sees the food on the table, his empty plate. 'Akbor and I were working. Sorry if you waited.' The tone sounds far from sorry.

It is their first overt coldness and he can't bear it. He has his speech prepared but the sight of her makes it impossible to use it. He says, impulsively, 'I shouted at you. I'm sorry. I didn't mean it to come out like that.'

She shrugs, and goes to the bathroom.

When she emerges he says, 'Annabel, we share this space and it's too small to carry tension we can't sort out. If you felt I was being overbearing, I apologize. But this may turn into a security crisis, and you do need to stay out of it.'

'Because?'

The intonation is that of a resentful teenager. For an instant he sees the absurdity of the situation, and almost smiles. But he holds back and says, simply, 'Because you have no status to get involved.'

The word 'status' touches the wrong button. Her frigid tone metamorphoses into angry heat. 'I'm a human being, and I thought there might be people in trouble. You don't need any special status to respond to that.'

'No. You just need a warm heart, which you have in large measure, and which I appreciate. But I'm responsible for what Lifeline does here, and however much you contribute, you're a volunteer. As a matter of principle we don't let volunteers get involved in situations that are potentially a security risk.'

With heavy irony – 'In case they do something foolish?'

'Perhaps.' He refuses to rise. 'But mainly in case they get hurt.' Another silence. 'Come on, Annabel, lighten up. I'm telling you it's not personal. And if you haven't eaten, you must be hungry.'

It takes another ten minutes but as he watches her tackling

her food with every sign of a healthy appetite, his own tension relaxes, to be replaced immediately by a desire to hold her. 'Kiss and make up,' they used to say when he was a kid. Making up without being able to even hug her is a joyless process.

'Tell me about your first-aid training. What made you do it?'

That works. 'I saw an accident when I was twelve. This guy on a bike crashed into a van. It was traumatic, there was blood everywhere and he was knocked out. There was a woman standing by who knew exactly what to do, she kept him going till the ambulance came. I thought, right, I want to be able to do that.'

'And have you ever used it?'

'No.'

'So I've robbed you of your first chance? No wonder you're mad at me.'

'What I was really mad at, if you want to know, was being treated like a child. You didn't want me going in case *I* got hurt.'

'Well of course I didn't! Is that such an insult?'

A suspicion of a smile. Then, suddenly, 'You know what? It's boring arguing. Let's just stop.'

'Brilliant idea.' And feeling light-headed with relief, he can't resist adding, 'Especially from one so young.'

She eyes the rest of the risotto on her plate and says, 'It's a pity this tastes so good, otherwise I might have used it as a missile.'

◈

Fahmeda returns from Sukhunobod, everyone gathers round to hear. No one has been hurt and no one will admit to seeing armed men moving about, but for some days farms in the outlying areas have been hearing strange sounds in the nights. Everyone is nervous in case there is another raid, or the Uzbekistan army comes after them. If that happens they will do what is demanded of them, and they are asking Lifeline to inform the government, to make sure there will be no reprisals.

After she has briefed them she goes with Nargis into another room, door closed. When they come out Nargis has that closed look on her face, back too erect, her formal persona in control.

A little while later she brings him some receipts to authorize; when he hands them back she does not leave his office. 'Sit for a moment,' he says. She does, but obediently, her body tense. He gets up to close the door, then asks quietly, 'Have you had news? Is it your husband?'

'Not news exactly. Things we guess.'

She wants to tell him, she knows the time has come; but how to find the words?

He waits. She knows he is going to wait until she gets it out. She says quietly, 'I couldn't tell you before because I am too ashamed. He is a drug dealer.'

Now that the words are out she is surprised at how simple it was to say.

He shows no reaction; simply asks, 'What kind of dealing?'

'First it was small stuff, getting it from a middleman, selling it on in the market. Now it is big traffic. We hear that he drives a truck for the people who control the trade.'

Suddenly it all makes sense. That is why he went to Tajikistan.

Nargis is talking now without prompting. 'That first time we went to Sukhunobod, you remember? You saw I was speaking to someone, after we were with the children? That was my mother-in-law's cousin. He goes over to Gharm sometimes. He hears things from people there.'

'Do they know who he is working for?'

She hesitates for a second before saying, 'When there is a war everyone needs guns. The government too.' She fumbles for a handkerchief, gets up, moves to stand looking out of the window. 'His parents have stopped talking about him. It has nearly destroyed them. Layla is a child, she knows nothing. And she must never hear it.'

'I completely understand.'

'I don't think you do.' She turns to face him. 'He isn't just selling drugs, he *needs* to, so he can buy for himself. Those people, they lose moral sense. We are afraid all the time about how he is living, what he might be doing. And there is no way back. Once you start working for drug traffickers, they can't afford to let you stop, you know too much about them. If they see that he is trying to give up, they will kill him rather than let him get away.'

Before he knows what he is doing he is next to her, his arms around her. She accepts it, allowing herself to be held by a man she knows she cannot have, this woman who has carried too much, for too long.

Quietly he says, 'I wish there was a way to make things easier for you.'

'There's nothing. It's the way things are. It's always been like that here. You just have to go on.' But she moves her head against his chest, and her voice is muffled now in tears. 'Whatever we hear of what is happening up there, for us it is always about Khaled. Those guns in the mosque. I am sure it was him who put them there.'

'There is no reason why it would have been him. You have to protect yourself from fear.'

'There *is* a reason. Khaled trades in guns, and he knows Sukhunobod. He would have known a place to hide them.'

~ 55 ~

There are times that you know, even as they are happening, that you will look back on this and hold it in your memory; an experience self-contained, carrying its own significance. For Tessa the journey to Central Asia was just that – time out of time, transported to another world.

From Khujand airport the small plane rose almost vertically, it seemed, to clear height enough to get over the mountains. She looked down into the barren high valleys. Somewhere in that complex knot of mountains Tajiks fleeing from war had crossed into Kyrgyzstan, and rebel groups back into Uzbekistan; and Rahul and Vitaly Ivanov had disappeared. Sadirov was there still, holed up in some remote valley that no one else dared approach; and there were still scores of his men stuck in Afghanistan. At any moment he might strike again, to get them back.

Nargis met her at the airport. Tessa felt she knew her already, and it wasn't just because of all those briefing papers flying between them. Everything she had learnt from Rahul about this part of the world seemed to be personified in Nargis. That they shared a connection to him cut through reserve, and with that as a starting point, a woman-to-woman understanding came instinctively. They were a similar age, both balancing work and family; to talk of their children was natural, to laugh together at small familiar things. She learnt Nargis's style of professional competence through days that were scheduled to the last minute.

Moving through the streets of Resham-serai, Tessa kept seeing things she felt she recognized. The market, the statue of the poet, the decaying hotel where Rahul had stayed on his short visits and where she now had a room. She played with a fantasy that perhaps she had the very room he had used. She listened to people talk of the social changes they were having to navigate and the effects of the catastrophic economic collapse. Fahmeda inducted her into Tajik hospitality at an overflowing meal in her home for all the staff, which Tessa noticed included Annabel. An elderly man with a lute sang strange half-droning tunes. This is *shash maqaam*, Fahmeda told her, six rhythms, it is our ancient tradition. In Soviet times it was neglected but a few musicians have kept the knowledge and now more people are calling them for weddings or other gatherings.

On day four she and Nargis set off for Sukhunobod, with Sultan driving.

Lance woke at dawn and followed them in his mind through the morning, past the army checkpoint, negotiating those hairpin bends. There had been no further security incidents and there seemed no reason for them not to go, but he could not deny that he was anxious. When you've made a decision, he told himself firmly, it's pointless rehashing it. Move on. They would be gone three days and he had work to attend to.

Duncan Eversley had reappeared in Resham-serai, the suave man who had arrived on the same flight. He invited Lance to lunch. Lance accepted in the hope of checking out whether he knew anything about the security situation, but they hadn't been together five minutes before his instinctive suspicion of the man resurfaced. Working for the IMF? In a remote province like this?

Eversley was looking tanned. He had been walking in the mountains, he said, which turned out to be a valley just beyond Sukhunobod. Lance had no doubt that it wasn't just the scenery he had been exploring.

'You people have connections up there, I believe?' Eversley asked.

'Just a couple of small projects,' Lance said.

That evening Annabel asked, 'How was your lunch with the IMF man?'

He stared. 'How did you know?'

'Akbor saw you going into the restaurant. He recognized the man.'

'You can't do a damn thing in this place without everyone knowing.'

'It has its uses. Akbor says –'

'Whatever Akbor says, if it's something I need to know, he can tell me directly.'

Her turn to stare. 'That's a bit extreme.'

He was mad at himself for being so unguarded. But Akbor this, Akbor that, it was too much.

'All I was going to say,' she continued calmly, 'is that Akbor says Rahul didn't trust that guy Eversley. I thought you might like to know.'

That did interest him. 'Do you know why?'

'Why don't you ask Akbor yourself?'

She was mocking him, and he couldn't hold out against it. 'I'm a fool,' he said.

'You are,' she agreed calmly.

Next morning he did a spot of direct communication with Akbor. Eversley had come to the office once to meet Rahul. Afterwards Rahul had said, 'If that man comes snooping around when I'm not here and asks questions about our work, act like you're really stupid and know nothing. And let me know.'

Eversley hadn't come back while Rahul was alive, and Akbor knew no more than that, but it was enough to prompt Lance to phone Brighton and ask Glen if he could find out anything about him. Glen loved a challenge and he always knew someone he could ask.

He called back a few hours later. 'I checked it out with James Horley. He's another upper-class Russian expert, I guessed they might know each other.'

'And?'

'It's true Eversley has done stuff for the IMF, but only occasional. So it may well be a cover now to get access. He's working for a mining conglomerate that's taken out a concession. Don't think he knows anything technical. Just risk assessment.'

That would explain why Eversley was wooing him. No mining company wanted to be in the path of Islamic radicals when they got active, so contacts with people in Sukhunobod could well be helpful to them. But it didn't explain why Rahul would have been hostile enough to warn Akbor.

Hugo called to ask how Tessa's visit was going.

'Slightly surreal. Like she's been here before.'

'I guess she has, in a way.'

Hugo was back in Dushanbe now, liaising with the government delegation in preparation for the Tehran peace talks. For more than a year it had seemed they were nearly there yet each time they got all the parties together something intervened to stall it. People outside the process had lost confidence that it would ever finish.

'It's forty degrees and tempers are fraying. I can feel something building up. We never get through a summer without a security crisis.'

'Don't tempt fate,' Lance said.

'You believe in fate?'

'Of course not,' he laughed. And then added, 'But you have to wonder, sometimes.'

In between other work Hugo was embarking on a clear-out of his papers. Later he would look back and wonder at the timing of it. It was almost as if he felt that he might be confronting a new challenge and was clearing the decks to prepare for it.

Buried under other piles he found some papers of Rahul's that he had retrieved from his rooms in the UN guest house. Six months ago. He had known there would be nothing relevant here yet he had been assailed by a moment of sentimentality and had taken them with him to look through later. Now, as he was about to discard them, he noticed a small padded envelope and remembered the envelope just this size left on Rahul's desk, addressed to his mother. He turned it over. It was sealed. He opened it.

Another cassette, labelled 'For MJ, 18 December 1996.'

He stared at it. He pictured Rahul recording that first cassette for his mother and then, influenced perhaps by a presentiment that something might happen to him, deciding to do one more. But he could think of only one person that he would have done that for, and her initials were not MJ. A letter he might have skimmed for clues but he had scruples about privacy and could not bring himself to listen to something so clearly intended to be private. If there was someone other than Rahul's mother and Tessa that he was sending spoken letters to, he didn't want to know. His only responsibility was to get this to whoever it

425

was meant for. After that he would try to forget it.

He went through a mental list of people Rahul had seemed close to in Tajikistan; in Afghanistan. No MJs. He phoned Rahul's father. Did he know anyone close to Rahul with initials MJ? He did not. He phoned the Lifeline office in Tashkent, keeping the reason for his enquiry vague. No one there called MJ. He wanted to ask Ulughbek, the driver, but decided it would not be helpful to draw attention to him in that way.

He phoned Lance again.

Lance considered for a moment. 'There's a poet he was interested in, Mirza Janov. Usually written as one word, but sometimes two.'

'A living poet?'

'Long dead.'

'No good. I'm looking for someone he might have sent an audio cassette to.'

'Then I've no idea. But I can ask people here.'

Half an hour later he called back. None of them could think of anyone.

Parveen Jalali. The name simply arrived in Hugo's brain, unasked; Rahul's friend in Human Rights Watch. PJ. Could she perhaps have another forename beginning with M, a name her close friends used? But there was no way to tell, and he was certainly not going to ask Tessa.

The cassette stared at him, soundlessly creating a nagging unease. He attempted to neutralize it by labelling it as if it were simply another work task, in a file marked 'Rahul-related, still to complete.'

~ 56 ~

On the road, another of Rahul's roads, climbing into the mountains. Sultan halted the car near a small lake whose dark depths stared back at her when she stood at its edge and looked down. All her senses were alert, to the solidity of cold rock on which they sat to eat by the roadside, to the silence, the echoing air. The vastness; the timelessness.

Back into the car, she in the front seat. Nargis had insisted. 'I want you to see our mountains properly.' And see them she did, from more angles than she had bargained for. Once after Sultan had negotiated a particularly dramatic bend he turned round to grin cheerfully at Nargis in the back. She said something sharp in Tajik, then translated for Tessa. 'I told him, if you don't keep your eyes on the road we'll take you off out-of-town driving.' Sultan just grinned back, but this time into the rear-view mirror.

In Sukhunobod town it was people's faces she noticed most sharply, the older ones weather-beaten, the young girls extraordinarily clear-skinned and beautiful. That this had been for centuries a route linking distant continents was evident in features that ranged from Mongolian to Aryan. The day was spent listening to the teachers discuss their problems, and observing the children. It was summer now so they were back in classrooms. There were a few books in a locked cupboard, and visual aids, decades old to judge by their state, pinned to walls high above the line of sight of these small people. We have to keep them from being damaged, the teachers said. There is no money to buy more. The old system supplied materials someone distant had devised but gave teachers no concept that it might be possible to teach without them. You can learn basic maths with stones as easily as with pictures of apples in a book, Tessa said. But she felt the answer in their tense expressions. Our forefathers counted stones. We cannot go backwards.

On the road again, to the yurt where they were to spend the night. They were received into a dimly lit, warm, enclosing circular home, walls lined with felt carpets in green and red patterns; and the space full already, it seemed, of people. But it was just the woman and her five children, ranging from very small to almost grown. Her husband, Nargis explained, had died in an avalanche. All the children had roles in keeping the family economy going. The youngest was four but he with his scarcely older brother were responsible for looking after the lambs, a job which could take them well beyond sight of home base. The woman saw Tessa's surprise. 'Do your children not have jobs?' she asked. Tessa said, 'Not important ones like yours, but when I get back maybe we'll do things differently.'

She worried about the burden they were imposing on this struggling family. Nargis said, 'Hospitality is a religion with these people, they feel honoured to have guests.' The schoolteachers would see she got other kinds of support in return.

They slept on wooden platforms between rugs of felt that the woman herself had made, and that smelt of sheep and smoke.

They woke to the soft sounds of people moving about, the fire getting going. They emerged from their cocoon into clean mountain air, and the high world spreading away endlessly.

On to the refugee settlement where Rahul had set up relief services; and from there towards Uzbekistan. 'This is the road the rebels would have taken when they crossed the border to raid the prison,' Nargis said. And Sultan joked, 'Look out for men with guns.' But it was no joke.

They arrived in a derelict-looking town clustered around a closed factory. Here she was shadowing Nargis, who had been asked to visit a residential institution for children with disabilities. Its budget was to be withdrawn; no one would be paid, there would be almost no money for food. Tessa stared at Nargis. 'We can't solve problems like that,' she said. Nargis said, 'Nor can they, I couldn't say no. At least we should see, and give them courage if we can.'

It was a deeply depressing experience. The children seemed disabled as much by having been kept away from normal social contacts as from anything they had been born with. Perhaps it would be better if it closed.

'What happens to such children in the West?' the director of the institution asked.

Tessa said, 'Mostly they live at home and go to school like other children. The teachers try to give them special help.'

The director looked disbelieving, defensive, verging on hostile. If such a thing were to happen here, she would lose her professional status, the only thing she had been trained to do.

She said, 'These children came here young. The families are not used to coping.'

They all looked at Tessa. What do they do in the West? The constant question. As things dissolved around them they clung to the belief that there was a magic formula elsewhere. There were things she could suggest, it was possible to see a road from here to somewhere different, but there was no point saying it now, to a woman who faced the abyss of losing her livelihood. To Nargis, later; and Nargis would find a time and a way.

She said, 'There are no simple answers.'

That too was not a good response. If she had no answers, why had she come?

Breakfast next morning was another Tajik-hospitality experience. Tessa could hardly eat, thinking of the children.

They set off back. 'A two-hour drive,' Nargis said. 'We'll be in Resham-serai by midday.

They had been driving perhaps half an hour when Tessa saw someone standing in the road ahead. No, she saw now, there were two of them, waving them to stop. They were in some kind of uniform, but grubby, crumpled, and carrying rifles. The movement of the car changed – for a moment she thought Sultan might attempt to speed past them – but he had pulled to a halt. One of the men came up to his window, rifle ready. An interchange in Tajik. Sultan was shaking his head, gesticulating, getting tense. He swivelled round to Nargis. She wound down her window and summoned the man to talk to her instead. She harangued him, there was no other word for it. She gestured towards Tessa, turned back to him, asked him a lot of questions.

After each one he seemed a little less confident; and Tessa saw now how young he was, scarcely more than a boy. He spoke to his companion. Stepped back, gestured sulkily for them to pass.

Sultan's foot was on the accelerator, revving like life depended on it. They sped away.

No one spoke until they could no longer see the men in the rear-view mirror. Then Sultan and Nargis both started laughing, the under-pressure laugh of release from tension, and through it words coming at Tessa in overlapping voices. They are soldiers but they have run away from the army, they don't get their pay. They say people who use the road should pay. Nargis had told him, 'It makes me ashamed, to see you point a gun at women. Where is your respect? What would your mother think? See, we have a foreign guest? What is she going to think about our people?'

Tessa felt breathless, just listening. 'So cool, with that gun pointing at you.'

Nargis was no longer laughing. 'It *does* make me ashamed. And angry. These guns, they spoil everyone's lives. But also I feel sorry. They are just young boys, no work, no future.'

Sultan said, 'Listen.'

The car was producing a strange noise, getting louder. It juddered, threatened to go into a skid. Nargis barked instructions. Sultan was heaving at the steering wheel, fighting the pull of the skid and gravity, the slipping earth beneath the spinning wheels. Tessa felt blinded by panic, saw nothing ahead of her, just her children thousands of miles away, never to see their mother again –

The car shuddered to a halt.

Silence. They sat completely still, absorbing the fact that they were still there, not crashing down the mountainside.

Slowly Sultan opened his door. Got out. Tessa sat watching through the windscreen as he stared at the tyres, the skid marks, and lifted the bonnet to peer into the engine. She turned round to face Nargis. Her face was drawn and white; naked now, hiding nothing.

'Let's get out,' she said.

Tessa wasn't sure her legs would hold her. Once on her feet she followed Nargis over to some low rocks. They found a flat one and perched on it. The land seemed empty in every direction.

Nargis said, 'I can't believe it. On your first journey.'

Tessa said, 'I feel shaky, just to be alive.'

Sultan came over to tell them, the car had blown something, Tessa couldn't afterwards remember what. He and Nargis switched to Tajik. A rapid discussion, then Nargis turned to Tessa. 'No way to get it going again without a spare part. If he can get to the army control post, they have a radio, they can get a message to the office, to send Taimur up with the other car.'

'How far is it?'

'Too far to walk. But he's going to go back to the farm we passed, to see if they have a vehicle he can borrow.'

He set off. Nargis got out a thermos of tea and some biscuits.

They sat drinking, saying little; looking out over the long

vista of the plain below. Tessa began to notice small things near her. The rocks. The grasses. The air sifting around them, carrying scents of wild flowers. She stretched out a hand, as if to touch it.

So far away was the life they had left down below. Up here it was so still; no noise of a car, no clang of the town. But as her ears began to tune in she realized the place was alive with small noises of its own. Insects somewhere near, in the grass. Goats in the fields above. The wind in the trees. A bird calling, high, far.

Nargis said, 'When I was a child we used to come up here. My uncle lived in one of the villages we passed through. There was a stream we played in.'

There was sadness in the memory. Tessa tried to imagine Nargis as a child. She was tall, big boned, one of those people who look as if they have always been adult. And all those worry lines around the eyes.

'Where did *you* live, when you were a child?' Nargis asked.

'All over,' Tessa said. Indonesia, Malaysia, Thailand. But she saw that the names alone evoked envy. 'You have something here that I always wanted and never had, a place where you belong.'

'I'd rather have experience,' Nargis said.

A few moments later: 'Yesterday, with the children, you had some ideas you weren't saying. Tell me.'

Tessa looked at her, marvelling. 'Guns pointing, near-death on the road, nothing stops you thinking about your work.'

'It's important. And you're here such a short time.'

They got started. Tessa thought, I will remember this for ever, devising a strategy for children with disabilities, while sitting on a rock half-way up a mountain.

Time moved slowly, ceased to be worth measuring. Sultan reappeared, driving a mule-cart with a young lad next to him. The sight was so appropriate to the mountain, so inappropriate to Sultan, it was impossible not to laugh. It was all they had, he said, and they hadn't been keen to lend it until they discovered that he worked for an international agency. Only money from outside the country had real bargaining power.

Sultan and the mule were still getting used to each other. 'Horses, I know. Mules, no. They are stubborn and stupid beasts.'

'And steady on mountain roads,' Nargis said. 'You'll be grateful round those corners.'

As they watched him set off she said, 'He'll make an adventure of it, nothing keeps him down, that boy.'

The cart moved off, slowly down, getting smaller and smaller. It rounded the first bend, and they could no longer see it.

Silence again.

The sun was high. Nargis began to calculate. A mule cart travels at slow walking pace, say four kilometres an hour. But never down that road. OK, say three. When you're walking steep uphill you have to add X for every metre increase in altitude, but I can't remember what X is, and what do you add for going down so steep you have to hold the mule back the whole time?

'How many kilometres does he have to go?'

'I don't know, so why am I calculating?'

They laughed. Tessa said, 'Whatever it is, it'll be hours. Why don't we walk? Up?'

They packed the mugs, biscuits, tea cloth, back in the car. 'There are goats up here,' Nargis said, 'They'll eat anything.'

'You know everything. It's very relaxing. If I was on my own I wouldn't have a clue.'

'If we were stuck on a mountain in Indonesia or Malaysia or Ireland, you'd be the one who knew.'

It was rough going, making their way up a boulder-strewn incline; but a good feeling to be moving. They turned round every little while to see yet another level of view open up. Tessa said, 'Rahul told me a bit about you. Your family.'

Nargis looked up sharply. 'What did he say?'

'About your husband, the war in Afghanistan. He admired you, the way you cope with everything.' Pause. 'And your father-in-law, that he studied with your great poet.'

'He told you about that?'

'A bit.' She had no inclination to involve Nargis in having to think about her relationship with Rahul; a simple formula would be enough. 'He was a kind of mentor, ever since I was in India. We didn't see each other often but when we did, he talked about things that were important to him. Like getting to know you all here.' She waited a moment. Then, 'Do you mind?'

Nargis shook her head. 'What does it matter? What does anything matter, when people are dead?'

'Your father-in-law, Rahul said he knew so much.'

435

'He does. When Rahul was here we thought – But most of it is going to die with him. It was good for him, talking to Rahul; but now he's gone, it's like it never happened.'

'I don't know,' Tessa said. 'It may not be all lost.'

Nargis stared. 'What do you mean?'

'Lance told you about the notes he has, that Annabel has been translating? I asked her about them. The ones she has done were all about things in Uzbekistan. But there's another lot that she hasn't started on, she got side-tracked into working with Akbor. I asked her to check them. They're notes he made on his visits here. Every time he came, it seems.'

'Notes – about?'

'Things he was learning from someone called Behdad Gulmanov.'

'That's my father-in-law.'

Tessa nodded. 'I thought it would be. Annabel says it looks like he was telling Rahul about his early life, and everything he knew about Rahman Mirzajanov. You should have a look at them.'

Nargis's lit face was reward itself; but still she could not fully take it in. 'Lance said they were in the old writing – I won't be able to read them.'

'But your father-in-law will.'

Suddenly her body stiffened, alert as an animal that has picked up a scent. 'Listen.'

Far away, down the valley, a sound. A sound becoming clearer now. A car engine.

They hurtled down the slope, back to the road.

~ 57 ~

Nargis took them to meet him, Behdad Gulmanov, retired Professor of Central Asian Literature. Lance, Tessa, Annabel, all these outsiders, let in finally past the privacy she had guarded so carefully. They came into the main room where her mother-in-law sat on cushions against a wall hung with red carpets, supervising Layla's homework. They talked for a few moments, and then they all went out to the verandah.

Behdad Gulmanov rose to greet them, his eyes cautious but engaged. Lance put the package of notes into his hands. He held them, looking down at them. Tessa was watching his face, the face of a man who had lost too much, and had hardly spoken to anyone outside the family for months. He looked up, his eyes met hers. She was moved, knowing that she sat where Rahul had sat with the old man, drawing out what he alone knew. But without language, how was she to tell him? She gestured to the courtyard with its cherry trees and vegetables, and over the tops of the walls, to the mountains, cut-outs against the sky. 'This is beautiful,' she said, and turned to ask Nargis to say it in Farsi. But Behdad Gulmanov was already nodding. He had understood, from her face.

Nargis pointed to the storeroom. 'That's where the poems have been all these years.' Then she turned and said something to her father-in-law, to tempt him to begin talking. But he was immersed still in the strangeness of it all.

In English again she said, 'Maybe it will be easier if I am not here. Annabel can help you.' She went inside to get the meal ready.

At first the old man and Annabel spoke, short exchanges which she did not attempt to interpret. Then she turned, signalling that he had things he wanted to tell them. He gestured to the notes and said, 'You have given me back something I thought was lost for ever. I cannot find words to thank you.'

But after a few minutes more the words began to come of their own accord. Rahul had heard about Rahman Mirzajanov from his father, he said, before he ever came here, and he wanted to hear everything I could tell him. My teacher had trusted me with things he did not talk about to others. You know he was in the Emir's prison in Bukhara and tortured? It was the Bolsheviks who released him, when they conquered the city. Perhaps from that experience, he believed they would bring changes that would be good for the people. Those early Bolshevik commanders, they were uneducated men who had risen in the revolution and they were Russians, nearly all, they had no understanding of our people. He was useful to them – a scribe, an interpreter. But he was broken by all the betrayals, and he was powerless. He knew he would be lost if he challenged openly. Only in his poetry, the secret poems, only in those could he hold on to his integrity. Then his enemies trapped him. They set him up, sent him abroad knowing he might try to make contact with people outside.

His words drifted into nothing. They waited.

He began again: 'He never came back. People disappeared, you never heard of them again, they just never came back.' Perhaps his mind was moving to those other losses, the other people who had just disappeared. His own son, of whom he could not speak; but of Rahul he could. 'He was supposed to be coming here the week he died. Then he phoned to say he had been called to go on an important journey. I think often of that. If he had not cancelled it.'

Nargis had reappeared at the door and was listening. Quietly she prompted, 'Tell them about the poems.'

'What must I tell? I have had them for fifty years. I was a young man when he disappeared and now, you see how I am.'

'But things have changed,' she said.

'It is the same self-seeking, power-hungry kinds of men in control as before. If they saw the poems I have, they would still say they are subversive. All my life I have heard lies from those in power, and these are no different. They put up a statue to him but they care nothing for the meaning of his poetry.'

Lance asked, 'What happened when Rahul came?'

When the question was translated he turned to Lance. 'You were his friend, Nargis says?'

'I was. His close friend.'

'He was a good man. A talented man. But he tried to do too many things.'

Lance nodded. 'I too wished he would slow down. Take more time for other things.'

'When peace is signed in Tajikistan, he always said, he would have more time. When peace is signed.'

Nargis said, 'And you remember what he said about the poems? A poet writes because he has things to say that people should hear. You cannot leave them buried.'

Behdad Gulmanov was backing off. He said, defensively, 'It needs someone who can read both scripts.'

'*You* can.'

'I am too tired. Rahul said he would find someone, but he didn't.'

'What was that person going to do?' Lance asked.

He looked at Lance, confused, as if he couldn't understand the question. Nargis repeated it. He said, as if it were obvious, 'They would write the poems I have in Cyrillic, so people here can read them.' Pause. 'And the ones that are already known, those they would write in Persian script. Then he was going get them all published, every poem in both kinds of writing so that the whole Persian-speaking world could read them. First of all outside the country, where we didn't have to ask anyone's permission. Then when the government saw he was recognized in other countries, they would not dare to suppress them.'

His voice had become animated, but suddenly the energy dropped again. 'And everything that is in those notes, the story of Rahman Mirzajanov's life, that too he was going to write, so that people who didn't live through those times would understand how the poems were wrenched out of pain. And then it could be translated, so the English-speaking world too could know.'

Lance turned to Annabel, a question in his eyes. She nodded.

'Tell him,' he said, 'and don't bother to interpret. Just tell him it can still happen.'

And as he and Tessa sat there with words they didn't understand flowing over them, he knew Annabel was telling him that she could do it, she was the person Rahul had not had time to find; and he, Lance, would find a way to get it published. He was closer to happiness than he had been for a long time; a quiet, grounded contentment. He was thinking, how our minds look for complexity when the answer is so simple. He had puzzled over why Rahul had chosen to write in Farsi. With the Uzbekistan notes, yes, it was probably for security, but with these it was simply because that was the language in which he was hearing the story. And why had he taken each instalment back with him to Delhi? Just because he was conscious of how unique was this record he was building up.

There may be stories here, Hamza had said, that we should keep hold of, for future generations. They had been there all along, if he'd had eyes to see.

~ 58 ~

Thousands of miles to the west, and six hours behind in time, Ben made his way to the office of Ethical Economics. It consisted of a series of interlinked rooms on the fifth floor of a run-down nineteenth-century building, serviced by a lift like a cage with expanding metal sides. It entertained him every time he used it, the irony of this group of individuals trying to track some of the world's most powerful corporations from a building with a lift as primitive as this.

It had taken him by surprise, how much this work meant to him. Since his first conscious thought the only thing he had wanted to do was earth sciences. He could not have found words for the power that drew him, he knew only that when he was working nothing disturbed his concentration, as nothing rivalled the elation of being out in mountains, directly in contact with rocks. Yet here he was, working on something that had only the most tangential connection to the science that had always absorbed him, and the switched-on feeling was similar.

In all the months without serious work to challenge his mind, he had done a lot of thinking. There's a paradox about time, he reflected, which men who have never stayed home with children never experience. When you're responsible for kids you have zero time to yourself, but in another way you have too much because actually they don't need your attention all the time. If they know you are there, with no intention of trying to escape, they get into playing. If they get wind of the fact that you are trying to do your own thing, they invent ways to bind you. So there are all these spaces when you are hanging around with them when your mind could be doing something but you can't get away to do it. So things float into it. Thoughts about his present state, how it got to be like this. About being alone, and not alone.

Now, with Tessa away, off on a journey of her own, it felt almost like the times before the children came when she would be gone, to be with Rahul. Factually, of course, everything was different – Rahul was not there, and the children were here. But one aspect was the same. Tessa was temporarily gone.

For all the years till he met her his own company had always been enough for him. His friends perhaps thought him shy with women but it was never that, it was self-protection, from watching his parents. Better by far to be alone. Tessa's intrusion into his life was the first disturbance in this pattern. She always said she had been in pieces at the time but it was not what he saw. He saw someone whole, real, someone whose horizons seemed unlimited. He realized for the first time that he had been stuck, isolated, while she moved through the world, and he wanted to move with her. For a few months they were intensely getting to know each other. Then that was absorbed, and gradually became normal, something added to life that took nothing away.

Then Rahul reappeared. For a while he felt blank, not knowing what he felt. He did what he had always done in difficult times, retreated into work. Tessa was still there but it was no longer just the two of them, it was two plus one. Sometimes he was part of the two, and sometimes he was the one at the side. Actually he found he could fill either role, but the switching was difficult. She could not help him adjust – he did not expect her to; as in these last months he has been unable to help her over Rahul's death. Existentially we are alone. You cannot merge yourself, you are lost if you let the desire for that drag you down. The idea that two people can blend into one is like an unstable equation. Don't try to define it, or its limits. You cannot hold the spirit of another person, you cannot ask them to fill your aching spaces. Do it, and you destroy the very thing you crave.

Companionship, that is something else, something you can hold on to. Sharing a life. Being alongside each other. Keep it nourished, it may grow into something more than you asked for. Like loving children. At root what you're doing in caring for them is essentially practical but every day you do it, the inner bond grows. Adults aren't that different.

The lift arrived on the fifth floor, juddered to a halt. The metal grid concertina-ed open and he walked out. In the office one of his colleagues greeted him with, 'That report you were chasing, it arrived.'

'That's great.' He dumped his bag and found the report on his desk. Within minutes the task had taken over, his sharp mind in full concentration.

Nargis lay wakeful, too much stimulus buzzing through her mind, too many confused emotions. She thought of the change in her father-in-law, that she had almost given up hope could happen; and now Tessa, who had made it happen, was going.

She had known her so short a time and yet she felt bereft; left behind, yet again. Tessa was returning to a place where everything worked, and people got paid, and there were no men with guns in the mountains. She would go home each day to a husband who was always there, who looked after the children and played with them. It was impossible not to feel envious.

And soon Lance too would be going. How would she cope? That quiet, solid strength he gave out, how would she live again without it? Perhaps it was not only Khaled who had thought that she was infatuated by Rahul but they were all wrong. Yes, she had admired him, been grateful to him for what he made possible, but to have allowed herself to want more would have been like fixing your desire on a shooting star. The life in him lit the spaces when he was there but he was gone before you had time to absorb it. Lance was different. Here every day, a companion, unobtrusively taking the load off her. At work at least she had a partner who respected and admired her, and the effect was so beguiling that she knew herself to be in danger of wanting more —

Which she could never have. Khaled was gone but she was bound to him still, by law, by the expectations of all around her. But it was not only that which made any thought of more impossible. She had no illusions – Lance's own desires were fixed elsewhere. Once she had overheard two of the younger ones in the office speculating about what went on in that apartment, and she had snapped them out of it sharply. It was none of their business. But she was also amazed at their ignorance. Anyone who knew anything about desire could see from Lance's eyes that he did not have what he longed for. Did Annabel herself not see? Was she deliberately stringing him along?

In her hotel room Tessa lay listening to rain lashing the windows, thinking, there is no way the plane is going to be able to take off in a storm like this. Almost, she willed the storm to continue. All the people and impressions of the past ten days held her here. How can you leave? they said, people he had loved and left behind.

She reran the events of the day. Nargis's programme had said 'Training session with the staff'. Training in what? she had asked. Anything, Nargis said. Anything you know about that we don't. There's very little of that, Tessa said, but there are things we can think about together. So she got them all, drivers included, to tell each other one incident from their childhoods that had had a formative influence; and then they all considered how such an experience might be different for children growing up today, on the streets; in yurts; in institutions threatened with closure. Then she set them to discuss how adult roles might need to change around all that. Listening to the buzz, she realized Greta was right. An outside eye was all it had taken to release their own sharp insights.

And they, all week they had been doing something for her that they were unaware of. They had seen no husband, no children, no burden of a complex story; within days they seemed to have almost forgotten that she came from the Brighton office. As she had moved through this unknown-yet-known landscape she had been simply herself, following the light that she was slowly recovering

~ 59 ~

Perhaps it was the same weather system that blew down from the mountains into Dushanbe. The storm had started in the early evening with lightning and distant thunder, and Hugo too had lain wakeful much of the night, listening to the wild elements. During the evening, while most people were hunkered down inside, six people had disappeared. The story was that in the UN house where they had got together for a meal they had been surprised by the sudden intrusion of masked men, been bundled into waiting vehicles, and driven away. Tajiks and foreigners, but all working for international organizations. Sadirov had struck again.

For Hugo the impact was overwhelming. There was no one among those taken that he was close to but it could not but trigger painful reflexes; and Ruiz Pérez, who had guided them through the last hostage crisis, was out of the country. Until he could get back Hugo was the senior UN officer handling the situation.

The demands? The same as before. They wanted the rest of their men out from Afghanistan.

The world's media were busy with other crises; it hardly made the news. Tessa, travelling between lives, did not hear it until she had been back two days. But in Central Asia itself news of that kind spreads without the intervention of journalists.

447

Lance phoned Hugo the moment he heard. They spoke for a couple of minutes only, then Hugo was called away.

For Nargis the day seemed interminably long. Concentration on work, usually her fail-safe method of dealing with tension, eluded her. Eventually she went to see Lance. 'I think I have a migraine coming on. I'd like to get home before.'

'Go right away.'

She hesitated. 'There's the meeting with the street children organizers.'

'Get Akbor to postpone it.'

But still she did not move. She said, 'This awful business in Tajikistan, it brings up everything about last time.'

He saw that she was about to cry. He got up, steered her to a chair, closed the door. She said, 'Last time we talked about Khaled —'

He waited. Just there, not going away.

'You asked, Do we know who he works for? I could not tell you. We know, but we hide from knowing. He has been seen with men from Sadirov's gang when they come to Gharm for supplies. He is probably part of this, what is happening now. Maybe it's he who drove the trucks that took them from Dushanbe.'

'Nargis.' He was choked up, had no words to comfort her. He brought his own chair close to hers, took her hand. Her other hand moved across her eyes, wiping tears.

'We do not talk about it, we try not even to think about it.'

'At least you're telling me. I'm glad.'

She shook her head. 'You still don't understand. It's not just this. It's Rahul. When we heard how he had died, we knew Khaled was somewhere in those mountains.'

'No, Nargis, no. Don't even think it.'

But she pushed away the false comfort. 'It could have been him driving when they took the hostages.'

'Nargis, it is six months since Rahul died. Khaled may not even have been there then.'

'We know. He has been with them longer than that.'

They were motionless, eyes locked.

Quietly she said, 'Killing he had done in Afghanistan. God knows what he has had to do to survive in drug trading. And the way he used to look at Rahul, I knew he could have killed him if he had the power.'

Her fear was contagious but he wanted urgently to deny it. 'It's too little, too vague.'

But there was no escaping it. It could have been him.

For what was left of the day he struggled with torn loyalties. At all costs he wanted to avoid doing anything that would add to her pain, yet for the first time he had learnt something that could be significant to the quest that for all these months had been the central focus of Hugo's life. How could he keep from him what he knew?

Loyalty to Hugo won. Or perhaps it was something more basic, something about truth. Just before he left the office he dialled Hugo's number. 'I know you've got more than enough to think of,' he began, 'but I felt you ought to know this.'

By the time he had told the story his protective feelings

towards Nargis were once again dominant. 'There's no evidence that it connects, it's just her fear.'

But Hugo had no time to listen to the caution. In this new crisis, all pieces of information might be relevant. At his most brusque he said, 'Get me a description of the man.'

'I really don't want to press her.'

'You don't have to ask her. Ask someone else.'

'Listen. I told you because I felt I had to, but I'm asking you not to pursue this. She's had enough to deal with.'

'You can't do that. You've told me. It's up to me now how I handle it.'

Lance had been clinging to the hope that he could have it both ways, but he couldn't. 'What are you going to do?'

'Pass it on to my contacts in security. But they'll need a description. Detailed. A name is not enough, people can change names.'

Lance's unhappiness pulsed through the silence.

'Listen, my friend.' With an effort Hugo moderated his tone. 'It's probably nothing, but we can't just pretend we didn't hear it.'

He told Annabel, sharing his confusion.

'You had to do it,' she said, quiet but definite. 'Even for Nargis it's better. Maybe Hugo's security people will find it couldn't possibly have been him, that he was nowhere near at the time – then she's freed from her terror. And if it was him, never knowing would be worse.' She paused. 'Do you want me to find out what he looks like? I can do it discreetly.'

He accepted. What else was there to do?

She watched his expression, thoughtfully. 'You need to be tougher. You can't protect everyone.'

Ruiz Pérez returned to Dushanbe. A negotiating meeting was set up. Sadirov himself had agreed to meet in Gharm provided someone senior came from the UN and government sides. The envoys were nominated: the Tajik Minister for Security, and Hugo.

At first light Hugo rose, prepared himself. It was a challenge greater than any he had faced in over thirty years of this life that he had chosen. Quietly, methodically, he got himself ready. As he washed his face he remembered Tessa's little girl staring at his beard, and him saying, It saves me having to shave. As he took a clean shirt out of the cupboard he thought, How do you dress for meeting a hostage-taker? As he put a wallet in his pocket he thought, Money can buy nothing in the situation I am going into. As he made coffee and cut a slice of bread and cheese he thought, I wonder what Sadirov has for breakfast?

An hour still before the vehicle would collect him. He made calls to a few close friends, to tell them what he was about to do.

'Christ,' Lance said. 'I suppose it has to be you?'

What could he say? Someone had to do it.

After a little consideration he decided also to tell his ex-wife, Oriel. 'For God's sake, take care,' she said, and oddly that acted to release tension and they both laughed. It was an old one between them, her telling him to take care and him doing things regardless of her concern.

'I am taking care,' he said. 'That's why I'm phoning. But there's no need to tell the boys.' Nor did he call Tessa. He did not want to worry her.

A car hooted in the road outside. He locked up, went out. The Minister for Security was already in the car. They set off, on the road to Gharm.

It was June 1997, coming up for six months since he had set off on this same road with Rahul.

Sadirov did not appear for the promised meeting. Instead a group of heavily armed men arrived. The discussions were brief. When it became clear that they were not immediately going to get what they were demanding, they simply took Hugo and the Minister for Security as additional hostages.

~ 60 ~

Lance heard it on the World Service news, and was plunged back into the panic of those days in Kathmandu. Annabel and Zohra between them were monitoring all the Tajik-language radio reports. He was constantly on the phone.

'Can no one stop the bastards?' he demanded of Glen. As if Glen could answer.

He phoned UNHCR in Geneva and refused to get off the line until they put him through to someone who could give him information. A government militia was on standby, they said, but it was too risky to order a shoot-out.

He phoned Tessa. She had not heard and was almost too shocked to speak. Hugo had suddenly become infinitely precious to them both.

She told Ben. This time round it was something they could share. She phoned Hugo's friend Karin at whose house they had had lunch. Ben told his colleagues at Ethical Economics. Tessa told Greta, who didn't know Hugo but said she felt as if she did. They were all holding on. Tessa knew how little holding on had helped when it was Rahul, but the instinct could not be quelled. Concentrating on anything else seemed an impossibility.

For Lance, something else significant was happening. He understood that Annabel was there for him. It did not matter now that she would never be more than a friend, she *was* a friend, the best he could have wished for.

Two days later – early morning it was, and Lance was still in the bathroom shaving – Annabel started calling and banging her crutches. Oh God, she's fallen, he thought, dropped his shaver and came rushing out, still in his underpants. She had the radio on and was thumping around on her crutches calling, 'They're out, they're out!'

The government negotiators had caved in and guaranteed a safe passage back into Tajikistan for all Sadirov's remaining men. The hostages were released.

The ordeal was over. For this time.

Afterwards Hugo could barely remember the days that followed. From others he knew that he was put on the first plane back to Geneva, was met, taken care of, debriefed. Apparently he gave a brief press statement and after that would not talk about what had happened. The most he would say was that when the unthinkable happens you discover, perhaps to your surprise, that you find within yourself the resources to cope with it, because you have no choice.

Then, suddenly, his mental faculties switched on again and went into overdrive. The euphoria of release seemed to have generated extraordinary amounts of adrenalin. For days he couldn't sleep, couldn't stay in one place, was talking all the time, though God knows about what. He was a man of careful habits and this behaviour was entirely untypical. He was vaguely aware that payback time would come, but while it drove him he could do nothing but give in to it.

Tessa and Lance were phoning almost daily. He was touched by their concern. When Lance asked, 'Were you roughed up?' he replied, 'No wounds, if that's what you mean. But it's not good for the nerves being surrounded by crazies with guns who you know are given to using them. Terrifying, in fact. But I began to realize, they had orders to keep us alive.'

'Thank God for that.'

'You realize the implications? About Rahul and Vitaly? Something different happened that time, that they know did them no good. They were being careful not to repeat it.'

With others he was reacting oddly, irritated rather than relieved at anything like official concern. 'They want me to have counselling,' he complained to Lance, 'in case I'm traumatized. I've told them, for me the best therapy is work.'

His manager was urging him to take leave, which he thought ridiculous. In a few days he had to be in Tehran for the peace talks. He and Rahul had been the key people working on issues of refugee return, and they had already lost Rahul.

He was so adamant that his manager became intimidated, and let him have his way.

Lance said, 'She should not have.'

For someone already stressed, Tehran in summer was not a good place to be. The heat was extreme, the air conditioning had stopped working, tempers were short. Hugo, struggling through the sessions of the peace negotiations with people who seemed to have no intention of making any concessions, thought, it's time I retired.

By the end of the first day all they had achieved was a joint statement condemning hostage-taking. Both sides had reason to hate Sadirov. The Tajikistan government representatives announced that a militia had been sent to try to track down

Sadirov's group, with authorization to engage militarily if they resisted arrest. That at least felt like action.

On the second day the opposition contingent sensed conspiracy and walked out. The senior UN official and the Iranian president spent hours conferring separately with each side. Hugo shadowed them, redrafting the wording of proposals.

The talks got going again, but he was finding it increasingly difficult to concentrate. He began to realize that there was more than heat and restlessness afflicting him, he was feeling strangely unwell. He stuck it out a little longer till he had no choice but to ask the senior UN official if he could be excused for an hour or so.

He retreated to his room. He had needed to be alone, but the aloneness hung heavy on him, the weight of living half his life in anonymous hotels. He lifted the phone to dial Lance's number, which he knew without having to look it up. There was nothing specific to say, he was simply calling for a little human comfort. But before he had finished dialling he realized that he hadn't the energy to talk, and he put the phone down. He picked up a pen to make a note of something but the pen dropped from his hand. He stared at it in surprise. Tried to pick it up, but his hand would not move. He tried to lift his arm. It did not respond. He tried to push back the chair. He had no strength. With an immense effort, leaning over to the left of his body, which still seemed to work, he tried to stand. His right leg collapsed under him and he slumped back onto the chair.

He did not try to move again.

It lasted perhaps fifteen minutes but it felt like an eternity. Then gradually he realized that he could move his hand again. His arm. His leg.

He sat very still, taking in what had happened and what it implied. He knew what it was called, because it had happened to a friend recently. He had had a TIA, a very short stroke. If he was lucky, it might leave little scar on the brain. But it could happen again, and next time it might not be short.

He considered his life, its fullness, its emptiness. He had wanted to finish these two things: to see the peace process through, and to establish beyond doubt what had happened to Rahul. The first was like a great, uncoordinated beast that would not be flogged into moving any faster. It would get there eventually, he presumed, but he knew now that he could no longer last the course. The second? Sitting here, virtually immobile, it seemed the height of folly ever to have undertaken it. What had he hoped to achieve? To name Rahul's murderers, just that. Retribution was another matter, he had not aimed that high. But just to name them, so that the crime should not pass unnoticed, so that morality, of a kind, would be upheld.

And now? He was almost sixty and in a couple of years he would be compulsorily retired. He had just pushed on all his life, one set of tasks after another, each one at the time seeming vital, imperatives he could not question. He had given no thought to what he would do afterwards. It was laughable, so common a situation that it was a cliché, but he never thought to find himself living a cliché. Now his body had announced: Learn to let go, starting now, or there may be no afterwards.

457

But the tenacity that had kept him going over decades was not so easily quelled. There was still one line of enquiry he had not exhausted and he needed to do it soon, while he could. If that too came to nothing, he would admit defeat.

When Tessa got the call there was a colleague in her office. If it had been anyone else on the phone she would have told them she was in a meeting and would call back later; but this was Hugo. She said to her colleague, 'I need to take this call. I'll come and find you when it's over.' She had put her hand over the receiver as she spoke but Hugo had heard, and felt inordinately touched.

'Tessa, there's something I need your help with.'

'Anything, Hugo.'

He explained. Parveen Jalali might have something relevant to tell him but she wouldn't talk about it on the phone. He had been planning to come to London to see her but for the moment it was probably not a good idea for him to travel.

Tessa immediately latched on to that. 'What is it, Hugo? Are you not well?'

'Nothing major, I just need to be cautious for a few weeks. I was wondering, could *you* meet her for me?'

A pause.

'And if I do?' she said, 'and if there is anything to tell, then how am I going to tell you if it can't be done by phone?'

'If you think it's significant, I will fix with Lifeline for you to come to Geneva for a day.'

Another pause. 'Hugo, I want to help but there's a bit of a history. I'm not sure she'll want to meet me.'

'I've checked. She says she will.'

Another pause. 'I guess that's OK, then.'

'I appreciate it, Tessa. I'm sorry if it's difficult.'

'Forget it. It probably had to happen sometime.'

Phone down, she sat staring at it for a few minutes then got up suddenly, out of the office, down the stairs, out. Walking, to clear her head.

There would have been no need ever to revisit all this, yet now she had been put into a position where she could not avoid it being dug up.

Rahul, she said, to the sky, to the light on the sea glinting at the bottom of the hill, help me stay sensible. I don't own you, I never did. I don't own your memory. You belong to anyone who ever loved you. We all connect with different bits of you. Those tensions belong to the past, there is no point letting them disturb my peace again.

What was so difficult for her about the idea of Parveen? That she too had been his lover? 'You've not the slightest need to feel threatened,' he had said, and life had proved him right. Yet even in those days, the insecurity had other roots. Perhaps it was the fear that this woman shared with him things she could not? Parveen, the political journalist like Rahul, working where dramatic crises were happening. Parveen, like Rahul, had imbibed political awareness from infancy, but more traumatically. Her parents, he had said, had been imprisoned by the Shah's regime, and tortured. She had been too young to know the details but she had lived with the results; damaged people, a fractured family. She, like Rahul, had gravitated to the work she did because it connected.

So what was there in that to be anxious about?

~ 61 ~

When Parveen called they said nothing beyond what was necessary to fix a time to meet. Tuesday, at four. Where?

Parveen said, 'The South Bank? You know the bookstalls under the bridge?'

No! That's our place. I'm not ready to share it.

Come on, this is Rahul's friend. Just try.

'Fine,' Tessa said, her voice sounding to her like an automaton.

She stopped at Greta's on her way there. 'I need some of your courage,' she said.

Greta listened, then asked, 'Just what is it that troubles you?'

'I don't know. Being faced with her, I suppose. Someone who had a part of him I didn't have. I don't want to know her, I don't want to have to think about what it was like for her.'

'She almost certainly won't ask you to.'

'But still, when there's an actual person in front of you, you can't block them off in the same way, I suppose. And that's what I always did with the thought of other women in his life.'

She looked up at Greta. What was she saying? You have been blessed, my dear, beyond what most people will ever experience. That's what you need to hold on to.

'You're right,' Tessa said.

Greta nodded. 'Just be yourself. It's all you can be.'

Standing near the bookstalls, she thought, How will we recognize each other? There was a dark-haired woman there already, browsing. She glanced up, saw Tessa watching her, stared for a moment, then looked down again. Tessa moved further away, unnerved.

She checked her watch. When she looked up again she saw a woman standing by the railing gazing out over the river. She too checked her watch and turned back to scan the bookstalls. She wore a full-length slim-line skirt, nothing showy about her clothes, they just suited her figure perfectly. Her thick dark hair was the kind Tessa as a child had always wished for, swept back and twisted on top of her head, fastened by a large leather clip. It left the shape of her head and neck uncluttered, classically beautiful. Composed. Making Tessa feel naive.

The woman had seen her now, seen that she was looking at her. They moved towards each other, eyes questioning but holding back. Parveen? Tessa? Strangers, whom life would not permit to remain so.

They ordered coffee. Parveen said, 'I should be frank, I wasn't keen to meet.'

What to say? I wasn't either?

Parveen said, 'I don't know what Rahul told you about me.'

Careful. 'I knew you were there.'

'And I knew you were.' Pause. 'And that you always came first.'

This was going to be harder even than she had imagined. She took refuge in formality. 'Hugo said you might have things to tell him?'

'I'm not sure I do. All I have is theories. I haven't talked about them to anyone but Rahul had a great respect for Hugo, so I'm willing to.' She stopped, as if unsure where to start. 'Hugo asked if Rahul had a Human Rights Watch connection. Yes he did. I imagine you knew that?'

'I thought it likely. But he said nothing explicit about it.'

Parveen's eyes flared scepticism. 'I had the impression he talked to you about everything.'

'Not if it was a question of security. Anyway, there were things he didn't raise unless I asked him.' One of them, said her inner voice, was you. 'One of them,' she said, 'was risks he was taking.'

'You need to understand there are people he was working with who are still at risk. So nothing we talk about should be relayed to anyone except Hugo. Or written down.'

'I understand.'

'Sorry, but I had to check.'

'It's OK,' Tessa said. 'How would you know?'

'I do know that Rahul trusted you. It should be enough.'

Another tentative step. It required a response. Tessa said, 'I know that about you too. But we have to do the rest on our own.'

With a sudden movement Parveen shifted in her seat and began. 'At the time he started working in Tashkent we couldn't get anyone into Uzbekistan officially. We were repeatedly refused visas. Their record is appalling and it's our job to make that public. When I heard Rahul was going there, I asked if he would act unofficially for us. We've done a report about what's going on there that is based largely on stuff he sent us. Hugo can see it if he's interested. Rahul's name is nowhere, of course.'

Tessa nodded. 'But would any of that connect? With what happened?'

'We don't know. It could do.' She stopped, hitting some kind of a barrier. 'Vitaly Ivanov, the Russian journalist who died with Rahul. Did you ever meet him?'

'No. But Rahul talked about him.'

'What did he say?'

'That he was a friend. And a dogged investigative journalist.'

Parveen gave a short, unamused laugh. 'He was dogged, all right, but he pushed the limits. He had done it before and got away with it, and it's like winning at gambling, it deadens you to risk. I can't do it, which is why I never made it as a journalist. It's also why I'm still alive and Vitaly isn't.'

A pause; perhaps to get control of her feelings? 'Hugo is assuming, maybe everyone is assuming, that it was Rahul that

463

gang in the mountains was getting at, and Vitaly was got rid of because he happened to be with him. But it may have been the other way round. It may be that Rahul died only because Vitaly offered to go with him.'

Now Tessa was riveted, personal tensions pushed aside.

'I don't have to tell you, Rahul was an instinctive negotiator. It's the art of the possible. He knew how to adjust what he was saying to what people could cope with. He listened to how they reacted, he didn't try and push where they couldn't go. He was there to negotiate the release of the hostages, and he would have held that aim firm in his mind. I can't believe he would have handled things in a way that pushed them to do away with him. But Vitaly had no role in negotiating, he just wanted the story. He was a sharp guy, but not clever enough to hide how sharp he was. He had stumbled on an unexpected story: Who are these people? What are they trying to do? Where are they recruiting people from? What scale of resources do they have? Those guys will have seen that his eyes were taking notes. Secrecy is a tool of power. He could have done them huge damage if they had let him go. And if he had to be got rid of, so did Rahul.'

Tessa stared. She didn't know about Vitaly but what Parveen was saying about Rahul made complete sense. Rahul's death wasn't just the inevitable result of his putting himself in dangerous places. Left to himself, he would have got out of there alive.

Parveen saw the effect she was having and said quickly, 'Of course, that's all speculation. We'll never know. But there's something else I can't get out of my head. Two men died, and they both had a Human Rights Watch connection. To me that's beyond coincidence.'

'Vitaly was also sending you information? About?'

'About dissidents in Uzbekistan. He gave Rahul his first contact there. The President is an old-style Stalinist, and paranoid. He sees Islam as a conspiracy against the state. The security apparatus hounds those people, plants evidence on them, tortures them to get confessions, victimizes their families. It's so mindless. If they would just ignore them they would be no threat, but they're pushing them into fundamentalist militancy.'

'But that's Uzbekistan. It was Tajik rebels who killed them.'

'We don't know that. The borders are artificial. Some of the Uzbeks who fled might have joined up with Sadirov, and maybe someone among them recognized Rahul or Vitaly.'

'But if they did? Why would they have been hostile?'

'I'm not saying the Uzbek exiles themselves would have been. But Sadirov is another matter. Why does anyone take hostages? One reason only, to use them as pawns to bargain with. So he looks at them and he thinks, what can I get out of these infidels that fate has delivered into my hands? And if he got wise to the fact that they had been reporting stuff to us, he would have known that the Uzbekistan government would have liked to get their hands on them. There are hundreds of Islamic militants in Uzbekistan's prisons. Maybe he thought, I could do a deal with the Uzbekistan secret police, tell them, You release a load of those prisoners and let them out to join us, and we'll hand these two over to you. You can do whatever you like with them and we'll put out a landmine story so no one will come asking questions.'

This is off the wall, Tessa thought. Parveen is driven by her fear that it was she who put him into danger through the work she asked him to do. But against her will images of fear flashed before her. Secret police torturing Rahul and Vitaly to get them to name names, more names. Real or not, she was being dragged into thinking about details she had never let herself go near.

She registered that she was feeling cold and clammy. It was a warm day but her body was shivering uncontrollably, some kind of muscular spasm. She wrapped her arms tight round herself, trying to stop the shivering.

Parveen watched dispassionately. 'It won't stop if you just sit there. Move about.'

They stood up and began walking. The shivering made Tessa unsteady, but there was a slight wind coming off the river, touching her face and arms, like the comfort of a human touch. She felt Rahul somewhere near, just out of sight, helping to steady her.

They walked in silence till Parveen said, 'It's weird being here, talking to you. Rahul gone, and you and me left.' Tessa did not respond. 'I never thought I could cope with meeting you.' A pause, then, 'How pathetic that sounds.'

The shivering had almost stopped but Tessa felt limp with tiredness. She looked around for a bench and sat down. Parveen sat too, but as far from her as the bench would allow.

With sudden force she said, 'I blamed you, for what you had done to him.'

Tessa turned. 'Done?'

'You disabled him.'

She looked at her, blankly. 'Disabled?'

'Because of you he could never have a real relationship with anyone else.'

'It wasn't like that,' she said. What was the point of trying to defend herself? Yet she could not let it pass. Just be yourself, Greta said, it's all you can be; and this woman needs to hear who I am, not be allowed to hold on to this distorted image she has created. She forced herself to sound calm. 'We made a mess of things earlier on. When we got together again, we held on to whatever we could have together. He chose that as much as I did. OK, that limited his other options, but that's what life's like, every choice you make closes down another.'

Parveen was looking past Tessa, out to the river. When she started again her voice was full of misery. 'It wasn't your fault, I know that. It was things between us. His dying brought up all the painful times, right back to when we were students together. He used to say we could be much better friends than lovers. Maybe that was true for him, but I needed more than a friend.' She stopped, then turned to face Tessa. 'There were other women too, you know that, don't you?'

Occasional, he had said. And why not? 'He lived alone. That's comfortless.'

Parveen stared. 'I don't understand how you can say that so calmly.'

Tessa shrugged. 'I wasn't always calm about it. But I knew that he had to live where he was, with whoever was there. That was how he was. I just came more and more to understand that when he gave his energy to other people, that didn't take anything away from me. And that was probably true for everyone close to him. You too.'

Parveen shook her head angrily. She was beyond trying to handle subtlety. She started talking again. Tessa suddenly realized, it's a record. She's been saying these things all these months, but just to herself. Now she's got me to tell it to. She needs me to hear all this. *This* is why we are here together. Maybe she would never have sought me out, but when Hugo set it up, she couldn't turn it down, she needed to get out her private pain about all that was unfinished between her and Rahul. But it's not my story, there's nothing I can do.

Parveen's voice was low. 'A few months before he died something awful happened between us. I had finally got a visa to get into Uzbekistan and was there meeting people in government. He knew I was coming but he was busy, we had hardly any time together, and I was hurt. Then as I was leaving he asked me to do something. There was a young woman he was trying to get out of the country because she was in danger. He asked me to take her in when she arrived here and look after her till she got sorted. It was so like him, he couldn't see that there was anything difficult about it. When she got here, I couldn't see her without wondering what there had been between them. I did it. Of course. When you're faced with an actual person you do it. But I was still hurt and angry, like he was using me. It suddenly all got too much. I wrote him a long, accusing letter. The moment I had posted it I would have given anything to get it back. Half of it wasn't even true. I knew if I wanted to fix things between us, that was the worst thing I could have done. I wrote again, almost immediately. I said, Please ignore it, I didn't mean it. But I knew it was useless. Once you've written it, it's there. And then – nothing.'

'He didn't reply?'

'I had a two-liner back. He said he was going to Delhi at short notice. And after that, to Tajikistan. He would write once he got back.'

And then —

Parveen said, 'Can we talk about something else?'

She didn't leave, that was the extraordinary thing. They had so obviously come to the end of what could be said, but Parveen didn't just get up and go. She was holding on, to the woman she had wanted to cancel by her hostility.

I've failed, Tessa thought. She thought of Rahul's long friendship with this woman, the childhood she had had to endure, the work that she did. She, Tessa, had never had anything like that to deal with, and she had Rahul wanting her there, never pushing her away. Surely she could have summoned the generosity of spirit to empathize with her pain, and help her get past it? But she had panicked, protecting herself.

Parveen said, 'All these feelings. It's all so pointless, now he's gone.'

'Yes. But they happen anyway. I know.'

Parveen shrugged. What was there more to say?

'Thanks for being willing to meet,' Tessa said. 'I'll tell Hugo what you said.'

She watched Parveen's back until she had turned a corner, out of sight. Then without warning the cumulative effect of her hostility and the nightmares she had evoked came surging back and the shivering took over again. Trying to will herself to calm down, Tessa walked towards the underground station. She got herself onto the train somehow. One part of her brain was detached, thinking, these people around me must think I'm about to have an epileptic fit. And maybe I am. The rest of her mind had closed down.

Out at Swiss Cottage, running the last part of the road. Press the buzzer. The shivering didn't stop until she was on the floor next to Greta's chair, when her body changed motion, heaving into sobs that she felt would never stop. She could hardly tell Greta what the matter was, just that Parveen was so full of pain and had landed it all on her.

Greta let it happen, stroking her hair; until gradually the storm inside her subsided.

She became aware of the bony feeling of Greta's thin legs through her skirt. Of the texture of the carpet under her. Of dust dancing in a shaft of sunlight coming from the window, that brought with it a verse of Rahul's:

Our life here is as transient as is a dancing spark's.

She said, 'I've been holding on so hard to his life, I haven't

470

let myself think about his death. And now she's put it in my head, there's going to be no way to get it out.'

The shivering started again. Greta's hand on her shoulder increased its pressure. 'Just let it move through you, my child. It will pass. Everything passes, in the end.'

Greta knew; about this too. About the kind of death you never wanted to have to think about, happening to people you loved. She had never talked about it, but Tessa could feel her knowing in the movement of her hand, in the acceptance of her lap.

Our changed and unchanged selves

In the small pool of light from her bedside lamp Nargis reads an English novel that was one of her father's favourites. How did your English get to be so good? Lance asked once. The answer was her father. He read in four languages and made sure that she could; and in the years when he was always ill, she would come home from school and read to him, all the old novels that he loved, Dostoevsky, Tolstoy, Dickens. You read Dickens aloud, it does things for your vocabulary. And then there was this book that he liked not for its story, he said, but for its philosophy:

> All our lives long, every day and every hour, we are engaged in the process of accommodating our changed and un-changed selves to the changed and unchanged surroundings. Living, in fact, is nothing else than this process of accom-modation.

Her thoughts move back to Lance. Today as they walked back together after a meeting she watched him noticing everything.

There was colour in the flower beds, and the avenues that when he first arrived must have seemed dismal and barren, are lined now with trees in full leaf. She was glad that he should see it like this, should see people who in winter walked hurriedly, huddled in coats against the cold, now ambling along. Young women pushing prams and stopping to talk to each other.

Watching him watch them, she said, 'You have become one of us,' and she saw that he was touched. Perhaps when you are an outsider everywhere, it is the ultimate compliment.

She turns back to her book:

> In quiet, uneventful lives the changes internal and external are so small that there is little or no strain in the process of fusion and accommodation; in other lives there is great strain, but also great accommodating power; in others great strain with little accommodating power.

She closes it. She is sad, for all the people around her who have had too many external changes thrust upon them, and too little time to adjust their inner selves; but also afraid for herself. For the changes never stop coming and she does not know if she will keep finding in herself the capacity to accommodate.

Annabel is working late on the Mirzajanov/Gulmanov papers. Lance positions himself, unobtrusively, he hopes, with a book

473

where he can watch her head bent over her work, how she lifts an arm and runs her fingers through her hair, combing it back, or looks up, not seeing him or anything else but pondering some nuance of meaning in the words on the page. Then she finds what she is looking for and bends back to the task. He is moved by her quiet sense of purpose. She has found what he wanted for her, something that uses her talents, something she knows to be profoundly worth doing. Her life from now on will move in a direction that it would never have taken if she had not come here, and if he had not had the box of Rahul's notes under his bed. That at least he can hold on to, it was through him that she found this.

Strange, he thinks, the lines our lives make in the sand. Starting fifty years ago in Prague, where Greta and Hamza were moved by the deep voice of a poet; then a year ago, when Rahul began to sit with Gulmanov and got him to talk about his life experience, to weather the sadness that had overtaken his old age; to a few months ago, when he, Lance, held a sand-dollar in his hand on the coast near Vancouver, and let the direction of his life be changed by the work Rahul had left unfinished – and then happened to be on the same flight as a young woman with coloured thread braided into her hair, with no previous connection with this place yet uniquely equipped to carry on what Rahul had started. Because of all of that, the power of Rahman Mirzajanov's poetry and the insights from his and Gulmanov's complex life stories will one day reach people who know no Tajik, and have only a dim understanding of the troubled history of this place.

And he? He faces his own situation. When this interlude in Annabel's life is over she will be gone, back to the life she has temporarily put aside, back to the friends her own age. Her companionship has become necessary to him, and he cannot hold her here.

~ 63 ~

Hugo sits on the patio of his friend Karin's house to which he has retreated, and closes his eyes as he waits for Tessa to arrive, letting the dappled English sun settle on his face. Mostly he avoids looking in the mirror but he knows his skin is an unnatural grey; presumably sunlight will be good for it.

It is just a week since he packed up the last of his personal possessions in the office in Geneva that he has kept coming back to but has never felt to be his own. It is finished now; he will shift papers there no longer. In any case, for more than three decades his real life has been elsewhere; but even that he doesn't know if he will ever get back to. Extended leave, they are calling it, but he has been around long enough to know that is a euphemism for compulsory retirement.

He has acquired the humility of a retired person. Tessa is so busy, time with her family is precious, yet she is fitting in a visit to him.

As he waits his mind travels vaguely over concerns he knows

he should try to detach from. Today is the 27th of June and in Moscow they have just signed the Tajikistan peace agreement. The work is done, the work of many, many people. He is not tempted to think that without his and Rahul's contributions it wouldn't have happened; history pushes on, a set of forces way beyond the individuals who get caught up in it. We simply do what's in front of us and hope it contributes. But however it happened, it is good that it is done at last. Now the real work can begin.

Karin's phone has been busy with calls from his friends scattered across the globe, reminding him that not everything in his life has closed down. Oriel even suggested she come and see him but he told her not to. 'I'm not on my way out yet,' he said, and then regretted it as soon as he had put the phone down. But he wasn't going to backtrack now. Both his sons came without stopping to ask, which meant more to him than he could tell them. Perhaps they knew. As some things come to an end, we discover other new beginnings; and perhaps the two are related.

The doorbell.

When Tessa sees him she cannot hide her reaction. She hugs him carefully, as if he might break. 'Hugo, you need to take care of yourself.'

'So people have been telling me.' They move out to the patio. Wryly he says, 'Karin says she's not letting me go back till my colour improves. She's giving me herbal remedies and lectures about life–work balance. I can't remember when I've had so many people ordering me about.'

They settle in the sun. Tessa asks, 'What's the life part going to be?'

'I might do something in the garden. A bit of walking. But it's not a lot of use thinking I'll just laze about, I can't detach my mind.'

'Go and see Ben on one of his days at home. He'd love it, and the children are experts at detaching the mind.'

'Thank you, I'll do that.'

He asks her to tell him more about her encounter with Parveen. When she has finished she says, 'You're such a comfort, Hugo. You and Greta between you have helped me go there again, and get past the fear of what I will unearth.'

'The comfort is mutual. And don't let Parveen's theories bother you. Confronting the Tajikistan government is something Sadirov knows how to do. Making secret contact with the Uzbekistan police is not.'

'I get the impression she's lonely. Like she has no one else to talk to about him. It won't do either of us any good to see each other again. But maybe you could, when you're stronger.'

He says quietly, 'You're a good person, Tessa.' For some reason that makes her want to cry.

They sit for a moment not speaking, but comfortable with the silence. Strange to think that this is only the third time they have met. He is visited once again by the feeling that her presence elicited on the other times, a moment of believing that happiness might be possible.

She says, 'You asked me once about Rahul's missing notes, the ones from his Tajikistan years. Did you ever find them?'

'No, and I've given up thinking anyone will. Now that I've handed over I see it all a bit differently.'

After being driven for so many months, he has reached a point where he can accept that they will never know for sure what happened up in the mountains. 'Death is like a flood,' he says, 'washing away the detail of life. It's only arbitrary fragments that remain, there's no use clinging to them.'

Tessa reaches for a large carrier bag she has brought with her. 'There's something I want to show you.' She lifts out a wooden box and puts it on the table between them.

'Beautiful box,' he says.

'Yes. I found it in a market in Vientiane.' She opens it and lifts up the papers from it. 'Rahul's letters to me from Tajikistan.' She holds them in the air for a moment as if weighing them. Then she puts them back, leaving the box open.

For a moment he is too surprised to speak. 'That's a lot of writing.'

She nods. 'It was a substitute for talking. He wrote most days, early morning. It's you who started him on that, in Peshawar.'

He is staring at the letters, half-mesmerized at the thought of what they might contain. The detachment he expressed just seconds ago is gone. He longs to be able to hold those letters in his own hands. With some difficulty he summons his failing sense of propriety and says, 'It's personal things he was writing about, I presume?'

'Everything was personal to Rahul. He was another one who didn't get the life–work balance thing. He wrote about everything that was happening to him.' She pauses, then says,

'What do you think?'

'I think,' he says slowly, 'if he was writing all that to you, there may not be any other notes.'

'That's what I've been thinking. But I've been through them again and I can't tell if any of it is relevant to what you're looking for. I don't know enough.'

The end of that road. Face up to it, move on. 'Well, at least that's one mystery solved.'

'I've brought them for you, Hugo.'

For a moment he is tempted. Then he shakes his head. 'I couldn't possibly.'

'There was a time when I couldn't possibly have offered them. But privacy makes a lot less sense now he's gone. You won't be able to find the bits you're looking for without reading a lot more than you will want to about Rahul and me, but if you can cope with that, I can.'

She pushes the box towards him.

She gets back home to take over from Fern, the childminder. 'Ben phoned,' Fern says. 'He's going to be late. He said not to wait up.'

But she does, and it's well after midnight when he gets in. 'I'm starving,' he says. 'Is there any dinner left?'

'I gave you up long ago. You didn't eat?'

'I didn't want to stop. Had a couple of packets of crisps on the train.'

'Ben, that's ridiculous. I'll do you a quick fry-up.'

She stands frying bacon and tomatoes and listening to his

479

animated talk, thinking, *This* is the Ben I first met, living in the library and dossing down on anyone's floor while he worked on his dissertation, oblivious of time or comfort.

'What kept you so late?'

'A detective trail I've been on. Was working on a document that has to be returned first thing tomorrow. Someone filched it secretly from their office for us.'

'I didn't know you went in for that kind of stuff.'

'Depends. Sometimes it's the only way. This guy who got it for us, he's pissed off with the firm and thinks he's about to be sacked anyway.'

'So who are you trailing?'

'An offshoot company of one that has a major interest in Extrincor. They're prospecting in the mountains of Kyrgyzstan, not far from where you were.'

'And?'

'Nothing very obvious. Yet. These mega-conglomerates have interests everywhere, it's not to say the practices of their subsidiaries are going to be similar. But this document I got hold of, it's a risk assessment and Lifeline features in it.'

'Lifeline? In a report on mining?'

'Because your guys are working near where they want to operate.'

'So what's that got to do with – ?' But before the question is out the answer comes to her. She thinks of Laos and that group of students working on human rights. Extrincor was certainly not happy to have them in the area, talking to the villagers. They would much rather that the local community was *not* being encouraged to look out for their rights.

Ben's eyes meet hers. 'Exactly. But that's not all. That grant you fixed up for Kyrgyzstan, remind me. What was the company called?

'Toddlers Plus. Why?'

He laughs, a short unamused laugh, and shakes his head, amazed at what life is presenting him with. 'I came across their name today; it rang a faint bell, then I remembered you talking about it. So did they suggest the grant go to Kyrgyzstan?'

'No. Central Asia, they said, but that's the only Central Asian country where we support projects with children.'

'Did they give a reason? Why Central Asia?'

'Yes. They get their cotton from there. Ben, what's this about?'

'Just that they are a subsidiary of the company that has the mining concession in Kyrgyzstan.'

She is definite: 'It can't be. They've got nothing to do with mining. I told you, they do kids' clothing. It's a small family firm, started by a woman who still designs the clothes.'

'I don't doubt it. But their annual reports for the past few years show they haven't been doing too well. They were bought out five months ago.'

She stares, stumped. 'I must be thick. What does all that mean?'

'It could mean nothing. But think. If you were a senior executive of a company that is looking to start mining in some remote place, and your risk assessment tells you there are a bunch of do-gooders working near by and you don't want them asking questions about your displacement of local people, might you not try and neutralize potential criticism in advance? A little money, perhaps, for their projects with children? So that if later on they feel inclined to criticize, they'll think twice because they won't want to risk losing their grant? But obviously, Lifeline's not likely to take money from a mining company with a dubious record, so why not find some innocuous small outfit to be the conduit, one that already has interests in the area, so it's going to look natural?'

'That is *so* contrived. I can't believe … To buy a whole company, just for that?'

'It's peanuts money to these guys. And if it is what happened, I'm not suggesting the Toddlers Plus people even know. Of course the people buying out this homey kids clothing company aren't going to tell them why they are coming to their financial rescue. But once they own them, it's easy to suggest some appropriate philanthropy to their promotions people.'

'Sweet Jesus.'

He nods. 'Perhaps you should warn your guys, before they get into it too deep. Tell them it's all circumstantial evidence so far, but I'll keep going.'

She is hopelessly out of her depth. She took on this job because she knew something about children. Now all this happening.

Oliver, the man in Fundraising, is distinctly hostile. Why wouldn't he be? The Toddlers Plus grant is one he fixed, he doesn't want anything happening to it. 'It's all far too vague,' he says. 'You'll have to wait until you've got more hard information. And with budgets the way they are, if you do decide to raise it, it's going to have to go right up to Lionel. He's not going to want us turning anything down unless you can prove there's blood on it.'

'If they're linked to Extrincor, Ben knows there is.'

'That's not going to be enough for Lionel. He's going to need some hard evidence.

She gets back to her office. Charlene says, 'Glen's been looking for you.'

Glen, looking for her? Well, he will just have to wait, she has a call to make first. She has long since given up trying to get time from him and he never makes any move to find out what she is doing.

A few minutes later she looks up to see him at her door. Actually at her door. She says, coolly, 'This is a surprise.'

He gives no sign of acknowledging her tone but settles in, as for a social chat. As Tessa's surprise wears off, indignation takes its place. How can he just switch like this, behaving as if nothing different has been going on all this time?

He says, 'I had Hugo Laval on the phone this morning. I gather you know each other.'

So that is it. Nothing she might achieve in Lifeline's work with children is ever going to make Glen feel inclined to treat her as an equal, but if *Hugo* suggested that she isn't just a waste of space, that will have made an impact.

Glen says, 'And I, it seems, am the last person to hear that you've been to Kyrgyzstan.'

483

Outrage whips through her. 'Glen. You made it clear on my first day, and have continued to ever since, that you don't think my area of work is important and that you are not going to apply your mind to what I get up to. That left me with two choices. Resign, or do it my own way.'

He tilts back on his chair, watching her, a smile growing. It is the smile of a man who has discovered that the woman has some fight in her, and thinks it rather becomes her. She glares at him, daring him to patronize her.

'OK,' he removes the offending smile. 'I get the message. I apologize.'

He has apologized. He has actually apologized. Eventually she says, 'Did anyone ever tell you that you are outrageous?'

'It has happened,' he says calmly. 'But I can't seem to find the other way.' He flips his chair back onto all its feet and switches his tone accordingly, back to work. 'OK, tell me about Kyrgyzstan. What you think about what they're up to.'

He spends the next twenty minutes listening, asking the occasional question. She has difficulty holding on to the fact that this is Glen here, actually wanting to learn something she knows. Then suddenly she understands, this is how he is with people he has accepted.

He is standing up to go. She says, 'Sit down again. There's something I need your help with.' He is clearly surprised. A step too far? She says firmly, 'Just a few minutes more, this could be important.'

He sits, and she tells him about Toddlers Plus. She knows the moment she starts in on the story that she can rely on his response. She remembers what Greta said of him, when she, Tessa, was too angry to want to hear: 'He's a man who is prepared to face personal cost for what he thinks right.' There is no question now of him saying, 'We can't say no to the money, we have a budget crisis.' What he says is, 'We'll have to put that grant on hold. As soon as Ben can get us something on paper, I'll raise it at directors' meeting. Tell him we're grateful to be alerted.'

'I will.' Then, unable to resist the temptation, 'This is what one needs a manager for. Just sometimes it's helpful to have a clear decision, and some practical support.'

He smiles, a slow smile quite different from the one she glared off his face. This one speaks recognition of a worthy sparring partner. Possibly even a colleague.

'Ask, whenever you need it,' he says. 'There's just such a lot of noise coming at me, you'll have to make it clear when it's urgent.'

After he has left she sits still, absorbing what has happened. She feels her smile growing. She turns to the computer contraption that has been the (almost) silent witness of her progress in the months since Glen first told her that he didn't think her job was needed. 'I think we won that one,' she says.

Then, unable to resist the desire to share it, she phones Hugo. 'I hear you've been speaking to Glen?'

'I have. He seemed remarkably uninformed about who he has working for him.'

'So you put him straight?'

'I tried to.'

She laughs, and tells him what has just happened, more or less word for word, enjoying it every minute more. By the time she has finished he too is laughing.

'Hugo,' she says, 'that's the first time I've heard you laugh. It's a wonderful sound.'

~ **64** ~

'Blast that man Eversley,' Lance says. 'I knew he was a snake. We've already got plans in place for using that grant. Losing it is going to zap morale here, and things are difficult enough as it is.'

'The security situation?' Glen asks.

'That, but a lot more.'

'Such as?'

'I'm not free to talk about it. Things going on with the staff. Personal, but heavy. I just don't want to add anything that's going to burden her.'

'Her?'

'Nargis, the programme manager. She's the one who carries it all, and she doesn't have an easy life. Work is what keeps her going. This project is close to her heart.'

'So don't say anything about the grant yet. Perhaps we can find you an alternative source.'

'Thanks, that would help.'

Through his open door he sees Annabel deep in conversation with Fahmeda; in Tajik of course. They appear to be the only two in the office, and their body language and lowered voices make it clear that what they are saying is for them alone.

Glen is saying, 'I saw James Horley yesterday. What's this I hear about a young English girl living in your apartment?'

Lance's hands become suddenly clammy. 'Hold on,' he says, and gets up to close the door. He takes a deep breath, lifts the receiver again, and says coldly, 'James Horley said that? The man hasn't even been here.'

'But your snake Eversley has.'

'And how the hell did Eversley know?'

'Who knows? He's a professional collector of information. They get into the habit of squirrelling away anything that comes their way. Maybe his driver talks to your driver.'

At the word 'driver' a picture comes into his mind, Annabel talking to a group of drivers, laughing. When has she ever been discreet about where she lives? The whole of Resham-serai probably knows.

It takes him a minute to get his feelings in order before he can say, 'Well I'm sorry to disappoint all you gossip merchants, but she's a backpacker who broke her ankle and needed a place to rest.'

'That's all it is?'

'That is all it is.'

'Odd. Whoever it was Eversley heard it from gave the impression of an arrangement that was a lot more of a fixture than a couple of nights.'

'I told you, the girl broke her bloody ankle. She could hardly hobble about. What was I supposed to do, throw her out onto the street? And I can't see why it should be the faintest concern to you or anyone else.'

'To other people, OK. But you can't expect me not to be curious if you give signs of breaking out of your single state.'

'I do expect you to know that I will tell you if that ever happens. You don't have to rely on sniffing bloodhounds.'

'OK, OK, so he got it all wrong, I got it all wrong. You have no interest in this girl whatsoever.' Pause. 'But you have taken her on to work for you, right?'

Oh God, here it comes. Why hasn't he sorted this out earlier?

'Yes,' he says icily, 'she is working for us. As a volunteer. While she has to hang around waiting for her ankle to get better.'

'Has to hang around?'

'She was about to go back when it happened. Had to cancel her flight.'

'So? They do take you on planes with your ankle in plaster, you know.'

That has never occurred to him. He asks, cautious now, 'What are you saying?'

'That whatever you are or aren't thinking about her, she's choosing to stay.'

Silence, while he takes that in. 'And if she is?'

'Who knows? I accept what you're telling me. But it seems she's attractive enough to make you the object of considerable envy, and I don't like the idea of someone in your office gossiping about your personal life to Eversley. It's got the smell of grievance to me, and I thought you ought to know. You made anyone redundant, by any chance?'

'No. But all this talk of slashing budget cuts doesn't help. Everyone waits to see where the axe will fall.' He takes a couple of steady breaths, trying to calm down. 'I don't like it either. But I think you should assume it's nothing major. I'll watch out for signs.'

'You do that.'

'And thanks for the warning. Sorry I flew off the handle.'

'Forget it. Understandable.'

She's choosing to stay. Of course she is. How could he have been so thick? But there could be many reasons, one called Akbor, for instance.

His mind trawls over everything she has ever said that could give him clues as to whether her staying is linked to him. 'You're a star,' she said as she hugged him goodbye, only to trip on the stairs and provide him with his first and only chance to hold her in his arms. 'Here's to Fate, for tripping me up on the stairs.' She has been telling him things all along that could mean everything, or could be just Annabel responding generously to life; to him no more than to anyone else. And always tossed his way in that light tone that leaves him completely confused as to how much to read into it. Perhaps she says similar things to the others? How would he know? Their banter is in Tajik. But from the constant laughter between them, it must be so.

Just tell her, tell her how you feel, desire urges. But he is far too afraid of what he will hear, and see in her eyes: 'I thought I could trust you at least to keep this to friendship'; or worse still, compassion: sorry that she has to hurt him, wishing that he had not made himself ridiculous. And after that, she will have to be forever careful in case she draws him on again. An end to the ease between them, the delight of those teasing eyes. He can't bear it. Anything rather than that.

When he comes out of his office Annabel is no longer there. Fahmeda seems to sense the question before he asks it. 'She's gone to work with Behdad Gulmanov.'

He goes home, can't face cooking, and goes out again to eat on his own in a local restaurant.

When he gets back she is there. He says, 'I've eaten. What about you?'

'They always ply me with food there, I'm fine.'

He sits down with a book, to try to get himself into the right state of mind to do what he has to do.

Annabel watches him. He seems to be in one of his withdrawn states, and long as she has lived in the same apartment, she still doesn't know how to read them. There is something she needs to say but she isn't at all sure this is the right moment.

She retreats to safer territory, talking about what she has been learning from Behdad Gulmanov. Lance is usually interested but today he seems hardly to be hearing what she is saying.

She stops. 'Difficult day?'

'You could say that.'

She tries a new tack. 'Sultan was talking in the car about that system Oman has for getting the drivers to record their journeys.'

'Yes?'

'Most of what they record is pointless. I checked with Akbor, he says we don't actually need all that information. I could show Oman how to make it simpler.'

'Annabel,' his voice is cold now, as she has never heard it. 'We have been here before. There are limits to your role as a volunteer, which you have to respect. I cannot have you trying to sort out our systems.'

She stares, amazed. 'I only said ... And Oman's system *really* bugs Sultan and Taimur.'

'And it will *really* bug everyone else if I let you suggest how they run the place.' He pauses, to gear himself up. 'Just think a moment: what do the others in the office see? An attractive young English woman moves in with me. They all know this place has only one bedroom, it's Akbor who found it, Zohra's been here to help you, the drivers come up here each time they help you get back up. They presumably draw conclusions about our living arrangements. That they don't happen to be true is irrelevant to how they see us. Then you start spending any time you like in the office. OK, there's your ankle, but other staff members don't feel free to invite their injured friends to come in and make themselves at home. It's director's privilege you're using and I never authorized it and I cannot let it continue. And I particularly cannot let you start suggesting improvements in how they do their jobs.'

He waits for that to sink in. She is mortified, shocked into silence.

In a more moderate voice he says, 'Jobs are deadly serious in this place, Annabel; they're about survival. Each of those people we employ is almost certainly the only one in their families earning decent money. They've all got brothers and sisters and cousins in need of jobs. If there's serious work needing doing why isn't the director creating a job for a local person to do it? Instead he lets this young woman who lives in his apartment dabble in things that they are responsible for. How do you think that comes across to them?'

He realizes as the words come out, it is himself he is accusing. His responsibility entirely that he has not made the limits clear before it got to this point.

'But they like you, Lance, they think you're great. No one is saying those things about you!'

'It's not a question of liking, it's the role. They have every cause to be wary of me – they were doing things their way till I pitched up, now they have a foreign director who has the ear of head office, and if I tell Glen the projects aren't worth supporting, he could decide to close the whole programme down tomorrow. And thereby remove their livelihood.'

She stares, aghast. 'You wouldn't do that, would you?'

'No I wouldn't, because I happen to think there are some remarkable things going on here. Small scale isn't the word for it, it's drop-in-the-ocean stuff compared to the size of the problems, but no one else has come up with any of the ideas these people have, and good luck to them. But I've had to close a programme before and it's not impossible I might have to do it here. There's a budget crisis and I'm having to do quite a lot of explaining. Glen can't see the point. And if the security situation worsens, which there is every possibility it might, Glen might well come to the conclusion that we can't afford to stay here.'

'Afford? Is it just about money, then?'

'Not just. But it would cost one hell of a lot more to keep operational here if things were to get out of control politically. Think. Casualties of civil conflict. Refugees whose homes have been destroyed. People needing tents, food, medical supplies. And the cost of supplies is just the start. You need lorries to get them across bad roads, people to get all that going and manage it. None of our staff or projects are oriented to emergency relief, we'd be starting from scratch, having to take on scores of extra people, send in emergency specialists from elsewhere. Back in Brighton Glen has to decide, is that realistic? And if it's not going to be possible, we'd better start getting out of here sooner rather than later, because it sure won't be the right time to do it when things are falling apart around us.'

She is staring at him in full concentration as when he first saw her, but no easy judgements this time. In a voice the nearest he has ever heard in her to humility, she says, 'I had no idea. About your job, I mean. All the things you have to think about.'

He shrugs. 'That's just the way it is. You want to support people doing good things, but it's seldom as simple as that.'

He feels overcome, trapped by his own confusion. He has

been driven to keep talking because he cannot let her see what is really going on, the tension of having had to hold desire in check, for so long. He puts his head in his hands and closes his eyes. 'Annabel, get to bed. I'm tired, and I need to be alone.'

She does not move. Her voice comes at him through the protection of hands and closed eyes. 'Lance, I'm so sorry. I didn't mean to make things complicated for you.'

He opens his eyes, lifts his head. Oh God, why is she there still, looking at him like that?

'It was my responsibility, not yours. But now you know, you can help me by phasing yourself out, and finding a way to do it that will cause the least possible comment.'

'The street-children's centre. Do I pull out of that?'

He hesitates. Glen has more or less promised they can keep going, and if he pulls Annabel off it now, it will raise uncomfortable questions. 'No, that's OK. It's the office that's the problem. Just keep away. You've enough things to keep you busy elsewhere.'

'I'm sorry, Lance, I really am.'

Just take yourself away from me, he wants to shout. Aloud he says, 'Don't bother about it any more, we've sorted it out.'

She gets up and, balancing against the table, is trying to clear away the dishes.

'Don't be absurd,' he says, 'how can you do that on crutches? Just get to bed.'

She has hobbled only a few steps away when she turns. 'What about getting places? The drivers' time, the office car?'

He is at the end of being able to hold it together. It is

impossible to draw clear lines. 'That's OK. But get Taimur to drive you, not Sultan.'

She looks amazed. 'What difference does that make?'

'A considerable difference,' he snaps. 'Taimur, like me, is old enough to be your father. For God's sake, Annabel, you cannot be unaware of the effect you have? You are an extremely attractive young woman, and we have three normally susceptible young men in the office, with all of whom you have been on the easiest of terms. Sultan gets to spend his days driving you around, you and Akbor are in each other's pockets over poetry, and do you think Oman doesn't feel envious? It's a small office, rivalries of that kind could get seriously in the way of their work.'

'That's ridiculous! They're not all after me, you know.'

'I don't know, and nor do you.' He abandons caution. 'And if you want proof of the fact that someone is harbouring envy, I have to tell you that gossip about us has got as far as Duncan Eversley. The bogus IMF man.'

'About us? Who told you?'

'Glen. Third-hand, from someone in London who knows Eversley. Things travel, things you don't even know anyone is thinking, let alone saying. But it's not the gossip that matters, it's the possible resentment that might be leading to it.'

Now her eyes have that look in them, her assessing eyes, probing to see what men are thinking. The moment lasts, indefinitely, it seems, sexually charged.

He turns away, so she can't see his face.

Step clump, step clump. She is walking back towards the

table. She sits. Her hand rests on his. The moment of touch, so long desired, sends a shock of disbelief through his body. He turns to her.

She says quietly, 'Whatever they're thinking, they're ahead of us. What I said the day we were up in the mountains, it was true then, but it's been out of date a long time. We couldn't be closer than we have become and we're still not even touching. It's crazy.'

He is in shock, his muscles not responding to messages from the brain. 'Annabel, I can't begin to tell you –'

Her hand is moving up to his face, her fingers tracing the shape of his nose, the line of his eyebrows. Her voice, quite different from how he has ever heard it: 'Please stop sleeping on the floor. Your bed's big enough for both of us.'

Suddenly he emerges from his stillness, pulling her towards him, his mouth on hers, on her cheeks, kissing each eye in turn, his hands in her hair, disbelief banished by desire let loose, by exultation. Then everything blanks out in sensations too immediate and overwhelming to name. Annabel, in his bed, the two of them lying naked, touching, loving, marvelling, moving, throwing caution to the winds where it belongs. Her body, her laughter, her touch, her softness, her warmth, her openness. Her.

He is late for work next morning. He makes no attempt to explain. There are curious looks as he says hello and goes through to his office. It must be shining out of him, his joy, his lightness, his very body announcing what has happened. And he doesn't care who sees.

~ 65 ~

Greta is moving slowly. Today she feels her age; every joint complains. There are letters she should be attending to but she hasn't the energy. So irritating to be getting old.

Tessa will be here soon and there is a book she wants to show her, one that Rahul particularly enjoyed. Now where has she put it? Perhaps the bookcase beneath the window? She gets up, steadying herself before she moves towards it. Once there she is distracted by what she sees out of the window, the plane tree branches swaying heavily, a storm brewing, dark clouds massing. She remembers Rahul standing at this window on a day when the sky darkened just as it is doing today, and he called her to come and stand with him to watch the lightning streak across the London skyline. 'That's one of the most potent images in Urdu poetry,' he said. 'Lightning. Like sudden intense emotion. So powerful it can destroy, yet momentarily it lights everything around it.' Then he quoted a verse, in one of his own translations, and she got him to write it out for her and pasted it inside her bureau:

> All that gives radiance to life comes from the love that ruins
>   your home
> Only the lightning that destroys the crops lights up this gath-
>   ering

And she said, Yes, it was like that in my own life too, love and loss were inextricably bound together. She had known that from the day her closest friend, a Jewish girl, was beaten up by thugs, and there was no longer any option to live a 'normal' life. And fifty years on, there was Rahul doing much what she had been doing in the years before she had to leave Austria, helping those at risk to escape.

Her eyes travel slowly over the photographs that surround her, keeping her people close. No photo of Walter in this room; she keeps that next to her bed, Walter as she first knew him, the lawyer who was there for her and so many others in their first refugee years. A man twenty years older than her, with children already grown, and he made it clear that he was past being able to contemplate having any more. But she chose to join her life to his because she knew that love comes as an unexpected gift, and if you say no you cut yourself off from the source of life. In 1950, that was. And later that same year she held the infant Lance in her arms, her friend's child but so generously shared with her, a consolation for the children she would never have. And then the ten-year-old Rahul, another child to weave his way into the deepest corners of her heart; Rahul, who, after Walter's death, came back to her, to keep her company as she came to terms with loss. Now he too was gone, yet miraculously another unexpected comfort had been given to her.

She holds them quietly in her mind, her legacy from all that journeying, the renewal of life after each shaft of fearful lightning. Lance, Rahul, Tessa.

Tessa arrives. At Greta's request she has brought photos to show her, of the children. She studies them, this woman who only has other people's children to love. But the moment Tessa thinks that 'only' she takes it away. Greta asks their birthdays, notes them down in her little notebook. Now Sam and Alisa will be getting birthday cards for as long as Greta is alive.

Most of the photos are from their time in Laos. The luxurious vegetation is there in the backdrop, but not the heat or humidity, the smells. All of that too interests Greta. Tessa can see she is imagining it all, Tessa's life against that backdrop.

'I've often wondered, after you went to Laos,' Greta asks, 'was it just letters between you and Rahul? Did you never get to see each other?'

'We did. Quite a few times.'

'There you are now, *that's* the story I want to hear!'

'You don't want anything left out, do you?'

'Not unless you don't want to tell me.'

'There's nothing now I would want to keep from you.'

But what to tell? Fragmentary memories move through her. Rahul on his first visit to them in their home in Laos ... She remembers him watching the crawling nine-month old Sam, a different being from the infant he had held with such confidence in Liverpool. Later she looked out through the gauze of the verandah to see the men finding their own level as together they fixed up a swing in the garden. While Ben was at work, she shared the places she loved with Rahul. With Sam in a sling she walked with him along a path that edged a paddy field. He was there listening as she squatted in the market to practise Lao with women who sold baskets, there looking out over the river, slow, wide, the life-source for so many people.

That was it, really. He came, he saw the life she was living, and for five days he became part of it. But that was a gift like no other. To have him there, his physical presence lighting up the space around her, his body draped easily across the floor as he played with Sam, his gradually growing ease with Ben. His laugh, his listening face, his quiet comments, his opinions. To be able to talk, instead of having to write.

Six months later he was back. Now Sam was spending mornings at the pre-school so she and Rahul had the luxury of several hours on their own each day. But another child was on the way. As she drove him to the airport to fly back she said, 'If you want to see me again before I get submerged with baby-care, don't leave it too long.'

'Next month?' he said.

'Next week?'

They laughed and he put his hand up to her face, to caress her cheek. She inclined her head to receive it.

'Watch the road,' he said. 'I'd like to stay alive at least till next time.'

They booked a time, a month before the baby was due. But that month there were refugees fleeing across the mountains to Kyrgyzstan, and Rahul was sent to deal with it. By the time that crisis was over Alisa had been born. She was a difficult baby, hardly slept and needed constant carrying. For Tessa each day was a question of trying to keep going through tiredness. Sam's ego was out of joint and he had become super-demanding.

She was wading through mounds of laundry, unwashed dishes accumulating on the sink, tripping over Sam's scattered toys. Ben was doing what he could, taking Sam over the moment he got home, taking turns when Alisa cried with colic; but he had a trip into the mountains coming up that he couldn't postpone any longer, and he was bothered about leaving her. When Rahul phoned to say he could get away the following week, Ben said, 'Well, thank God for that. He can give you a hand while I'm away.'

'It's extraordinary,' Greta says, 'what you all managed.'

'It's Ben who's extraordinary.'

'It's the combination,' Greta says firmly. 'Ben wouldn't be like that without you having some part in it.'

'And Rahul too. Something happened to him over those years in Afghanistan. He learnt to let go of what he could not have, without letting go of the love.'

The last time was a few months before he died. He talked about his growing involvement with people in Resham-serai. About the children on the streets, and in the yurt school in Sukhunobod. Akbor and his passion for poetry. Nargis, with her sharp mind and compassionate heart, and heavy troubles in her family. From all they talked about, and equally from the things he didn't need to say, she felt, this is a man at the height of his powers. All that had ever been potential in him seemed to be there to draw on. It was a life that suited him profoundly, and it was difficult to imagine how it would have been possible if things had not happened to keep them apart. He too had come to understand something similar about her. Whatever time they had together was mediated through his desire for her to be happy in the way she had chosen. Being with Ben was right for her in many ways; and when are things ever completely right?

'Ambiguity and compromise are part of the deal with life,' he said. 'However much time we had, it wouldn't be enough. Just be glad we can love.'

> *Joy in the raging flood and, like the bridge's image, dance*
> *Know where you are, but move beyond the bounds of self,*
> *and dance.*

When the days were over and she was driving him to the airport he said, 'I don't feel I'm leaving.'

'You're not. I feel it too.'

'It's a miracle. We are thousands of miles apart, our lives are separate, and different. Yet whatever I am doing, you are with me. Whatever you are doing, I am with you.'

'I bet you know a verse for it.'

'I don't,' he smiled. 'But if I find one, I'll let you know.'

At the airport they learnt that the plane was delayed and they were getting an unexpected extra two hours together.

'Another gift from life,' she laughed.

'A reward for virtue,' he said.

But what is virtue? It was luck, surely, to have found each other in the first place, luck to have found each other again, and to have found a way to keep hold of it when all the chances were stacked against it. But were they lucky to have had so much, or unlucky not to have had more?

'Live now,' he said. 'It's all we've got.'

And all these months on from that moment in Vientiane airport, *now* is here, in Greta's flat. It is late, and Greta looks tired. Tessa goes into the kitchen thinking she will make her some supper before she goes, but there is very little to make it with. She says, 'I'm just popping out to the shop,' and she comes back with two carrier bags full of food.

'You really shouldn't have,' says Greta as she watches Tessa unpack it all. 'I normally do a little each day. It's just that this week I've been a bit idle about going out.'

'So be idle occasionally. I can do a bit each time I come.'

She leaves Greta to her supper and sets off down the stairs. She is thinking about what drives Greta's sense of connection with everything she can tell her; and that there is one thing she has not asked. Tessa has sensed the unspoken question, and knows that it comes from her protective love for the boy who flew his kite with her on Primrose Hill, who read books that he took from her shelves, who came back to her as a young man. It comes from her sadness that his moments of intimacy had to be so carefully rationed. She wants to know, but she is too discreet to ask, after the children were there, did he never again have the comfort and joy that only lying close with your beloved can give?

Tessa comes out of the building into the long light of a summer evening, the sun still high. She stands still, taking it in. Across the road the plane trees are in full summer leaf. She looks up at the shape of the branches, arms stretching to the sky, like desire.

~ 66 ~

For days Lance has been moving in a surreal state. In the office he attempts to behave as if nothing has happened but he cannot stop marvelling. Doubt is impossible; her body says it clearer than words. But his insecurities cannot be so quickly banished. 'I'm slow at change,' he told her, weeks ago. He has schooled himself to know he cannot have her, and his emotions are still trying to catch up with the almost incredible fact that he can.

After their first explosive love-making they lay for hours in the dark, rerunning the months they have lived so intensely together, yet never quite able to breach their separateness. 'Once things began to change for me,' she said, 'nothing I hinted at got through to you. Sometimes I thought, he's just being super-careful not to take advantage. Other times I thought, all he wants is companionship. I didn't know what to do about it. I've never had to woo a man before, I've only learnt how to keep them at arm's length.'

But even as he accepts it, he can hardly believe that it will last. She will tire of him, surely? By her own admission she has not ever had a committed relationship. Why would she be willing to give herself to one now? Nothing can cancel the fact that he is twenty years older than her. For the moment she is carried away enough to overlook it, but her plaster will come off, she will have to go back, to help her sister, if nothing else. And when she is back in her life in London, with friends her own age, she will see it all differently.

'Of course,' she says, eyes laughing at him. 'You're just a boring middle-aged development worker. What I really want is someone with a sensitive soul, a poet maybe. But there isn't one available, so you'll have to do.'

And they begin making love again.

Time is measured now in 'Before' and 'After'. It is about a week After that he and Nargis are summoned to the office of the Minister for Internal Security for a briefing on the security situation. Together with representatives of other international agencies they wait on chairs lined up against the wall; the very arrangement of furniture expresses intimidating levels of power. Eventually they are told that the meeting has been postponed. Nargis goes on to see someone else and Lance sets off to walk back to the office, taking a long route to prolong these moments alone, to savour the feelings that are still swirling around inside him.

He arrives an hour earlier than anyone will have expected him. Annabel, he knows, will make no appearance. She is at Nargis's house, working with Behdad Gulmanov. So he won't have to try to appear normal in her company.

There is an unnatural silence in the central work area as he comes in, the kind where you know people have been talking about you. He notices several unusual facts. Akbor is not at his desk. The door to Lance's office is closed; he always leaves it open when he is out. He opens it —

To see Annabel and Akbor in intimate contact. She is sitting in his, Lance's, chair, and Akbor is in another chair pulled up close, with his arms around her. Her head is on his shoulder.

He stands rigid in the doorway. Everything has gone into slow motion. Akbor rises from the chair in deep embarrassment, mumbles something inaudible, makes for the door. It closes behind him. He and Annabel are left staring at each other.

She gets in first. 'Lance, there's no good way to tell you this.'

'Do you need to tell me? It seems obvious.'

'Sit down,' she says, voice low but vehement.

He cannot move.

Rewind, many hours back and across several time zones, where it is still yesterday. Tessa stands at the entrance to Greta's flat and presses the entry-phone buzzer. No answer. Perhaps she has fallen asleep? Should she leave her to rest? But Greta will be disappointed to miss her.

She presses the buzzer again, and this time she holds it down. Nothing. A slow panic rises. She presses number five, the other flat on the third floor.

A man's voice. 'Who is it?'

'Greta Fielding in number six is expecting me and there's no answer. Could you let me into the building?'

The neighbour has a key to Greta's flat. They open her door, to see her sprawled on the floor near the window. Tessa is down on the floor next to her instantly. Greta looks up, her dark eyes unnaturally large as they stare out of her white face.

Her voice, barely audible: 'So – stupid – of – me.'

The neighbour is on the phone for an ambulance. Tessa sits stroking her hair. Greta's eyes keep staring. The ambulance arrives. A young woman bends over her. 'You fell?' The smallest movement of her head. 'How long ago, do you know?'

'Long – time.'

The young woman gives her an injection and they wait for it to take effect. Then in extreme slow motion they manoeuvre her onto a stretcher, and out.

In the ambulance Tessa holds Greta's hand all the way. As the painkiller cuts deeper her face softens, her eyes become less staring. Tessa sees she is noticing the young paramedic now, watching her fill in a form on a clipboard. She feels a surge of relief at the sight of Greta's spirit made visible.

Voice faint, Greta asks, 'What's your name?'

The young woman looks up, smiles. 'Belinda.'

'Belinda. You're very young to be doing such a responsible job.'

'I'm twenty-five. I bet you were doing responsible things when you were twenty-five.'

'Well, yes.' A hint of a returning smile in Greta's tired eyes.

Belinda, to Tessa: 'Are you her daughter?'

Tessa to Greta: 'Shall I say adopted daughter?'

'That would make me very happy.'

Belinda again: 'Next-of-kin?'

So simple a question, but not if you have lost all your kin.

Tessa to Greta: 'What shall we say?'

A pause. Then, 'Lance. But he's not here. Could you?'

'I'd love to.'

'Well, that's sorted, then.'

Her eyes close, and she hands over responsibility for herself, for possibly the first time in a very long life.

~ 67 ~

'*Sit down*,' Annabel says again.

This time Lance obeys, hypnotized. He cannot work out what is going on. He knows only that he is blocking his ears against hearing what she is about to say. Then he realizes, slowly, that she is in fact saying something quite different.

She repeats. Speaks in short sentences, enunciating as for the hard of hearing. 'Tessa phoned. They couldn't find you. Akbor came to fetch me. It's your godmother. She has broken her hip. They have to operate. It's possible she won't come through it.'

Blankness.

'She is in serious pain but she won't let them operate till you get there.'

Suddenly it registers and he switches into brisk action. 'There's a flight this afternoon and then not again for three days. I have to get it.'

'Akbor is already sorting the tickets.'

The competent part of Nargis's brain has taken charge.

'I don't know when I can get back,' Lance is saying, 'but I'll phone every day.'

'Don't worry about anything here,' she says.

For an hour they are together in his office as he hands over, checks she knows where everything is in his files. Possible actions if the security situation worsens. But all the time she is thinking, These are our last moments. He will not be back. He is going, and I will be alone again.

For four months she has had a companion who supported her, who valued her, who wanted to know her. Now he is going. It is over. And he is completely unaware of what it means to her.

Lance is looking around for Annabel – she has disappeared. He goes back to the apartment to gather up his things and finds her there with Taimur, the older of the drivers, coming down the stairs with her backpack. So she is coming too? He has moved in the past few hours through so many states of intense feeling that it seems half of his psyche is still trying to catch up. His room – her room – has been stripped of everything she brought with her, all sign of her female presence gone. Does she not plan to come back, then? She made it beautiful with the smallest of touches, the notebook that she kept on the

509

table next to the bed, its cover designed by her artist sister, the coloured braids and hairgrips on the window ledge, a length of cloth from the weaving project draped over the chair. And now? Will he be coming back alone when this is over?

Back to the office with his bag – they all gather round. Annabel is saying goodbye in a way that makes it clear she is going for good. Zohra is tearful, the young men look bereft. Akbor is embarrassed still but Annabel is not giving him the chance to opt out, they too have a farewell hug. Lance turns away, unable to watch.

Fahmeda holds her like a daughter and says something in Tajik. Annabel nods and says, 'I will' – in Tajik – but that much he by now understands. I will – what?

As they move to the car Taimur insists on carrying Lance's case as well as Annabel's backpack – Lance tries to take it from him but Annabel says, 'He's concerned for you, let him show it.'

At the airport Lance gets her to repeat, word for word, what Tessa said on the phone. A broken hip is a common fracture for people her age, the doctor said. Her bones are brittle with osteoporosis, her joints worn by arthritis. There is no choice about operating but no one can know for sure if her heart will hold out under the anaesthetic. Greta listened to it all, pain dulled by morphine, and said, 'Thank you for explaining it so clearly. But if there's a chance I might die, it'll have to wait till Lance gets here.'

It is the second time he is hearing it but he is like a child, wanting to ask to hear it again.

Apart from that they hardly talk. He feels bruised, and wants only to retire into himself.

He watches as Annabel clumps over to talk in Tajik with the airport officials. Standing there on her crutches she looks vulnerable, confiding and grateful all at the same time. A wheelchair is brought out to help her board the plane – she doesn't need it, but he realizes it is strategy – if she asks for it they will take her disability seriously. In the plane he discovers that they have both been given seats right at the front, the only place with enough leg room for her plaster.

His feelings move formlessly … to Greta the last time he saw her, and him saying, 'I don't want any phone calls saying, Come quickly or you'll be too late' … He is remembering when Greta's husband died. Walter. And he, Lance, was the one who found him. Walter was a lot older than her but he seemed perfectly well, then he just drifted off to sleep in his armchair and never woke up. Lance was in his twenties and had never even contemplated the idea of anyone dying, but at least there were practical things he could do, to save Greta having to think about them. So much legal, bureaucratic stuff to deal with after a death –

Please God, don't let it be Greta's he has to deal with next.

In Tashkent airport they get a cup of tepid tea and an indigestible sandwich and wait for the call to board. Lance leaves his sandwich uneaten. On the entire journey so far they have hardly exchanged five words. He cannot move past the sight of her and Akbor caught in a moment of intimacy, and he is still confused about what it signifies. Akbor would never have initiated something like that, not with his shyness, not in the office.

He makes an effort to appear more normal. 'Thanks for fixing everything.'

She takes his hand and presses it. The relief is almost a shock. He holds on tight but still confusion circles just beyond where they sit.

He turns to face her. 'This morning. In my office —'

'I know. Me and Akbor. You thought something mega was going on.'

He waits – he needs her to say, clearly, that it wasn't. For a moment she says nothing at all, her eyes just latch onto his. Then, voice low, intense. 'There is something I have to say to you.' The loudspeaker blares at them – time to board. 'I'll tell you on the plane.'

Find your seats, fasten your seat belts, an avalanche of safety announcements making conversation impossible. God, it all takes such a tedious, long time. The plane takes off, the announcements come to an end. He turns in his seat to face her. 'What is it?'

'This morning – I couldn't believe your face when you saw us together – you instantly jumped to conclusions. Crying on a friend's shoulder is allowed, Lance, and it doesn't turn him into a lover.'

'Crying?'

'Yes, crying. It happens sometimes, you know? We'd gone into your office because I just suddenly got emotional. It's been

512

an intense time – in every possible way – and now, with no notice, we're leaving. I was so upset for you, about Greta. And yes, I felt emotional about saying goodbye to Akbor. He's a special person and it has meant a lot to me, working with him. You must know he is only a friend, yet every single time I have mentioned his name you get that look in your eye that says, of course she prefers him. We can't live like that, Lance, you've got to do something about it.'

'Annabel –' This damn aeroplane, people everywhere. He feels as if he has been through a wringer and is just discovering that he still exists. But still needing to check —

'You packed all your things?'

'Yes, I packed all my things. I don't have many, and we don't know yet how long we'll be gone.' She pauses. Then, 'I'm going to tell you something Fahmeda said.'

'You talked to Fahmeda? About us?'

'I know, it's shocking. But she raised it, not me, just before everything started happening. She got me alone and went straight for it – telling me off, in case I was messing about with your feelings. I said the problem is I don't know what he's feeling. She said, it's obvious, the way he watches you.'

'Oh my God. And I thought I —'

'Maybe you fooled yourself. You almost fooled me. But not Fahmeda. She said, the trouble is he is too modest, he can't believe it can happen. You like to tease, Annabel, but don't joke about this.' All trace of laughter has gone. 'So listen now, carefully. I am on this plane because I'm coming with you. When you come back, I'm coming back with you. I have never stuck with anyone before but I'm sticking with you. Why? Because we have fun together. Because I want to keep sleeping in the same bed, for ever. Because you are the best person I know. And don't give me that stuff about being middle-aged and boring – goodness is not boring, it's the thing above all others that I need in the man I'm going to spend my life with.' But that is as long a speech as she can make without her eyes laughing again. 'And if you keep squashing my hands like that, the bones will crack.'

He releases them. 'I don't know how it is possible.'

'It's not just possible, it's real. And you've got all of life to get used to it. Now try and get some sleep – Greta's going to need your energy.'

~ 68 ~

Time has lost shape as they wait for Lance to arrive. Tessa has cancelled everything else to be with her. Ben is with the children. Work can wait.

Mostly Greta sleeps, doped against pain. Tessa sits in a chair by her bed, doing whatever small things she can to make her comfortable. When Greta wakes she has spurts of lucidity, starting conversations in the middle, and then slipping back again.

Once she says, 'It seems such a waste to sleep when you're here.'

'I'm not going anywhere. You sleep.'

A few times while Greta is dozing she has slipped out to phone Ben. 'The children are fine,' he says. 'Fern and I are managing fine. Alisa's teddy has a broken leg, we're practising splints.'

By mid-afternoon Greta has acquired a little energy, and sends Tessa back to her flat to get her address book. Tessa thinks it is to get phone numbers, but when Greta holds the book in her hands and starts paging through it, that seems to be all she wants to do, just to summon in her mind all her people. A roll call. Sorting out her life.

There has been no need to let anyone know; Tessa's one call to Lifeline explaining why she was not coming into work was enough. The word has whipped around. The nurses are constantly bringing messages from people who have phoned, asking how Greta is and if they can visit. At first she kept them at bay because Greta was so tired, but it began to feel the wrong thing to do. If these might be her last days, how can she deny them? She lets them in, and keeps the visits short, people from Lifeline, from her other committees, adopted nieces and nephews who live near enough to get there.

A nurse comes to say, 'There's a minister on the ward. The churches do a rota. Do you want to see him?'

Greta says, 'I'm happy to meet anyone.'

Tessa says, 'I think she means, do you feel a religious need?'

'Well of course I don't, but I'd be interested to know what he says to people in my situation.'

The nurse says, 'I'll get him to come.'

The minister is young, new to the job, Tessa guesses. She leaves them to it and goes off to get a cup of tea, feeling a certain compassion for the young man. When she comes back Greta says, 'I had no idea how interesting hospital would be.'

'Tell me.'

'He was surprisingly open-minded. He agreed with me that all we can know for sure is what makes life valuable here and now.' She looks around her. There is more she wants to say but she is searching for the words. She turns to look straight at Tessa. 'I've had a long life. I know it has to end sometime. But it's hard to take in that it may be about to happen.'

'Maybe you don't have to. They said your heart seemed strong.' Then, 'Are you afraid?'

'I don't think it's that. Just, I don't like the idea of leaving people.'

'Don't assume you're going to. This is maybe just a blip, and then we can carry on as we were.'

'I don't feel as if I have the energy at the moment.'

'You've got a broken hip. Wait till they've fixed it, and then see.'

The next time she wakes she is brusque, even irritable. 'My mind's gone all vague. So annoying. It must be this stuff they keep pumping into me. There was something I particularly wanted to ask you, but now it's gone.'

'Close your eyes again, it'll come back.'

A moment later she says, 'It did.'

'Tell me then.'

'What happened to that notebook, the one with Rahul's translations?'

'I have it. He gave it to me, the last time we were together.'

'I'm so glad it's not lost. I would very much like to see it.'

'I'll bring it, as soon as you're over this.'

Greta closes her eyes. A few minutes later she opens them again. 'Why did he not give it to you earlier?'

'Because he kept adding poems.'

'So why did he give it to you at the end?'

Tessa says quietly, 'You're a clever woman, Greta.'

Greta stares at her, concentration full on. 'He knew? That something might happen to him?'

'Not exactly. But he had been surrounded by unexpected death, it changed how he saw things. Now is the only time we live, he said. If it matters, do it now. There may not be another time.'

'I always knew he was a wise boy.'

Watching the clock, waiting for Lance. Greta is quiet but it is obvious that her mind is following a trail.

'One thing I don't need to worry about is Lifeline and the children. You'll do it.'

Tessa remembers their first conversation, Greta saying, Where are the children in our work? I have kept asking, and the directors have kept thinking I'm an irritating old woman.

'How did it get to be like that, that you cared so much?'

Greta's head shifts slightly, that small movement of concentration, but she says nothing.

Tessa backtracks. 'Don't try and talk if it's going to make you tired.'

But she wants to. 'It was the war. Dreadful things happened to adults but it seemed worse for children, they are so defenceless.' Silent again. Then, 'You see, I lost my own.'

'Your own?'

'My sister's, really. She had to go underground so I was looking after them. They were just four and two, the age of yours. But I knew I didn't have much time. I left them with my neighbour, there was nothing else I could do.'

'And your sister?'

'Sent to a labour camp. I never heard of her again. Nor the neighbour. I went back after the war but the building where we had lived was a pile of rubble. I tried everything but I couldn't track them.'

Her eyes have closed again, her face in retreat. In the silence Tessa hears again her words from their first meeting: 'This post is something I've been hammering on about for a long time, and I wanted someone who would do it with love. And that's you.'

The story goes back sixty years, and she has never given up trying to care for the children she had to leave.

And that is how Lance sees them when he comes quietly into the ward and stands just inside the door. Greta is a tiny body on a bed. Tessa is sitting beside her, holding her hand, her back to him. They are both silent, neither moving. He stands there for several minutes, not wanting to disturb them.

Tessa senses that someone is there. Turns, sees him, and quietly detaches her hand from Greta's to get up. At that small shift Greta opens her eyes. Slowly they focus – she sees it is him. And when he sees the look on her face, the relief that the waiting is over, the reassurance, he knows with complete certainty that if she survives the operation he is never again while she lives going to take himself off somewhere far away. He is going to stay here, where he can check on her every day, and make sure she knows she is not alone.

In a voice hardly audible she says, 'My dear boy.'

He is at her side, holding her hand. Tessa stands quietly on the other side. Greta looks from one to the other and says, 'Now I have everything.'

Then to Tessa, 'I don't want you to go, but I'm worried about the children. You must get back.'

He says what he has to say, in case this is their last chance. Actually there isn't much that can be put into words, and they both know it all anyway – that Greta has been the lodestar of his life, without whom he would never have become who he is. That he has been the son she never had.

'I want to know about that young woman you've found.'

She knew all along, she says.

'No, Greta, that's impossible. I didn't know myself.'

'My dear boy, months ago you told me you needed a shared

519

life. Then I heard there was an independent-minded young woman staying with you – and she was still there months later. What else was I to think?'

'She's twenty years younger than me, Greta. It didn't seem conceivable that that wouldn't matter to her.'

'It's one of the least important things in the world. Walter was more than twenty years older than me, and we couldn't have been happier.'

'I never thought of that.'

'There you are now – how silly was that?'

Tessa has given him a list of people who have come, and new ones who want to. He doesn't let anyone stay longer than fifteen minutes but they all get their turn. There are two very elderly men who say she helped them get out of Austria. One is a violinist, 'A wonderful musician,' Greta says after he has gone. 'At least I saved him for the world.' The other, she says, made a fortune in finance. 'Far more than anyone could need. I told him, no one gets that rich without someone else becoming poor. But at least he gave us our building.'

'Our building?'

'The Lifeline building. He insisted on it being anonymous but really, what does it matter after all these years?'

'And you put him up to it?'

'He wanted to do something for me. I told him that was quite unnecessary, I had everything I needed, but if he wanted to be useful he could help us support other people living through crises.'

A nurse and an orderly arrive to wheel her bed to the theatre. Greta says, 'After all this fuss I'm certain to come through it.'

'I'm sure you are,' he says as he walks alongside her moving bed. 'But it didn't do you any harm to have an army of people coming to tell you they can't do without you.'

~ 69 ~

She surfaced from the anaesthetic to find both Lance and Tessa waiting to receive her. Maybe there's a euphoria in those first hours of recovery, maybe it was just Greta's indomitable spirit – but she smiled when she saw them, and said, 'You're both here. My two next-of-kin.'

They understood well that it was a temporary reprieve. All other plans were adjusted. Lance told the directors of Lifeline that he was taking a month's leave and after that would be renegotiating his future. Tessa asked for compassionate leave to spend two afternoons a week with Greta. Practically she wasn't needed; Lance was there, and he had hired help by day and a nurse for the nights; but he himself saw that Tessa had ways of taking Greta's mind off her discomfort that her other carers did not.

Nothing, Lance thought in those weeks, had ever daunted Greta, but the life of the spirit had been so dominant that she had paid very little attention to her body. Her muscles were weak from too much sitting and it was a struggle to get her legs moving again. As he gradually got her back to being able to move about in her flat, he had the satisfaction of knowing that she had really needed him. Without him there to tease and cajole her through her exercises, she might not have made it.

Those were also his first weeks of being with Annabel in their new state, of regularly sharing a bed. It was all that had been missing from an intimacy already so developed that it seemed now obvious that this was where they had always been heading. But to sleep each night with her body close to his seemed still an almost illicit pleasure, and to wake each morning to find her there and making him laugh was delight itself. Her plaster was off, and she was full of creative zeal, organizing her sister, finding old friends, working at translations. She was back in contact with her Farsi professor and sharing with him what Rahul's legacy had opened up to her. She joined the rota on Greta's care so that Lance could get to Brighton more often, and read to her, instalments as she translated them of the life of Rahman Mirzajanov. She and Akbor were emailing each other almost daily, sending each other drafts of translations. Lance marvelled to think that once this friendship had seemed so threatening. Now he was simply glad for her that she had that on-going connection with a world she had given herself to with such energy.

He was on the phone to Nargis every couple of days.

'My father-in-law keeps asking about Annabel,' she said.

'She'll be coming, when she has translated what she's got here. Then she will stay on for however long it takes for them to finish their work together.'

'And you, Lance? Will you be back?'

'Not yet. I'm getting you officially appointed as director. Coming away jolted me into realizing you don't need me there. You can do it all.'

'But better than I could before, because you were here.'

'It was a special time for me too. You know that. And I'll be back for a visit. As soon as I can.'

~ 70 ~

Nargis returns to the decisions facing her. I am back, she thinks, to where this all started with Rahul – she and Fahmeda need to plan what can be done to support the displaced people in the settlements beyond Sukhunobod. The peace treaty has been signed, with clauses guaranteeing a safe return. Now Lifeline needs to work with those women and children to help them get back to the life that was so cruelly disrupted. Whatever words are in the documents that were signed in some smart hotel in Moscow, back in the mountains and plains of Tajikistan it's not going to be an easy road.

She feels, as she has felt so many times before, that the problems of her community are overwhelming. But she has learnt an inner strategy that helps her not give up. She asks herself a simple question – What would I do if they were my family? My sisters? My children? *Something*, that's what she would do, however little that something. She has knowledge they have no access to. She interacts daily with people who might have some influence. She knows others with no influence but with good hearts who might be persuaded to do something practical, if she can create a framework. She controls a budget, however small, and if she is clever in how she allocates it, perhaps she can improve their chances of getting back to where they can live again with dignity. Her mind is already forming the words she will use to write all this up as a project proposal, that will be agreed in Brighton, and perhaps someone there will find them extra funds. Perhaps Tessa can talk to organizations that care about children, and say, I have seen the conditions in those camps, they need your help. Perhaps Lance's friend Hugo will tell her who she can speak to in the UN agencies, to arrange transport to get people back. Perhaps she can make contact with another organization like Lifeline, but one that works in the places the women must return to.

Something. And courage, that too she and Fahmeda and all the others can give. Because when those people see we are doing something, they will know they have not been forgotten.

And she, herself? Her own life, her own anxieties? There is nothing to be done about that except what she already does. Support her family. Try to build a future for Layla. Care for her parents-in-law, whose lives have been hard. Try to forget Khaled, so she does not waste energy uselessly. Work, and be glad that she can.

❖

Rest, they all say, rest. Greta rests and rests but the tiredness will not go away, and she is so tired of being tired. There are things still to make happen and she is not ready to let go.

'I have been thinking so much about Sushila and Hamza,' Greta says to Tessa. 'His parents. You never met them, did you? Such a shame they couldn't know you, and know how well he was loved.'

'I did meet them, once.'

'You've never told me that!'

'It never came up.'

'Tell me now.'

'Shouldn't you rest, Greta? I don't want to tire you.'

'Your stories don't tire me.'

So Tessa begins. It was last year, she says, late November. I was asked, at short notice, to go with a group of Lao teachers on a study visit to Delhi. I hadn't been back for twelve years. Ben said, Do it, and took leave to be with the children. I told Rahul. I didn't ask what he had to cancel or postpone, but he was there to greet us as we came off the plane ...

The days whizzed past faster than she could register. Rahul joined them for the hotel breakfast each day and chatted about what they were going to see. He was there again when they got back at the end of the day. The group adopted him, their knowledgeable Indian friend, who could tell them so much about the background of things they were seeing. One night he took them all to eat in a Thai restaurant so they could have the sticky rice that they were homesick for. They had an interpreter but were nervous at being off known territory and clustered round Tessa wherever they went. In a moment alone with her he said, 'They're like kids, they don't leave you for a second.' But they were tired from the day's outings, taking in so much that was new, so they retired early to their rooms, and the evenings were theirs.

'We've come full circle,' Rahul said when they were finally alone. 'Now it's me waiting around for you to be free from all your pressing commitments.'

He insisted on removing her for one evening, so he could take her to have a meal with his parents. Tessa was amazed that he wanted to do it, but history had moved on, he said, and he wanted to bring the pieces together.

'What are you going to tell them?' she asked.

'I already have told them. The truth, and nothing but the truth.'

She was appalled.

'But not, of course, the whole truth.'

He had said simply that she was an old friend from village project days. His mother said, 'I'm glad you keep your old friendships going.'

And his father?

'It's possible he will guess. But if he does, he'll never show it. Nor will he let it get in the way of meeting you, as you.'

Tessa could not but be charmed into relaxing with them, and their unique blend of quiet spaciousness, intellectual engagement and warmth. Rahul took her into the kitchen to meet the man who was cooking the meal. 'Manzoor has known me since I was five,' he told her, and to Manzoor he said, 'She's the one who used to send all those letters with Irish stamps.' Manzoor was laughing, their secret finally out. Rahul was sailing close to the wind and enjoying it.

Over the meal Hamza asked about the political situation in Laos. Sushila asked about Tessa's children, and talked about her own grandchildren, now young adults, beginning to make their own choices in life. She wanted to hear about Tessa's time in Hasilgah. Sushila herself, Tessa discovered, had been involved with the project ever since Rahul pulled out. 'It's a family thing. It was my father who gave the land, Rahul who made something of it. I just felt there should be someone from the family who stayed involved.'

Rahul said, 'You're being far too modest, *Ammi jaan*. Tell Tessa about the scholarships.'

'Oh that. I've just been harassing my relatives, the ones with money, to set up a scholarship fund in my mother's name. She was a pioneer of girls' education.' There were girls from the village who wanted to go on to secondary school but that meant they had to go to the town and lodge with other people. 'A girl in that position would be completely unprotected, so we employ a social worker to find families who will take proper care of them, and check up on them regularly. She's a local woman, of great character. And two of those girls are back now in the village, teaching the younger ones.' She smiled at Tessa. 'They will have been young children when you were there. So you see, things happen. Small things, but you have to put your faith in something.'

It was all very simple, but it completed something. Tessa saw where he came from, how he got to be how he was. Rahul was watching them all together, happy that it was happening.

Greta says, in a voice suddenly filled with her old definiteness, 'Sushila knew.'

'She couldn't have known. There was nothing to suggest it.'

'She would have guessed, because he wanted to bring you. She misses nothing. She never understood why he didn't marry, he told me, and he wouldn't talk to her about it. And then there he is bringing a woman friend to meet them, someone important enough that he wants them to know her, and she's married to someone else. Hamza too, he would have seen the ease between you. No one needed to say anything.'

'And if they did guess?'

'It means you should go back, as soon as you can. Go and see them again, and share with them what you've shared with me.'

'No, Greta!'

'Why no?'

'They have enough to deal with. Why would I want to complicate their grieving?'

'Anything anyone brings them of him will help them. You can bring more than anyone. Don't hold it from them.'

'Greta, you're exhausting yourself. Rest again.'

'Tell me first that you'll go.'

Tessa takes her hand, her small, mottled bony hand. 'This is emotional blackmail. I'm not promising anything. Now you rest.'

'You've taken so much time off for me,' Greta says to Lance. 'You'll need to be getting back.'

'I'm not going back.'

'My dear boy, I can't have you organizing your life around me. What will you do?'

'I'm taking over Glen's job.' He smiles at her amazed expression, and comes to sit next to her. 'The trustees have agreed it. They assumed I would have your vote.'

'And Glen?'

'He's getting back to a country programme, the first one that comes up.'

'He wants that?'

'He wouldn't have if Lionel had suggested it. But coming from me, he didn't resist long. He knows himself, it's time he got some new stimulus.'

For a few moments she is quiet, digesting it. Then, 'I must say, this offers considerable possibilities.'

'Yes?' He is amused; she has clearly moved on to things that have nothing to do with his being here to look after her.

'You'll be much more skilful at handling Lionel. And it will be so good for Tessa to have you as a manager.'

'For that alone you approve it?'

'I certainly do.'

There is a look of concentration in her eyes that he knows well. She is brewing some plan. He waits to hear what it will be.

'Do something for me, my dear boy. Send Tessa to India. There must be Lifeline work for her to do there.'

He raises his eyebrows. 'She has managed her own role exceptionally well. I have no intention of interfering.'

'She needs to see Hamza and Sushila. It's important for them, as well as her.'

He smiles, shakes his head. 'As it happens, we have spoken about this. She *is* going to India, and quite soon, but she's not sure about seeing them.'

'She's *quite* wrong, it will help them. Don't you think so?'

He takes her hand in his, feeling grateful for every definite opinion she has ever had.

'It's not a question of what you or I think. It's what she's ready to do. Just trust her, she'll work it out.'

~ 71 ~

'So it's India next,' Hugo says.

Tessa hasn't wanted to go anywhere but now that it is happening it feels right. Lifeline needs her there. She will be meeting people who live and work in villages not unlike Hasilgah. She will sit once again, perhaps, in the cleared space under a peepul tree, will sleep again on a string bed. Each step she takes forward will also be a reaffirmation of what mattered in the past.

Hugo has the box of her letters waiting on the patio table to return to her. He pats it and says, 'I feel honoured that you were willing to share these.'

'You found something?'

Hugo shakes his head. 'Not that. I realized almost as soon as I started that I had given up hope of that. But reading the letters fulfilled another need, one I hadn't been able to name before – they allowed me to spend time with him again. And for that, I am very grateful. And I did learn something else.' He lifts up a small padded envelope that has been on the table next to the box. 'This is for you.'

'A present?'

'But not from me.'

Tessa opens it. Inside is something folded in a blank sheet of paper. She unfolds it. A cassette, labelled in Rahul's handwriting, 'For MJ, 18 December 1996.'

She looks up, eyes querying. He says, 'I found it among his papers, left behind before he went on that journey. But who was MJ? No one knew. I almost threw it away. Then you trusted me with his letters, and I saw how he addressed you.'

Meri jaan … M J.

Tessa looks at the circle of magnetic tape visible through the cassette cover, and then up, to meet his eyes. She feels overwhelmed. 'Thank you, Hugo.'

'There's nothing to thank me for. I'm just the messenger, and honoured to be so.'

Her mind will not proceed beyond the practical. She sees in her mind's eye Rahul's cassette recorder, the essential tool of his journalistic days. 'I haven't got a cassette player.'

'I've borrowed one for you. It's in the room I'm using.' He leads her through to the room where he has placed it ready for her, on a desk with a view out onto the garden. 'You can listen here in complete privacy.'

He takes a book and goes back out, moving his chair as far as possible from the house, under an acacia tree. But the book lies open on his lap, pages unturned. Inside the house Tessa is listening to Rahul speaking to her one last time, neither of them visible but each so vividly present. The love that moved between them, and the love of a different kind between him and each of them, seems to pervade the soft summer air of the garden. He feels it in the scent of honeysuckle, in the delicate colouring of the clematis blooms that trail over the patio roof, the filigree patterns of the leaves of the acacia outlined against the sky.

The sun moves. He does not know how long he has been sitting there. He lifts his head, to see her standing at the patio door. She looks suddenly so much younger, as if released from a burden. She smiles, and he thinks of Rahul seeing that smile for the first time in the face of a nineteen-year-old girl.

She brings one of the patio chairs over to sit next to him and says lightly, 'The last time I memorized anything that long was at university, when I had the lead in a play.'

'I didn't know you acted?'

'I loved it. Becoming part of other people's lives.'

'Maybe you will do it again one day?'

She laughs and shakes her head. 'I've found other ways to

get there.' She passes him the cassette. 'Thank you, Hugo. It meant more than I can say.'

'You won't take it with you?'

'I'd rather it stayed with you. Keep it for me, so if one day my memory doesn't hold I can come back to it.'

Now it is her last visit to Greta before she goes. Tessa says, 'I've brought you the notebook. Rahul's translations.'

'That is excellent.'

Slowly Greta's gnarled hands turn the pages. The words absorb her, these fragments of thought in the mind of a man long gone, ephemeral as the beat of butterflies' wings, yet captured in marks on the page so we can hold them and have the illusion of listening not just to the poet but to the man who chose to translate them. At one she smiles, at another shakes her head. Tessa, watching, is thinking about Greta's question, the one she has always been too discreet to ask. Perhaps it is time to tell her? But probably by now she knows the answer. She saw it in Greta's eyes as she was telling her about the last time she and Rahul were together, those days in Delhi, though she said nothing about the two days they had just for themselves after the Lao teachers had gone back. She holds it in her memory now, the comfort of those days, the freedom to lie close together and talk into the night, a thing she had thought might never happen again. She is grateful that he did not have to go before they had that time – grateful for herself, but even more for him. They had no sense that it might be an end. Rather it felt like a new start, a recovery of something that they had for far too long had to put aside. Things that had seemed complicated became, for that moment, simple. Perhaps that was an illusion. Perhaps if he had lived the complications would have surfaced again, and maybe more powerfully for the fact that they had allowed themselves that temporary freedom.

Greta looks up, and holds out the notebook to show Tessa the couplet she has been reading. 'This is him. He only knew one way to be, and that was total. Totally engaged. Totally himself.'

> I pledge myself entire to love, and love of life possesses me
> I worship lightning – and lament the lightning's handiwork

Tessa smiles. 'He would say, that's Ghalib speaking.'

'It may be Ghalib. It's also Rahul, and he had his eyes open. He understood where living like that would land him.'

Tessa says, 'I have something to tell you.'

Greta is watching her face. She knows. 'You are going to see them?'

Tessa nods. 'For you, but for me too.'

'My dear girl, I knew you would.'

They sit quietly together for a few moments. Eventually Greta says, as if it is the end, 'You've been a joy to me.'

'I'll be back, and you'll still be here. It's only ten days.'

But it *is* an end, and they both know it. Sitting up here together, detached from the world that passes by in the streets below, she has relived in the safety of Greta's receiving presence each stage of the story, hers and Rahul's, and it has done for her what Rahul used to say their times together did for him, everything in the right place for once. And then she has walked out, as now she must again, back to the world in which each day we are required to make a new beginning.

~ 72 ~

In the street outside Greta's window the plane trees are in full-blown summer leaf. Lance has been seeing them in all seasons, for all the years of his adult life, while she has been his

> *ever-fixéd mark*
> *That looks on tempests and is never shaken*
> *A star to every wandering bark.*

Without her, would he ever have read Shakespeare? Or politics? Or history? And in a future that he must navigate without her, what will be his ever-fixéd mark?

He turns from the window, to see that she is awake and watching him. She has been noticeably more tired these last few days. Her heartbeat is irregular, the doctor says, her lungs are struggling. It could be weeks, it could be months. It is unlikely to be longer.

When I have to go, her eyes say, I don't want you to grieve.

535

He shakes his head. No, Greta, that's not possible. He is grieving already. But he knows he will have to find the grace to accept the inevitable and move on. This he has learnt from Greta herself, not from anything she has ever said, but from how she has lived her life. Out of the loss of her own family, she made a life of loving other people's. In her loneliness at a critical moment she found joy with Hamza, and then accepted what she could not have, and freed herself to become not just his lifelong friend but Sushila's; and through them to be there for Rahul, and after him for Tessa. She came through the intense private loneliness after her husband Walter died, to breathe life into Lifeline – for that, he now understands, that too started with a death.

Annabel arrives and the moment is lightened. She bends to kiss Greta, and then comes to stand behind him, her hands massaging his shoulders. Small strong movements that shift the tiredness out of the muscles. 'You're all knotted up,' she says. 'Go and get some exercise.'

He doesn't want to go because he doesn't know how many days Greta has left, and he doesn't want to miss any of them. But she has not given up, she is still telling him what to do. 'Annabel is right,' she says. 'Go.'

So he goes. He walks down the road and into Regent's Park. This was Tessa and Rahul's place, she told him once, they walked here, they saw these trees, growing still. 'I feel him there for me even now,' Tessa said once. Perhaps that is how it will be for him with Greta. She will be there in what he does and what he doesn't do, because of how she influenced him to think and be aware. She will be there in the face of every old person he sees in the rubble of a home destroyed by earthquake, and every child whose life he hopes their activities may set on a path of resilience. She will be there because the passion she invested in life was invested also in him.

He looks up, to take in the simple beauty of trees outlined against the sky, and he knows it will always be like this, Greta saying to him, Live now. Don't grieve.

They go up on the downs the evening before she leaves, Tessa, Ben and the children. They lose track of time up there in the light that just goes on and on. The children skip about like young lambs, and Ben seems half-child himself, playing chasing games. Skylarks rise at their footsteps and circle, higher, higher, till they are small specks against the sky. Seagulls call, plaintive cries wheeling above them. Like early morning on a beach in Thailand, this is a moment that she knows will stay with her for ever, the transition to a new stage in life perfectly represented in the quality of light and air.

Morning. Breakfast. Fern arrives to be with the children. It feels like a normal morning. Tessa folds both the children in an embrace. The parting is not too difficult. They have done this before, and they know she will be back.

The train to London, she and Ben together. At Victoria station, about to go their separate ways, they hug and she says, 'I don't know how I got to be so lucky.'

He looks slightly surprised. 'Your job?'

'No. You.'

He laughs and says, 'Snap.'

At the airport, waiting to board, she slips back into her quiet inner space, listening to Rahul's voice, the voice on the cassette, and back from that to their last time together in Delhi. She knew, through the lightness of those days, that he had mortality on his mind. But it was not his own death he was thinking of, it was that of a close Tajik friend who had just been murdered. Rahul talked about him, conjuring the man's living presence, the breath of his life. He was the kind of person that the new Tajikistan so badly needed, he said; a journalist, an enthusiast, a restless thinker, who through the worst of times had kept the capacity to focus on things that make life worth living. Then one morning his body was found in the streets of Dushanbe, and that was it. A senseless death, the end of an extraordinary man. It had brought home to him that the future could not be taken for granted. If it matters, say it now. So he said it, on the cassette that he did not live to send her; what their life together had meant to him.

Her eyes return to where she is, watching through the airport windows as one plane after another lifts into the air, taking people off to other lives. Soon she will be in one of them, but she is flying no further. We have come to an end, *meri jaan*. Nothing can happen now to disturb the careful balance we worked so hard to create. If there was anything separating us, it was my residual fear of that. Now it has all been brought to

538

a non-negotiable end and there is nothing left to fear. Perhaps that's why you feel so close.

The call to board.

Author's note

This story is entirely fictional but the background of place, history and politics is factually based. The names Resham-serai, Sukhunobod and Hasilgah will be found on no map outside this novel, but reflect actual conditions in the areas where they are imaginatively located.

The hostage-taking happened as described. News media in December 1997 reported that twenty-three men were taken hostage, but only twenty-one were released. The fate of the other two remains a mystery.

I owe to Save the Children the opportunity to work, over a period of thirteen years, in the countries that feature in the story. Countless people have inspired my imagination and helped me understand complexities they dealt with daily. My thanks to Zainab Babaeva, Matthew Bullard, Urvashi Butalia, Shon Campbell, Joanna Clark, Michael Etherton, Terry Giles, Dilrabo Inomova, Zarangez Karimova, Divya Lata, Bronwen Lewis, Primila Lewis, Lawrence Lifschultz, John MacLeod, Layla Mamina, Carolyn Miller, Shireen Vakil Miller, Alfia Mirasova, Bruce Pannier, Tom Porteous, Ahmed Rashid, William Reeve, Jose Riera, Ferhana Faruqi Stocker, Steve Thorne, Monica Whitlock. Several of these have read drafts and checked for authenticity. I received useful feedback on early drafts from Carole Beu, David Birmingham, Martine Brousse, Barbara Dinham, Becky Joynt, Tina Hyder, Lorraine Lawrence, Colin Marquard, Susan Nicolai, Liz Nussbaum,

Francesca Hopwood Road, Nicky Road, Mary Simpson, Anna Taylor, Ann Waterhouse.

Many people responded to Advance Editions' invitation to comment in the final stages. I am grateful to them all. In giving the book its final form I drew on suggestions by Anne Kristine Arbon, Wolfgang Bayer, Alyson Elliman, Sughra Choudhry Khan, Christina D'Allesandro, Georgina Donaldson, Carolyn Galbraith, Leesa Harwood, Kate Holt, David Humphrey, Heidi Kingstone, Brian Marquard, David Marquard, Susan Murray, Kate Nowlan, Marina Palmer, Angela Piddock, Philippa Ramsden, Paula Scott, Kari Shah, Wendy Staal, Helen Sunderland, Diane Swales, Rosemary Wailes, Ann Waters-Bayer, Rosemary Welchman, Zsuzsi Yardley, Angela Young and Ralph Young.

Thank you to Alastair Niven and Juliette Mitchell for encouragement; to Greg Lanning, Jenny Marshall, Linda Wright and my daughters May and Star for support through the years of writing; to the production team at Advance Editions for their expert touch – Anna South, editor, Andrew Corbett, cover designer, Trevor Horwood, copy-editor; and to Hector Macdonald, who made it all happen. My husband Robert has been the perfect writer's partner: philosophical when I was absorbed, unfailingly generous about picking up the pieces, and making life fun when I emerged.

Sources of poems

The poem 'I do not believe in miracles' (ch. 18) is a translation of 'Aarzu' ('Longing') by the Urdu poet Faiz Ahmad Faiz (1911–84). The translation is mine and I gratefully acknowledge the permission of the Faiz Foundation Trust to publish it here.

Other verses are from the Persian poets Firdawsi (d. 1020), Sadi (1210–91), Amir Khusrao (1253–1325) and Hafiz (c.1315–90); the Urdu poet Mir Taqi Mir (1723–1810); and Ghalib (1797–1869), who wrote in both Urdu and Persian.

Rahman Mirzajanov is a fictional poet but his story was suggested by several real ones. The poems ascribed to him are mine.

This list gives the poet for each verse, with the chapter in which it first appears. For those by Ghalib a ghazal number is given, and those marked P are in Persian.

Part 1 'This year it is the lightning' – Ghalib 140
ch. 3 'The wind blows hard' – Ghalib P87
ch. 7 'I grapple with that fragment of ill fate' – Ghalib 21
       'The waves are rising high' – Ghalib P234
ch. 8 'Your body holds such joy' – Mir
ch. 17 'With us there is no talk of near or far' – Mir
ch. 20 'I do not believe in miracles' – Faiz
ch. 24 'Now let me go away' – Ghalib 121
       'To live in freedom' – Ghalib 118